Caroline Scott completed a PhD in History at the University of Durham. She has a particular interest in the experience of women during the First World War, in the challenges faced by the returning soldier and in the development of tourism and pilgrimage in the former conflict zones. Caroline is originally from Lancashire, but now lives in south-west France. *When I Come Home Again* is her second novel.

Also by Caroline Scott:

The Photographer of the Lost

NON-FICTION:

Holding the Home Front:
The Women's Land Army in the First World War

The Manchester Bantams:
The Story of a Pals Battalion and a City at War

WHEN I COME HOME AGAIN

CAROLINE SCOTT

SIMON & SCHUSTER

London · New York · Sydney · Toronto · New Delhi

First published in Great Britain by Simon & Schuster UK Ltd, 2020

1 3 5 7 9 10 8 6 4 2

Simon & Schuster UK Ltd
1st Floor
222 Gray's Inn Road
London WC1X 8HB

Simon & Schuster Australia, Sydney
Simon & Schuster India, New Delhi

www.simonandschuster.co.uk
www.simonandschuster.com.au
www.simonandschuster.co.in

A CIP catalogue record for this book
is available from the British Library

Hardback ISBN: 978-1-4711-9217-3
Trade Paperback ISBN: 978-1-4711-9218-0
eBook ISBN: 978-1-3985-0137-9
Audio ISBN: 978-1-4711-9223-4

Typeset in Bembo by M Rules
Printed and bound in Australia by Griffin Press, part of Ovato

For J & Z, as ever.

'Unknown and yet well known, dying and behold we live'

Inscription on the grave of the Unknown Warrior, Westminster Abbey

Durham Cathedral, November 1918

Chapter One

He shuts the door on the wind. Stepping into the absolute stillness of the cathedral is like entering a different atmosphere, and he breathes in the smell of damp stone and burning beeswax. He puts a hand through his hair – he feels all tugged out of shape by the wind – and blinks in the dim light. This place is all space and distorted sound. For a moment it is full of the rush of his own breath, the whole great height of the cathedral echoing with the rhythm of his own breathing, an almighty stone ribcage, but then it is just the whisper of other people's prayers, and the whistle of the east wind around the door, and the echo falls from his ears like a dropped seashell.

A movement drags his eyes up; a flicker at the top of the pillars. There's a bird trapped inside the building, and he turns then as he watches it streak between light and shadow. It flits between the arches and lunges at the vaulted ceiling. He moves down the nave, following its fluttering progress above, until it soars up the height of the tower, up the great tapering trunks of stone, and into the sudden brightness of the lantern windows. Twenty feet up. Fifty feet. A hundred feet now, and more. He spins and it dizzies him; gazing up at this circling height is like looking down a well, and his knees feel unsteady.

The stone cross spirals above with pigeon wings all around

it. Trapped within the height of stone, there is something both miraculous and distressing about the bird's flight, and he feels for the creature as it lurches at the glass of the windows. Its confinement. Its confusion. The noise of the wings, amplified by the architecture, is brittle and fragile. The bird hurtles and loses height. How many times has it already plunged up the tower, lunged at the light, and failed? How many more times before its strength gives out and it just keeps on falling? He wants to look away, wants to sit down and steady himself, but can't take his eyes from it.

He only becomes aware of the woman's presence when he hears her getting to her feet. She lifts her hand and he sees her fingers extending towards him. Has she been watching him all this time? He turns away, but the carvings of the choir stalls look like burned bones, and he retreats back down the north aisle. His boots squeak on the marble floor, and he is torn between the desire to be away from the woman's staring eyes and stretching fingers, and the sense that it is wrong to break the sanctified silence of this place. But he can hear her footsteps too, knows she is following him, and when he turns she is there, right behind him. He can feel the woman's eyes moving over his face. He watches the dart of her pupils and feels eaten by her eyes. She puts her hand out towards him and there is a tremble in her touch. He shuts his eyes as her fingers move over his face. It is not objectionable until he hears her crying, and then her touch is more forceful than kind. Peter, she calls him.

She shouts the name after him as he walks away. Her scream is like a tear in the cathedral silence, there is something desperate in that sound, something animal in it, and he needs to get away from her. He is running now and can hear his own ragged breath. When he reaches the chapel he pushes the door closed against her clamouring hands. He wants to shut out the woman in black and her needy tears. He knows he is not Peter.

This chapel is like a petrified wood. The image of another wood glimmers fleetingly, where the ground was soft, and the branches sharp, and where he'd been afraid, but he shuts it down. It is an effort of will, but by blinking in the here and now, by focusing on the edges of the carving and the texture of the flagstones beneath his feet, he can make it stop. He doesn't mean to let it start again. His fingertips circle the stone columns as he takes in all the details of this chapel. He could be standing in a forest, or a plantation, only great arcing branches of geometry shoot from these slender trunks. Pineapples and pomegranates sprout from this strange Moorish architecture, but there is no hiding amongst these trees.

He crouches down behind a tomb. His parapet is a vase of flowering camellia; his forward defence is a row of altar candlesticks. He thinks about the trapped bird as he listens to the woman's circling footsteps. He knows it will not get out, that in a few days it will fall from the stony heights, plunging down, swooning dead to the marble floor. He pictures its fallen body. Its feathers stir. He holds on to the square stone of the tomb and thinks that he can smell the bones of saints.

He watches the shadows turn and time takes the tension from his fingers. She has gone. He is sure of it. He heard her crying as her footsteps retreated and that name again, Peter, stretching through the silence. He leans his back against the sarcophagus now. There are hints of apostles and kings stained into the stone above. A crucifix, perhaps, where the white-wash has been picked back. Fragments of sinners. Flakes of martyrs. The pigments are more suggestion than statement now. They are barely there, these wall paintings, but so forcefully present.

The evening light slants through the windows and pushes out the colours of the glass. It is the colour of miracles, and shimmering tints of green and gold and purple reach across the flagstones towards him. He puts his hand out experimentally and turns it in the ethereal jewel colours and the projected faces of angels. It makes him want to paint. He remembers the piece of chalk in his pocket.

He looks out from behind the tomb. The silence is thick now and he knows that he is the only person in the cathedral. He takes the chalk from his pocket and smiles as he puts it to the stone. It makes a smooth line; its mark is satisfying; it is soft and decisive. He curves a line, his arm arching. A cross-hatching of shadow. Forks of feather. He draws the bird in upwards flight, a phoenix roaring from the flames, Icarus soaring, or a saint arising to heaven, its wings full of acceleration. He is rapt in the act of drawing. Absorbed in it. There is only this and only now. He doesn't hear the footsteps approach.

The chalk falls, the man shouts and he is running again, back through the cathedral and its streaming candles and black baroque – past the organ pipes, and the stone bishops, and the memorials of soldiers – past the chrysanthemums, and the lilies, and the names of the blessed dead. He knocks a candlestick over in his flight and it clatters to the ground. He doubles back across the altar and plunges through a stockade of pews. The door is heavy, but he is out then into the light. His feet hammer at the flagstones, his heart hammers in his chest, but the noise of the man's breath and boots is still there behind him. He flashes through shadow and sunlight, skids on the corners, and dives for the next turn. The breath roars in his lungs and he is just raw fear and speed and spent now. This cloister is a maze, then, and a trap. He is an animal circling in a cage. There is no escape.

'It's the end,' says the voice of the man behind him.

He knows it. He turns. He nods.

Chapter Two

'Name: __________'

The hairs rise on his forearm and he hugs his knees to his chest. It is cold in the cell. They have taken his clothes away and he feels every breath of air from the window above. His naked body is familiar to him and yet not. He knows his own hands, but he can't remember the scars on his arms, or the lice bites that cover his body. He scratches the backs of his knees and sees that there is blood on his fingers.

Your name, they said. *We need a name. We can't start without it. You need to give us your name.*

It comes back at him again, that insistent question. All through the night. No starting, but no stopping. He would have told them, if he could.

The walls of the cell are blistered with damp. The plaster ripples and glistens. The walls are as pockmarked as his skin and the whitewash comes away on his shoulder when he leans against it. There are scales of lime in the creases of his hands and chalk down his fingernails. Five white condemning crescents. It is the chalk that has put him in this police cell.

Where's your identity disc? they asked. *Your pay book? Your service number?*

Looking at the new bruise blooming on his arm makes him

ashamed. The constable had walked him through the town with his arms in a grip. It wasn't so much that it hurt, but he had felt humiliated when the people's eyes flicked towards him and then away, and chastened by the words that they mouthed. He wanted to tell them that he'd done nothing wrong. He wanted to shout it out. He wanted to tell them that this wasn't him.

What's your battalion? What regiment? Where are you stationed?

They had emptied his pockets while the sergeant questioned him. Every item was catalogued and inspected. Every coin was turned over. Every pebble. Every piece of chalk. This scrutiny made him feel as though his pencil stub and box of matches were specimens in a museum requiring labels. But what should their labels be? Could these innocent items condemn him? They told him that they were taking his belt away so that he wouldn't hang himself.

He watches the silverfish scurry. There are cobwebs in the corners and chains on the wall of the cell. They are crumbling, rusting old chains, the kind prisoners have in storybook dungeons, and he suspects they are there more for warning than purpose. He hears the spyhole in the door click again. They have been doing this all night; coming to look at him, checking on him. Why did they imagine that he might hang himself?

Home address? You must have a home address. You must have come from somewhere.

He tries to remember. He genuinely tries. He recalls the barns and sheds and ditches of the past few weeks, but nothing before that. He slept on a bench in a church porch some days ago. An old woman handed him a bowl of warm milk in the morning. A young cleric gave him a blanket that smelled of laundry soap. He tries to remember what home feels like, what it smells like. It smells of damp and disinfectant and urine in this cell, and the sweat on his own skin.

Place of birth? Date of birth?

'Born to raise the sons of earth,' the voice in the next cell crescendos. 'Born to give them second birth.' It's Christmas carols now. The disembodied voice has been singing hymns all night; eight hours of rhyming trials and tribulations, mysteries and mercies, and green hills far away.

It was a desecration of a place of worship, they told him. It was a serious offence. He'd laughed when they said that this was the sort of filthy thing the Germans had done in France. They told him it didn't help his case that he laughed. They asked him why he did it. What was he thinking? What made him want to do such a thing? He could only reply that he didn't know.

Next of kin?

Nothing. He apologized. He could see their frustration. He didn't want to frustrate them. It wouldn't do him any good, the sergeant said, if he didn't speak up, if he didn't co-operate. He would have to go back to his regiment, they said. The authorities would need to be informed. Was he home on leave, they wanted to know. Was he due back with his battalion? Had he gone absent?

What were you thinking, lad? they asked. *Are you a deserter?*

The electric bulb buzzes and casts a cold white light. It has been left on all night, the moths dancing foolishly around it. He picks them up off the floor now and they crumble to dust between his fingers.

The sergeant had brought him a tin mug of tea, bread and butter and a jug of hot water. He'd told him that he should wash. That he stank. When he put his hands to his face he realized that he hadn't shaved for several days. He can't remember his own reflection. He felt the new shape of his face with his wet fingers. The sergeant had leaned against the wall as he watched him wash. He said that he lost his son to the war last year. That Colin was a good boy. That his mother wouldn't ever get over it. There were dark shadows under the man's eyes.

Where's your mother, lad? Does she know where you are? Don't you want to be a good boy for your mother?

They showed him the charge sheet, turned it round to face him, the empty white spaces that ought to be filled. Where he ought to have a date and place of birth. Where he ought to have a residence. A next of kin. A name. The inspector's finger jabbed at the paper.

What are you called? he asked it again. They keep on asking it. *What's your fucking name?*

Chapter Three

'Adam Galilee'

'They've made me Adam,' he says. 'Like in the garden of Eden.'

'Haworth. James Haworth.' The man shakes his hand.

'Well, we had to call him something,' the police sergeant explains, 'so we christened him Adam Galilee, because he was in the Galilee chapel, you see? It sounds a bit fanciful now, doesn't it?'

The man called Haworth smiles. 'We all need a name. Are you happy to be Adam for the moment?' he asks.

'I have probably been called worse things,' he replies.

Haworth nods. 'Well, I hope that it will only be a temporary cloak. I'm here to help you remember who is underneath.'

The police sergeant pats his shoulder. 'Good luck, lad. Good luck, Adam,' he says.

They will call him so many names. He had been Peter to the woman in the cathedral, but soon he will be Mark and Robert and Ellis. He will fill the spaces of Franks and Phillips and Daniels. So many hopes and voids. They will want him to be a George and an Edward and a John. They will believe him a Stephen, a Sidney and a Benjamin. They will need him to be a Luke and a Jack. So many false hopes. So many unfillable voids. For the moment, he is Adam, but he doesn't particularly want to remember who he may be underneath.

The train pulls out and he watches the cathedral slide. He stands, puts his hands to the glass, so that he can see it angling into the distance.

'It's like something geological,' he says to Haworth, as he turns away from the window. 'Don't you think? Like an almighty eruption of rock.'

Haworth raises an eyebrow. 'They told me that you didn't speak.'

'Only if I don't know the answer to the question.'

Haworth nods. 'Sergeant Lonsdale has a theory that you just fell out of the sky.'

'Like a fallen angel? He said that? No. It was a bad thing that I did. They used the word *desecration*. That means I took something sacred away, doesn't it?'

'It was only chalk, though. They told me that it brushed off. It might have worked out differently had you decided to give the cathedral a coat of red paint.'

He sits back down and looks at Haworth. His face is one that could be caught on paper in a few economic lines: strong brows, sharp cheekbones, a long, straight nose and a wide mouth. It's a face of particular architecture, of angles rather than curves, but his heavily lidded grey eyes are expressive. When Haworth smiles, his eyes crease, and he looks as though he means it. He is conventionally a handsome man, Adam supposes, particularly when he smiles, but his resting face is scribbled all over by melancholy.

'What?' He looks back at Adam and laughs. 'I feel appraised. I'm not sure that we're getting this the right way round.'

'I'm sorry. They tell me that I have a bad habit of staring.'

He is a doctor, they told him, a doctor of minds. Haworth would take him to a place where he would get put back together again, they said. It made him think about a sing-song rhyme and all the king's horses and all the king's men.

Doctor Haworth has bitten-down fingernails and his hands move all the time. They must always be turning a pencil, or twisting together, or adjusting the crease of his trouser legs. He slits a new packet of cigarettes open with his thumbnail now and proceeds to fold the silver paper into neat pleats. He winds it between his fingers then, and Adam can see that this is a regularly repeated, but unconscious ceremony. As he watches his hands, Adam supposes that Doctor Haworth may suffer with his nerves.

'Sergeant Lonsdale is an old friend of Doctor Shepherd,' says Haworth. 'That's why I'm here. That's why we're making this journey. Shepherd treated Lonsdale's wife long ago, very successfully, from what I'm told. He will look after you too. We will look after you. It's not a hospital or a prison, you must understand that. We focus on rehabilitation. We offer rest, tranquillity, pastoral care, remedial occupation. We'll help you to get it all unravelled and put right.'

He looks at Haworth. He is not sure that he wants to be unravelled. As he looks at Haworth's fidgeting hands, he's not sure that *he* has entirely been put right.

'I'd offer you a cigarette, only I'm not certain you should be near naked flames.' Haworth holds the packet out towards him.

'I'll take the risk.'

He is glad to breathe in Haworth's cigarette smoke. There is a dank smell in the compartment, an old dirt smell from the upholstery, and below it all the chemical reek of his own clothes. They have fumigated his uniform and it smells strongly of creosote. They have shaved his head and scrubbed him with carbolic soap. They watched him, supervising, while he cleaned under his fingernails and brushed his teeth. It had been strange to see the colour of his hair on the floor of the police cell. The sergeant gave him polish for his boots and told him that he could keep the tin. At this moment it is his only possession.

From Durham there are hedgerows and then brown fields with a green haze of winter wheat showing, stretching to low hills and cirrus clouds streaming east. The terraces of Chester-le-Street roll past and then they are into the darkness of a cutting, the black-green of the earth bank and the flicker of a man's face. He sees his own reflection in the window, moving over the slowing branches, and it is like seeing the face of a friend from long ago. He puts his fingers to the bridge of his eyebrows, to his nose, to his mouth. Haworth watches him, but then looks away. It is a private moment and he is grateful for the sensitivity of the man at his side.

'You haven't had a mirror?'

'No.'

'Do you recognize yourself?'

'I can't tell you. Yes and no. I look like an older version of someone who I might have known years ago.'

The view turns to rail yards and goods yards, to wobbling lines of cemeteries and allotments. Two men wave at one another in between rows of leeks and bronze dahlias, or they might be waving fists. Newcastle is warehouses, big ships, steaming funnels and spires, and so much arching iron. He looks down at the hubbub of the quayside, and up to castle crenulations and the spikes of a cathedral steeple. A filigree of crossing railway lines stretches ahead.

'It might occur to you to run,' Haworth says, as he rises to disembark. He is taller than Adam when they're side by side, but thin for his height, so that he seems all knees and elbows. He looks like a man who doesn't sleep well, Adam thinks. 'You might want to lose me now and, if you mean to, there's not much I can do about that. But, please, believe me that I'm on your side. I want to help you and I'd like to be your ally. Will you trust me? Will you stay with me?'

'Yes.'

The railway station is a rush of steel and steam, porters and trolleys and the taste of smoke. He follows Haworth's back through the noise and push of the crowded platform, all the while wondering where this pledge of allegiance might lead, and whether he ought to be running away instead.

He looks out from the train and the warehouses turn to pitheads, then back to hedgerows, and there are fishing lines dipping in the shallow waters of the South Tyne. He spies grand houses on the tops of hills, grazing sheep and the landscape is all soft folds. He leans his cheek against the cool of the window and watches it slide by.

'I suppose I should tell you about myself, should I?' says Haworth.

Adam doesn't feel he needs to, but it seems the man must. He nods. 'If you wish.'

'I was a medical student before the war. Shepherd was my tutor. He meant to set up in private practice and asked me to join him, though events rather got in the way. But it did end up happening in a roundabout way. He always said that, when the war was over, I should think about it again. Doctor Shepherd owns Fellside House,' he clarifies. 'Fellside is where we're going.'

Adam looks out and watches the gentle, curving,

nursery-rhyme landscape. He would like to follow the lines of the stone walls and know what is hidden in the folds of the fields. He is not sure that he wants to be in a house being practised upon by a junior doctor. The low sun picks out the patterns on the ploughed fields and the bare trees are like ink sketches of themselves. He sees the shapes of elm and beech and hornbeam and his hand itches for a pen. There are stipplings of late foliage clinging on and catching the light, but he sees the glint of gorse here and there, and catkins are brightening on the hazel. Gulls dip and rise in the wake of a plough and rabbits scatter across a tawny field.

'Thank you,' he says, as it seems to be the expected response. 'I'm grateful to you.'

He sees factory chimneys and terraces, the smoke of steel-works, mountains rising in the distance, and as they slow into a station, a sign for Carlisle.

'We have to change again, I'm afraid.' Haworth rattles the coins in his trouser pockets as he stands. 'We've half an hour before our next train comes.'

They wait in the refreshment room and Adam thinks about what changes and challenges he might face at the end of this journey. Haworth doesn't look back as he stands at the counter. He nods at the woman with the tea urn and Adam sees her smile as she places spoons in saucers. He grips the arms of his chair and feels the momentum in his muscles. He could go now, make a break for it, and perhaps lose Haworth in the bustle of the station; he could run for the exit, or try to get on a train; he could be away, back on the roads, free of well-meaning nods and watching eyes. But he had been frightened on the road and his eyes connect with Haworth's now as he turns with the tea tray.

'I wondered if you'd bolt,' he says as he sets cups and saucers down on the table. 'I was half expecting to see an empty chair.'

'I did think about it.'

'Naturally,' Haworth says as he stirs the teapot. 'You're not in my custody, you know. You're not my prisoner. But I will be your guardian and friend. I think that, right now, you might perhaps be in need of a friend.'

'Yes,' he concedes over the rim of his cup.

'Do you want to remember?'

'I'm not sure,' he replies in all honesty. 'Sometimes I see things that I might remember and I don't like them.'

'Things?'

'Places. Faces. They don't join up, but then I don't really want to make them fit together.'

Haworth nods as if he can understand. Adam can hardly imagine how he might understand. 'But you must want to remember your name? Where you come from?'

'What if I had good reason to forget? What if I'm not a good man? What if I don't like the person I was? What if I've done something bad?'

'Something worse than desecrating a cathedral?'

He is grateful for the glimmer of humour in Haworth's eyes, but he nods. Sometimes the disjointed faces and places are horrific, are terrifying, like the scenes of hell on the walls of old churches, and Adam doesn't know if he has caused them to be that way.

'Do you fear that you've done something bad? Do you feel that you might?'

'I know I'm not a fallen angel,' he replies.

'Wasn't Lucifer a fallen angel?' Haworth shrugs. His tea-spoon rattles in his saucer. 'In all likelihood, you've a home and a family somewhere, possibly a wife, maybe even children. Don't you want to see them again?'

Adam considers. 'Do I? I'd remember that, wouldn't I? Surely I would, if it meant something. What if it's a home and a family that wasn't happy? What if I made it unhappy? Would they want me back? Should I want that back?'

'Maybe if it wasn't right before, you could make it right now?'

'Redemption, you mean?'

'What a very biblical choice of word.' Haworth raises an eyebrow. 'I do momentarily forget that you came into being in a cathedral. Is there incense in your veins?' His smile stretches and then sobers. 'Maybe you have a second chance? Maybe you can be delivered from sin?'

Redemption sounds like a journey, and if that means travelling back through the scenes that sometimes flash at him in the night, Adam is not presently sure that he wants to go there. 'I don't know.'

From the train he looks into back yards with hen runs and pigeon lofts and clothes lines, and into cobwebbed attic windows. He glimpses an old man sitting in a doorway polishing shoes to a satisfactory shine. A woman is shaking out a tablecloth, a girl is carefully carrying out crumbs for the birds, and a boy at a table turns the pages of a newspaper. All these lives continue without an upward glance for the train, without so much as seeming to notice it go by, so that to look in on them makes Adam feel like a god or a ghost. Was his life once such as this? Might it be again? At this moment he would rather look out at other people's lives, at their dramas and domesticities, than try to find a way back to his own.

South of Carlisle the trees cast long shadows in the sun. A

river meanders along the side of the railway line and the landscape begins to change. The square fields give way to curves south of Penrith and the horizon rises. The sky seems low at Shap, farmland turns to moorland and he stands to watch a hare streak into the distance. There are rushing becks then, and steeply rising peeks, and Haworth asks him if he would like living in this landscape. Adam looks out at the hawthorns and yew trees and the old stones, this landscape that he's sure he has never known before, and answers, 'Yes.'

There are flags out all along the length of the platform as they pull into Oxenholme station, swags of bunting and strings of paper flowers in red, white and blue. It has the appearance of a celebration, all the trimmings of a party about to start, but the people on the platforms look more startled than festive.

'What is it?'

'Didn't you see the newspapers yesterday?' Haworth asks.

He shakes his head.

'It finally happened. The war ended yesterday. There's an armistice.'

'An armistice?' He looks at James Haworth's reflection in the window against the flags and flowers. Haworth's face doesn't seem sure of what emotion it means to communicate.

'A truce. A ceasefire. It's all finished,' he says. 'The war is over.'

'Which war?' Adam replies.

Chapter Four

James Haworth, Loughrigg Hall, Westmorland, November 1918

He can't quite fathom it as he approaches – this odd grouping of fur and feather on the frosty lawn. As James gets closer he sees that one of the housemaids is tickling a stuffed calf with an ostrich-feather duster. There are foxes, ferrets, pine martens, a pug dog and a two-headed lamb.

James shakes Alan Shepherd's hand. 'It looks like an escape bid from one half of the ark.'

'Charlotte insists that they must be put out to sweeten in the winter sun. She hopes the frost might kill off any fleas.'

'Is she not just trying to edge it all out of the house?'

'Very possibly.'

While Fellside was built for a Liverpool sugar merchant in the last century, and is all whimsical gables and finials, Loughrigg Hall is the Gothic original, complete with castellated chimneys, crenulated towers and extents of ornate ironwork. There are green men and griffins in the architecture, James sees, and all this dark frontage seems oddly balanced between the secular and sacred. When James had worked for Shepherd in the hospital in Cheadle, he'd no idea that this rational, modest man stood to inherit two eccentric Westmorland houses; it is slightly difficult to equate the pre-war city nerve doctor with the Cumbrian gentleman who seems so at home amongst all this slightly unnerving history. James steps between posed polecats and the motionless wings of owls. Stuck butterflies quiver on their pins and look as if they might take flight.

'Did you collect it all?'

'No. God forbid! It came with the house. It's all my father's fault. They were a terrible generation for accumulating clutter. As a set of siblings they haunted auction rooms. They even bid against each other. Only now they've left it all behind to overcrowd and haunt us.'

'You could always take it back to auction.'

'Heaven forfend. Then the senior Shepherds really would come back to exact retribution from beyond the grave.' Shepherd casts his eyes skyward and gives James a side-on grin. 'I did strip your flat of it all. We took boxes of this stuff out of Fellside. Is Caitlin settling in?'

'Yes. I think so. We took a boat out onto Windermere at the weekend. She says this place looks like a notion of English landscape on China plates; that it's all an exaggeration; the hills fly up too fast and too high, she says, and the trees look as if they've been placed there by an interior decorator. I think it was meant as a compliment.'

Shepherd laughs. 'But the house, I mean – is she settling into the house?'

'Yes. The flat was crammed full of packing cases last month but, bit by bit, they're exiting. Caitlin's pottery wheel is coming up next week and there's a chap in Ambleside who is willing to let her have some of his kiln space. It's fortunate how it's worked out. Caitlin hit it off with him and he's been introducing her to lots of local contacts.'

'Not hit it off too well, I hope?'

'No danger. He must be in his sixties. I think he might actually be looking for a successor. We could find ourselves putting down roots here.'

'Good. God bless the amiable potter.'

'She's very grateful to you for letting her set up at Fellside. It's all been in storage since she left London and I rather feared she'd packed her ambitions up too.'

James has left Caitlin arranging her plates on the kitchen dresser, talking of patterns and glazes and clay pits, and he had felt lifted to hear a note of excitement in her voice.

'She told me this will be the first proper home that you've had together.'

'It's true. Our brief snatches of marital togetherness have been in parental parlours and parks and gardens. Our chattels are the contents of two adolescent bedrooms and three canteens of inherited cutlery. We've been married for five years and have never lived together yet. Bizarre isn't it? I'm really rather hoping that we get along.'

'It's a shame that your first real home is an office on-the-job, as it were. Are you certain Caitlin doesn't mind?'

'Having the space to set up her studio is definitely a sweetener. Thank you. She wants to make it work and I believe she will.'

'Excellent. I hope so. I do understand that living in Fellside is not what every young wife might want.'

James hadn't been convinced that she would agree to it. When Shepherd had offered him a permanent position, Caitlin had brightened; when he added that it would mean living in the institution, James had seen that brightness fade. Her eyes had clouded with questions.

'Come in.' There are paintings of moors and castles and Highland cattle all along the length of the hallway, and antique maps of Westmorland with hills and houses that look fantastical. It smells of lingeringly damp mackintoshes and wet dogs. Somewhere in the house a piano is picking out phrases of Tchaikovsky. 'Come through.'

The door to Shepherd's study is propped open with a large piece of quartz. The interior is more shabbily domestic than the monumental facade of the house suggests, but the ceiling beams are painted to look like they belong in the Middle Ages, their design picked out in reds and greens and gilt. Shepherd gestures for James to sit. He shakes his head to a glass of whisky.

'Caitlin says that your house makes her think of Wuthering Heights.'

'It's draughty enough. Does she see me as Heathcliff? I'm complimented. I must remember to curl my lip at her. I do start to think that this house is getting too big for us, though. We've closed the dining room and the library. We seem to be retreating into fewer and fewer rooms.'

There are photographs of Alpine peaks in Shepherd's study, crumbling abbeys and college cricket teams. These additions, so obviously Shepherd's own, don't seem to fit with the imposing furniture and grandeur of the decorating schemes. The bookcase is like a church altar. The dimensions of the desk take inches from Alan Shepherd's height.

'I thought she looked well when we saw you last week.'

'Caitlin? Yes. She's like a photograph of herself. She never seems to get any older. I sometimes wonder if it's witchcraft.'

'Undoubtedly.' Shepherd smiles and pours himself a whisky.

He does look older, James thinks. His dark hair is flecked with grey at the temples now, and the lines that define his face have all become deeper over the past five years, but his voice still has that old warmness and the vaguest hint of long-ago Liverpool schooling.

'Anyway, how was your patient? You didn't have any difficulty on the way over?'

'He was fairly docile,' James replies. 'More eloquent than I expected, but I do think he's scared.'

'Scared?'

'Not so much of the here and now. I wouldn't say he's jumpy, but it's very apparent that he's gone through some trauma and isn't willing, or ready, to address it.'

'I bumped into Sally in the village yesterday and she told me that Mr Galilee had arrived with terribly dirty fingernails. She said that she'd made him wash his hands, but five minutes later he'd got himself in a mess again. By Sally's diagnosis, this is a very messy mind.' Shepherd laughs. 'Did he resist recall?'

'I don't know that it's a matter of volition, at least not in any active way. He seems to have only snapshots of recall, not joined up, but they're evidently sufficiently distressing that he doesn't want to make the effort to piece them together.'

'And you said he's having nightmares?'

'Yes. He has no memory of them afterwards, he tells me, none at all, but he wakes in a panic and has clearly experienced something terrifying. And that sensation, that fear, is contributing to his reluctance to look back; he doesn't want to remember his dreams, or the episodes that he's probably revisiting in his sleep.'

'It's a grandly biblical name, Adam Galilee. Why did you choose it?'

'It was the police sergeant who gave him the name. He was found in the Galilee chapel.'

'Of course. It was in the newspaper, wasn't it? Did he cause much damage?'

'No. Not at all. It was only chalk. The story got entirely

exaggerated. The poor lad's face took a bit of a battering, though.'

'I saw he had a black eye. He resisted arrest?'

'He was cornered. He panicked. I don't think he'd normally be violent.'

'Good. Lonsdale said that our Mr Galilee looked as though he'd been on the road. Have we any idea for how long?'

'A few weeks, I'd guess.'

'And is there anything specific as regards that journey? Does he recall locations? Where he started from? Where he was aiming for?'

'He's drawn several venerable trees and a number of tumbledown barns for me, but that's as documentary as it gets. He's a good draughtsman, he has a great facility in sketching, which could be useful, but there are no place names and no sense that he was heading for a particular destination. He'd evidently walked some distance, though. His boots were nearly worn through. He says that his first memory is the image of his feet on the road.'

'Do you sense he was running away from something?'

'Perhaps. There does seem to be some dread nagging at him; he's frightened that he might have done something bad.'

'Bad? It's no use looking at recent military absconders?'

'Where would you start?'

'Can we be sure he even was a serving soldier? I mean, we're making an assumption that the uniform he was wearing was his own, that his condition has been triggered by an experience while on active service, but are we making too many presumptions?'

'I've asked myself the same question, but, no, I don't think the assumption is mistaken. His uniform was fitted to him. It was worn and shaped to his body, as if he'd been wearing it for a long time. The boots fit his feet and he looked like he'd been in his underclothes for weeks.'

James had smelled it on him too; though they'd de-loused him in Durham, and he stank of creosote and carbolic on the train, there was another smell that came off him as he changed into new clothes back at Fellside. It was something that James recognized. He knew Adam had been in France.

'There's also a scar on his leg. A glancing bullet wound, well healed, from at least a couple of years ago.'

'So you have no doubt, then?' Shepherd asks.

'I have many doubts, but not that he was wearing his own uniform.'

'There's no question that he might be faking the memory loss, do you think? There's no suspicion that he knows more than he's letting on?'

'No. I don't think so. I was watching him on the train. He sat forward in his seat for the whole journey and barely took his eyes from the window. I watched his eye movement and it was as if he was seeing everything for the first time. He's perfectly lucid in the moment, he's very much awake in the here and now, but there seems to be a cut-off point, and beyond that it's all gaps and disjointed images.'

'Retroactive amnesia following emotional shock?'

'I'd say so. Although there's nothing physical to give us any clues as to what that shock might have been. Apart from that wound to his lower leg, and some old scars on his arms, there's no sign of physical injury.'

'And the triggering incident is forgotten?'

'Entirely.'

'There are no other symptoms?'

'The inability to recall particular events seems to be his only disability, as far as I can tell at this early stage. He has absolutely no recollection of his name, his home, his family or having spent any time as a serving soldier. There's a pretty extensive tract of his former life that he's unable to access, but much else is intact. He can speak quite fluently when he gets onto a subject that interests him, and there's evidently a lot of retained knowledge. All of that gives me some grounds for optimism, but something strong within him is resisting recalling the pertinent parts.'

'You'll have to be patient. Talk to him. Give him time.'

James nods. 'I will. I mean to. As long as you're willing to have him at Fellside, I don't see that there's a need to hurry. It's likely that there are memories that will be intensely distressing, so I'd prefer to gently encourage rather than press him. I only wish I was more convinced that he wants to remember.'

Chapter Five

Adam, Fellside House, Westmorland, November 1918

They keep asking him for his first memory and he knows that they want a scene from his childhood, a few recalled words of friendship, or a glimpse of his mother's face, but at this moment, Adam can't recall that he has ever had a childhood, a friend or a mother.

'Roll back,' they say and smile. As if it were that easy. 'Tell me what you first remember.'

But it isn't like that. It isn't linear. That's not the way it works. It doesn't have momentum or a narrative arc, and he doesn't know where it starts. It surprises him, if they are doctors of minds, that they can't understand that.

Adam lies back in the warm bath and wriggles his wrinkled toes. It all starts to become joined up with the memory of his feet on the road. That's the first scene that exists in any detail. He woke up in coppiced woodland (it might have been weeks or months ago), where there were other men with split boots and blackened faces. The men said that they needed to keep moving on, that it didn't do to dally here, and so there his feet were on the road. He has no idea, not remotely, how he came to be on that particular stretch of road.

'And what did you feel?' they asked him today.

Feel? Frightened. Bloody terrified. He admits that. He didn't know any of the men and their faces were strange, like they'd known long hardship and sorrow. Of course, he soon realized that they didn't mean him any harm, but that's not to say that he trusted them. These men carried knives in their broken boots and told tales about bare-knuckle fights and the inside of police cells. He didn't know what the inside of a police cell looked like at that point, and neither did he want to know the feel of a knife or a fist. So, because these men spoke their words as if they were wisdom, and liked to spend time sharpening their knives, when they said they must move on, Adam did. He wouldn't have dared to contradict and wouldn't have known where to go otherwise.

'Did you know the names of any of these men?' the doctors ask him.

'Of course. Dear fellows. We do mean to keep in touch, but I'm afraid I might have mislaid their business cards.'

No. It wasn't like that. Names weren't offered and he wouldn't have had the nerve to ask. He remembers numbness in his fingers and a racing in his chest as he had set off on the road on that first day and, in part, that was caused by the company he was keeping.

He scrubs his finger ends with the nailbrush now. The woman who says he must call her Sally keeps telling him that he has to do this, as if his mental well-being balances on the cleanness of his fingernails.

It was not knowing how he got there that frightened him most, though. The chasm of blank. The edgeless emptiness that might swallow him up again at any moment. It was like not knowing what was solid, where the boundaries existed between one object and the next. The road beneath his boots might as well have been a tightrope. What was to stop him from falling off again at any moment? And what had he done, where had he been, *who* had he been in the void? He isn't sure that he would recognize his own personality.

But he doesn't want to dwell on the questions. When he wakes up with the panic, he knows that his sleeping imagination has been back into the void, and then he's glad that he can't remember. Adam thinks about the blanks on antique maps now, as he lingers a minute longer in his bathwater, and sailors who feared falling off the edges of the earth once upon a time. Aren't the blanks best avoided, and can't life continue if we steer clear of the edges? Isn't it best just to keep on walking forwards? On the afternoon of his first day on the road he had turned round on a crossroads to make sure that he still had a shadow. If he walks towards the light, it stays behind him.

'And so you just kept on walking?' Haworth had asked.

What else was he meant to do? He didn't know where he was going, but equally there was nowhere to go back to. The men told him the names of the hamlets that were charitable, and those that were best avoided, about farm dogs and vicarages and workhouses. He should keep to the small roads, they said.

The water spirals clockwise down the plughole now and then jinks anticlockwise. He is not sure which is right. He dries himself and dresses, knowing that the clothes he puts on belong to someone else; the trouser legs are slightly too long and the shirt is short in the sleeves. It is only in his nakedness that he feels he's not pretending to be another person.

'Would you remember the road that you walked down?'

'Possibly. I'm not sure.'

None of it had any meaning until he had started naming the trees. But he had found that he could do that, that the names were there in his head, and then so were the flowers and the insects, the butterflies and the birds. The void had filled with names then, with species and varieties, and those words were like a life raft or a guy rope. And so then his head had been full of the oaks and the elders, the beeches and the limes, the hairstreak, the tortoiseshell, the merlin and the mistle thrush. Suddenly every mile was like a poem and that was what had kept him moving.

'Could you retrace that road? Follow it back?'

'I suppose. Maybe. But why?'

He knows that they want him to push back, but all that comes before is unknowable and unmanageable. Surely what matters is what he makes of the day ahead and the person who he'll be in the next week? Isn't the important thing discovering and being and becoming? He now knows that he has a shadow, but he doesn't need to keep checking that it's following him. Adam wants to keep walking towards the light. He can't see the point in looking back.

Chapter Six

James, Fellside House, December 1918

It is cold in Adam's room. The wind breathes in the chimney and stirs the ashes in the hearth. James has told Sally that the fire must be kept lit, but Adam lets it go out. He doesn't seem to feel the cold, though James sees that his finger ends are white and knows that his feet are red and swollen with chilblains.

'Are you not frozen?'

'No,' he says, as always.

James busies himself with remaking and lighting the fire. He triangulates kindling and blows on the embers, which bloom and then die. Sap hisses and at last there are the small flames. It leaps, gasps into life, and he sits back on his haunches and warms his own hands. Behind the crackle of the fire, he can hear starlings twittering around the chimneys.

'My wife says this house is damp. She's always pointing at dark patches on the wallpaper.'

James looks around and sees that there are a lot of damp patches on the walls of Adam's room. He isn't sure what is pattern, and what is mould. With the cracks in the plaster and the regions of damp, the walls of Adam's room resemble the pages of an atlas, James thinks, with fantasy mountain ranges and mighty rivers. He must mention it to Shepherd.

'It's because we're under the hillside,' says Adam.

'I think these used to be the servants' rooms. With all the slanting walls it reminds me of being in a tent. Doesn't it you? Are you happy enough up here?'

He nods. 'I don't know when I last slept in a bed, or had my own door to close.'

Adam's room is in the eaves. It is all triangles and tricks of light. Six mirrors, evidently salvaged from various attics, bounce the angles of the room around. James knows that surrounding Adam with his own reflection is a deliberate action. But the glimmer of the mirrors triggers a flash of memory for James, and he is back five years ago, tentatively stepping through a blasted house, where there might well be tripwires and traps. The mirrors are still on the walls of this house, but all askew, and James catches glimmers of himself at odd angles and doesn't know his own face. He feels like a ghost in the blasted house, but he's also all too aware that he might set off a detonation at any moment.

'You don't object to the mirrors?'

'Do I have a choice?'

'If you find them too disturbing, I can talk to Doctor Shepherd.'

'Am I not meant to find them disturbing? Isn't that the object?'

James can't entirely deny it. 'The object is to help you, not to torture you.'

'Don't worry. They don't upset me. But I'm grateful for your consideration.'

Adam often looks at his reflection, James notices. It's seemingly not out of any sense of vanity – indeed he shows little regard for his own appearance, but rather his eyes look as though they are searching. When James walks into the room, he often finds Adam at the glass. Their eyes meet in the mirror.

'I like being this high up,' Adam says. 'I leave the window open when it's raining because I enjoy hearing it gurgling down the gutters. And I open the curtains again at night so I can look out at the hillside. I can see the stars paling away and the morning light creeping in between the oak trees. When I lie with my head on the pillow, I can see the tops of the trees against the sky.'

'You sound like a poet.'

'Again?'

Adam has been several poets over the past few days. James believed he had made a breakthrough at the start of the week when Adam had given him a name. At first he had thought that he was speaking of a comrade, but then realized that he was putting himself in the third person. He had said that Henry Alford was injured in France. He had described the incident, and details of the subsequent hospitalization. He had given James a date of birth and a town of residence. James had started to seek out the relevant medical records, in order to pin some substantiating fact to the testimony, and it had felt like a victory. But then he had been Thomas Ashe the day after. And William Broome the day after that. When they had got to Clough and Coleridge, bells had rung and James had finally realized that they were working through *The Oxford Book of English Verse.*

Adam shakes his head as he looks out of the window now. 'I have stopped being poets.'

While Adam might like to direct lyrical thoughts at the hillside, James has noticed that Caitlin closes the curtains early. When he has asked her, she has said that the proximity of the patients isn't a worry to her, that she has no objection to living here, but he's not absolutely sure he believes her. He remembers, on the day that they had moved in, how she had turned as the morning light slanted through the sitting-room windows and it had made a halo of her hair. Only, there's so little light in the winter. He hopes that with the arrival of her wheel, and the occupation of setting up her studio, she will feel more settled.

'The house was a hospital during the war,' James says. 'An ordinary military hospital, I mean. There are photographs of the library full of bedsteads and men in bath chairs playing ping-pong on the dining-room table. A lot of people have moved through here. This morning my wife asked me if anyone had died here.' He makes a face. 'What do you say to such a question? I didn't know what to reply, to be honest. I think she suspects it's haunted.'

'Isn't it?' Adam asks, but there seems to be no question on his face.

James instantly regrets bringing up the idea. He's not sure that the possibility needs planting in Adam's imagination. As James stands, Adam's image bounces around the room in the mirrors. For a moment he sees Adam at all angles, crowding around him. 'But you're comfortable enough?'

'Yes,' he replies. 'I'm glad that I'm allowed out, though. I saw a fox in the garden yesterday morning; it stepped out of the mist, and I followed it. But it slinked through the bars of a gate and then I couldn't watch it any longer. It went into a walled garden. The gate is locked. Are we not permitted to go in there?'

'The old garden? No, there's nowhere that's out of bounds. I'll ask Doctor Shepherd about it. I don't know if there's a key, or if the gate has just rusted shut. Did you want to look in there for any particular reason?' James asks.

'I was only curious. I could see the greenhouse at the far end and the fruit trees on the walls. I wanted to explore what it might have been.'

James nods. 'There are no boundaries. Nothing is off limits. You can explore as much as you like, walk as far as you feel inclined, but I hope that Fellside will seem like a home and you'll want to come back here at the end of the day.'

He's pleased to see the interest that Adam is taking in the garden and the surrounding landscape. When he'd first left the house, James hadn't been certain that he would return, but then he had come back in the evening with pockets full of fossils that he'd found in the old quarry. Adam hadn't woken with the panic that night, and the next morning he'd told James that he'd been tired with the air and exertion, and had gone to sleep with a head full of new sights. James has resolved that he perhaps ought to take more exercise too.

'Thank you,' Adam says. 'I'm grateful to have my own space. I'd also like to look at more of the collectors' cabinets.'

'Good. Excellent. I've brought more up today. It was a lifetime's collection, so there's plenty to keep us going.'

It had worked well last time. James had brought a couple of the drawers up to Adam's room yesterday and it had prompted conversations. He'd seemed contented to discuss these objects, was obviously genuinely interested, and it gave James the opportunity to hear his voice, how he expressed himself, and to gauge the extent of his knowledge and experiences. There are conch shells and butterflies lined up on the green baize between them now, beetles in lustrous gem colours, corals, agates, fluorspars, flints and sharks' teeth.

Adam's finger moves over a drawer full of birds' eggs, variously speckled and green and blue.

'I'm happy someone likes them,' James goes on. 'Sally was dusting them yesterday. I wasn't aware that she knew so many swear words.'

The house is full of the collections of Alan Shepherd's aunt. A lifetime of obsessions is catalogued in the cabinets that line many of the rooms; fossils and minerals, seahorses and sea urchins lie in wait in rosewood drawers; there are shelves of carved jade and Islamic silver, and the finger bones of saints crumble in silk-lined boxes. The whole house is a cabinet of curiosities, and James supposes that it's perhaps not so inappropriate that a collection of psychiatric abnormalities has now taken up residence in its rooms.

'Do you know this one?' James' finger points.

'Easy. Robin's egg.'

'And this?'

'Magpie. And redstart, and starling and wren.' Adam's finger moves along the line as he matches a name to a particular tone and complexion of eggshell. He looks up at James and smiles as if he feels he has passed a test.

'I wouldn't begin to know that,' James replies. 'I might have been able to pick out the robin, but that would be it.' They had gone through a similar exercise yesterday with the trays of butterflies and then, walking through the garden, Adam had produced the Latin names of all the trees. Whatever might be blocked in Adam Galilee's mind, whatever might be refusing to roll backwards, it isn't impairing his evidently expansive knowledge of the taxonomy of the natural world. 'It's like talking to an encyclopaedia.'

'I know everything's name but my own,' Adam says. 'I have all the words apart from the ones that you want.'

'It's not that *I* want it. It's not for *my* sake.' He watches the delicacy with which Adam lifts an egg from the box and holds it to the light. 'You have had a great passion for this, haven't you?'

'They're beautiful, aren't they?'

He nods. 'You remember all the things that you like.'

'And not those that I don't?'

'Very probably. How lucky you are. And it gives you pleasure to draw these things?'

'Yes.'

'Because you like to record them?'

'When I draw them, I look at them properly. I really see them. I see how they're made. How they work. Why they appeal to me. And lots of things don't last, do they?'

'No.'

James looks around the room. He had given Adam a sketchpad last week and there are drawings everywhere now. He often sees him in the garden with a white flash of paper in his hand, bent over a subject, or sitting there for hours observing. He seems to spend much of his time drawing, James notices, and clearly derives some contentment from it. Looking at the papers cast around the floor, he observes that it is mostly details of nature (a study of ivy leaves here, the winter shapes of ash trees, and there a repeated meditation on a pheasant feather), but also a repeated female face. It is the only face that he draws, James realizes as he looks around, the only image of humanity that finds its way into Adam's catalogue. There are no other figures, no man-made objects, no human hand or thought spoils the scenes that Adam chooses to record. It is nature crisply intact. In the story that Adam tells on paper, the wood is primordial and all the people have been pushed out of this valley; other than this woman's face,

Adam's drawing is a world where no humans walk, and that makes her seem all the more important. Is it the case that he sees this woman as a part of nature, rather than as a person? He repeats the same features over and over.

'You draw this woman a lot.'

He nods.

'Always the same woman?'

'Yes. I remember her face. I generally can't remember what I dream, but I know that I've seen her in my sleep.'

'You remember her? Do you know who she is? How she relates to you? Is she your wife?'

'I don't know that.'

'Is she a woman with whom you have had a relationship – a sexual relationship, I mean?'

Adam looks away. His face reflects in iterations all around the room. James looks up and sees himself surrounded by slightly different versions of Adam.

'I'm sorry. I don't mean to be indelicate.'

'I understand that.' Adam shakes his head. 'But I just don't remember.'

'What do you feel about her? What does it make you feel when you draw her?'

'That I like her face. That I miss her, I think. That I don't want to forget her.'

James nods. 'That's good.'

Chapter Seven

James, Fellside House, December 1918

'His room is full of mirrors now,' says James. 'Alan has brought them in from all over the house and he's surrounded by his own reflection. I can't imagine it puts him at ease. I don't think I could live with it. It would nag at me, having to look myself in the eye all the time.'

'Isn't that precisely Alan's intention?' Caitlin's blue, steady, level-lidded eyes look out. James watches her fingers picking out a tune on the windowsill.

As Adam's room is all triangles, so this room is all squares. The wide window, looking out at the facing hillside, is divided into sixteen squares, and Caitlin has filled all the ledges with glass bottles, adding her collection to Fellside's own. The first of them were dug from their childhood garden, James knows, Caitlin and Nathaniel exploring the banks together, like two junior archaeologists. He can picture their faces as they rinse their finds in the river and hold the newly recovered colours to the sky. Some of them are old poison bottles, Caitlin has told him; there are jewel-green ink bottles, cobalt blue apothecary jars, flasks of sulphur yellow and cranberry glass. The colours stretch and glimmer now on the evening floorboards and James wonders if their presence, and the memories they project, is making her feel more at home.

'I like the light in here,' she says. 'But I do occasionally feel as though we're actors in a play. Don't you ever have that sensation? I'm not complaining. It's great to have big windows, but it's also rather comforting to be able to draw a curtain across them at night. All our actions are our own then, aren't they?'

'Do you mean that?' He looks at her with concern.

'I'm sorry. I'm being daft, aren't I? But don't you ever feel like someone is watching us?'

'No. Never. Seriously? Have you ever actually seen someone out there?'

'No, it's just a feeling. A sense. A notion. I feel someone's eyes are on me, but I can never spin my head quite fast enough to catch them.' She turns from the window and her gaze holds his for a moment before she breaks away. 'Or maybe it's Nat? Sometimes he's there right behind me, you know. I'm absolutely certain of it. I can almost feel his breath on the back of my neck; he's as real and as present as you are now. And occasionally, when I catch my reflection, he's there in the mirror too, like a blur in a photograph or an echo; I see his outline overlapping mine, there at the very edge, but I never get to see his face.' She smiles. 'You're looking at me like I'm silly. This is your line of work – you're meant to tolerate this sort of silliness and nod learnedly at it! Oh, I know, I can hear myself sounding loopy, but really I do sometimes feel that Nat's watching over us and that thought comforts me.'

'I have never once thought you silly. I wouldn't dare.' James winds his fingers through her hair and kisses her. 'I'm only sorry that Nathaniel's not really here.' He so sincerely wishes it could be otherwise. He closes his eyes and breathes in the scent of her neck. 'If the thought of him being around comforts you, carry on.'

'Really? So I don't get a case file yet? I need to get to work. That's the truth of it: I need to be occupied. Get busy. I don't think idleness is good for my imagination. I'm afraid I might not be a natural *hausfrau*.'

'There are five black fingerprints on your cheek.' He wipes soot from her face with a licked handkerchief and he feels such tenderness towards the soft apple-blossom bloom of her skin as he does so. 'You made a perfect print of your hand.'

'I remade the fire earlier. It had gone out and I had to start it all again.'

James imagines Caitlin making the gesture, putting her hand to her face like that, and the emotions that may have occasioned it. Does she really feel Nathaniel standing behind her? He's not certain that he's comforted by that thought. 'There, you see, your reluctant domestication is progressing faster than you credit.'

'I scorched one of your shirts with the iron and tried to make a cake but forgot to add the baking powder,' she says.

'I'm sure you scorched it beautifully.' He pushes a strand of hair back behind her ear. 'And I don't care a jot if your cakes don't rise.'

'But I ought to look in a mirror before you get home, shouldn't I? That's what a good wife is meant to do, isn't it? I never know when you will be home, though. This house is full of footsteps, but when I think I hear the approach of your feet on the corridor, I always get it wrong.'

'Nobody troubles you? Nobody else comes to the door?'

'No. No, it's not that. Percy left me a wet newspaper cone full of gorse flowers on the step the other day. He told me that he'd walked past it and was instantly transported back to his kitchen at home and watching his wife taking coconut macaroons out of the oven. He smiled so beautifully as he said it. And it's true; it smelled like desiccated coconut. Then Adam left me a branch of witch hazel and a piece of flint this morning. It looks like an arrowhead. He said he dug it up in the garden. I caught him at the end of the corridor. He was sneaking away, but I could see his shadow and hear his breath, so I made him stop and speak. He's promised to take pelargonium cuttings for me in the spring.'

'I didn't know that you had admirers. I may have to start coming home earlier.'

'You must.' She smiles.

The plates on the dresser reflect the last of the winter sunlight. The room is swinging back into its familiar shadows. He remembers when they had first looked at the apartment. Is it really only three months ago? Shepherd had asked them to Loughrigg Hall for dinner and then he had sprung the offer of the job on James. He recalls following Caitlin along the corridor later that evening. The electricity was off and so she was carrying a lantern. The candlelight flickered ahead, picking out cornicing and ceiling mouldings, and her three-quarters face had turned towards him with an expression that was somewhere between fear and excitement. They had stood side by side in front of the overmantel mirror, the shadows making their faces unfamiliar, framed in ebony and mother of pearl.

'We're like a portrait of a couple from long ago,' she had said.

He'd pushed a door open and revealed what appeared to be a room full of icebergs, but they'd found a mahogany bedroom suite hidden beneath. They had sneezed and laughed as they pulled off the dust sheets and the room full of ice had become a space full of flapping sails. He remembers her hand placing the lantern down on the floor, the shadows all shifting and her laughter in his ear.

James crushes his cigarette out and puts his arm around her now. 'Are you happy?' he asks. 'Is it okay here? I do want you to be happy.'

'Of course I am.'

'I love that you're sensible and determined, but you must tell me if anything worries you, won't you? You don't always have to be sensible.'

'If you'd seen me swearing at the iron earlier, you wouldn't think me at all sensible. But are *you* happy?' she goes on. 'I was watching you in the garden this afternoon. You kept lighting cigarettes and then tossing them away.'

'I did?' He wasn't expecting her to throw the question back at him. 'Perhaps that's why I always seem to be at the end of a packet.'

'His hands are stiller than yours.' She takes James' hand in hers and turns it. She examines his palm with the lightest touch of fingertips, and a focused frown, and looks as if she is about to pronounce a prophecy, but then her fingers tickle and he can't help but laugh.

'*His?*'

'Adam.'

'Are they? He always seems to have a pencil in his hands at the moment.'

'Maybe you ought to take it up,' she suggests.

He thinks about how he would portray Caitlin on a page, how he might break her down into lines and define her colours. 'Perhaps you're right.'

If he were parted from her, might he repeat her features on paper, as Adam does with his woman? He senses the longing that Adam must feel for this woman whose face he is compelled to draw over and over. Surely it's worth pushing him to remember, and encouraging him to recross difficult bridges, if that journey can bring her back to him? Surely he would ultimately want that, wouldn't he? Surely it's the right thing to do?

Chapter Eight

Adam, Fellside House, December 1918

The gate has rusted closed. Adam puts his shoulder to it, but it won't give. The metal has crusted over, like a badly healed wound, and sealed the old walled garden in. Amongst the tawny mass of frost-touched weed and the white mist of milk thistle, the odd dahlia and chard stalk are splashes of enduring colour. The climbing roses have outgrown themselves and great curlicues of thorn bend from the walls. There is something slightly frightening about how feral it all is, how lavishly ruinous, but there's also an enchantment in that. Nature alone has been left in charge and all the polite formality has burst.

The groundsel and nightshade have taken over, the teasels and the nettles, the ragwort, the willowherb and the brambles. It is lordly, this disorder, it's enthralling, but the garden is suffocating itself, he thinks. How long is it since it has been tended? Five years? Ten years? All the clues are still there as to its former structure and purpose. He can see the winter branches of the espaliered apple trees, which must once have been carefully trained, the shapes of blackcurrant and gooseberry bushes, and the collapsed cold frames. The red-brick walls are still in good condition, albeit much scrambled over by bindweed and ivy, and even on this frosty day he can picture them pulsing back August's warmth. Adam leans his face against the bars and grips the cold metal, but he is no longer a prisoner in a cell and when he looks into the garden beyond, he feels an urge to dig and scythe and tire his bones into dreamless exhaustion.

He hasn't been asked into the room where they question him today. Has it then finally stopped? In order to end their interrogations, he has been seven men over the past week; on Monday he decided to be Henry Alford, Thomas Ashe on Tuesday, William Broome, William Cartwright, George Chapman and then Arthur Clough on Saturday. He had taken the names from the shelves of the library, and invented birthdates, families, memories and homes for these men. But on the Sunday he was Samuel Coleridge, it was too close to home, and with that they'd found him out. They haven't asked him his name today. They haven't asked him any questions. Is it then perhaps at an end?

He leaves the gate and walks on, skirting the walls of the garden. The grass has been mowed around the house, but it all runs ragged at the edges. Ferns fringe the far side, tinted pink and amber now, and beyond it is a jungle of overgrown holly hedge, rhododendrons and camellias. In times gone by this garden was planned, he sees; the yews and the pines are thoughtfully placed, and there must have been vistas from the windows, a studied working-together of the decorative wild and the tame, but undomesticated nature is winning now and pushing in the boundaries. Rooks rise and cry from the hillside ahead, circle and are gone again.

He follows the chatter of blackbirds, and a blue flash of a jay's wing, and picks a path through the rhododendrons. He sees his own footprints from earlier that day trampling the grass ahead, and a robin is now busy where his hands had then pulled the roots of ivy from the bank. He has ventured out this far before, had brought in armfuls of greenery for Mrs Haworth that morning, all festooned with berries for Christmas, but when Adam puts his boot up onto the bank, and finds a handhold in the rocks, he is pushing out the boundaries of his own territory.

Over the past month they have examined his body for distinguishing marks, recorded his voice so that they may pick through its sounds, and had him copy out paragraphs of the Bible in order that they may analyse his handwriting. He wonders what science they will extract from the gradient to which his letters lean, the diameter of their loops and the spaces between his words. He presently feels like an experiment, a weary object of wonder, and at this moment he desires nothing more than to look outside and beyond his own physicality. He places new footprints on the frosty bank and the untrodden hillside opens up ahead of him.

He uses the tree roots and low-hanging branches to pull himself up. The damp earth slips under his feet in places and, here and there, stone crumbles away, but he ascends quickly and is soon looking back at the peaky gables and smoking chimney pots of Fellside House. It is a strange sort of a building, Adam considers; the Gothic gabling verges on whimsical, and the leaded diamond windows make it look like a jewel box. Too fanciful to be an everyday home, it has the aspect of a gentleman's weekend residence, he thinks – the sort of house to which a wealthy man might bring cousins for boating and picnics. It is preparing for Christmas today; a fir tree has been brought into the hall this morning and Caitlin Haworth is hanging paper chains from it, while Sally, the kitchen girl, is spiking cloves into oranges. Haworth says that it is the first

Christmas of peacetime, that they must make something of it, and bring all of the festive colours of the garden inside. The smell of pine needles and citrus, of cloves, ginger and allspice has reached up as far as Adam's attic room.

He knows they want it to be homely, and that's what the collectors' cabinets, and carpeted corridors, and the dressing of the Christmas tree are all really about; that they mean to keep the fires lit, and to have all the customs and comforts of a house in which a family still lives, but the faces of the men who inhabit Fellside suggest they aren't quite entering into the spirit of things. They don't look like a family, and Adam is finding it difficult to connect with these other men. They are unpredictable, as yet, these strangers; they have sudden moods and make sudden noises, and all their eyes look at him when he walks into rooms.

They are required to sit around the dining table as a group, and encouraged to play board games and walk in the garden side by side, but none of them really want to let each other in. They are all curled in upon themselves, these men, and they talk behind each other's backs; they all give each other's secrets away, as if each thinks himself the superior, the saner, man. Thus Adam has learned that Warner is a tailor who is no longer able to thread a needle because his hands shake, that Evans puts his fingers down his throat after every meal, Jones wets the bed at night, Marlow has been sent here by his wife because he doesn't want to sleep in her bed any longer, and Laffin has taken off his belt and used it on his children. Adam is not sure that he wants to spend more time with these men and their spilling secrets.

He turns away from the rooftops and scrambles up the last of the bank, his breath clouding around him with the effort of the incline, drawing the cold, clean air down into his lungs.

He feels his blood pump, his skin tingles and his head is full of chilly clarity. As the gradient levels out, he finds himself looking into an endless wood. The sky is blue between the branches and his steps are drawn on through the filigree shadow of the antique oaks. He knows that he is the only person in the wood, and he feels as though he has stepped out of society and time; this is his private, safe place and only nature's rules apply. The benign wind touches his skin and he feels admitted to this wood's secrets.

Adam pauses to look at seed heads and pine cones, all architecture and marvels of design, at catkins and holly berries. The frost picks out the edges and the veins of leaves, so that they are chalk sketches of themselves. He makes new tunnels through the wood; his feet print paths where none have been before. He dips under a lone, leafless apple tree, autumn's fruit breaks beneath his feet, and the scent is a sweet distillation of summer. Haworth has told him that there are bluebells in the wood in April. Will he still be here in four months' time to see it glowing?

His fingers touch tree trunks and the lichen is mineral green and copper and gold. It is bronze and blue and grey, and he wishes that he could paint these colours. He crouches on his haunches, takes out his sketchpad and pencil and begins to try to convey its textures on paper. Slowly, carefully, he makes a record, and there is only the noise of his pencil on paper, his steady breath and the chatter of the birds.

Haworth says that if Adam talks, he will remember – and they are determined to make him remember, whether he wants it or not. Haworth seems to think words are some kind of lubricant, and if enough of them fall out of Adam's mouth, he might start slipping backwards. But Adam is careful about his words and he doesn't mean to be false-footed. Because

Haworth wants him to talk, there must always be questions and requests for his opinions. He places trays of birds' eggs and butterflies in Adam's hands, invites him to pick out his favourites, and then asks why he makes those particular choices and judgements. He does the same with seashells and fossils and books of poems. Occasionally Adam feels like a puzzle that James Haworth is trying to work out. He knows that Haworth listens to every inflection of his voice and observes each shift of his eyes, but sometimes Adam doesn't want to be picked over; he doesn't want to speak; he doesn't want to be watched; he doesn't want there to be any more questions.

With the yellow flick of a goldcrest's wing, the branches stir. The lacquered red rosehips are like Christmas baubles, the sloes blue-bloomed enamel, and Adam thinks: is this here and now not enough? For one day, could they not look instead of talk? The low sun makes a shimmering lace of cobwebs. He walks on and the sky is full of spinning oak leaves. They twist and writhe and flock like starlings.

Haworth believes that if Adam answers enough questions, and sufficient words leave his mouth, he will start to turn back the hands of the clock, retrace his steps, and will face up to what came before. He has told Adam that. He needs to look it in the eye, Haworth says, he needs to address it, and come to terms with it – as if his past is an old enemy with whom he must now negotiate a peace treaty. But Adam knows it is not that simple; it is not just that he doesn't want to go there; there are blanks that he genuinely can't bring back, footpaths that are completely forgotten and gaps that he can't cross. Sometimes, if he focuses, he can grab at a word that is almost out of reach, but there are also places where he doesn't want to focus, where he doesn't want to direct his attention. There are questions that he doesn't want to ask himself. He doesn't see why the clock needs to be wound back.

He climbs then, out of the wood, out of the peaceful shade and shelter of the trees, and onto the crag where it all opens out. Rocks thrust upward from the summit, all the layers upended, as if the earth has been churned and twisted here, like so much kneaded bread. The edges are crystalline sharp in places, but looking down from the top of the crag, he sees the softness of tree canopy below and the shadows of clouds moving over Coniston Fells, all shades of purple and bronze and blue. The wind tugs at his clothes and he can see for such a long way. There is so much more still to see.

Haworth has told him that he will be encouraged to walk, to explore the landscape, and his feelings for it. But as he looks at the distant blue hills, Adam considers: what is there to stop him from carrying on walking and not going back? What he feels at this moment is that pull. Perhaps the granting of this freedom is what matters, though – the trust and faith and care that he will return and take his place at the table. His footsteps hesitate and turn.

Adam comes down by the tarn, back into the wood, and retraces his newly printed path. The slope is steep to descend, and so his fingers reach out for the trunks and ferns, and pebbles skitter away under his feet. He can smell the smoke of the chimneys again and see the house through the trees, the window that is all coloured glass and Caitlin Haworth's face looking out. He moves slowly, carefully, so that she doesn't see him. He doesn't mean to scare her. When the angle of her head turns towards him, he steps behind a tree trunk, but the fallen leaves spill beneath his feet and it all falls away like a river. He presses his face to the bark, breathes the scent of wet moss and lichen, pushes his fingers into its texture and wills himself invisible. He closes his eyes and his lungs are full of the orange-brown smell of the forest and pine sap. When he dares to look again, he sees her turning away and takes his chance; his feet skid through the leaves and it is more of an ungainly tumble than a planned descent.

But his heels push into the earth, then. He grips for a branch to stop himself falling and crouches to listen. Somebody else is in the trees below. He holds his breath so that he might hear. He tells himself that it was only the flutter of a bird's wing, or the fall of a pine cone, but he knows it was not. A rabbit? A hare? A deer? It's there again, a shadow splitting from the trees. A dark flicker. Adam feels his pulse quickening, and hears his own breath, and for a fraction of a moment he is in a different wood, where red hands grasp at his ankles, and the undergrowth sighs, and everything is sticky and sweet. But he blinks it away and forces his eyes to focus on the details of this kinder here and now. He watches. He waits. He listens. There it is again: a fleeting movement. A shift in the shadows. A figure between the trees. The crack of a twig beneath a boot.

'Hello? Who is it? Who is there?' Adam shouts.

He doesn't know Haworth's face for a moment. He looks up towards the direction of Adam's voice and it is as if his mask slips just for a second; fear makes James Haworth look like a different man. But then his features arrange, he is himself again, and he smiles with recognition. 'Adam! So you're there. I've been looking for you for ages. All woods are the devil's work,' he says.

Chapter Nine

James

'We have to do this properly,' says Captain O'Keaffe as he walks along the line. 'We have to hold it. We have to keep together. It's the only way that we can be sure that we've swept this wood. It needs to be cleared. We must have absolute certainty that we can hold it.'

'Hold it?' James hears Jackson repeat the words in a whisper and the note of incredulity in his voice. His face is inches from James' own. His breath is sour and there are dark circles under his eyes, like a premonition of himself as an older man, James thinks. Jackson looks like a man of forty this morning. Did they really raise glasses to his twenty-first birthday a few weeks ago?

'Officers, watch your compasses,' O'Keaffe goes on. 'We need to make sure that we continue to head north. No deviation this time. Stay in close contact. You need to constantly have the man to your left and right in view. Link arms, if you must. Hold hands, if that's your sort of thing.' A ripple of dissent and laughter goes along the line of men. 'We can't let the chain break.'

'This place is going to break *us*,' Webb says under his breath. 'I've got a really bad feeling about this.'

The whole battalion has been lined up at the southern edge of the wood, waiting here since 6 a.m., watching the light slowly reveal the tangle of bramble and branch ahead. The wood is four hundred yards wide on the ridge, James knows, and runs for 1,400 yards north. He has seen the typed orders. And the repeated orders, as attempt after attempt has failed. This wood has already changed hands several times, is full of Allied and enemy dead, but today they must secure it. The order uses, and italicizes, the word *imperative.* James looks at the compass in his hands and the needle is spinning. The men laugh now, but they will hold hands.

They set off picking their way in, but the terrain is terrible and within yards the line is ragged again. It is all tangled and frightful, and they stumble and swear. It is difficult to keep together, to keep thoughts on compass pins and the integrity of the line, when they must scramble through sharp, shattered branches and winding undergrowth. James' feet tangle in briars, sink into unseen hollows and catch on spirals of wire.

'We don't stop under any circumstances,' O'Keaffe repeats ahead. 'No hold-ups this time.'

'Would you want to linger here? Shall we pause for a picnic?' Webb's eyes say it all.

James wonders how this place will ever be innocent again. Will it ever again be a benign woodland where courting couples walk? Will this tension ever fall and the birdsong come back? But, then, perhaps this place has always been malevolent? It is a blue-skied July morning, but twenty yards into this wood it is midnight.

It stinks in the wood, of terrible, unnameable things. James doesn't want to open his mouth because he can taste it; he doesn't want to breathe through his nose because he feels he might be sick. It reeks and the flies cluster. They are on James' face and on his hands. Great fat, slow bluebottles. He tries to bat them away, but they're dozy and there are too many of them. As they had camped on the far side last evening, Nathaniel had lit two cigarettes and smoked them both at once, hoping that the smoke would repel the flies. They had laughed to see him trying to keep two cigarettes between his lips, but it did no good. Nathaniel is along the line, a few feet to James' left. He catches glimpses of him now and then. He catches the sound of his voice. When he glances towards him, it always feels like Nathaniel has just looked away.

A beat of black wings sends James stumbling. The crow angles its head and looks him in the eye – a black bead eye with nothing behind it – before its wings lift and it is gone. James realizes it has lifted from a body. It has lifted from a face.

'Don't look,' says Summerfield.

But how can they not look? And how can they not see that ruined face for ever more?

'This wood is the devil's work,' says Webb.

The dead are everywhere then. They are all slumped together, the khaki and the grey-green dead. There are men with broken limbs and broken faces, and as James looks at them, he never asks himself if they are *ours* or *theirs*. The wounded have been lying here for days. They have cracked lips and wounds that fester and stink. They are wheezing and coughing and calling out.

'Fuck!' Jackson swears and stumbles at James' side. When he looks down he sees that there are fingers around Jackson's ankle and his foot is then kicking the hand away, kicking at the arm and shoulder of the man who groans on the ground. Jackson's face is all frenzy and fear. James grabs his shoulders, tries to steady and calm him, and sees there are tears on Jackson's face.

'That's enough,' James says. He can feel Jackson trembling, feel the shock and fear coursing through his body. He gasps, crumples and vomits, but they have to go on.

'Why has no one been in to get these poor buggers out?' Webb asks. 'Are they just going to leave the dead and the wounded in here? Shouldn't we be getting them out?'

But they can't. They can't slow down and they can't go back. They say that more than two thousand men have already died in this wood. It is a charnel house.

'Anyone who looks like walking wounded, get them up and get them in the line,' says O'Keaffe. 'The rest can be dealt with when and if.'

'*Dealt with?*' Miller repeats. '*When and if?*'

'If anyone looks capable, he needs to get on his feet.'

That means they must sort the living from the dead, raise them up, make them walk, link the chain. They must pick those who can be patched back together from those who won't make it. And so they root them out of hollows, put a boot to backs and turn shoulders, but too many men are between life and death. Too many faces turn terribly towards them. Then there are the dazed and the wandering – all the men who seemingly have lost their wits in this wood – capable of walking, but not able to stay in line. James wonders: will these men ever leave this place?

'It's Old Testament, isn't it?' he says. He can feel the sweat trickling down his back. It prickles on his top lip. 'It's Isaiah and Ezekiel. It's Bruegel and Bosch.'

'It's bloody wicked,' Webb replies.

'Leave granted to fire at will,' shouts O'Keaffe ahead. He pauses and raises his hand. 'Keep your eyes open. You need to have your eyes all around you now. Any object might potentially conceal an enemy sniper.'

'This wood is haunted,' says Miller. 'I can tell. It's shifting shape around us. Don't you see? That big old bastard oak tree was to our left ten minutes ago. Now it's on the right.'

'Happen it's a different big old bastard tree.'

'No, it's not. Look at it. I bet you it's got a number chalked on it.'

'But is it the same number?'

'Perhaps we're going round in circles?'

It's like something from a fairy story, James thinks. Like Hansel and Gretel, and they're going deeper and deeper into the witch-wood. All his senses are saturated. He can hear his own heartbeat. His chest feels tight. Every snap of twig makes him jump. The needle of his compass won't stay still.

'There was a place that we used to dare each other to go into when we were children,' says Webb. 'There was a sink-hole in Lindley Woods. A couple of children had drowned there, so it was probably our own parents who made up the stories to keep us out. But we believed it and we felt it. I don't know why we pushed each other into that wood. Nobody wanted to be there.'

'But you kept going back? That's kids, isn't it?'

'And did you ever see anything?'

'Only out of the corners of my eyes,' Webb goes on. 'But whenever we went in there I knew that something was going on just out of sight, at the very edge of my vision, and if I turned around fast enough I might catch it. Something was definitely watching us. Do you know what I mean? Have you ever felt that? I wouldn't have gone in there on my own. I wouldn't go in there on my own now.'

'Lucky we're here to hold your hand, eh?'

They laugh, but it stops suddenly and their footsteps still.

The shape in front of them is a wraith for a minute,

something otherworldly summoned from Webb's story and the wood's own sour spirit; but then it is a man in a grey uniform with a gun turned upon them. They hit the ground as rifle fire cracks through the trees and then the wood is full of screaming.

James feels a current of air pass across his cheek, as a bullet strikes the ground inches ahead. There are raised voices all around him, but the whistle of that bullet was like a whisper in his ear, picking him out, intimate and foreboding. He's too frightened to move for a moment, he doesn't want to lift his head, but then the line of fire moves away and now they have to take their chance. The crack of rifles is all around him, and the recoil in his own hands, but the man in grey won't stay in his sights.

'The fucker won't go down!' shouts Reeth.

'He will now,' says Miller.

And it's true – finally – as James looks along the length of his rifle, he can't find the figure at all any longer. He shuts his eyes and the only noise left then is the breathing of the men around him. The sound of it takes up all the space and seems amplified by the trees. It is as if the wood itself is breathing and it makes James not want to open his eyes again. When he eventually does, he thinks he sees berries on a hawthorn branch for a moment, but it's July and they are beads of blood. The realization makes him gasp and he looks along the line needing to see Nathaniel. His face, on the ground, is turned towards James, but his eyes are closed too. For a moment James fears the worst, but then he watches Nathaniel's eye flick open. The relief is brief, though. There is something about the rapid movement of Nathaniel's eyes that James doesn't like. He has seen men's eyes move like that before. He sees panic in Nathaniel's eyes.

As they scramble up, and dust themselves down, there is one shocking last rifle crack and then shouting along the line. It comes back to them that a man from C-company has turned his gun on himself.

'Stupid bastard,' says Miller.

'Poor bastard,' says Webb.

James knows, as he breathes it in, that this place will come back to him in dreams for the rest of his life. He knows, having seen that look in Nathaniel's eyes, that this will revisit him too. He is suddenly afraid that Nathaniel will be the next poor bastard who turns his gun. James desperately needs to talk to Nathaniel then, to steady his nerves, to make sure he's being careful, to tell him all the things that he should have said earlier, but how can he now?

The broken trenches are tangled in with undergrowth and branches, and they stumble into them like sleepwalkers. They move on up through the old German communications trenches. The shells have churned everything up. It is all splintered and shattered, flung and tossed about and the angles aren't right. Nothing is as it should be in this wood. The sweat runs down James' face and stings his eyes.

There are pools of water, of unfathomable depth, as they move north. James recalls Webb's story of sinkholes and things shifting just out of sight. The wood echoes with the sound of artillery further north and they have to walk towards it. They are not allowed to stop walking. The surface of the water in the pool ahead is vibrating.

'Get down!' Miller screams.

The incoming shells roar and suddenly everyone is running. The line is broken and men are leaping in every direction. James hears the noise accelerate until every atom of his body seems to be vibrating. He hits the ground, his hands over his ears, and feels the force of the contact. The whole wood rocks and leaps then; branches fly and the black water in the hollows streaks upwards. Everything is up in the air, is stretched and twisted and overturned, and then falling down.

When James finally does look up again, it has all been rearranged. Like a child's game of memory, it is the same as it was, but all subtly different and parts are missing. What he doesn't expect to see when he looks up is Nathaniel. But he's there, on his feet, looking around, with a face like a child lost in a haunted wood. James wants to scream at Nathaniel to get down, to take cover; he wants to sprint to him and pull him to the ground, but the sight of him, with that look on his face, just circling in the glade of trees as if he has no idea how he has got here, makes James freeze for an instant. And it takes a moment for James to process the fact that the odd sing-song words in his head are actually coming out from Nathaniel's mouth. In the middle of this splintered, shattered, corpse-filled wood, erupting with shell fire, Nathaniel Holker is singing. The cracked, childlike voice is not the one that normally comes out of Nathaniel's mouth – and yet is terribly, desperately, vulnerably his own voice.

'"Once I had a sprig of thyme,"' he sings. '"It prospered by night and by day; 'Til a false young man came a-courting to me, and he stole all my thyme away."'

It's a song that James has heard old men singing in village pubs. Certainly a tune that he has never heard Nathaniel sing before. What mischief has put these words in his mouth now? What madness is making Nathaniel stand in a shaken-apart wood rhyming about lilies and wine and the end of time? It's at that moment, as Nathaniel's eyes slide and connect with James', that he hears the sniper start up.

*

When his eyes open it is Caitlin's face that he sees – so like Nathaniel's, yet so far removed; her eyes are wide with fear too. 'You did it again,' she says.

'I'm sorry. I'm so sorry.' James sits up. He rubs the nightmare from his eyes.

'Don't apologize. It's just heartbreaking to see you like that. Was it the same dream again?'

'Yes.'

'Did you see Nat again?'

He nods. He can't lie to her, but he also can't tell her any more of it. How can he share that?

'I'm sorry that's the version of him that you go back to. The other day I was thinking about when we all went to Bamburgh beach together. Can you remember? There are scenes from that day that I can still recall as if it were yesterday. You're both trying to walk on your hands and the sea is filling up the prints that you're leaving all down the sand. Your upside-down faces are laughing. I can see you so clearly. I can still hear you. That's the version of my brother that I want to remember. He was so blissfully happy that day! I'm trying hard to make that my dominant memory of him. Can you not remember that day too?'

'I can.' He takes her hand. 'I wish it could have stopped then, that the clocks could all have seized and we could just have stayed on the beach. I occasionally think how lucky Adam is, to have wiped the past five years out. I know that he's had no armistice, but he also has no war. Sometimes it frustrates me that he so obviously doesn't want to look back, but then I think, why would you want to be cured of that?'

'But I remember meeting you in London when you came home on leave and that stolen week we had. I remember seeing your face on the train the day you finally came home, and knowing you were home for good then and wouldn't be going back. Those memories are precious to me too. I wouldn't want that wiped out. We should look through the old photographs one day soon. Remind ourselves of our good memories of Nat. Make those images the ones that we remember.'

'Yes, I'll try,' he replies.

Chapter Ten

Adam, Fellside House, December 1918

'You don't like the wood, do you?' Adam asks.

'Why do you say that?'

'I could see it on your face.'

Adam looks up at the ceiling and listens to the noises of the house. There are steps across the oilcloth on the floor below. A kettle whistles. A sash window is pulled down. The plumbing clangs and somewhere water is gushing. It leaves behind the sound of the rain on the slate roof and Adam smiles to himself. Having said it aloud, having put the question out there, it's only fair to look away from Haworth's face. To give him time. To give him space to decide how, and if, he wants to reply.

'I'm not sure whether we perhaps ought to swap chairs!' Haworth says and Adam hears a smile in his voice.

'I'm sorry. Maybe I shouldn't have asked. Maybe I shouldn't have said that.'

'No, you're quite right. I seemed to spend a lot of the war in various woods. We had a difficult time in the woods.'

Adam nods.

'And you?' he asks.

'Me?'

'You seem like you're in your natural element there.'

'There's so much to see. My senses feel all full up in the wood and there's a satisfaction in remembering the names of things. Am I your first patient?'

Haworth laughs again. 'Hell. Is it that obvious?'

'I heard someone screaming last night.'

When the nightmare had kept coming back to him, Adam had decided to get up and to walk. Out in the garden, the moonlight shadows had been crisp as a woodcut and the snow gave all the lines of the land more significance. It had made Adam look at the landscape anew, and its stillness had forced him to listen. Breathing in the sharp, cold air, he had stood by the gates of the walled garden and had decided that he'd ask Shepherd if he could do some work in there, come the spring, if he was still here. The snow crunched underfoot, and creaked on the trees, and he had retraced his footsteps back across the garden. There had been something momentous about the moonlit garden in the full grip of winter, he had thought. It was like a dream light, it had glittered and sighed all around him, and taken away all the half-formed impressions of the nightmare that he can never quite remember.

But then Adam had heard the scream as he was crossing back towards the house, and seen the light flick on in the upstairs window. He had known that the voice was Haworth's, that it was his scream, that he screamed because he was remembering. Adam had considered: how could Haworth encourage him to remember, when that was what remembrance felt like? Caitlin Haworth's silhouette had crossed the curtain at the window and then back again.

An owl had screamed too, out of the indistinct darkness of the wood, but the light had been changing at that moment, and Adam could see the cloud of his breath all around him.

Though it would snow again, the sky had started to brighten, and he had known that it was nearly dawn. The silhouette of the house had looked as if it had been sketched onto the sky in blue-grey ink.

Adam had glanced back at the doubled line of his footprints across the lawn, the path that he had printed that night, and for a brief flicker he had seen other paths. Paths everywhere. Duckboard tracks, sunken roads and lines of mud in the snow. It was all scribbled across with barbed wire and telegraph lines. But Adam had blinked, forced it back, and the garden ahead had been pristine white again. That was how it worked. That was why the memories had to be held back. That was why he always had to look forward.

'Several people in the house have occasional nightmares,' Haworth says now, screwing the top on his pen and closing his notepad. 'It's not unusual. It happens. It didn't disturb you?'

'No. I thought it was a fox at first. I think I've heard it before.'

'Quite likely. Will you come down to us in five minutes?'

'I will.'

When Adam lies in his bed and looks up at the triangulating roof beams, he thinks of trigonometry and tree houses, the stone roof of the cathedral chapel and the turn of a kaleidoscope. The clouds roll over the hill now, the ceiling is all shifting shadows, and he is up in the elements in his rain-loud room. When he goes downstairs, in five minutes, they are planning to look inside his head and speak to his subconscious. Haworth has told Adam that this will help him, will help him to remember and thereby let him find peace of mind. But do they not see that peace of mind is about going forwards, not backwards? That it exists in the present and not the past tense? As Haworth closes the door, Adam remembers his scream breaking the silence of the midnight garden. He listens to the calm, predictable, knowable noise of the rain on the slate roof and wonders if he could climb out of the window.

Chapter Eleven

Caitlin, Fellside House, December 1918

She turns her tools in her hands, these deceptively simple planes of bamboo and bone that she had carefully shaped five years ago, so that their curves would, in turn, produce twin but reverse arcs when put to the spinning clay. Caitlin remembers sitting on a doorstep in Limehouse and spending hours filing away with sandpaper to smooth the perfect curve to form the foot of a bowl. She can still feel the sun of that day on her scalp, and hear the contented murmurs of the pigeons in the yard next door, and Nat's voice singing some frightful old music-hall song as he was whitewashing the walls inside.

'You made all your own tools?' Charlotte Shepherd asks.

Caitlin looks up and blinks away the memory. The snow has turned to rain today and it is gushing in the gutters now, washing against the windows, and giving the room a strange light. She runs her thumb over the well-known textures of her combs and stamps and throwing tools.

'Yes. I had friends who used fragments of knapped flint and deer horn and oyster shell, and I sometimes wonder how far we've come from the cavemen. But I like the primitiveness of it all, how basic and uncomplicated it is. People have been doing the same thing for thousands of years and I love that sense of continuity, that it's all just passed from one hand to the next.'

'Some hands being more capable than others. I wouldn't have the first clue! Is it one of those riding-a-bike things? I mean, does it simply come back to you straight away?'

'More or less. It takes ages to get it right at first, but then when you have a feel for it, that memory seems to lodge itself in your muscles. It's as if the collected sensations and their repetition become physically part of you.'

She had worried that it might not still be there, that the memory might have been dislodged or diminished, what with everything that has happened since, but she had started and then it was as though she'd never stopped, as though the past five years hadn't happened. The recall in her hands and her instincts had kicked in. And for a moment then, with the spiralling of the wheel, and her control of it, she had been her younger self again and everything was so much simpler.

'James is obviously pleased that you're starting again. He looked so proud when he was talking about your work.'

'Did he?' Caitlin can't help but smile. 'I adore him for suggesting it. I wouldn't have asked, and it means all the more that it was his idea. I'll never be able to thank you enough for letting me have this space.'

Charlotte shakes her head. 'There was nothing down here but rusting gardening equipment and crates of wizened apples. We want you both to be happy. Alan is determined that he wants to keep James here and so you both need to feel settled at Fellside.'

Though everything has now been cleared out, this cellar still smells of apples – a sweet, musty scent, like old apple brandy. Alan had said that some of the crates must have been mouldering away down here for decades. James had breathed it in and mused as to whether the air of this cellar might well be fifty per cent proof. But it's mingling with the smell of clay today, and there's something heady in that too, Caitlin thinks.

'We're so grateful for it. I can't tell you how much it means that Alan is supporting James' work. I think he might have struggled if Alan hadn't given him this chance.'

'Favouritism.' Charlotte winks. 'He was Alan's brightest student. He always talked about James. As soon as we heard he was home again, it was all I could do to stop Alan from pouncing upon him.'

Caitlin watches Charlotte touring her transformed cellar. She runs her fingers over the texture of the bench and reads aloud the names on the drums of slip and glaze. Though Charlotte is nearly twenty years younger than Alan, she seems to lean towards him in her looks, Caitlin considers. Perhaps it's the cut of her clothes, and the style of her hair, but if Caitlin didn't know otherwise, she would assume them to be a couple of the same age. There's something more mature in Charlotte's manner too, the way she unhesitatingly asks questions and draws conclusions, but perhaps that's what comes of having been a doctor's wife for fifteen years? Caitlin wonders: will she too take on that persona with time? She and James are still settling into the rhythm and order of their new life together, still tentatively defining their roles, but like old trees or standing stones, will they lean together with time? She thinks that she'd like it to be so.

'They've got a group coming in from Liverpool University tomorrow,' Charlotte says. 'Did James tell you? They're coming in to observe.'

'He did. It's great to see their work getting recognition, isn't it? Alan must feel very proud.'

'If his chest puffed out any further, his buttons would burst.'

'They've got a lot to look forward to, I hope.'

'And so have you,' Charlotte adds.

Caitlin had felt that as she'd watched James setting up her wheel at the weekend. It's a sensation that she hasn't known in a long time, and though she'd felt slightly mistrustful of giving herself over to optimism and excitement (something inconceivable for so long – and surely reckless!), she couldn't deny it was there. James had found a solid workbench and a slate slab, has fixed up shelves along the walls, and she'd seen how determined he was to make her happy. The heavy work done, he'd then sat back and watched as she'd unwrapped her tools. He had seemed fascinated by the unpacking of her previous life, and it had been a pleasure to share those memories with him.

Of course, they had talked about Nat, because he was there in all those recalled scenes, but this was the version of her brother who existed before the war, and Caitlin had found that she enjoyed saying his name again and briefly forgetting what came after. There had been something frightening, but then delightful about saying Nat's name out loud, and seeing James' hesitation turning into a smile. And she has felt Nat's presence in this studio too, as he always is there with her, looking on. She sometimes feels a stab of guilt now, it catches her out when she smiles or laughs, but Nat had been so encouraging of her work, of her doing her own thing, and so wouldn't he be pleased to see her starting again? Isn't he smiling too?

As James had brought in the last of the boxes, it had struck her that, while they had already shared so much, there remained spaces in the past to explore together. Good places to revisit. There was so much still to tell him. There was so much yet to learn about one another, and they could find joy in that, couldn't they? That was allowed, wasn't it? Surely that would make Nat happy too.

'Is this room suited to your work?' Charlotte asks.

'It is. It's cool, but light. It's ideal.'

The light slants in from the long row of ground-level windows at the back of the house, and Caitlin has positioned her bench so that she can watch people's legs as they come to the door. Already she has come to recognize the boots and trouser hems of every member of the household, their particular gait, and who approaches with confidence and who with hesitation. She knows James' feet as they pace back and forth on the gravel and sees his cigarette streaking away. The shadow of James' legs has moved back and forth across the walls of the studio this morning and it transmitted a tension. It made her pause and go wrong in her work. She is a little worried about the pacing, and isn't sure what it means.

Yesterday Adam had kneeled down and looked in through the window. He'd raised his hand when Caitlin caught his eye. She'd let him come into the studio afterwards, and had observed the keen interest with which he looked at her wheel and tools. He had put his fingers to the pot of brushes, and she's sure that she'd seen some sense of connection as he tested the bristles on his palm. He'd nodded and said, 'It's a splendid space,' and she had felt rather sorry when he'd left. Caitlin means to ask James whether she might offer Adam a lesson on the wheel.

'James told me you were at the Slade,' Charlotte says, 'and you had your own studio in London.'

'Studio makes it sound rather grander than it was, I'm afraid. I shared a basement flat in East London with another student and we rented the workshop above.'

'But that's quite something. You've never talked about it.'

'It's a long time ago,' she says and smiles at the recalled squalor and laughter of that summer spent flat-sharing with Rebecca. It seems *such* a long time ago. It might well be someone else's lifetime. It's like there's a disconnection between then and now, Caitlin thinks, like the world has tilted on its axis and the rules of physics have all shifted; like the war went on for four decades, not four years. That carefree, ambitious young art student, who danced and drank cocktails and laughed so much, might well be a storybook girl, and not her younger self. Caitlin likes that girl, she's fond of her, and she rather admires her boldness, but she also pities her because the girl has no idea what's coming next.

'Did you meet James in London?'

'I did. Becky and I were making an exhibition of ourselves in a park. You know how young girls are? We were pretending to read poetry and laying our picnic out as though it was a still life. James was down for the week, and playing football with his cousin and his crew. And so this uncouth youth kicked his dirty football right into our decorative salad leaves and vegetarian paste sandwiches. It might actually have been a mercy – but I wouldn't dream of telling him that!'

She can still recall first looking up into James' face, his hair stuck to his forehead with sweat, and then his smile spreading. Months later he had told her that he instantly knew he wanted to spend the rest of his life with her. She had felt rather sorry then for how Becky had sworn and scolded him that day.

'I take it you stopped working because of the war?' Charlotte asks.

'My mother wanted me to come back after Nat went. She told me that she needed me at home.'

'I understand. It was like that, wasn't it? Do I recall rightly that your brother was in the same battalion as James?'

'He was. Nat was like a puppy dog following James around. Of course, James was rather glamorous back in those days. He cut quite a figure in his uniform. I've never managed to work out whether Nat wanted to be James, or whether he was in love with him.'

'I remember James coming to dinner before they left for France and him being the dashing young lieutenant. But you didn't think about setting up a studio when you moved back up north?'

'My mother never really approved of it. She was glad to have me back rolling bandages with her nice safe local ladies and knitting socks for soldiers. My wheel and all my kit were put into storage and I was expected to be quiet and fragrant.'

'How very bored you must have been.'

'Frightfully! I hated the bloody war.' She laughs and apologizes.

'Nathaniel was your twin, wasn't he?'

'He was.'

'I imagine that it's been very difficult. Losing a sibling must be bad enough. The past five years must have been rather tough for you.'

'It's a peculiarly physical thing; it sometimes feels like part of my own body has been removed. It's hard to explain.'

'I'm sorry. I probably shouldn't have brought it up.'

'No! Don't apologize, Charlotte. Everyone tells me that I ought to talk about it, though I'll admit it isn't always easy. People keep telling me that time heals too, and that made me so angry at first – I mean, how glib! How would they know? But I couldn't even bring myself to say Nat's name two years ago, so I suppose they weren't entirely wrong. I still have off days, but it's not as bad as it was, and I think that starting work again will help too. I can't do it without focusing one hundred per cent. You have to blinker everything else out and it's physical work. It tires my body and my brain. When I've done a full day of work, I just want to sleep and I never dream.'

'What bliss that sounds!' Charlotte smiles, but then Caitlin sees a hesitation on her face. 'I'm really not sure that I ought to mention it, but Alan thinks James looks tired. He is sleeping, isn't he?'

'Not terribly well, if I'm honest. I guess it'll take a while for everything to settle down.' She considers whether to tell Charlotte about James' nightmares, but decides that this isn't perhaps information that she has the right to share.

'He'll get there,' Charlotte says. 'And he's determined to make things right for you. He's strong. It will all work itself out, and the peace of this place will help James as much as it helps everyone else.'

'I hope so,' Caitlin replies.

Chapter Twelve

James, Fellside House, December 1918

James walks through to the office. There are photographs of Shepherd's grandfathers on the desk, looking frank and fearless in uniform, and the room is full of the crackle of Adam's voice on a wax cylinder.

'"And I shall have some peace there, for peace comes dropping slow,"' Adam recites. His voice is measured. It is the voice of a man self-consciously reading words from a page. '"Dropping from the veils of the morning to where the cricket sings; there midnight's all a glimmer, and noon a purple glow, and evening full of the linnet's wings."'

'Yeats, isn't it? Why this in particular?' Shepherd asks.

'I handed him the *Oxford Book of English Verse* and tried to turn his game on him, as it were; I watched him flicking through the pages and asked him if he'd pick a favourite and read it aloud for me. I was interested in his choices, what spoke to him, and also in his voice. I do still want to hear more of his voice.'

'His accent?'

'Yes. I can't pin it down. Can you?'

Shepherd nods as he listens. 'Northern vowel sounds, I'd say, but beyond that it has rather stumped me too. I can't hear any specific locality. He has no particularly striking local characteristics.'

'"I will arise and go now,"' Adam reads, '"for always night and day I hear lake water lapping with low sounds by the shore; while I stand on the roadway, or on the pavements grey, I hear it in the deep heart's core."'

'How does it make you feel?' It is James' own voice on the wax cylinder now.

There's a silence.

'I can't hear you shake your head.' It's James again. 'Would you speak, please, Adam?'

'I don't know.'

'Does it remind you of anything?'

'I'm not sure.'

'Do you like the words?'

Silence again. 'Will you speak for the record, Adam?'

The recording crackles out.

'That's a shame,' says Shepherd. 'Could he give you a reason? Could he explain why he picked this particular poem?'

'Eventually. He told me that he liked the mood of it,' James replies, 'and the choice of words: the bean-rows and the bee-loud glade. He took a while looking through the book – I started to wish that I'd given him something slimmer. I wasn't sure that he'd select anything at all, but then this seemed to move him. I could see him thinking about it. It unmistakably seemed to speak to him. There was obviously some connection.'

'And what do you take from that?'

James looks up at Shepherd and smiles. 'I search for meaning in every choice that he makes, you know. I squint at his every decision and facial inflection, hunting for patterns, trying to root out clues, but then in interpreting, in applying meaning to his choices, isn't there a danger that it's more about me than him? Contaminating the experiment with my own overactive will to see a result, I mean. I ask myself: am I seeing things in him that simply aren't there? Am I overkeen? Am I trying too hard?'

'Adam Galilee the enigma.' Shepherd raises an eyebrow. 'He's stopped the fabrications now?'

'Yes. He looked like a scuppered schoolboy when I pointed out that he'd been seven minor English poets over the course of a week. I don't think that just asking him his name is the way to go about it.'

'Don't doubt yourself too much. Your instincts are spot on. You're going about it the right way.'

'Am I? Thank you. I'm grateful for your vote of confidence.' James glances down at his notes, but they're so scant and every line seems to end in a question mark. 'He unmistakably has an affinity for, and knowledge of, the natural world. There's no randomness to him picking out a poem full of bean cultivation and a linnet's wings. We've walked together and he points things out. He can talk like an encyclopaedia when he's in the mood. His head is full of nomenclature, the life cycle of this and that, and what distinguishes an alder from an elder – and yet everything personal has been wiped clean. I'm struck by how neatly compartmentalized and intact all that knowledge is, when everything that relates to his own history might as well have been taken out with a scalpel.'

'Trauma,' says Shepherd.

James nods. He has no doubt that Shepherd is correct, but he hears such confidence in his voice, and doesn't feel he can share that certainty. Can one word really answer all the questions that he has, and sum up all that complexity? Can it be that simple?

'Does he know the Latin names?' Shepherd asks.

'Of plants? Yes, in many cases. Why do you ask?'

'I'm only thinking about his level of education. Are the dirty fingernails a red herring? Was he a man who worked with a spade, or with a pen? I find this voice curiously classless. Don't you? And the drawing – he's accomplished. He's been making splendid studies in the garden. Was that taught? Could he have been a scholar? Is he a gentleman?'

'If it's defined by knowing the Latin name for a daisy, then I'm evidently not. He could be self-taught? He's evidently had a passion for these things.'

'And the woman – the woman who he draws – is that a passion too?'

'The repetition is almost obsessive. It's the only face that he puts down on paper; the only figure that appears at all. I asked him if he'd like Sally to sit for a portrait, if he wanted to study another face for a change, a face from life, but he said that he wouldn't know how to start to draw her.'

'Who do you think the woman is, then?'

'His wife? His lover? Certainly someone with whom he's had a close relationship. From the drawings, I'd say that she's a woman of approximately his own age. He says he misses her.'

'It's something that he acknowledges that much; that he feels something for this woman. The expression of that emotion is some crack in his armour, isn't it? I'm glad we've found one at last.' Shepherd takes off his glasses and rubs his eyes. 'Do you remember Doctor Wilkinson from Cheadle Royal? We had him round for dinner last night, and he spent the entire evening trying to persuade me that Galilee is a fake.'

James sits back in his chair. 'But Wilkinson has never met Adam, has he?'

'Quite. I said: Why would a man pretend that he's forgotten everything that matters to him? Fair enough, if he'd just played that game for a day or two, but it's been well over a month now.'

'Exactly. And Wilkinson said?'

'That we're keeping him. That we're cosseting him. What worries does Adam have? What responsibilities does he bear?'

'No, it's not like that.'

'I agree. It's no strategy. It's no game. But it did leave a niggle behind. I'm glad that Adam has agreed to be hypnotized. I would like to feel that we're making some progress. Have you told him how it works?'

'Yes, I explained the procedure.'

'And what was his reaction?'

James considers. 'Not keen, if I'm honest. Concerned. Wary. Nervous. He asked me whether he'd remember it afterwards, or if it would be like a dream that he might forget.'

'It's a pity that he's not more enthusiastic. I do have concerns. Is he likely to fight against it?'

'I'm not sure. Left to his own devices, he's calm enough. He tends to get absorbed in what he's doing and can look almost serene, but when I try to encourage him into conversation, he gets agitated. If I'm straight with you, I don't know whether you'll manage to put him under.'

The wax cylinder hisses again and then Adam's voice is singing. There is something odd about this part, James thinks; something otherworldly, something uncanny about Adam's crackling voice. And it's more than the choice of song. Though they made the recording only yesterday, it feels as though Adam's voice is coming from somewhere very distant to the rational order of Shepherd's study.

'"Oh, thyme it is a precious thing,"' he sings, '"And thyme

it will grow on, and thyme it'll bring all things to an end, and so does my thyme grow on."'

'It's a folk song, isn't it?' Shepherd asks.

'Yes, we looked through the Cecil Sharp. I was interested in whether he remembered tunes.'

James hadn't expected Adam to pick out that tune. As soon as Adam had begun, James was back in Trônes Wood in 1916, amongst those tattered trees, and it was Nathaniel's voice singing. He has maybe heard this particular song four or five times in his life. What are the odds that Adam's voice would pick out the same melody as Nathaniel's? What odd game is this?

'Isn't it a song about a woman losing her virginity?'

'Or loss of innocence.'

'"The gardener was standing by,"' Adam sings. '"I bid him choose for me. He chose me the lily, aye, the violet and the pink, but I really did refuse them all three."'

When James had asked Adam where he knew the song from, he had shaken his head. It was just there, he'd said. He couldn't remember when he'd ever heard it before. The recording crackles to a close and James looks up to see Adam's face at the door.

James listens to Shepherd's voice. He tells Adam that he is lying in a summer meadow, that the sun is warm on his face and that bees are buzzing in poppies and cornflowers all around him. Behind Shepherd's voice, James can hear the noise of the rain on the roof, but he's pushing that away, conjuring the lulling hum of midsummer and birdsong. He tells Adam to give himself up to sleep, to breathe deeply and let sleep come over him. He is feeling drowsy, Shepherd tells him, his muscles are relaxing, his limbs are feeling heavy, his eyelids as heavy as lead. Shepherd speaks slowly and calmly, his words stretching out and Adam's eyes flicker. James can see that Adam's eyelids are resisting. They hardly look like they're heavy as lead. He's trying to keep his eyes open, but he's losing the fight. When Adam's eyes finally close, James can see the rapid movement still going on beneath. He doesn't look like his subconscious is lying in a summer meadow; he looks like something inside him is thrashing.

'He's under,' Shepherd says to James over his shoulder. 'Finally.'

'Yes.' As he watches Adam's face, he's not convinced that this is a good idea. Have they forced him? Have they pushed him into it? Was it right to have gone against his obvious reluctance?

Shepherd takes Adam back to the cathedral, back to pushing the door open and entering, back to walking through the streets with the cathedral towers in his eyes. He rewinds all of Adam's movements back, to the time before he was Adam, and then asks him to take over. He animates the sights and sounds and smell of Durham marketplace all around him, puts his feet on those cobbles, and then wants to know how they have got there.

'Walk backwards for me now, will you?' Shepherd asks. 'You can talk. You can tell me what you see. Take me to where you've come from. Speak.'

James watches Adam's face respond. He looks like he's waking from sleep. He blinks hard and seems to consider the question. James is struck by how different his face looks now, how the shadows have realigned from five minutes earlier, and the personality that expresses itself on Adam's face has changed. Those are still Adam's gentle brown eyes, but something different is vibrating behind them now. Adam puts his fist to his mouth as he thinks and James can't quite tell whether he is trying to keep the thought in or struggling to get it out.

'On the road,' he finally replies.

James tries to focus in on Adam's vowel sounds: is there more of an accent there now? Or is it just drowsiness?

'Yes. Go on,' Shepherd encourages. 'Have you been on the road for a long time?'

'Yes.'

'You've been walking?'

'Yes. There are lots of us on the road.'

'Lots of you? Go on. Tell me what's happening around you. Are you with other soldiers?'

Adam lifts his hands and rubs his eyes as if he's weary. When his hands pull away, he looks like an older man, James thinks. Is this his face without the mask, or is this a different persona that he has put on? Which is the real Adam?

'Some. There are other men who have been on the road for years. Some of them know nothing but the walking.'

'When did you start to walk the road?'

'A long time ago. I'm tired.'

'Did you start in France?'

Adam closes his eyes and takes a breath. They watch the rise and fall of his chest. It is as though he is steadying himself. James thinks that he looks like an athlete about to step up to the start line, but when his eyes open again, he is anything but focused.

'His pupils are dilated,' says Shepherd.

James steps in closer to see Adam's eyes. They watch his eyes slowly move about the room, as if taking it all in for the first time, but then the movement is more rapid. Adam's eyes tear about the room like he's seeing invisible terrors.

'Is he quite well? Should we stop? Can you get him out of it?'

'What are you seeing, Adam?' Shepherd asks. 'What's there? Will you tell me what you're experiencing?'

'He's distressed, Alan. I'm concerned.' James can see Adam trembling. He looks like every nerve in his body is vibrating. With the stretch of his mouth, he is like an agony in an Old Testament painting. He is a face from William Blake and Bruegel and Bosch. It is the face of the men in the wood.

'Can you tell me your name?' Shepherd asks. 'Will you tell me your name? Will you tell me where you've come from?'

The scream that comes from Adam's mouth makes them both step back. It is a roar of raw terror and it won't stop. It's like something awful has been unleashed and won't now go back inside. James looks to Shepherd in panic. Adam's scream fills the house and echoes into the hillside.

1920

Chapter Thirteen

Anna Mason, Victoria Station, London, November 1920

'There were six of them,' says the woman in the black straw hat, 'from the Aisne, Marne, Cambrai, the Somme, Arras and Ypres.' She counts them out on her fingers. 'I read it in the evening paper. Six poor boys dug up out of nameless graves. My Alfie's last letter was from Arras, so it could be, couldn't it?'

Anna leans against the barriers. The whole station has filled with people and she can't see the end of the crowd behind now. She looks at the face of the woman by her side, so in need of affirmation. 'Yes, it could be,' she replies.

'They carried each of them on a stretcher and brought them to a chapel. They were all covered over with a flag. No one must know who was from where. You see? And so the old general goes in with his eyes blindfolded. Can you imagine? Then it's up to him. He steps forward and he puts his hand on one of them, and that's it. Just like that. That's him. The lad is put into an unmarked coffin, and then they're bringing him home, and calling him the unknown warrior.'

The woman dabs at her eyes with a handkerchief. Anna can smell violet scent and sweat. She finds herself feeling strangely alienated from this show of sentimentality.

'And what happened to the others?'

'The others? I'm sorry, love?'

'To the men on the stretchers – the other bodies?'

'Oh. I've no idea. The newspaper didn't say.'

Anna looks at her watch. She can feel the crowd pressing behind. They are all having this conversation. They are all speculating. Do they all have someone missing, then? Can there be so many of them? She has told herself that she will know if the man in the railway carriage is Mark. She will feel it. She will sense it. But the breath of the crowd is on the back of her neck, and the murmur of their words, and she knows that they are all contemplating the same question.

She puts her hand out to steady herself on the barriers. She feels too hot and slightly light-headed. With the swell and crackle of energy through the line of people, it is like the moment before the pistol cracks for the start of a race. The constables walk along the line again.

'Please, ma'am.'

She takes her hand from the barricade and apologizes.

There is silence for the first moment, as they glimpse the engine coming into the station. Then there is a collective intake of breath. But it holds only for a second. It starts then, the great swell from behind. They are pushing into Anna's back, nudging her forward; she has to move to keep on her feet, and then the barriers are crashing to the ground. The people push past her, they surge around her, and she sees the black straw hat ahead. The special constables are shouting now, they are blowing their whistles and pointing, but how can they stop something like this? How can they hold this back? She steps over the fallen barriers.

A woman is screaming up ahead, they are pushing too close to the platform edge and it is all starting to become hysterical. Through the crowd she can just see the white top of the railway van approaching. It moves very slowly down the platform and, as it does, she watches the crowd step back. It is as if the carriage has some strange repelling magnetism, and suddenly the frenzy is silenced. Hats are lowered. Heads are bowed. Hands go to mouths. The only noise is the sound of a man sobbing.

The train comes to a halt some distance down the platform. Anna hears the doors sliding open and for a moment she feels that she doesn't want to approach it. She doesn't want to see inside. She stands still and watches the crowd move forward. Many of them don't stay long; the crowd starts to break and they drift back. A man leads a woman away with an arm around her shoulders. A young girl turns and her face is swollen with tears. A woman shoves into Anna, shaking her head. She turns, instinctively about to protest, but the woman's face is so tragic that the words dissolve in Anna's mouth. Do the people who walk away have a sense that this nameless man is not theirs? Is it doubt or hope that makes others linger? Do they want to think that this man who will be interred in an abbey tomorrow could be theirs?

As she steps forward, she gets a first glimpse of the interior. It is an ordinary luggage carriage, albeit newly painted and polished for the occasion. The light inside is dim, but she can make out small electric bulbs illuminating the folds of purple drapes. There are palm leaves plaited into wreaths and a latticework of bay leaves. Amongst the shadows, chrysanthemums glow white.

The police are trying to give the occasion back its dignity. They're righting the barriers. Politely asking the crowd to move back. Saying that the barricades are there for the public's own welfare and comfort. After the initial rush of emotion, the crowd is silent now and compliant. They do as they are told. Everyone is talking in whispers. Rules are being re-established.

As she steps to the barrier, Anna sees that four soldiers have moved up to guard the coach. They stand with their heads bowed, the muzzles of their guns between their boots, their fingers intertwining over their rifle butts. They instantly become stone sentries these men, and might well be guarding the tomb of a king, or a pharaoh. Their reverent features could be marble, and their eyes don't move as the crowd pushes and sighs. They are the last watch. Anna considers what emotions must be passing behind their impassive eyes.

The doors and windows of the carriage are open now so that it can be seen in full. There are great laurel wreaths and white ribbons and, on the floor, a box draped with a flag. With all the surrounding ceremony, there is something surprising to Anna in that; the coffin ought to be raised up on a dais, or at the very least lifted on some sort of trestle. There is something so pathetic and prosaic about this wooden box, she thinks, on the floor of a goods van with the fabric falling in creases. There is a clash of humbleness and ceremony, and she wonders if they genuinely do mean to bury this ordinary soldier beside kings.

One of the sentries stifles a cough and is suddenly a mortal, flesh-and-bone man again. She looks at his khaki shoulder, his hair neatly trimmed against his neck, his cheeks newly shaved and his brown eyes cast down. His eyes are the same colour as Mark's. She watches the flick of his eyelashes, his chest rise and fall, the breath leave his lips. She can smell his sweat and shaving soap and can see ink on his fingers. Does this man draw it all too, and fold his images into envelopes for his wife? She shakes her head. She sees more of Mark in this man than in the nameless body in the van. Is there even a body in there? Is this not all theatre and a charade to pacify the public? Would they really bury a common soldier in the abbey? The newspapers are calling this anonymous man a hero, a brave man who sacrificed himself for his dear land, but how can they know that? How can any ordinary man measure up to that? How can they really know what this man's war was like?

She checks her wristwatch again. The return train to Halifax leaves in forty-five minutes. She had planned to stay the night with her cousin in Tottenham, and to watch the coffin being carried into the abbey, but she knows now that there is no need.

The woman in the black straw hat is at her side again. She squeezes Anna's hand and she looks into this stranger's face, so full of raw emotion.

'It's not Alfie,' the woman says. 'I so wanted it to be him, and I'd know if it was, but it's not. Do you think it might be your husband, dear? Do you feel it? Could it be him?'

'No. It's not Mark. It can't be. My husband's not dead,' Anna replies.

Chapter Fourteen

Celia Dakers, Ryedale, November 1920

'You've got your lovely grey serge on,' says Stella, as she links her arm through Celia's.

'Yes.' Stella is all in black. Celia considers again: should she have worn the black dress instead? Would that not have been more proper? More appropriate? She had pulled it out, and held it up against herself in front of the dressing-table mirror, but it seemed like bad luck, like it might jinx things, like it might force a decision that she isn't prepared to make. 'It's Robert's favourite. You don't think anyone will consider it disrespectful?'

'No, of course not.'

But Celia feels her heart race as they go up the path through the graveyard. There are wreaths of white lilies in the church porch, a peppery scent and waxy petals that don't seem to leave any room for doubt.

Stella squeezes her hand. 'You are quite well? You still want to go in?'

'Yes. I should. We should pay our respects to the others, shouldn't we?'

Eyes turn towards Celia, as she and Stella enter, and they quickly slip into a pew at the back. The church is full of people who have already taken their seats, this not being the time or place for small talk. With so many people here, it is strange how quiet it is inside the church. Celia looks up at the glow of the window, seeking comfort in Jesus' luminous features, but his eyes are angled away, and the men arranged around him are all stiffly unconvincing. She looks up to the roof beams (Robert always said they reminded him of the belly of a boat), and can hear the breathing of the people all around her. Do they all feel the same tension she does? Do they too worry that Jesus isn't listening?

'It feels like a funeral,' whispers Stella.

Celia supposes that, in many ways, it is.

The organ wheezes out its first notes, the stoppers and keys creaking, and they all stand for the opening hymn. '"O God, our help in ages past,"' she sings, '"Our hope for years to come, our shelter from the stormy blast, and our eternal home."'

Reverend Seabrook had asked her, the previous day, if she would like a bell to be tolled for Robert. The question had surprised her.

'For Robert? But why?'

'Because Robert hasn't come home,' Reverend Seabrook had said in a voice that was obviously meant to be kindly. 'Because Robert might not come home.'

'But of course he will!' Celia had replied. Tea had spilled in her saucer. She had stood up. She felt an urge to head for the door.

'Please, Celia, will you sit with me?'

She had reluctantly complied, smoothed the fabric of her skirt over her knees, pushing away all the creases, and had told him, 'I know he's coming back. It's just difficult for him at the moment. But he will come home. I have never been surer of anything in my life.'

'I wonder,' Reverend Seabrook began. He hesitated. 'I do wonder if you shouldn't perhaps prepare yourself for the alternative? It has been two years now.'

Celia had shaken her head as she had walked away, angry at that man of God for his lack of faith. She had made her mind up that she wouldn't attend the memorial service today, but then she had read about the journey of the unknown warrior in the newspaper last night, and it didn't seem right not to pay her respects to David Summerfield and Edmund Williamson and Alice Smith's poor boy.

'"Time, like an ever-rolling stream, bears all its sons away,"' Stella sings at her side now. '"They fly forgotten, as a dream dies at the opening day."'

They sit and must listen to Reverend Seabrook's well-practised kindnesses. The bereaved families have all been seated in the front pew, Celia sees, with the aldermen and councillors and the corporation men. She watches Alfred Harper put a hand around his wife's shaking shoulders. There is an empty pew between the bereaved families and the rest of the congregation, as if, for all the well-meant smiles and nods and handshakes, no one knows quite how to cross that space; how to negotiate that difficult barrier. Celia is glad that she doesn't have to sit in the front pew with all their eyes on her back.

Reverend Seabrook talks about the resurrection and eternal life. He talks about heroism and sacrifice and a debt of gratitude. He looks up from his words from time to time, leans over his lectern, his eyes scanning the congregation, and Celia finds herself looking down when he does this. She doesn't want his eyes to connect with hers. She can't connect Robert with the sentiments he's rehearsing. She is realistic enough to know that her son hasn't played a hero's role; he also hasn't been sacrificed. She doesn't want these words to be for him. The lectern is carved with an eagle, sharp talons and hooked beak and spread wings that look full of tense energy, as if the thing might be about to pounce. Celia sees the vicar's fingers tightening around the edges of the lectern, and there is something hawkish about him too as he leans and looks out at them all.

'Grant, we beseech thee, merciful Lord, to thy faithful people pardon and peace that they may be cleansed from all their sins, and serve thee with a quiet mind.'

Philip Stewart is two rows in front. Celia can see the edges of the tin mask that hides the hole in his face. She can't help but look at that, her eyes can't help but be drawn there, and she has noticed that everyone does the same. She wonders: does he feel pardoned and peaceful? Does he have a quiet mind? There is something so tragic and terrifying about his mouth that smiles only at one side, and Celia thinks *that* is sacrifice. She wonders: would she want Robert back if people were to look at him that way? But she knows he will come back whole and soon.

'O Lord, have mercy upon us. O Lord, let thy mercy lighten upon us: as our trust is in thee. O Lord, in thee have I trusted: let me never be confounded.'

The vicar talks about sorrow and triumph, about grief and healing and pride. There's to be a new chancel screen to commemorate the fallen, he says, so that they may always be in their thoughts, so that future generations may always look up and remember them. It will be carved from an oak tree that fell in the village during the last year of the war. Celia remembers that old tree, down by the churchyard gate, and seeing it brought to the ground by the storm. Such a mighty thing to be felled.

She had walked past that tree for decades, but then seeing it on its side made it seem as strange and remote as a fallen Grecian column, or the skeleton of a dinosaur, and crowds had gathered around it. She remembers looking at its upended roots, powerful and fine and scented with something that must be history, and the disturbance of the earth so close to the gravestones. What tremors had they felt? What had unsettled there? She also remembers Robert leaning against that same oak tree, two years earlier, and turning an acorn between his fingers. She knows that Robert hasn't fallen. Everything has been unsettled, but she has that certainty: that he has no need for a gravestone, or a mourning bell, or a carving to bring him to mind.

'I believe in the Holy Ghost,' Stella's voice repeats at her side, 'the holy Catholic Church; the communion of saints; the forgiveness of sins; the resurrection of the body, and the life everlasting.'

The vicar tells them about the unknown warrior being laid to rest in Westminster Abbey today. No one will ever know who that man was, he supposes. He might well be a lad from this village, he says, and pauses at that thought. It is a beautiful thought, he reflects, and every bereaved mother whose son lies in an unknown grave should take that comforting thought to heart.

Celia feels Stella glance towards her, but she holds on to her Bible and knows that she is not a bereaved mother. She doesn't want them to think that, because she refuses to believe it herself. It is beyond contemplation. It is beyond possibility. She doesn't want comforting thoughts or sympathetic looks.

Reverend Seabrook talks about men whose bodies lie in foreign lands, men buried hurriedly as they fell, and those whose resting places are not known. No padre offered up prayers for these men, he says; it wasn't possible, but as a bugle was sounded over them, it seemed as though they were laid to rest in consecrated ground. Celia kneels through the prayers, her head bent to her chest, and crouches into herself as the words pass over.

Peter Summerfield has been brought in to play the 'Last Post'. As the notes quaver, Celia wonders if Peter is thinking of his older brother who hasn't come back. The notes are tremulous at first, are full of vibration and uncertainty, and Celia pities him for how exposing this music is, but the sound gains in intensity and expression, and finally she feels it vibrate inside her own chest. In the long silence that follows, she thinks about the last time she saw Robert; they went out walking together on his last leave and they had named all the varieties of trees together. She cannot now walk down that lane without hearing Robert's voice distinguishing the alder and the elder. She had laundered his clothes after he left, and found conkers and pebbles in his pockets, the way she always used to when he was a boy. He is too young, too intensely alive, not to still be out there walking lanes and turning pebbles over in his pockets. She shuts her eyes to the white lilies and the black coats, and tries to imagine the lane that Robert is walking down today. She asks God to turn his footsteps and bring him home.

Peter Summerfield plays the 'Reveille', though his brother will never wake up again, and his mother looks as though she would gladly follow him into the ground. The sanctified silence ends and bowed heads are raised, but then there is an awkward moment of staging and whispered instruction as the next demonstration of collective grief is arranged. The vicar had told her that the bell would strike, and so it finally does now.

It tolls six times, once for each man from the village who has died, their names spoken aloud in between the strikes and listed on the order of service that shakes in Celia's hand, and once for the unknown warrior. Though she had asked Reverend Seabrook not to speak Robert's name, she half expects that he still will, and it is a relief when the bells finally end. She is glad there were only six bells, though there is a strange emptiness as the resonance fades away and it feels like something is missing, like something else is about to happen. But it doesn't. She squeezes her hands between her knees to stop them from trembling. Celia feels all hollowed out by the bells.

They all blink into the daylight and she almost expects Robert to be there when she steps out of the church – for the light to shift, and for him to be standing there smiling, and telling her that she was right to wear her pearl-grey dress. It would be just like Robert to surprise her. That would be so typical of him. She can almost picture the expression on his face, the light in his eyes, the shadow of his eyelashes, but there is only the dazzle of the sun and Stella waiting to take her arm. They walk out amongst the old gravestones and the yew trees which have seen it all before.

People squeeze Celia's hand and touch her shoulder as they move through the churchyard. They want to detain her and to talk about the memorial. Mrs Palmer tells her that they are close to signing off the plans, that they have chosen a Gothic lettering, and it will now say, *In Memory of the Men of this Parish who Fell in the Great War.* Celia can see that Mrs Palmer wants her to appreciate the sentiment and to nod at that. *Greater love hath no man than this: that a man lay down his life for his friends* will be carved at the base. Mrs Palmer wants Celia to like that, she can see; she desires her consent and approval. But Celia can only shake her head. She feels it is not something that she needs to be part of. She doesn't require consulting on the Bible quote or the font of the lettering. She doesn't want to be included in this. It's not her business.

Many of the old graves in the churchyard are leaning. They tilt together like fond friends, or village gossips sharing news. The Men of this Parish who Fell are all to have new graves cut from Portland stone, they have been told. They will be clean and straight and true, with no doves or ivy leaves or cherubs to clutter their tidy uniformity. Celia thinks this rather sad. She and Robert had always liked to walk amongst the old graves and observe their curious individuality and archaic quotations. She still likes to look out at the stiff-winged angels and the incline of the crosses. Celia's garden backs on to this graveyard, and in the spring she plants crocus bulbs around Tabitha Fenwick and Augustus Spedding, because they are her view and her neighbours. She knows all the inscriptions, and carvings, and names – and, above all, she knows that Robert's name definitely shouldn't be in this churchyard. He doesn't belong amongst the *In Memoriams* and *Loving Memories*. He shouldn't be listed on a monument, or tolled by a bell. He doesn't need to be made into a hero, and she doesn't need to be told to remember him. There is no grave. There is no news. But she knows that his footsteps have turned now and that he's coming home.

'He's coming back,' she says to Stella. 'It's happening. He's coming now. I can feel it.'

Chapter Fifteen

Lucy Vickers, Lancashire, November 1920

George calls the Adelphi a fleapit. He says that Lucy will come out covered in bites, that she will come home crawling, and really ought to save her sixpence. But Dora goes on: 'What if it's Ellis? Have you thought? What would you feel like if it was Ellis?' And so Lucy has to go and see it, doesn't she?

'What if it *is* your brother?' Dora had said. 'Imagine if it's him in the coffin, and all the to-do and the crowds have come out for poor old, ordinary Ellis Vickers? I mean, it could be, couldn't it?' Lucy had wanted to hit Dora for saying that. She had wanted to shake her, and shout, and ask her how she could think such a thing. But somehow Dora had persuaded her to come to the cinema. And now she is sitting in this fleapit. 'Happen you will know if it's him when you see it?' Dora had said. 'And there's Douglas Fairbanks afterwards, anyway.'

It smells unpleasant in the Adelphi, a sweet, sickly smell, like the whole place needs a proper clean. Like the whole thing needs fumigating. The arms of the seat are sticky. Lucy puts her hands in her lap and tries not to think about fleas, or who sat in this seat last, and why Ellis isn't here with her now.

'It said in the paper that they'd got in a string quartet,'

Dora complains, as she leans down towards the front. 'I feel a bit short-changed. I paid for *Pomp and Circumstance*. It said, in the *Gazette*, how the music was so rousing.'

All Lucy can see is the usual organist and a chap waxing the bow of a violin, the rosin flickering away under the electric lights and a spray of mimosa on the music stand. 'I'm not sure that this audience ought to be roused.'

She feels a peculiar sense of nervousness as the house lights go down. It's not that she doesn't know what's coming, only that it's different to actually see it up there in the full, unflinching glare of the cinema screen. She had read it all in the newspaper, of course, the week before; about all the stations full of people watching the van with the white roof slide by, the gun carriage and the barrels of soil brought from France, and the queues to see the coffin. As the film flashes into life, something seems to flip in her stomach.

'It could be anyone in that coffin, couldn't it?' Dora whispers in the darkness. 'Have you thought? It could be our coal man, or nasty Uncle Neville, or that man who used to walk around Victoria Park with his flies down. Just think, if it was him, buried next to the kings and queens?'

'But that wouldn't happen, would it? They wouldn't let that happen?'

She feels Dora's shrug at her side.

The film opens with scenes from the day that the war ended, with people waving from the tops of London buses, and raising flags to the camera. Can that really be two years ago now? The mouths of the people all move together, as if they are singing, but Lucy can't make out the words, or remember what songs they sung that day. There are crowd scenes then, a street packed with people, and all of them wanting to take their turn to grin at the camera. They wave their hats and their flags and it's all a bit frenzied, like the film is playing too fast.

She thinks about November 1918, when the church bells had rung, every steeple in the country breaking its long silence, how she had trembled all over, and it was done. It had been three years since she had heard from Ellis, but she knew then, with the waving flags, that he would finally be able to come home. If he'd been in any trouble, any difficulty, had got himself into any bother, it would all be in the past tense, all be over with and wiped clean, and he would surely come back now. She had waited for the post. She had waited for his knock at the door.

The piano changes key and the film cuts to a cemetery then, the gravestones all not quite in line, and the earth sinisterly humped and broken. The crosses are made of wood, some elaborate, but mostly humble. Lucy can see a maple leaf on one, and a horseshoe hanging upside down, so that all the luck is running out. Only a few of the graves have flowers, and there are so many of them. The camera focuses in on one cross, the words *British Soldier* marked out in paint, long shadows slanting behind.

It is five years now, but Lucy knows that Ellis is not in a grave. She would have heard something, surely? She would have *felt* something. He is her own flesh and blood, after all, and surely in her bones she would know? Surely something in the fibre of her being would tell her that, wouldn't it? She hears Dora sigh.

A break in the film flickers and then there are lines of French soldiers marching through a town, and a cart pulled by horses carrying a coffin draped with a flag. The French soldiers march like they are weary, like they have come a long way, and Lucy supposes that they have. Their rifles are slumped on their shoulders, and over their arms, like they're no longer sure why they must carry them. Some of the men have musical instruments too, she can see, drums and bugles and a euphonium, but they don't look as if they have the heart to play them. The cinema organist is going for an air of military band now, making it bright and brassy, but the notes don't seem to fit.

When Ellis had last written it was from a bar in a French village. ('That's about right,' George had said.) He'd told Lucy that a gramophone was playing and some of the men were singing along with the song. It had been such a cheerful letter. He had put in all the details of the scene and she could quite picture him there. He had felt sorry for the canary in its cage, he had told her, what with all the roar of soldiers filling the estaminet. Its wings had beaten against the bars, he had said, and he had known that it was frightened. The lady had thanked him for taking down the cage and carrying it through to the back room. She had told him that he was a kind young man, that he was thoughtful, and had given him a silk postcard for his trouble, embroidered with swallows and little blue flowers. He had folded that postcard into his letter and sent it to Lucy with the words *Forget Me Not* written on the back. When she shuts her eyes, she can picture Ellis in the bar, and he seems so much more real than the men on the cinema screen. She can see him cooing to the yellow canary, putting a gentle finger to its soft feathers, and she can smell the beer and the birdcage. She can see Ellis in such sharp focus. Every detail of his face. All in colour. His eyes flick from the canary to meet hers and he gives her his grin and a wink. How could she forget him? How could she give up on him?

Men in uniforms like Ellis' are walking alongside the cart now. Lucy can see one of them opening his mouth and she wonders what his muted words were. People are sitting on the roofs of shacks and watching this strange parade go past. Behind the van, two men abreast, they carry huge wreaths of flowers, great enormous garlands, taller than a man. They look heavy, and the soldiers seem to be finding them a trouble to carry. Lucy can make out the shape of laurel leaves on the screen and can almost smell the nodding heads of chrysanthemums. She holds on to the arms of her cinema seat.

The year before the war, when their mother had died, Ellis had come home with a potted chrysanthemum. He had put it in the kitchen window and Lucy had seen it as she came back from work. She smelled it as soon as she walked into the house. It was deadly, that smell. There was something so terribly definite about it. She had made Ellis carry the pot out into the yard.

'But it's for Mother,' he had said. 'I thought it would please you. They're Japanese chrysanthemums. You can tell that because the petals curl upwards.'

'It's not right, though,' she'd replied. 'Those flowers are for graves, not for in the house. I don't think it's good luck to have them in the house.'

'There's no pleasing you,' Ellis had said.

She knew that he was angry with her, but he'd said that he would take the plant to their mother's grave the next day instead. When she had looked out of her bedroom window that night, she could see the yellow petals glowing in the dark. She thinks about Ellis, with the pot of chrysanthemums in his arms, and the smell of death all around. Had her mother been alive, she wouldn't have let him go off to war just twelve months later. Was that bad luck paying him back?

The coffin is on a ship then and men are saluting as it slips out of the port. Sailors look at the sea and Lucy can almost taste the white spray and the salty wind. Lines of soldiers bow their heads as the coffin is carried along the Dover dockside.

Dora thinks that Ellis is dead. Lucy knows she does. This is why she has insisted that Lucy come to the cinema today. Dora thinks she needs to come to terms with her brother's death, to accept that inevitable truth, to know that Ellis won't cross that expanse of sea again. She looks at Dora's profile in the flicker of light from the screen. She turns towards Lucy and smiles.

The film cuts to London and soldiers are marching with medals and military bands. The coffin looks somehow pathetic amongst all the pomp and ceremony. The king watches the coffin, and the men who bear its weight on their shoulders clumsily take their caps off. Lucy sees that there is a tin hat on top of the coffin and a belt buckle, just like the one she had polished when Ellis came home on leave. She can recall the grain of that leather still and the smell of the dubbin as she worked it in circles.

'You don't need to,' he had said. 'We don't do that any longer.'

But that wasn't the point. She had wanted to do it for him.

The piano notes become solemn as the camera pans over the crowds outside the abbey, and the men on the screen take off their hats and bow their heads. Lucy supposes that many of them are old soldiers. The women come after, made to queue and marshalled by policemen. They bring bunches of flowers and wreaths. There are lilies for loss of innocence and chrysanthemums for sorrow. There is the most enormous mound of flowers. It is too big, too much, and Lucy wonders what will happen when the petals wilt and it all starts to fall and rot. The queue snakes right down the street.

The violinist is stretching out the notes now, and making

them quaver, like he wants everyone to cry. She feels Dora squeeze her hand. Does Dora think she ought to be crying? That she too ought to be taking flowers to a graveside? But there is no grave to visit. There is no death. She feels a sudden anger welling up in her chest. It is like something trapped and struggling in her ribcage, like the canary in the cage, and she wants to run out into the daylight so that she can breathe, but Dora is holding her hand tight.

It ends with the king at the cenotaph and huge flags falling to reveal the white column. One of the flags doesn't fall tidily and a man has to go up and give it a tug. Lucy is glad when the screen blackens and it ends.

When the house lights go up, she sees people with handkerchiefs, and then a man starts to clap his hands. Suddenly they are all on their feet and applauding. Lucy looks around the cinema. She can't understand why they are clapping. Are they pleased by this anonymous man's death? Are they praising him for it? Do they mean to thank him for dying?

'Why are they doing that?' she says as she turns to Dora.

'Out of respect, of course. I mean, he could be anyone's son or husband or brother, couldn't he?'

'But it's just sad and a shame. It's not something to applaud.'

'Mrs Lawson says they dug him up from Ypres. Imagine if you'd lost your husband at Ypres. It might be some comfort, mightn't it? Knowing that soldier could be him, don't you think? Seeing how he's been brought home and honoured that way.'

She knows that Dora wants her to imagine that it's Ellis in that coffin. That he has been brought home. It's Lucy who she means to comfort with her words. But Lucy knows that Ellis isn't the Unknown Soldier. There's no way that the man in that coffin could be Ellis, because he isn't dead. However much they try to tell her otherwise, she knows that Ellis will come back. Ellis will come home too, but he won't come home in a coffin.

'Ellis was never at Ypres,' she says.

Chapter Sixteen

James, Fellside House, November 1920

'I'm not sure what the appropriate word is – inmates? Patients?' The journalist hesitates.

'I can't say that we particularly use either,' Shepherd replies.

'What I mean to ask,' the journalist goes on, 'is how long they're here for. Have they all been here since the war? Do they stay all the time? Do they just come in temporarily?'

Shepherd nods. 'The faces come and go. Some are here for only a few days. Others stay for months. Adam has been here the longest – for the past two years. Some are sent by their families, seeking a solution for sleepless nights, strained relationships and anxieties that are difficult to manage. Others admit themselves. Undeniably, a few are sent here to be hidden, it's sad to say – trembling hands and twitching faces, that sort of thing. But we try to sort it all out. We offer a place where they can rest and they can talk. We encourage them to converse and try to explore the gaps in memory. Of course, some want to talk more than others.'

'And do you try to make them talk?'

'We use hypnotism sometimes,' James replies, and the journalist's eyes connect with his. 'Familiar objects to inspire and provoke conversation. Unfamiliar objects too. And the landscape. We find ourselves doing a lot of walking. It's amazing how the landscape can open people up. It's so much bigger than us and the men react to that. Often it's simply rest that they need, just ordinary unbroken sleep.'

The journalist nods. James watches the marks from his pen speeding across the page.

'Hypnotism, you say?'

'Hypnotism shuts down the field of consciousness,' Shepherd explains. 'It allows us to converse with a patient's subconscious, to bring buried memories up to the surface. Using this method, a patient can take out forgotten facts, look at them, rationally address them and know that the need for fear has now passed. Thereby it restores self-control. With some patients a single session is enough; with others it's a process that we must repeat several times. In almost all cases we see great improvement, if not complete cure.'

'But this chap's subconscious isn't feeling talkative?'

'The brain can be very powerful,' says James, 'and self-protecting. If something truly traumatic has occurred, it can compartmentalize and shut off the events that the individual isn't emotionally able to process; the unconscious self protecting the whole, if you will, not letting him engage with experience as he hitherto would. Thus some parts of the structure of his mind remain effectively active, but other sections may temporarily shut down.'

'Is it something physical?'

'Possibly. I can't pretend that we understand it precisely or entirely. Personally, I believe it's a combination of the physical and psychological – of damage to the nervous system and emotional shock.'

'So you know nothing about him?'

James shakes his head. 'I wouldn't say that. We know a lot about him – what his personality is like, what he enjoys, what he responds to – we just don't know where he's come from, what particularly happened to trigger this condition and what he's called.'

'And that's where I want to help.' Longworth, the journalist, looks up from his notepad and nods. 'That's where we can help.'

'You want to publish photographs, I understand, Mr Longworth?'

'That's right. Our strapline will be "The Living Unknown Warriors".' He frames it with his fingers. 'We thought it would strike a chord at the moment, you see? We mean to publish photographs of each of the amnesiacs, and to give a brief profile of each; hair colour, eye colour, height, distinguishing marks, that sort of thing. Our hope is that readers might recognize them. It's a way of getting these images out to a big audience. Imagine if we could make that connection. Imagine if we could give your mystery man a name and send him home.'

James watches the enthusiasm spark in Longworth's eyes. He can see the journalist senses a potential scoop. He can't help but wonder, though, whether Adam really wants his picture in the papers, a name pinning to him and to be sent on his way. Could it really be dealt with that easily and be over? It all seems too straightforwardly black and white somehow. When James had mentioned the possibility of this newspaper article to Adam, he had seemed impassive and James can't help but wonder what emotions that mask of calm hid.

'So are we in agreement?' Longworth asks.

James watches Shepherd nod.

Adam

The man with the camera shakes Adam's hand. He leads him to a chair and invites him to sit.

'Are you excited about this?' he asks.

Adam watches the man making adjustments to the camera. 'I don't know,' he replies.

'Imagine if your wife sees your picture in the paper. Imagine if your mother sees it.'

'Please, I'd rather you didn't set up these possibilities,' Haworth intervenes.

Adam can see concern on Haworth's face, and questions. He can tell that Haworth isn't comfortable with this.

'I don't know that I have a wife,' Adam replies. 'I don't know that I have a mother.'

The journalist laughs. 'Did you fall out of the sky, then?'

Adam looks to Haworth and then down at his lap. 'No.'

'Do you mind?' The journalist's fingers are on his face. He lifts his chin, squares his cheekbones, pushes the hair away from his eyes. 'Can you keep your head at that angle? Don't smile for the camera. Just look straight at the lens. I want a true record of what you look like.'

Adam thinks about the word *truth* as he looks down the lens. What truths does the camera see? What truths will the photograph image of his face unlock? He has an urge to turn away – he's about to, but the flashgun catches him before he can move, and the white magnesium flare is like a momentary shock of memory.

James

'You're not happy about it, are you?' Shepherd asks.

'I'm just not sure what will happen next. He's seemed so much more settled in recent months and I don't want to upset that. I haven't seen him look scared for a long time, but he was again today. Didn't you think so? I'd hate to see him take a step back.'

'On the other hand, everything might fall into place; a caring family might come forward, a family who have been searching for him, and it could all click; he could be reunited with the people who miss him – surely that's the result we want?'

'Possibly,' James concedes.

'I did notice that you didn't tell our newspaper chap about any of his scars?'

'I figured that it was best not to give everything away. I mean, if anyone does come forward to claim him, having something in reserve might help us to test that they are genuine.'

Shepherd nods. 'That was very long-sighted of you. How artful.'

'Or cynical?' James replies.

In Birmingham, Alice Wallace brings the photograph closer to her reading glasses and sees her dead husband, Alfred.

In Darlington, Mavis Stephens glimpses her son's eyes and has to grip on to the arms of her chair.

In Bradford, Angela Davis knows that her brother has been dead since 1914, but why is his likeness then staring out of the evening newspaper?

In Cromer, Melissa Boden carries the paper to the window, to better see it in the light and, yes, it is her Anthony.

In Chester-le-Street, William Bowen points a finger that won't quite stay still.

In Dartford, Elizabeth Wilkinson watches her mother's eyes as she brings the newspaper closer to her face.

In Todmorden, Anne Uttley lets the glass fall from her hand.

In Marlborough, Mary Long screams until her throat is raw.

In St Ives, David Harrison has to cross his arms over his chest to keep the trembling in.

In Poulton-le-Sands, Sidney Solomon clutches his son's face in his hand and curls himself into a ball on the kitchen floor.

Chapter Seventeen

Celia

It was Daniel who'd left the newspaper when he called in with the church magazine. 'There's not much in it, these days,' he'd said, 'only happen it passes a half hour.'

Celia hadn't got around to reading it that night, and so she's using yesterday's news to lay the fire this morning, down on her knees, scrunching the pages into twists. But it's then that she sees him. There. Amongst the kindling and matches. Dusted with yesterday's ashes. His face. Robert.

His features leap out of the page and she isn't able to understand it for a minute. Is she unwell? Is she seeing things? Is her mind playing tricks? She can't make out the words under his picture because the paper won't stay still in her hands.

She has to flatten it out on the hearthrug, smooth it out, blow the ashes away, and must now read and reread the lines until it makes some sort of sense. But is she being quite sensible? Can she trust her eyes? Could this be some cruel trick, or a mistake, or madness?

She could so easily have missed him. She might not have looked at the pictures and simply put a match to the page. But sometimes fate is like that, she thinks, and perhaps the

Almighty does have a sense of mischief and some kindness left after all. She rocks on her knees, and gasps with her face pressed against the fire screen.

Lucy

Her reflection ripples in the water below, but all Lucy sees is his photograph face. She and George had sat at the table last night and agreed that it might be him; it could be their brother's likeness. Those looked like Ellis' eyes. Wasn't that his nose? Was that his mouth? She pushes her fingernails into the palm of her hand to prove to herself that this is a moment she is living through – that she is here, and now, and feeling this – and that it is not a scene that she half recalls from the cinema screen.

She has felt a strange mixture of elation and outrage, knowing that he had been out there for five years. She thought of how she had secretly cried for the Unknown Soldier, wondering if it might be Ellis, when all the time (*all this time!*) he has been in the next county. All those months and years of hoping, of trying to stay strong, and not letting each other cry; all those years of silence, and questions, and struggling to explain it to his children.

Lucy walks on around the lake. The article in the newspaper says that he has lost his memory, that he can't remember his name, his family, who he is. She remembers walking around the lake with Ellis, how they had shared memories and ambitions with each other on those walks, talked about the lives that they meant to make for themselves and the people they wanted to be. How could he have forgotten all of that? When she had become mother to her brother's children, all the looking forward had to stop, and she simply needed to *be* – or try to be – the person that they required. But now that Ellis' photograph face is there in the newspaper, with the possibilities that opens up, it all changes again, doesn't it? Can't it?

George wouldn't go further than a *maybe* last night. He wouldn't budge beyond calling it a *likeness*, but he had agreed that Lucy ought to go and see. Though, if it was Ellis, George had gone on, it would be a big responsibility to take on a man who had lost his mind. He might no longer be the Ellis that they knew. He might need care. He might never be able to look after himself again, never mind his children.

But wasn't there a chance? Couldn't there be a chance?

Lucy looks out across the water and recalls her brother's long-ago laughter. Surely putting him back in this place, where all his memories were made, might jog something in his mind? Surely, looking into the eyes of his own children, he would know them? Couldn't that all be fixed? Could she yet have Ellis' laughter and her own future back?

Anna

Anna steps out into the yard and screams until it hurts. She looks down the valley and her chest heaves. She crouches with her arms around her knees and rocks. She doesn't recognize the sound that comes from her own mouth.

In truth, she had already known it when she had gone down to London to see the nameless soldier. As she had stood looking at that railway carriage, she had known with absolute certainty that Mark wasn't inside that van. She also knew then that he wasn't dead.

Could he have been in that hospital, just eighty miles to the north, all this time? Could he have been there since 1916? She thinks of all the letters that she has written, all the telephone calls and telegrams and miles on the train, all the enquiries that she has followed that have led nowhere. She thinks of all the money that she has paid out to Jack Giddings, who claimed to be following leads, who said that he was making progress. Were there ever really any leads, she wonders now. Has she just been fobbed off and cheated? Did anyone ever actually read her letters? It suddenly seems like so much wasted time and hope and money. So much searching in the wrong places. After so much looking, after so many written words and months of waiting, the emotion that she is experiencing in finally finding Mark again is not the one that she expected to feel.

The hospital is in Westmorland, the newspaper article says. She has already half written her letter of introduction, as the instructions say that she must, but she wants to get on a train this evening. Can she not go there now? It is a chance that she feels she needs to grasp quickly. She might not have turned the page. She might not have bought a paper today. She might so easily have missed him. But she knows, really, that this is more than just a chance; there are no odds, no probability about it; she has not a moment's hesitation or doubt. It's her husband's chin, his cheekbones, his mouth. This is the man she married. From this day forward, for better, for worse, for richer, for poorer, in sickness and in health, until death do us part. But it is not death that has parted them. The man in the paper is her husband. It is Mark Mason.

'I will come back. I will come home again,' he had written

to her in 1916, and she had believed him – after all, this was his land, and whatever complications there might have been between them, he would come home for that. As she walks back into the porch, she catches her own reflection in the hall mirror. There is mud on her collar and her hair is escaping from its slides. She puts a hand to her eyes. Mark would want to come back to the farm, but would he want her back, after what happened? If he has been there, so close by, for so long, can he want her back? Is it her being here that has stopped him from coming home? She turns away from her own reflection.

But perhaps, if he has lost his memory, he has forgotten the problems that they had too. Might all that have gone? Could they start again? Could she yet make it right? The newspaper article calls him an amnesiac. Anna thinks about the face of the man she married, and wonders how much of that person is left. Surely his instincts, his basic personality will still be the same? The war can't have taken away his gentleness, can it? It can't have wiped out his kindness, his love of landscape and his need to put it all down on paper?

From the window she looks out across the fields – the fields that Mark and his ancestors farmed – and feels with absolute certainty that he will know their hollows and rises and hedgerows. He will know the walls of the dairy where his father milked, and the kitchen table that is patterned with his mother's knife marks. He will know that this is home and surely that will make him better? This is the house where he was born. Can he not be born here again? She also realizes that she will have to tell him that the land has all been sold off.

She puts a hand to her face and realizes that her cheeks are wet. Anna remembers putting her face to Mark's five years ago and feeling the surprising wetness of his tears. His sketchbooks had always been full of her face, but that night he had told her that he couldn't look at her any longer. Is there a chance that that memory might have gone too? Could they yet restart from before the day Mark had cried?

Chapter Eighteen

Adam, Fellside House, December 1920

Adam can hear them downstairs. They are filling the corridor and queuing along the flowerbed outside. He can hear Haworth's door opening and closing, and the rise and fall of their voices. There was a shouted exchange earlier in the morning and a man's voice crying. When he saw Haworth, at lunch, he looked exhausted. Adam suspects that he regrets this business.

Haworth has told him that he asks them about heights and hair colours and scars. It is a guessing game of which he is the subject, and seemingly most of them get the answers wrong. Many of the people leave quickly. They do not all want to go, don't all want to accept a mistaken recognition of his newspaper features, but Haworth, apologizing, tells them that they must. It is only those whose descriptions score sufficient similarity that Adam will be required to meet, he has been told. They will whittle them down. Weed them out. But there seem to be so many people downstairs. He overhears Haworth saying that this could go on for weeks.

Celia

The woman in front of Celia knows he is her husband. She keeps saying it, but Celia wants to tell her she is mistaken. She wants to apologize and comfort the woman, to kindly show her how wrong she is, but she sees something beyond reason in the young woman's eyes. Celia wonders, how can so many of them be mistaken? How can so many have wishfully misinterpreted that newspaper image? Could they really rearrange Robert's features and make them into the man they are missing? It's a terribly sad thing, she considers, but there is also something slightly hysterical about it all. Something slightly overheated. She listens to the voices rise around her. Mostly female. Some of them shrill. A whole mix of accents and classes, and all of them talking over one another. At times it seems like a competition; they are all competing to prove that he belongs to them. How can they possibly think that he is theirs, when he is hers?

It is a handsome house, she considers: pointed gables and slate roof and diamond-leaded windows. The wisteria is a tangle of winter stems today, but she imagines the front of the house bursting into a mauve shimmer by May. The windows look out onto lawns, rhododendrons and woods beyond. She imagines that Robert might like this place, that he would be contented, that he would draw here. She looks at the windows and wonders which of them conceals her son. She can hear a gramophone playing on the upper floors. Could he really be that close at this moment? Is he looking out even now? Can he see her down here? She feels a foolish urge to wave. But all that Celia can see when she looks in the windows is the reflection of all of the people in the queue.

For a moment, surrounded by the voices and the tears and the claims, a fear starts to squirm in her belly. What if their louder words, their showier claims, will outshine her own quiet truths? The sense of jeopardy suddenly overcomes her. What if the men who make the decisions mistake tears and exclamations for sincerity? Must she cry too? Must she beat her fists and make a public show? Celia doesn't have it in her. She can't be like that. She only knows, in quiet sincerity, that it is Robert's face. Surely they won't fail to recognize that? Surely Robert will look at her and know – and they will see that, won't they?

Adam

'What is it about Galilee?' Adam hears Shepherd ask the question in the corridor. 'Sheffield has had thirty applicants for their amnesiac. Netley around fifty. Why have we had over a hundred?'

Adam looks down from his window and sees hats and hair of every colour. Does he really connect to any of these people? Does he want that connection? Why do so many of them seem to need him? Haworth says that later in the day he must come down and meet some of the more likely candidates. Shepherd wants to see their reactions. He wants to see Adam's responses too, he knows.

'It wasn't the clearest photograph, was it?' he hears Haworth's voice replying below. 'Perhaps if the picture had come out sharper, had it looked more like him, there might not have been so many. Being indistinct, it opens the door to doubt, doesn't it? People will see in it what they want to. It really isn't a good reproduction. I mean, it might be any man.'

'Does that photographer know how much bloody work he's given us?'

Adam looks at his reflection. In the circle of mirrors, slices of his likeness bounce all around the room, so that he is many men, and surrounded by himself. How can all these people recognize something in him when he hardly knows himself? He is not sure that he wants to meet the eyes and questions of all the people now filing into the hall below.

Celia

The woman in the green shawl reacts angrily when Celia tells her about Robert's likeness. She had taken out her photograph to show the woman, to prove it to her, but she shakes her head and tells Celia that she is deluded, that she's fooling herself. It is just wishful thinking, the woman says. Her face is all creases of negativity, a hard and stubborn face. Celia becomes angry too as she watches this woman shake her head. Who is she to make that judgement? What right does she have? And why can't she see it? Does her own certainty make her blind? The woman turns her back on Celia, who feels a sudden savage urge to pull her yellow hair and to take the certainty off her face. She can feel her blood rushing. She wants to scream at this woman. It is not like her to feel this way.

Imagine if they gave Robert to a person like that? Imagine if they believed the loud claims and the certainty? She thinks of Robert being taken home to that woman's house, how little care she would give him, how little connection there would be between them. The woman probably only wants him for his army pension and to fetch and carry, at best to fill the space left by some no-good son, who probably couldn't wait to leave home. There would be no tenderness, no gentleness, no garden. How terrible, she thinks, that there are women like that in this queue, that she must wait in line to make her claim and compete against people like this. She has already seen two young women fighting. How awful, how frightening, that it has come to this.

She looks at Robert's photograph face again. How will he react when he sees her? The scenario of him not knowing her, not recognizing her as his mother, is terrifying, but she knows that she might have to face it. She has imagined and reimagined that scene; his dear face not knowing hers; his eyes searching for recognition and not finding it. What a thing for a mother to face! But surely that will come back with time? Surely, in his own home, surrounded by his own things, the memories will all fall back into place? She tells his photograph face every day how she loves him, what good care she will take of him when he gets home, how she will never let him be in harm's way again. It will be a joy to cook his meals. It will be a delight to launder his clothes. She chastises herself every day for having let him go. She won't let him go again. Whatever it takes, she will make sure that no other woman in this queue will take him home. Even if she must fight for him. Even if there must be raised voices and tempers and solicitors.

The curtains have been drawn now and she can see a sitting room through the windows; wing-back chairs, landscapes on the walls and the black lacquer of a piano. Do they let Robert play the piano here? His sheet music is still on the piano at home. When she looks at the patterns of notes on the page, she remembers his fingers on the keyboard and wills the melody into her mind. Even if he has forgotten other things, that instinct and knowledge must still be there. She pictures his fingers on the keys and the music plays in her head again. Chopin ripples around her and for a moment the queue and the sadness and the questions are gone.

She watches a girl in front powdering her nose as she looks at her reflection in the window. There are women in thin coats with city accents, and women who affect the airs of duchesses. So many women. So many missing men. So many unanswered questions. It is a terrifying thing to be here and a terrible thing.

But she is here to take Robert home, and she will.

Chapter Nineteen

Adam, Fellside House, December 1920

Adam puts on the white shirt that Haworth has given him. His fingers tremble and he fumbles with the buttons. Sally made him clean his fingernails with a brush this morning, had sat there by his side and observed the scrubbing until he could show her ten pink finger ends. She had dried his hands for him on a new towel and told him that it was a minor miracle. Sally's face lights up with humour when she smiles at him. She is vigorous in her ministrations, but kindly, and he's not afraid of her, or of any of the other women who work in the kitchen, or make the beds, or dust the corridors. They all talk to him – Agnes and Esther and Letty – they take the time to pause from their work and they smile. But the women outside today aren't smiling. They are all there still, queuing along the front of the house. From above, he can tell that they are peering in at the windows.

Adam looks at his face in the mirror. He combs his hair, as Haworth has told him that he must, and considers his own reflection. There is nothing remarkable about his face; it is an average face; there are men of finer and nobler features – but then perhaps that is it? Perhaps it is his lack of distinction? Perhaps, as he overheard Haworth saying, it is just that he looks like too many other men? As his image bounces around the mirrors, he understands that there are angles and elements that too many women may think they recognize.

He laces the shoes that Sally has polished for him. Although he can't remember his first day at school, he imagines that it must have felt something like this. He feels slightly light-headed as he steps out onto the landing and shuts the door on his private space. As he pauses at the top of the stairs, he can hear them talking in the entrance hall below. A woman is laughing, a raucous laugh; somebody shouts and it takes a few moments before the voices below fill the silence again. He is not certain that they won't tear him limb from limb.

He finds himself trying to descend the stairs without making any noise. He places his feet carefully, knowing where the boards creak, keeping his back to the wall. He thinks about the woman in the cathedral who called him Peter and chased him. The crowd of women in the hall has the energy of a pack and he's frightened that they'll rush at him.

On the turn of the stairs he hears a woman say that she thought her heart was broken. Her companion replies that it's a miracle; his children have cried for him for three years, but they won't need to cry any longer when she takes him home. Adam hears competition in the voices. Like they will scratch each other to possess him. It is too much.

He cuts along the first-floor corridor and runs down the back kitchen stairs. It is all silence and shadows on this stairwell, and he would like to just curl up here on the linoleum, but then he can hear Sally and Esther talking as they wash dishes in the scullery. The smell of coffee and bacon is sticky in the air. The door is open and he sees Sally's shadow cross and recross. He waits until he can no longer hear her footsteps. All there is then is the rush of his own breath.

He feels a sliver of cool air pushing around the edges of the back door. The key isn't in the lock. Could it be open? If Sally turns, he will be cornered. Will she make him go to Shepherd's study if she catches him? He plunges down the last flight of stairs and runs for the door. He sees a glimpse of Sally turning, but he doesn't look back and his hands are working at the lock. He hears her shout his name as he plunges out into the daylight.

He glances round – there is no one on this side of the building – and dives over the wall, sprinting for the wood. He doesn't stop running until he is in amongst the trees, and only then dares to look back again. He can see the women at the end of the building. The queue stretches all the way up the path to the gates. How can there be so many of them?

Will Sally alert Shepherd now? Adam knows she saw him run. He hopes that she understands enough, that she has sufficient fellow feeling, to let him go. He scrambles up the steep bank and earth falls and skitters down from his feet. He hears a shout from towards the house and freezes. He breathes into the earth, doesn't dare to move a muscle until he is certain that the voices aren't getting closer. He knows that if they look this way, they will see his white shirt through the trees and curses Haworth for making him wear it. He feels like a target.

When no voices follow, he dares to climb higher. His hands grasp at tree trunks and roots. It is an almighty effort of will and muscle to climb up this part of the bank, but fear pushes him higher. Shards of slate slice his fingers and thorns cut his palms, but he has to get up above them. He scrambles up through the roots of an old hawthorn and finally he can swing up and sit at the top of the bank. There is earth and blood stained all up the front of his white shirt now, but still he feels too conspicuous in it. He unbuttons it and pushes it under the fallen leaves. He looks at his black fingernails and he knows Sally will chastise him. There are scratches all up his arms.

Adam gets to his feet again; it is less steep from here so he can run up the slope. He weaves between the junipers, and the skid of slate, and only stops when he sees the fox, suddenly there in his path. It's a dog fox, a big old boy (tod, reynard, *vulpes vulpes*), his coat a long history of territorial fights. He sniffs the air and Adam can see that he's searching for a mate. Adam himself might well be invisible, and he is glad of that.

The fox turns, goes on his way, and Adam is running again. Can he ever go back? Could he just keep on running? But – what then? Where does he go to next? He doesn't want to go back on the road and he doesn't want to disappoint Haworth; there are his drawings, the gate of the walled garden is open now and he has plans for the spring, and surely all the women will be gone by the end of the day? Won't they? He will wait here in the wood until all the women have gone.

A blackbird rises from the leaves and he springs back from the fork of black feathers. When he looks again, she is there; a woman stepping out from between the trees. Adam is about to turn and run again, but then he is not sure who is more frightened, him or her, and he can't help but stare at her. She stands still, and looks at him, and he hears a catch in her breath. What is this sensation? Is this recognition? As he takes in the woman's face, it is like the moment when he first looked up into the sycamore trees and the word – the name – was simply there in his head. Only the word is just slightly out of reach now. Adam stares at the woman, stretching for the word, and the light seems to shimmer through her, flickering like her just-out-of-reach name. She glows at the edges. He turns a feather between his fingers.

'I know you, don't I?'

She looks at him, her eyes don't leave his, and he is reminded of when he first saw his own reflection in a mirror, two years ago, recognizing his own face and yet not.

'I shouldn't be here,' she says eventually.

'Nor I.'

'Can I take a step closer to you?'

He can see that she is afraid, but her voice is low and level, and her stillness is quite unlike the women crowding around the house. He knows her stillness, her manner, her voice, her face. He's certain of it – and yet. He nods. 'Yes.'

'You're not frightened of me?' she asks.

'No. I'm not.'

Her blouse is embroidered with five-pointed stars and pomegranates, and he can see her chest rising and falling. Her eyes are the green of sunlight through oak leaves, her breath smells of liquorice and when she moves there is the scent of violets. He watches a strand of hair shift against her cheek. She shivers as though she's cold.

'You are all cut,' she says. Her eyelashes shift. She looks at his chest. 'My poor boy. You need comfrey and witch hazel.'

'Yes.'

She raises her hand as if she wants to touch the cuts on his chest, but then as quickly pulls her fingers away.

He stares at her. She stares at him. He wants her to put her cool hands to his chest and bathe his cuts with herbs, and say his name, but her eyes flick away. 'You weren't meant to see me here,' she says.

He wants to tell her to stay, to sit with him in the wood for a while, just to be with him, just to talk with him, but as quickly as she appeared, she has gone. Adam's eyes fix the place where she stood and can't quite seem to focus. Pollen glitters in the sudden sunlight. Is it bewitchment, or is it true that he knows the woman's face as well as he knows his own? Adam makes himself name all the plants that surround him (bittercress-bullace-blackthorn-rowan-hawthorn-hellebore-mistletoe) in the hope that her name will be next in the chain. But, at the end, there is only a stretching silence.

Chapter Twenty

James, Fellside House, December 1920

'Poor Adam. It was like a bear pit down there yesterday.' Caitlin steps back from the window. In the harlequin light of the glass, her face is all diamonds of red and yellow and jewelled blue. 'Are you still sure this is a good idea?'

'I don't know.'

'You're having doubts, aren't you?'

James shakes his head. 'I felt so sorry for him yesterday, he looked terrified, but Alan is convinced that something might come of it. He reckons there's a good chance that a genuine link might be out there; it's just locating it that's the problem, and saying "no" to all the people who have come here so full of expectation. They keep showing me their sons' last letters, you know. I found the first one so difficult – I mean, you can imagine, can't you? – but then they keep on coming. They arrive with boxes and envelopes and then spill it all out onto the desk, all these postcards that they've prayed over, bits of souvenirs and letters that say in black and white that their sons are dead, only they don't want to believe that. They're all waiting for me to tell them that the official letters are wrong. So they push these pitiful, pathetic, powerful things at me, and then I have to tell them that *they're* wrong.'

'I can't imagine the experience is good for their well-being. Can you? Building up such hopes only to have them dashed? It's like a surge of grief, isn't it? Like a great wave of sorrow that's crashing all over this house. All those poor people, queuing up to have their last little glimmers of hope snuffed out. I keep thinking how I'd feel if I saw Nat's face in a newspaper.'

'Of course,' he replies.

'What a terrible thing to have to go through – to come here so full of excitement and expectation, only to find out that his face doesn't actually fit.'

'Some of them are trying hard to make it fit.'

'Naturally. They will, won't they? Don't you think you would in their circumstances?' Her fingers arch on the mantelpiece as though she is holding down a chord on a keyboard. 'And how is Adam coping with it?'

'Scared. Disturbed. Confused. We've made such a lot of progress over the past couple of years, he's so much more settled than he was, but I'm worried that we're going to rush backwards now.'

'It can't not be upsetting for him.'

When Adam walks into the room there are gasps and tears, fainting fits and hands that rush towards him. He already hates this process; James can see it. Adam knows none of these people, but they all so hungrily need him.

'The families are always shocked when they see him. I keep watching the same thing over and over. Everyone says how much older he is. How much thinner. How he must have suffered. They all want to touch him, and he also touches them. I guess that he's trying to remember, but the interaction – that connection and misconnection – is the most peculiar, alarming, terrible thing to observe.'

'I'm sure.'

'They stare at each other, the families and Adam, and he explores their faces with his fingers. He scrutinizes them, as if he's considering drawing them. He touches them very gently. The buttons on their jackets. Their collars. Their hair. And they just keep on staring.'

'The thought of it makes me shiver. I guess he's trying to figure out whether he knows them, or not?'

'Absolutely. He's searching their faces, and they're searching him, but it's the most desperate and poignant thing to watch because there's such intensity on both sides and all the connections are misfiring.'

Some caress him. Many cry. Many babble on about homes and friends and shared memories that evidently mean nothing to him. They show him photographs that are obviously precious to them. He looks at them politely, but shakes his head.

'None of them have seemed likely candidates yet then?'

'No, but not for want of trying. They all put so much effort into making him fit and he's really being very patient.'

When they want to see familiar marks on his body, he complies, but it is evidently an embarrassment to him. They want to look at his hands, at his feet, at his teeth. There is something both hideously matter-of-fact and deeply emotional about the whole process, and there have been several occasions this morning when James has wanted to call time on the whole sorry charade.

'Sally said he bolted yesterday.'

James nods. 'We sat waiting for him for an hour, but he'd taken off into the woods. Now, this is the interesting part: he told me that he saw a fairy there, and—'

'A fairy?' Caitlin raises her eyebrows. James is pleased, at last, to see her smile. It seems to be days ago that he last saw her smile. 'You say that almost like it's an aside! Did she have wings?'

'Not that he mentioned. But she did have other interesting features – features he recognized.'

'*Recognized?* You mean he knew her?'

'And that's where it gets both promising and profoundly frustrating. He's certain that he's seen her face before, he's absolutely positive about it, but he can't place her or give her a name. He evidently felt something for this *fairy*, something intense. That seems significant, doesn't it? But, then again, he could have simply imagined the whole incident.'

Caitlin blinks in the sunlight and James sees a premonition of her future face, the tracery of lines that will only make him love her eyes more. It's not been the easiest year – or, rather, *he's* not given her the easiest past few months, James knows that – but he hopes that she sees and understands how much he still cares for her. When Adam had come back from the wood, and talked about the woman he'd seen there, he had looked like a man in the first throes of love. James still looks at Caitlin sometimes and feels that light-headedness. For all the difficult words that they've exchanged since they came here, that feeling is unchanged. He puts his hand towards hers, winds her fingers with his own and is glad that she doesn't pull away.

'Do you think one of your ladies might have escaped from the queue?'

'It's not impossible, I suppose, but Wilkinson was on the gate and he swears that no one wandered off in that direction. What was she doing up in the woods?'

'Direct action?' Caitlin suggests.

'Do you think?'

There's clay all around the edges of Caitlin's fingernails

again, James notices, as there always used to be when he first met her. He rubs his thumb along her finger ends and smiles because she lets him. There would be clay on her teacup in those days, and in her hair, and on her pillow, and she always seemed to hardly notice. James remembers how vibrant she was at that time, so full of ideas and plans and unshadowed ambition. Her enthusiasm for life had shone out of her. She is still the same Caitlin, but quieter now and not quite so brave. He'd hoped that he might be able to help rebuild her lost confidence, that with time grief might let her go, but he's not convinced that's happening. Is living in this house impeding that? Being surrounded by the men and their difficult memories? Or is it living with him that's the problem? Are his own unresolved issues contributing to the sadness that he sees in her eyes?

'You've got clay on your cheek,' he says.

'Have I?'

'You had a good day in the studio?'

'Not bad.' She smiles back at him, but it looks as though she's making an effort. 'Perhaps you need to watch out for some of these people taking matters into their own hands? Perhaps you need to tell Shepherd? It could have been more orderly today. At times it felt like they were swarming all over the house.'

'I want to ask Adam more about the woman, but there doesn't seem to be any time at the moment. There doesn't seem to be time for anything apart from crossing names off lists.' It's tiring, all the faces and the names, and watching their disappointment. James pulls his hands away from her and puts them through his hair. 'Meanwhile, I've told him not to run away with any fairies.'

'Did he actually use that word?'

'Yes. With every seriousness. In all earnestness.'

'He might be one himself, you know,' she says.

James laughs. He can't discern the expression on her face. 'What do you mean? Adam? A fairy?'

'I'm not altogether sure that our Adam Galilee is quite of this mortal earth.' The corner of her mouth twitches upwards as their eyes connect. 'You're giving me a look! I mean, he's solid and square enough, but there's something else going on in his eyes. Don't you ever think that? They're not always in the here and now. They're not seeing what we see. There's something ethereal about him. He's like some character in a fairy story who is condemned to walk the earth for a thousand melancholy years.'

'What an imagination you have!'

'It's not just me. Sally says the same thing. I've never been able to pinpoint what it is that's odd about him, but then Sally said it last week: he's unworldly. And Letty agrees with us. He's started doing that thing in the garden recently – you must have spotted it too? – standing there like his eyes aren't seeing, like he's been turned to stone. I swear, he stands that way for hours sometimes.'

James smiles. 'He's only thinking! Poor Adam. He's just processing his thoughts.'

'But not thinking like everybody else thinks. There's something very still in the centre of him, but it all speeds up around him. Haven't you noticed that?'

'It's certainly sped up here over the past couple of days.'

Caitlin turns towards the window. 'Perhaps it's the fairy who peeps in.'

'Who peeps in?' He is sorry to see the amusement leave Caitlin's face, sorry that she is returning again to this notion.

'From the woods. Perhaps, when it feels like someone is watching us, it's the fairy looking in from the hillside?'

'Perhaps.'

James looks out of the window. There are no fairies on the hillside, or along the path below, just three women sitting on the bench. A girl with red hair swings her feet. A grey hat in the middle turns to either side. At the end is a woman with hair as dark and shiny as a blackbird's wing. He watches as her chin tilts and then she is suddenly looking up at him. Her lips part. He feels her silent gasp and jumps back from the window.

Chapter Twenty-One

Celia, Fellside House, December 1920

'There are high walls around this house,' Celia observes.

'There's also a gate,' the young doctor says. He smiles.

'I didn't expect the gate to be open.'

'It always is. It's never closed. This is a place of sanctuary, not a prison.'

Celia nods. She can see that the young doctor is a gentleman. He has gentle manners and she is glad of that. He says his name is Doctor Haworth, but tells her she can call him James.

'Does Robert know I'm here?'

'We've told Adam about you, all the things that we've already discussed, and he's ready to meet you. We'll go through to the next room shortly.'

Could it really be true that Robert is there, just a wall away? Something lurches in her stomach. She feels that she might faint.

'Are you quite well, Mrs Dakers? You do look terribly pale. I understand how emotionally testing this is.'

She nods and is grateful for his kindness. She accepts the handkerchief that he offers her.

'Did you serve in the war yourself, Doctor Haworth?'

'James, please. And, yes, I did.'

He picks a paperweight up from the desk, turns it between his hands and then puts it down again.

'I expect that was a terrible worry for your family.'

'Yes, I'm afraid that it must have been.'

Celia looks at him and sees the marks of it under his skin, the nervousness that's there below the surface. She watches his hands as he pours her a glass of water and she can't imagine this young man holding a gun any more than she could Robert. Has the war left those marks on Robert too, then?

'Will it be long?' she asks.

To focus on the doctor's face takes away some of her trembling, but the thought that Robert might be there just on the other side of the watery landscape and the sprig-print wallpaper makes it difficult to concentrate for long. She finds herself watching the door. Is he looking at the handle on the other side? Is he too finding it difficult to breathe?

'No. My colleague will give us a knock when he's ready.'

The young doctor lights a cigarette, the match flares and she sees how the flame trembles between his fingers. He almost looks as though he ought to be a patient here himself. She imagines that he doesn't sleep well.

'Is he frightened?' she asks.

'He's not accustomed to having to meet so many people. It's not been an easy week.'

'Of course.' She nods. 'I can imagine. It must have been disturbing and I don't want him to be disturbed. I just want him to know how my heart is bursting with the joy of seeing him again and what good care I am going to take of him now.'

She jumps in her seat when the knock finally comes. The doctor puts his cigarette out and goes to the door. She watches as he exchanges whispered words with a colleague on the other side and then he is turning towards her and beckoning. 'Please. Will you follow me, Mrs Dakers? He's ready for you now.'

He is so much thinner. That's the first thing that strikes her. She wants to cry for his wrist bones and the hollows in his face. There are dark circles under his eyes and his eyelashes cast down. They flicker and he looks up at her shyly. The realization that he doesn't immediately know her breaks Celia's heart. She wants to rush at him, to kiss his poor sad eyes, but he looks so fragile. He is so nervous. She is frightened that she might scare him.

'Adam, this is Celia Dakers,' the younger doctor says to him. 'The lady we've told you about.'

He nods. She wants them to stop calling him Adam. She wants to be Mother not Celia. She wants to close her arms around him, but they are treating him like he is so breakable, so delicate.

'Do you remember me?' she says as softly as she can.

His neck looks slender in the collar of his shirt. She could weep just for that. She feels such tenderness towards the places where his bones show, and the grain of his skin. His hair still stands up on his crown, the way it always did when he lolled against the cushions on the sofa. She wants to lick her palm and flatten it, as she used to – and yet she hardly dares touch him. She feels his eyes moving over her face. Can he not look in her eyes and remember the first face he knew as a baby? Can he not see that hers is the flesh that bore him? Does he not know his own mother's smile?

'Do you recognize me, darling?'

She watches as he stands. His legs look so slight in his trousers. He glances to the young doctor for approval of his actions and he nods.

'As you wish,' the doctor says.

He steps closer to her. She can see the breath rise and fall in his chest and she feels her own breath falter and come faster. He is older. He has suffered, she sees. But his gentle brown eyes are still the same and she can smell him. It is the smell of her son. It takes all her strength not to weep and reach out to grab him.

'My darling boy,' she dares to say.

When his fingers reach out and touch her face it is both a torture and an ecstasy.

She watches him sip at the glass of water. He looks tired now. She so wants to take him home, to put him to bed in his own room and cook him chicken soup to fill out his clothes, and make him smile with damson jam and gingerbread. She looks at his neck. His poor thin dear neck. The edges of his jacket collar are frayed.

'May I bring in some of his clothes?' she asks.

'That's up to Adam,' the older doctor replies. 'Would you mind if Mrs Dakers were to come and see you again, Adam? Would you be happy for her to bring you in some extra clothes?'

The moments before he nods seem to stretch for a lifetime.

Chapter Twenty-Two

James, Fellside House, December 1920

He dreams he's in Trônes Wood again. The light between the trees is flickering, and James feels the ground lurch under his feet, but when he looks, Nathaniel is still there at his side. The snipers have started again, and they crouch down in the old German trench, which has been cut through the great bole of an ancient tree. It must be hundreds of years old, this tree, James thinks, must have seen centuries of deer and boar and hunters pass by, but now it is just a mighty severed trunk with roots as broad as his own thighs. In the trembling forest half-light he can see spiders and ants and finger bones. He gasps when the bones begin to move, but it's only the earthworms. He looks to Nathaniel then and laughs at his own shock, but Nathaniel's face is suddenly not his. It's Adam's face that James sees when he looks up. Unreadable. Unworldly. James doesn't know what's going on behind Adam's eyes, and feels suddenly much less safe with him at his side.

McLaughlin shouts and suddenly Fletcher is making a run. James sees his heels kicking up out of the trench and Fletcher lurches forward. He is down behind another tree now, but James can't tell if he's dead or alive.

'We should try to go forward too,' he says to Adam, but

his face is not in the here and now. James puts his hand to his arm, but then, before he is ready, Adam has turned and is clambering up the rear wall of the trench. His fingers dig into the soil and pull on the roots, but then he is up and over and away. James sees his back diving between the trees. He watches Adam running away, getting away, and suddenly he is full of anger. So angry that he wants to stop Adam. It isn't fair that he can just run away, while the rest of them have to stay here. He is furious with Adam, it is all wrong, and so James stands and aims his pistol at his back. He sees Adam still, his arms lift, his knees start to crumple and then, when he turns and falls, it is Nathaniel's face looking back again.

The electric light is switched on when he wakes and Caitlin is there with an arm around his shoulders. Her fingers wipe tears from his cheeks, but she looks at him like she's not quite sure how to speak to him, like she can't understand him, like she doesn't know what to do next.

'You screamed again,' she says eventually.

'I'm sorry.'

'Surely you could take something to help you sleep? It's the second time this week.'

'I took half a bottle of whisky. I just couldn't get off last night.'

'I'm not sure that's what you ought to be taking.' Her eyes flicker across his and, for a moment, they are the colour of the light through the trees in a wood in France. And the expression on her face is Nathaniel's. His misplaced face. His face that is still somewhere in a wood in France. James blinks it away, rubs his eyes, and then Caitlin's features are her own once more, and it's the face of the woman he loves, but her eyes tell him how difficult she finds this. 'We can't keep on having nights like this,' she says. 'I'm exhausted and God knows how you feel. This isn't getting better, James; it's getting worse. I'm so tired in the mornings and I don't know how you're concentrating. Don't you think it's maybe time to talk to Shepherd, to ask him for some help? He would understand. Or you could start by talking to me.'

James shakes his head. 'I'm sorry, Caitlin.'

'Don't keep apologizing! Can you hear yourself? You're endlessly apologizing. Stop saying sorry and do something. Talk to someone. Let it out. This thing is like a virus multiplying inside you. It's like a tumour and I'm frightened sometimes that it's going to swallow you up.'

Her shadow exaggerates her gestures against the wall. If James watches her shadow, he doesn't have to look her in the eye. If he doesn't look at Caitlin, he doesn't have to see Nathaniel in her eyes. 'I won't let it.'

'I wish you sounded more in earnest. Did you see Nat again?'

'Yes.'

She brushes the hair away from his forehead. 'He wouldn't want you to be like this. You know that, don't you? Nat would hate this. He wouldn't want you to remember him that way. You've got to try to break out of this cycle.'

'I want to. You must understand that I don't want to be like this. I don't want you to be tired and upset. I don't want us to have cross words.'

'Why do you keep dreaming about Nat?'

'I suppose it's not knowing,' he admits.

'*Not knowing?*'

'Where your brother is.'

She nods. 'I wish you'd told me that sooner. You must realize that I feel the same – but that ought to bring us together, not be pulling us apart. Is there anything more that we could do? Could we try harder to find him?'

She makes it sound so simple, he thinks. Like that's possible. Like he hadn't tried hard enough already. James can't help shaking his head, it's an automatic reaction, and he doesn't really mean to dismiss her. But when he looks at her again, the anger is there in Caitlin's eyes once more, and he has to turn his eyes away.

Chapter Twenty-Three

Adam, Fellside House, December 1920

'Hello, Brother,' she says.

Adam walks to the mirror, looks at himself, and then back at her.

The girl has long red-gold hair, which naturally curls into ringlets. It is the colour of gingerbread, her hair, or perhaps marmalade, and Adam thinks that this is hair other women might envy, but she wears it carelessly and it coils around the edges of her black woollen cap. He imagines that, if he were to touch it, this hair would be brittle, that it might spring back from his fingers, and there is something brittle about her face too. Something challenging. She is sharp-featured, almost hard-featured. Her nose is narrow and straight and there are shadows beneath her slanting grey eyes. She blinks blond lashes in the light from the window. When Adam looks in the mirror he can see no match in their colouring, or common angles in their features.

'Adam, this is Lucy Vickers,' says Haworth. 'She's looking for her brother, Ellis. Won't you come and sit with us? Please, Adam, won't you join us?'

'Looking? I'm not looking any longer. My search has just stopped,' she says.

Adam walks towards her. The cuffs of her coat are frayed,

he sees. He can tell that she is a working woman. He catches a harsh note of soap as he inhales her, and sweat beneath; her smell is not familiar. He can tell that she is nervous. He can hear the quickened pace of her breath, but she does not rush at him like the other women. He picks up a sense of resentment from her. Is she angry with him? What had he done to make her angry? Her eyes flick up and meet his. She fixes him with her steady grey eyes.

'I am glad to see you again,' she tells him, but he's not absolutely sure she means it.

The collar of her white blouse is embroidered with green leaves, entwining tendrils and flowers picked out in yellow thread.

'Did you sew it yourself?' he asks.

'Yes. I used to stitch your handkerchiefs. Do you remember?'

He shakes his head.

'I did,' she says. 'Your initials.'

'My initials?'

'E.V. E for Ellis and V for Vickers. Our Ellis,' she says and nods.

Adam looks to Haworth. He shrugs.

'Not A for Adam?' he asks.

'No,' she says, as if she is surprised at him. 'You silly, of course not.'

She does not put her fingers out to touch him, as the other women have done, and so he feels that he is not given the licence to reciprocate. Besides, there is something about this woman that pushes him back. Her fingernails are chewed. Her hands are red and look older than her face. The skin on her hands looks rough. He is glad that she doesn't try to touch him with her rough red hands.

'Sit down, eh, Adam?' Haworth nods towards the empty chair. The woman called Lucy Vickers pats the seat.

'Here we are, then,' she says. 'Here we are again.'

Adam watches Haworth unscrewing his pen. He looks down at the blank sheet of paper in front of him and then up at the girl. Adam finds himself willing Haworth's pen to make a cross rather than a tick.

'Will I be able to take him home? Can he come home tonight?'

Adam watches her. Her eyes connect with Haworth's, but not his own.

'Perhaps in time,' Haworth replies. 'But, for now, maybe you could tell me a little about yourself and about Ellis.'

She looks down at her lap and turns a pair of grey cotton gloves between her red fingers. Adam sees that she has expected this to be simpler.

'I knew him as soon as I saw the picture in the newspaper. Well, you do, don't you? You know your own.'

Adam sees Haworth glance from the girl to him. Does Haworth see any similarity in their faces? Does he recognize a connection there that Adam can't see himself?

'Perhaps you could start by telling me Ellis' date of birth.'

'The fifth of April 1898. Our birthdays are in the same week, aren't they, Ellis? Only two years apart.' She looks at Adam and then back at Haworth. 'We always shared a birthday cake. Mother would bake one cake and then cut it in half, but he got the better part of the deal because his birthday comes first. I always slightly resented that as a child. Well, children do, don't they? I would never have wished him away, though.'

'And your mother is still living?'

'No, we lost her, didn't we?' She turns to Adam and shakes

her head as if she's exasperated by his lack of response. 'In 1913. She would never have let him sign up. She wouldn't have let him go away. It would all have happened differently if my mother had still been alive. We'd all be living different lives now.'

Haworth nods. Adam watches the loops of his pen. 'And you, Miss Vickers? How did you feel about your brother leaving?'

'Well, it had consequences, didn't it? Significant consequences for me, as it happened.'

'Go on. Please.'

'His children for a start.'

Adam can feel Haworth scrutinizing his face for a reaction. 'His children?' Haworth replies. 'Perhaps we had better rewind. Can you tell me about Ellis' family circumstances before the war?'

She is playing with her gloves. She straightens each finger out carefully, but then wrings them into a screw of fabric. Adam observes how her fingers twist. They still as she looks up at him and her eyes connect with his then. 'He was married at eighteen, weren't you? And happily so. But Phoebe died with the second child. That's when he moved back into our house. I've brought them up as my own. Katie is six now and quite the young lady. You'll see Phoebe in her face,' she adds, nodding with something that seems to be certainty.

'That can't have been easy for you. That's a significant responsibility to take on.'

Adam watches Haworth's handwriting stretching across the page.

'Well, yes, but it's family, isn't it?' she replies. 'I live with my elder brother, George. We all get by together. George stayed at home because he always had problems with his chest. It's a good job that he did stay, because we needed his wages.'

'And you – do you work, Miss Vickers?'

'I work in a laundry. I was training to be a seamstress before the war – I liked it and they said I had a talent for it – but this is steadier. I don't earn much, and I have to take the children into work with me sometimes, but it's regular work. It's not ideal, but it's regular wages and regular hours.'

'And can I ask you when you last heard from Ellis?'

'Too bloody long ago.'

Adam knows then that she is angry with him. He sees the line of her mouth harden and wants to tell her that it's not his fault. He's not this missing person. He's not the father of these children. He can't fill the gap that her brother has left and make her life easier. He doesn't have the capacity to make her happier.

'I'm sorry,' she corrects herself. She apologizes to Haworth, Adam notices, not to him. 'He'd just been discharged from hospital. We had a letter in the January – 1915, that is. He told us he'd been wounded – a bullet wound to his lower leg – but he said it wasn't as bad as that sounded and he was out. It was only a glancing wound, that's how he put it. He told us not to worry. He sent me a postcard with the words *Forget Me Not* on it and promised he'd write again.'

'And?'

'Nothing for another two months. Then, in the March, there was a telegram saying that he'd been reported missing, believed killed. I thought that was it. The end. I told his children. Can you imagine having to do that? But then, a few weeks later, there was a letter from his officer. He said that Ellis had taken part in a raid on enemy trenches, only it had gone wrong. There was bombing on both sides, he said, a lot of smoke and confusion. They hadn't managed to get all the wounded back and Ellis was missing. This Captain Bretton said that there was a fair chance Ellis had been taken prisoner, you see? That was the explanation, and I knew it was right. I knew in my bones then that he wasn't dead. And I *was* right, wasn't I?'

She turns to Adam. He finds he can't reply. Her eyes are full of questions and need. The wound in his shin throbs.

'Do you have any photographs?' Haworth asks.

'I'm sorry?'

'A photograph of Ellis? A photograph of his wife and his children, perhaps? It might help, I mean, if Adam could see them.'

'Ellis,' she corrects. She puts the flat of her hand emphatically down on the desk. 'Jog his memory, you mean?'

'Perhaps you could bring them in another time?'

'He won't get to come home with me today, then?' Her red fingers drum on the desk. Adam can hear the impatience in her voice with that. He imagines the hot, wet walls of a laundry and two damp children within. He can't imagine himself a father. He can't imagine himself the brother of this girl who is now pushing the grey gloves back onto her red hands.

'I'll come back for you soon,' she says at the door. Adam is grateful that, unlike the others, she doesn't try to kiss him.

Haworth turns his papers, which are now covered over with black words. 'Phoebe?' he says to Adam. The name is clearly a test. Adam shakes his head.

Chapter Twenty-Four

James, Fellside House, December 1920

The leaves in the water are copper and gold and flickering movement. They spin slowly in the shallows, but further up the water is rushing white and James feels the spray on his face.

'I didn't know there was so much sadness in the world,' says Adam. 'I had no idea. How can so many people be missing?'

A leaf rotates on the surface of the water. James watches it complete a turn before he looks at Adam. 'It's rather brought it home, hasn't it?'

They stand on Clappersgate bridge and watch the beck. It is brown after the rain and quickening to foam. Adam drops a stick in and they both turn to see it emerge from the other side of the bridge. The air is damp today and James pulls the collar of his overcoat up and pushes his hands deep down into his pockets. He wriggles his toes in his boots to keep off the ache of the cold.

'We never expected it to be like this. I don't think we'd have started this had we known.'

'I kept thinking about flocks of rooks this morning,' Adam replies. 'They were all cawing in the hallway.'

The leaves that cling on to the trees are yellow now. The reflection of an ash tree glimmers in the water. The noise of the rushing beck and all the sadness that has passed through the house today makes James feel colder.

'You don't mind seeing Mrs Dakers again? You don't object to that?'

'No.' James hears Adam hesitate. 'I feel sorry for her. I could see that she misses her son. But I'm not that person. Why do you want me to see her again?'

'Are you certain you don't know her? She seemed to know you.'

Adam shakes his head. He blinks and James can see his eyes following the current of the water. 'I wanted to remember her in order to make her less sad, but I couldn't. I didn't.'

'So you're one hundred per cent certain?'

'Well, no, but – do I have to quantify it? If I say more than fifty per cent is that enough?'

'I'm sorry,' James says. 'I know this week can't have been easy for you. It isn't feeling like too much pressure? It's not making you sad?'

'Yes, of course it's making me sad. I feel sorry for them because I see that they all need my face to be someone else's face. I see the disappointment in their eyes when they walk into the room, the little twitches of doubt, and how desperately they're trying to make my face fit. They need it more than me.'

'We won't drag it out. I think there are only a couple more that seemed likely. Lots of the letters were completely way out. It's not fair on anyone to stretch it out for months.'

'No.'

Looking at Adam, as he turns on the bridge and smiles at the trees, James isn't at all sure that he wants his face to fit. He doesn't really get the sense that Adam wants to leave here with any of these women, and yet some of them had been adamant.

There were facts that fitted, scenarios that seemed plausible, and their reactions had been so entirely convincing. Surely he had to measure their certainty up too and take that into account? He imagines himself in their position and Nathaniel sitting in Adam's chair, only with all the memories taken out of his head. The claimants deserve the chance to make their case, James thinks.

'Is there anyone else today?' Adam asks.

'Just one more woman this afternoon.'

The swirl of falling leaves flickers and it all vibrates like a pointillist painting. They walk down to the shingle beach, the pebbles crunching underfoot, and Adam skims a stone. It skips one-two-three-four times. James watches the ripples widen.

'I got the impression that you didn't warm to Miss Vickers very much.'

'I didn't recognize her at all. I didn't feel any connection to her.'

'And the idea of being a father?'

Adam shakes his head. He narrows his eyes at James. 'I'm not. I'm sure I'm not. I'd have some sense of that, wouldn't I?'

'She's convinced that you're her brother. She also seems determined that she wants you back in the family home.'

'I could see that. I also felt like she was angry.'

'Perhaps. Maybe that proves her reaction is a genuine one?'

'Do you think?'

'If it could be proved that she was telling the truth, if it turns out that you are her brother, would you want to leave with her?'

'I'd have to, I suppose, wouldn't I? But I don't feel it's right. I don't think it's the truth.'

'We'll investigate each claim as thoroughly as we can – and

you won't be forced to do anything that you don't want to do. I promise you that. We'll never make you leave against your will.'

Adam nods, but doesn't look entirely convinced.

'And the woman you said you saw in the woods – you haven't seen her again? You haven't spotted her amongst the people in the house?'

'No.'

'I have to say, I'm curious to know what she looked like. Could you draw her for me?'

'Draw her? I already have.'

'You have? Will you show me?'

'Again? Yes, if you'd like.'

James can feel the cold biting at his feet. His toes are frozen. He tries to wriggle them in his boots, but he can't. 'Dear God, let's go back and sit in front of the fire! My feet haven't been this cold and wet since I was in France. It's not a memory that I care to re-enact.' He turns to Adam and sees him smile. 'You're not cold?'

'No.'

When Adam had first come to Fellside, there were chilblains on his feet, James recalls, but that didn't prove that he'd been in France; that could just have been the weeks on the road. He also remembers that there was a wound on his shin, though. He'd seen it when they'd first examined him. A silver line of scar tissue. Like the scar left by a glancing bullet wound.

'How lucky you are to be able to forget,' James says.

Chapter Twenty-Five

James, Fellside House, December 1920

He watches Anna Mason's fingers turning the locket around her throat. The gold chain ripples along the length of her fingers and catches the light. This is not the first time her fingers have gone to the necklace as they have talked, and it is as though there is something superstitious, or talismanic in the action. He can tell that the locket around her neck must have some link to her husband and, in touching it, she is connecting with him in some way.

'Do you have a picture inside?' he asks.

'Yes. Of Mark.'

'Would you show me?'

James doesn't think about it as he asks, but he has to lean closer to her now. In a slightly overexposed oval of photograph, he makes out a young man's features. The paleness of it, the indistinct focus, reminds James of looking for meaningful shapes in clouds, but the pigment condenses into a face of regular, symmetrical features, a face of no distinct, defining irregularity. Can it be Adam five years younger? It could be, he concludes, but with no fanfare of certainty.

'You're not sure, are you?' she asks.

When his eyes lift from the locket, he is suddenly conscious of how close to her he is standing. He suddenly becomes aware of her breath on his face, the flecks of gold in her green eyes, and the shape of her lips now forming into another question.

'It's not the clearest photograph.'

'No,' she says, as she snaps the locket shut. 'I will be allowed to see him today?'

'Yes. Of course. He knows you're here.'

She nods. There's something about her face that's troubling James; something about her features that's familiar, and yet he can't quite make the link. Is it that she looks like someone else, or has he met her before? She's a handsome woman and it's a strong face, he considers, a face that he probably would remember. The high arch of her dark eyebrows makes her face seem open and intelligent, and her smooth black hair is exactly parted, so that when she leans forward, as now, he can see the precise white line of her scalp. It is a strange feeling to know, and yet not know, this woman. James thinks about percentages of certainty and wonders if this is how Adam feels when he looks at them all.

'There are so many people outside,' she says. 'So many women! I didn't expect that.'

'Neither did we.' He offers her a cigarette. 'We thought we might have one or two enquiries, but we've had over a hundred.'

'A hundred? Really? You make me feel that my odds are rather long. I'm certain that it's him, though. The photograph in the newspaper looked exactly like Mark.'

'For your sake I hope you're right.'

'The letter they sent me said that he was missing in action,' she tells him. Threads of smoke wind from her lips and she bats them away with long white fingers. 'It wasn't missing presumed killed – it wasn't worded like that – just missing, and that left me with room for hope.'

'I understand. My wife's brother was reported missing and I don't think she's ever stopped hoping that he might turn up.'

He doesn't add that he'd seen Nathaniel's dead body, though. He had felt the weight of him, lifeless in his arms – only, it had been there, and then not, so that his brother-in-law must now be indefinitely missing. James has never felt he can conclusively prove Nathaniel's death to Caitlin, and he worries that she still hopes.

'I'm glad you understand how that feels, that you know those endless questions. I'm not glad that you suffer those doubts, I mean, but it's a comfort to know you have some empathy with how this feels.'

'I do.'

'I've been paying an investigator – a private detective, if you will – to find Mark. He's been looking for him for eighteen months. There are clues, there seem to be trails, but then they always lead to dead ends.'

'Clues?'

'I mean we've pieced together all of his movements, we know precisely where he was and when, but then suddenly all the information dries up.' She sips from her glass of water. 'For a while it seemed possible that he might have been taken prisoner and then, when time went on, I thought that he could have ended up in a French hospital and somehow been lost in the system. We've followed lots of paper trails. Sometimes round in circles.'

'It sounds as though you've put a lot of time and effort into looking for him.'

'I have – and I'm afraid I've spent all our money on it as well. I kept the farm going until last year, but then there was too much other expense. I've still got the house, but I've sold most of the land off. It was Mark's father's farm, and his grandfather's before that – their family farm. It will break his heart when he realizes. I don't know how I'm ever going to tell him.'

'Wait for the right time. There's no hurry, is there?' As he says it, he realizes that he sounds like he's encouraging her. James doesn't mean to give her increased reason to hope, but then he acknowledges that there is something satisfying about the idea of Adam having an attractive wife who has been determinedly searching for him, and a home and a history. While he can't stop Nathaniel from being missing, he would like Adam to be found and placed and named and have a chance of happiness again. But, seeing both the anxiety and need in Anna Mason's eyes, he adjusts his tone. 'Don't worry about it yet. Face the issue when and if the time comes.'

'I brought some of his letters with me, to show you and to help him remember.' She takes an envelope from her purse and turns the blue notepaper between her fingers. 'His handwriting,' she says.

James refocuses on the page in her hands and sees that it is crowded with words. He wants to take the letter from her, and to hear the voice of the man who once certainly was this woman's husband. He tries to remember the loops and leans of Adam's handwriting. Can it be the same hand and the same voice?

'Did he ever illustrate his letters?'

'Illustrate?' She dabs her half-smoked cigarette out in the ashtray with a clatter of celluloid bangle and tilts her head as she looks up at him.

'Did he ever send you drawings?'

'No, not then. Not after he went to France. But he used to draw years ago. Before.'

'Before?'

'Before the war, I mean. Oh, long ago, when he was young. When I first knew Mark, he used to carry a sketchpad in his pocket and liked to draw the plants and animals that he saw. He was good at it. He had a talent.' She smiles. 'He knew the names of everything too. And in Latin! I thought him quite the show-off when I first met him. But he also liked to draw my portrait. Why do you ask me that? Does he draw here?'

'Yes.'

James glances back as he is about to open the door, and sees her pinching colour into her cheeks; her eyes catching his, and then shifting away, as if this action is something that James shouldn't witness, that she shouldn't let him see. He pictures her face as a pencil portrait and then knows exactly where he's seen her before.

'I do know it's him,' she says, as James opens the door.

Chapter Twenty-Six

Anna, Fellside House, December 1920

She was expecting him to be in the next room, but instead the doctor has led her through another empty office, down a corridor and now out of a door at the back of the house.

'I hope you're warm enough?' he asks. 'It's hardly the day for sitting out on the lawn, is it? But he wanted a breather. We've been doing interviews for the past couple of days, so when he requested a bit of fresh air and space, I did feel that we owed him a concession. You don't mind terribly, do you?'

'No, of course not,' she replies.

They cross a lawn, and veer around trees, and she can hear the noise of the last few people making their way to the gates. How many of them have crossed this lawn today? Did they all feel this peculiar mix of impatience and fear?

'Are you expecting more people tomorrow?'

'I hope not. It's all rather more than we'd planned for. We'd love to make a breakthrough, but I'm also conscious of what hard work this is for Adam. Emotionally taxing, I mean – you understand?'

'Yes.'

Mark is a quiet man. He likes his house, and his books, and his land. He has never been much of a one for company.

When they had gone out to fetes, and fairs, and dances, it had always been at her request; she always had to tug his hand. She imagines him having to be interviewed by all these people now – all these women! – and thinks that he must hate it.

'He's in the walled garden,' the young doctor says.

She can see the gate then, in the old red brick walls ahead. Is he finally there – within those walls – beyond that gate? After so many months, so many years, of searching, after all those letters and appointments, those false leads and disappointments, could he really be behind those walls? She puts a hand out to steady herself.

'Are you feeling unwell?' Doctor Haworth asks.

'Just nervous, a bit light-headed; it's rather overwhelming that this is finally happening,' she says. 'It's been so long. I don't know what his reaction is going to be.'

Of course, her mind replays that last scene, the last time that she saw him; the tears on his cheeks, the smile that wasn't a smile at all, and those words. Does he remember the words that he said? Might they have to restart there?

'Everyone has been nervous,' the doctor says. 'He is too. Just take it gently.'

There's another man, another doctor it seems, standing inside the gate and he shakes her hand. His eyes move over her face, and it feels almost impolite when she looks away, but she needs to see *him*. She needs to see Mark. To know if it really could be him. She needs to see the expression on his face.

As they walk into the walled garden, she misses him at first. It looks like an old-fashioned kitchen garden, rather neglected now, but someone seems to have been making an effort to take out the worst of the weed and bramble. Two facing chairs have been set up on the cleared patch of ground. Empty as yet. Obviously meant for him and her. There's something unmistakably confrontational, she thinks, in the positioning of the two opposing chairs. Is that why they're here, outside, within these walls, with two lookers-on to supervise and, if necessary, intervene? Has Mark requested that it be like this? Was this the only way that he could face her?

She sees him then. He has a scythe in his hands and the sight of him makes her gasp, because it is him (unmistakably, wonderfully, gloriously, terrifyingly), she could exactly place him straight back in his father's fields again, and also because of the way that he's holding the blade in his outstretched arm.

'Please, Mrs Mason, will you take a seat?' The older doctor leans against the back of a chair and beckons. 'I am sorry. This is frightfully unconventional, isn't it? And I hope you're not too cold? Only, it was at Adam's request. This garden is his project, you see? And I'm afraid that the house has felt rather claustrophobic over the past few days.'

His words stream away unheeded, but she takes the seat, as he bids her. She doesn't let her eyes leave Mark, though. She daren't. She can't read the expression on his face. She can't make him out. What is he feeling as his eyes watch hers?

Doctor Haworth takes the scythe from Mark (there is some relief in that) and leads him towards the facing seat. His eyes haven't left hers since he first saw her, but he glances at the doctor now. It is a relief to be free of the link of his gaze for a moment, to be able to look at him and take in his face; to know his mouth and his cheekbones, the colour of his hair, that frown line on his brow and his brown eyes looking at her again now.

'May I?'

She'd hardly heard him ask the question, but he's seemingly been given consent, and he leans forward in his chair. As his eyes explore her face, it's almost a physical sensation. Is he reading her? Knowing her? But what is he thinking? He's focused, studying her face, but it's as if she has forgotten how to interpret the language of his features, or perhaps there is no feeling there? He is looking at her like he is curious. Like he is interested, but is it only that? Bearing the investigation of Mark's eyes is almost too much. What does it mean? She wishes that he'd speak. Is she allowed to speak?

'Can I approach her?' he asks the doctor.

She hears herself laugh. It's nerves; it's the oddness of the situation and his manner; it's not knowing what to expect next.

'Do you recognize Mrs Mason's face?' Doctor Haworth asks.

'I don't know,' Mark replies.

And it's at that moment that it hits her: that he genuinely doesn't know her; that her husband has forgotten her. She wasn't ready for the shock of that, for the scale of that shock, and for just how much it hurts.

Mark stands and takes a step towards her then.

'You don't mind? It's all right?' the older doctor asks.

'No, of course not.' She barely hears her own voice.

He is only inches away from her now and she can see that his hands are dirty from working in the garden. He's thinner in his face, and paler than he was when he was out in the fields every day. His eyes are the same, though. His beautiful eyes. She remembers how she had once longed to kiss his eyelids and his mouth.

'Mark, I'm your wife,' she says.

He takes a step closer, but she can't tell whether the movement of his head is a nod or a shake. She can hear his breathing and smell his skin. She knows the scent of his skin, the feel of his face against hers, the taste of his sweat and his tears. As he puts his face nearer to hers, she has to close her eyes. It's too much. She hears him lowering his head, though, and his long intake of breath. His cheek only touches hers for an instant, it's only a glancing touch, but that brief contact is like a jolt of electricity.

Chapter Twenty-Seven

Caitlin, Fellside House, December 1920

Caitlin feels his eyes on her as she's working. It's Nat. He's here again. Standing just behind her. The back of her neck prickles and she's waiting to feel his breath. She holds her own breath as she listens; she listens so intently, and something in her own body seems to shift as every fibre readies to acknowledge his presence. But then, as she slowly straightens and looks up, she realizes that it's not Nat at all; the eyes are Adam's instead and he's there, crouched at the cellar window. Caitlin hears the sigh of her own released breath, and she's not sure if it's relief or disappointment that floods her body now. She has to take a moment to steady herself before she can raise her hand and acknowledge Adam. His expression is momentarily unreadable, but why does she feel he has just witnessed her moment of confusion and understood it? When she looks again, his face twitches into a quick smile and it might as well be a wink or a nod of acknowledgement.

'Do you want to come and hide in here for a bit?' she asks him.

'Could I? May I? Would you let me?'

'Of course. Just don't tell James that we've conspired.'

She watches him moving around the studio and thinks

that he looks tense. Adam's face has been as placid as a church plasterwork in recent months, but today his eyes are flickering around the walls and he can't seem to settle. Though she pities him, it is a reprieve to blink away her own thoughts and focus on another person's emotions, to have another bodily presence breaking the silence and stillness, the noise of his footsteps, the smell of earth on his clothes, the unquestionably real whisper of Adam's breath.

'How's it all going?' she asks, as she washes her hands at the sink.

He shakes his head.

'James tells me you've been meeting some of them.'

'They want me to. I know they want to see me making connections.'

'And?'

'Well, they all know me, they're all certain, but I don't think I know them. The connections are all a bit one-sided.'

'Don't *think* you know them?' Caitlin repeats.

He paces the width of the room. 'And that's just it – I don't know what certainty feels like any longer.'

'You're pacing like a caged animal.'

'I'm sorry. I do feel rather trapped at the moment.'

He retraces the line of his steps, just as James is so often doing when Caitlin sees him from her cellar window. She watches Adam's mouth moving, and realizes that he's counting his paces. Does James do the same, she wonders, and, if so, why? What does the pacing mean? Does James feel trapped too? Is he also feeling uncertain? She remembers his face as he awoke from the nightmare, and knows that he's full of doubts and conflicts. But then her attention shifts back to Adam's as his foot turns her kick wheel and, briefly, she sees more curiosity than anxiousness on his face.

'Would you like to try?'

He seems to consider the question before he shakes his head. 'I'd be frightened to break something.'

'You wouldn't! What would you break? You should never be frightened.'

'Never?' Adam looks up as he asks it.

Addressing the question on his face, Caitlin thinks how Adam is detached from his own history. What fears might he have faced in those blacked-out years? How frightening that blank must be in itself. 'Well, only of wild dogs and strange men.'

'I think I might have a certificate somewhere with *strange man* written on it.'

She is thankful at last to see a glint of humour in Adam's eyes. 'But you're curious-strange, not nasty-strange.'

He smiles and nods his head at that, as if he's grateful for the qualification. 'Perhaps you might add an asterisk to my certificate?'

'Well?'

'Well what?'

'I won't offer twice. I wouldn't let anyone else use my wheel. I wouldn't dream of letting James have a go. Now, he *would* break something.'

As Adam rolls his sleeves up, Caitlin sees the marks on his arms again. James says that Adam must have brought those scars back from the war, but Caitlin can't help thinking that they look self-inflicted. She remembers similar marks on Rebecca's arms and the sadness that had caused her friend to make those cuts. Caitlin hopes that she's wrong, that Adam hasn't also experienced this sadness and – if he has – that he will perhaps never remember it.

'Whenever you're ready.'

Adam stares at the spinning circle and briefly looks as though he's been hypnotized by it. The tension that was written all over his face five minutes earlier now seems to be slipping away and his lowered eyelids are perfectly still. As Caitlin watches Adam's face, she realizes that she too knows this moment and this effect, but then Adam's eyes lift, and connect with hers, and are full of questions again.

'A woman came here yesterday and said I was her brother. She swore it. She insisted we were flesh and blood, but I've never thought of myself as a sibling and I can't imagine it. She didn't even look like me. She was so certain, there was no doubt there, but I looked at her face and I couldn't recognize anything of myself there.'

'Not all siblings look alike.'

'But generally there's some similarity, isn't there?' He watches the rotating wheel slowing and then stop. 'James told me you had a twin brother.'

'Yes, we did look alike. Everyone used to say that we were mirror images of one another, like the male and female versions of one single person.' She smiles, and Adam returns it, and because of that she goes on. 'When we were small my mother would dress us in matching outfits, but pink for me and blue for Nat. We both hated that because, although we looked so alike, we were our own distinct personalities. Sometimes, for mischief, we'd swap outfits. My mother's face!'

Adam laughs.

'And once we conspired to cut my plaits off. Nat took the dress-making shears to my hair. We thought she wouldn't be able to tell us apart then, and that would be funny. I don't think she knew which of us to scold first! We were such a close unit, and perhaps a closed unit sometimes; my poor mother didn't have a chance.'

'You were co-conspirators?'

'Always. I had my hair cut short after Nat died and my mother cried when she saw me. And then I cried too when I looked in the mirror at home, because I could see Nat looking back.'

'It can't have been easy to get used to being a whole rather than a half.'

'That's precisely it.' Caitlin nods at Adam and is grateful for his understanding. Perhaps he does see it, she thinks. 'Nat's still there in the mirror sometimes. Quite often. He's standing just behind me, like a vibration at the edges of my own reflection. I only see him briefly, no more than a teasing glimmer, but I'm absolutely certain that he's there. I read that sometimes when men lose limbs they have a sensation, as if they can still feel the foot or hand that's not there any longer. Have you heard of that? When I read about it, it made me think of Nat. Because he was such a fundamental part of me, and I was part of him, he's still here. Only he's not here often enough. I can't hear his voice. And I never get to see him smile.'

'I'm sorry.'

She shakes her head. 'I went off the rails for a few months after he died because my balance seemed to have gone. It's like I was all lopsided and couldn't keep on standing up on my own. I lost my sense of direction too. I spent a while looking for Nat's smile at the bottom of a bottle, but it wasn't there either.'

'I have no memory of knowing closeness like that, but I can imagine that it must have been very difficult to lose it.'

Caitlin looks at him. 'What about the woman who you draw? You must have been close to her.'

Adam turns his hands in the water and she can see him considering.

'I know her face and her skin and her hands, I know them in up-close detail, but I can't actually remember being with her. I only have a memory of what *she* looks like, how she is, not of how *I* was with her. I only have one half of the picture. Do you understand? I don't know how we connect up, or what she feels for me.'

There is both sadness and happiness in Adam's expression as he seems to contemplate what his relationship with this woman might have been, and Caitlin feels such sympathy for him at this moment.

'She might come here, you know. I understand that you don't like all these people filling up the house, but she might be here one day, and when you see her that memory might fit back.'

He hesitates. 'Perhaps.'

'Would you like that?'

'Of course.'

'Let's hope then, shall we?'

He nods at her. 'Yes.'

'And by then you'll be a master potter, and won't that be a surprise for her? Come on. Give it a go.'

He arches his back and pushes the hair away from his eyes, leaving a streak of clay across his forehead, and then the wheel is spinning again.

'You need to keep dipping your hands in the water. But not too much. You'll get the measure of it. Keep your elbows in and braced to your body. You need to be a solid triangle. If you wave your arms around loosely, it will all start waving around.'

The rhythm breaks as he laughs. 'Everything's waving around! You make it look a lot easier than it is.'

'A small matter of a decade of practice. But you're doing

well. Very well for a first time. Are you sure you haven't done it before?'

'Not that I recall. A small matter of two years of certified amnesia.'

'*Touché*. Sorry. Silly question.'

He pauses as he seems to consider his next move. He sits perfectly motionless and Caitlin thinks that is one of the striking things about Adam, this capacity for stillness. It is a meditation, almost. It brings to mind the glassy surface of a pool untouched by the wind. Whatever memories Adam is meant to be repressing, they seem to be well below the surface these days, she thinks. She also realizes, as she observes Adam's seemingly contented stillness, that this is something James lacks.

'I think I've got it now,' he says. 'I can visualize the shape I'm aiming for.'

'Good. Pull up from the base. Feel the thickness of the walls with your fingers. Keep your hands linked.'

Adam starts again and the walls of the bowl rise. He seems to have no issue with the mechanics of combining foot and hand movement, and Caitlin can see the control in his fingers. Adam's hands are strong and capable, she considers, able to apply both force and delicacy. As she watches Adam work, she thinks that he must have been a man who earned his living with his hands, but in some skilled way. She wonders what tools and techniques his hands have known and what memories there are in the fibre of his muscles.

'I'm really not convinced that you haven't done this before.'

'I'll take it as a compliment. I think that's about as well as I'm going to do, though.'

He sits back and looks at the bowl he has made.

'You should feel proud of yourself. I'll have it fired for you and you can help me glaze it.'

'Can I?'

'And you can come in here any time you want, you know. It doesn't just have to be when you're hiding.'

'Thank you.'

Caitlin realizes, as she says it, that there are so few people to whom she would extend that invitation. This, after all, is her private space and being here is something like hiding for her too. But she likes the atmosphere of Adam's calmness and it always feels like a sincere compliment when he smiles.

She watches as he washes his hands, and observes that all the tension he entered with has now gone – but then he's turning towards her, and there's suddenly something else in his face.

'Can I tell you a secret?' he asks.

'Yes, of course. I don't leak.'

He presses his lips together as if he's not sure whether to keep his secret in or not.

'I lied before. Or, at least, it was a half-truth.'

'Really, Adam? How shocking.' She widens her eyes at him to tease, but then can see that there's no light-heartedness in his expression. 'I'm sorry. Go on. Please tell me.'

'The woman who I was talking about – the woman who I draw – the woman I think I remember . . .'

'Yes?'

'She's already come. She's been here. I've seen her.'

Chapter Twenty-Eight

James, Fellside House, December 1920

'Could your Mrs Mason be the woman he draws?' Shepherd asks.

'I asked myself that same question,' James replies. 'I couldn't figure out where I knew her from at first, but then when they were sitting face to face in the garden, and looking at one another so intently, I was certain that my guess was right. At that moment I wanted to shout, "Bingo!" I would have sworn it was the same face, but then I asked him this morning and he denies it. No, it's not her, he says. Absolutely not.'

'No? He's definite about that?'

James shakes his head. 'I was all elated last night, excited, but he popped my balloon this morning. He looked at me like I was a fool.'

'Really? Is he telling the truth, do you think? Could he have a motive for not admitting that he knows her? It certainly was an emotionally loaded encounter.'

'Wasn't it? But he informs me that the woman in his drawings is the same woman he saw in the woods.'

'The *fairy*?'

'I asked him if he could draw a picture of his supposed fairy, and he did, but it's the same face he's drawn from the day he first arrived here. Exactly. Unmistakably. I'm not convinced that I believe in fairies,' says James, 'but the face in those drawings does look like Anna Mason.'

'But why invent this woman in the woods?'

'Convenience? So he can avoid making any commitment? The timing of her arrival is expedient, isn't it?'

'Or Galilee might have been seeing fairies all his life?' Shepherd smiles.

'Well, she was a very pretty fairy. I wouldn't mind if she were to creep up on me in the woods.'

'So where does this leave us with Mrs Mason?'

'After some pressing, he eventually conceded that there might be some slight resemblance between her and his fairy.'

'*Slight?* More than slight, I'd say. We need to see her and Adam together again, don't we? I mean, it's not just the likeness. It's the way they reacted to one another. I felt like a voyeur at the end.'

'Quite!'

'But why feign? What reason could he have not to acknowledge her?'

'I have no idea. I don't know what's going on in Adam's head this morning, but we do need to see more of Mrs Mason, don't we?'

'She said they had a farm,' James tells Caitlin, 'that it was her husband's family farm, only now she's had to sell all the land off.'

'How terribly sad.' Caitlin stands with her back to him, touching the ornaments on the mantelpiece each in turn. 'Imagine if he does go back – imagine if it is Adam – and he finds that he's lost all his land. That could break a man's heart.'

'More than losing his name and his family, you think?'

'No, of course not. I just mean that he must have a deep connection with that landscape.'

'That doesn't sound unlike Adam, does it?'

'No,' she replies. 'But he swears she's not the fairy?'

'He's very firm about it. Don't you think it's odd? When Adam came back from the woods it was like he was lovesick. He was mooning. And he and Mrs Mason definitely reacted to one another in the garden. It was electric. But this morning he's adamant that these are two different women.'

'So who is the woman in the woods, then?'

'I've no idea – and I'm inclined to think that she might not even exist.' James lights another cigarette. 'The thing is, all these women, all these stories, are plausible to some degree. They all have facts that fit. But they can't all be right, can they?'

'Unless he's been a very talented and busy trickster in his previous life.' Caitlin smiles.

'I find it hard to fathom how you could so convincingly persuade yourself that a stranger is your brother, or your husband, or your son. They all genuinely seem to believe it, but surely you'd know at some level that you were twisting the reality in order to fill a gap? Surely you'd have some niggle of doubt? And, yet, I can't see any twisting or niggling in any of their faces.'

'It's a powerful need, I suppose.'

'It must be.' James thinks about Anna Mason's face as she looked at Adam. Her look as Adam had put his face to hers. 'Mrs Mason has been searching for her husband. She's been pretty active. She even employed a private detective.'

'You thought about employing someone to look for Nat once, didn't you?'

'I still do. But that's a different sort of search.' It's one thing to hunt for a missing person, but quite another to search for a body. He looks at Caitlin and wonders if she entirely understands that. At some level, could she harbour a hope that Nathaniel might be alive somewhere? Sometimes, when he sees the sadness on her face, he wishes that he could give her more. If she actually knew where Nathaniel's body was, and had a grave to visit, would that make it easier for her to come to terms with her grief? James worries when she talks about eyes watching her, and when he catches her eyes looking aslant at her own reflection. But what if that can never happen – if there never can be a grave? Will she spend the rest of her life wanting to see ghosts?

'I take it that this detective hasn't come up with anything concrete, though?' Caitlin twists her rings around her fingers.

'Not anything that she wants to believe, it seems. And if it does work out that Adam is Mark Mason, this detective has evidently been looking in all the wrong places.'

'What's your gut reaction? Do you think it's a match?'

'At this moment I'm more confused by Adam than ever.'

Chapter Twenty-Nine

James, High House, Lancashire, January 1921

The house is right on the edge of the lake. The land immediately in front of it slopes down to the water, which sucks at the sand and shingle edge not fifteen feet from the front door. Wind shivers across the water, creasing the reflection of clouds and cold heights of blue. The view from the windows of this house must be like that from a ship, James supposes. On winter nights the water must whip at the windows. It is an ark, this house, and as isolated. This must be a wonderful, and terrible, place to be a child, and that surely would lodge its way indelibly in a person's mind? The water whispers where it meets the earth, there is an unending liquid murmur, and James understands that it must never be silent here. He remembers Adam's voice, two years ago, reading aloud a line from a poem: *For always night and day I hear lake water lapping with low sounds by the shore.* That phrase precisely sums up this place and this moment.

Adam skims a stone and it skips across the lake. The water glimmers bronze, silver and gold. Lucy Vickers' laughter breaks James' thoughts.

'See!' she says. 'He remembers. I was the person who taught him how to do that.' Her eyes meet James' as if this is proof; as if Adam's ability to skim a stone shows that this is where he belongs. It's certainly something Adam is accustomed to doing, James considers; there's a muscle memory there, and it's likely a trick learned in childhood, but is it this body of water that he practised upon?

'Did you grow up here?' James asks Lucy as they walk along the water's edge.

'We all did. My grandfather ran the ferry. It went to my father after that, and then to George.'

'A whole family tree of ferrymen?'

'Ellis never wanted to do it,' she says as she looks at Adam, 'but your Tom does. He sometimes goes out with his uncle George. He's needed a father figure,' she adds.

The buildings are surrounded by a stone wall, stained green with lichen and moss and damp. This was obviously a farmstead in an earlier century; the cow stalls and sties have evidently long since been abandoned, and the sheepfolds have fallen, but James can still see what it once was. The past still casts a shadow over the present here and, behind, the moors crease in wintry yellows and browns and purples. It seems an inhospitable place. It feels terrifically lonely. With its reflections and echoes, it is like a house in a poem, James thinks.

'You can see us all here,' says Lucy. She points to where a series of letters are carved into the lintel of a barn door. James thinks that these are Roman numerals at first, perhaps a date, but then picks out three sets of initials: *G.V., L.V. & E.V.* 'We each carved in our own letters. George first, a few years ahead, and then Ellis and I followed. He carved his own name in, even though he was only little. George said that I shouldn't have let him have the knife.'

'You look like you've been here for ever,' James remarks. Lichen has crept over their letters and the weather has rounded the cuts of their knife, giving these carvings a false antiquity. 'I suppose it's the nature of the stone, but you might well be three medieval siblings.'

'See, you've always been here,' she says to Adam. 'You never left really, did you? Do you remember that day?'

He shakes his head.

'Never mind,' says Lucy. 'You will.'

James can't ignore the confidence in her voice, the note of certainty, but he also sees her awareness of his presence; he knows that she means to convince him. Does she really believe that if Adam passes her tests, and performs all the demonstrations she seeks, James will just leave him here at the end of the day?

'George is here today?' he asks. It's part of the reason he's sanctioned this visit; he wants to see how the older brother responds to Adam, and if there is any more family resemblance there.

'He wanted to be here, he meant to be, but he's had to work.'

'Oh, that's a pity. I'm sorry to hear that. I thought he might be keen to see Adam?'

'He is.'

'Perhaps George might come to Fellside then?'

'Yes. I'll try to get him to come along with me next time.'

'Try to?'

Lucy seems to check herself. 'He takes all the work that he can. He has to. It's just the way it is.'

'I understand,' James says, but there's something about her reply, and the brother's absence, that leaves him questioning.

'There's been a farm here since medieval times,' Lucy goes on. 'It's called High House, which hardly seems to suit it now, does it? It seems low down today, on the edge of the water, but once it stood over a valley and when you looked up from the bottom this must have been the horizon. It's strange to think of that shift, isn't it? It makes me feel oddly dizzy.'

She can point out the old stones that have fallen, time and again, and been repositioned in the walls of the house. These stones, squared off centuries ago, keep finding a new angle and a new purpose. They fall down, but always somehow get put back, she says. James considers: does she think that Adam can get put back too?

'We spent our childhood imagining all the generations who lived here before us, trying to piece it all back as it might have been, hoping to see a ghost. But we never did, did we, Ellis?'

James sees that the history of this house is important to her, and their place within that long narrative. It matters that her brother is presently missing from it; she clearly can't settle to accepting that gap. James watches Adam as he turns in the centre of the farmstead. His eyes flicker all about and James can't help but wonder whether there are glimmers of memory there. He notices that Lucy is watching Adam's eyes too.

'It's a man-made lake, you see,' she says. 'They flooded the valley in the 1860s and it took much of the farm's lower land. Can you imagine what it must have felt like for the family who lived here? To watch the water rising and it all going under?'

Her hair is braided around her head today, like a copper crown, and she might well have stepped out of a church window. James thinks about the brittle girl from the laundry who came to Fellside. Lucy Vickers seems so much more alive here. Brighter. More liquid. This is her element. This belongs to her and makes her who she is. She rocks on her toes and expresses herself with her hands as she talks about the history of this place. James wonders if there is some remnant of this place in Adam too. Is the dust of its old stones in his lungs, its damp there in his bones, and its echoes locked somewhere within his imagination? Given time, would he become as one with this strange watery place too? Or perhaps he was once glad to take a wife and to get away from Lucy's ghost stories?

The mullioned windows look seventeenth-century, James thinks; they are small for the size of the house. The lamps are lit inside and the whitewash is blistering from the walls in places. It blooms green in one corner of the kitchen and under the smell of wax polish and washing soda there is a breath of decay here. Even in July this place must be still full of damp and shadows, James imagines.

'I can see why you hunted for ghosts.'

'There aren't any, though.' She smiles a quick flinch of a smile. 'Not a one. It's a constant disappointment for the children.'

There are two armchairs either side of the kitchen range, where Adam and Lucy must now sit, it seems. It occurs to James that Lucy hasn't included him in the scene that she's envisaged, and for a moment he feels like he is the ghost, the spare and unwanted person in this room. He hears reluctance in Lucy's voice when she tells him that he can bring a dining chair over from the table.

It's a big old scrubbed-pine farmhouse table, the sort that a coffin would be placed upon. Five heavy chairs are arranged around it, carved with oak and ivy leaves. James hesitates over which one to take, feeling as if the decision will somehow have significance. The odd number makes him count. He knows that four people live in this house today. Has the fifth always then been left out for the missing brother, waiting five years for his return? Is there then a chair in which no one but Ellis Vickers is permitted to sit?

The kettle hisses on the hob and Adam watches the flames flicker through the bars. There's a line of tea caddies and beer tankards on the mantel over the fire. James wonders if one of these tankards belonged to Ellis too, and is waiting to be filled for him and raised to his return. A black slate clock, all pediment and Corinthian column, like a small temple, marks time loudly.

'Tick, tock,' says Adam.

The hearthrug is worn smooth where his feet settle, James sees. Does Adam know the glow of this fire, the tick of this clock and the feel of that chair at his back?

Lucy spreads butter on bread at the table and offers Adam a plate painted with weeping willows. 'There's still some blackberry jam, if you want it,' she says. 'He needs building up and filling out, doesn't he?'

'He does.'

A basket of knitting is set down by the side of the fire, James notices. She is knitting children's gloves. Otherwise, there is nothing to indicate that children might live in this house, and James is glad of that, for Adam's sake. He had warned Lucy that it might be too much for Adam, but hadn't been certain that she trusted his judgement. He can see that Lucy thinks she knows what is best, and that resolve is evidently strengthened by being in this place.

James sips his too-hot tea and watches over the gilt rim as Adam licks jam from his fingers. He notices that Lucy watches him too. Her eyes rarely leave him, as she talks of *your* father, *your* mother, *your* brother, but James sees no connection in Adam's eyes. He places his plate down on the rug when he is finished and rises purposefully from his chair. The mantelpiece clock whirs as it gets ready to strike the hour, like a long intake of breath, and with that sound it feels as though time is suspended. They watch as Adam walks towards the far wall.

Lucy turns in her seat. She kicks the leg of James' chair and apologizes. 'Do you remember it?' she asks Adam's back. 'Do you know it? It's yours,' she says.

He is standing in front of a painting on the wall. It is greys and greens in an ebony frame. James pushes his chair back and follows Adam and the liquid colours shift into shape as he approaches. It is a painting of the lake, he sees; the horizon is set high within the frame, so that the composition is more water than sky; there is this building, High House, on the edge, and all the reflected colours of a winter day surround it. James wonders, did Adam's hand paint this scene? James is familiar enough with his drawing, and would surely recognize his style – but, then, it has always been pencil or ink. It's always black and white. Could this be Adam with a box of colours? Are those then his real initials in the corner? James looks at Adam's profile against the painting. His eyelids flicker fast. There is something strange going on behind Adam's eyes.

'There's a figure. I didn't see it at first. What's the man doing in the water?' James asks.

'He's walking out into it,' Adam replies.

'He was always painting,' Lucy says. Her voice is suddenly there at James' side. 'When he was young he had a notion of going to art college.' She smiles as she turns away. 'Isn't that so, Ellis? Isn't that right? Only it was just a notion. It could only ever be a notion because, well, I mean, that's not a job, is it? Not here, not in this place, at any rate.'

The sash windows rattle in the wind. Adam looks from the painting to the view beyond the rattling windows. What is it that flickers in that look? James can see from the way Adam hugs his arms to his chest that he's cold.

'Come back to the fire,' he says.

'So he trained as a draughtsman,' Lucy continues. 'Here, he might remember this.'

They watch as she walks to the kitchen dresser. When she turns, she is holding a box. Her hand strokes the gloss of the polished wood and her rolled sleeves show her thin arms. She turns a key, lifts the lid and holds the box out to Adam.

James sees the slight tremble in Adam's hands as he receives it. For a moment, for some reason, James expects it to be a music box and for a waltz to come tinkling out, but inside there are brass compasses and protractors and technical pencils bedded in purple velvet.

'It's a thing of beauty.'

'Father bought it for him for his eighteenth birthday.'

James watches Adam's hand move over the surface. Does Adam know the textures and the use of the instruments in this box? He wants to put them in Adam's hands and see how his fingers form around them, if there is knowledge there in his grip and balance. Adam lifts the top tray out, as if he is familiar enough with this, as if he knows how this thing works, and underneath there are papers in a handwriting that might be Adam's and a photograph of a young woman in white lace. James watches the vibration of Adam's eyelashes, the slight movement of his lips, but then he is returning the tray, and closing the lid, and passing the box back to Lucy.

'It's not mine,' he says. 'This belongs to someone else.'

Lucy shakes her head as if she can't understand him.

There are two men's hats and two winter coats on the cloak rail in the porch. As far as James is aware, there's only one adult male living in this house. Does one of these then belong to Adam? There is a line of shoes beneath, and a pair of black leather boots packed tight with newspaper. They look recently polished. Are they waiting for him too? Expecting his return? Do they fit? Does this fit? James asks himself: is there some reason why Adam doesn't want this to fit?

Adam

He shuts his eyes and listens to the noise of the wind moving over the water. Adam knows he has heard this sound before. He can taste peat and heather on the wind. That is familiar too. When he turns, Haworth's footsteps are there on the shingle behind.

'Your feet are wet,' Haworth says. 'Can't you feel it? It's lapping right over your boots.'

Adam looks down and is surprised to see that it is so. He steps back. He's sure that the water wasn't this high moments ago.

'There are lapwings,' he says. 'Can you hear? I was listening to them. It's a familiar noise.'

'You remember the sound of this place?'

'It's quite distinctive, isn't it? Particular acoustics. It's a bit like the sound of a seashell. It's very still here and yet full of things going on just below the surface. There will be Canada geese in the spring and curlew.'

'Do you know that or do you imagine it?'

He considers the question. 'I think I know it.'

There is something strange about standing on the edge of this water. It is like standing on a precipice and Adam feels as if he has walked out into this water before. He knows exactly how the ground shelves, and will fall away beneath his feet, how the water will feel in the sleeves of his shirt and when it streams into his mouth and his nose. He can feel the weight of the rocks in his pockets again, but is that knowledge, or imagination? Is this his memory or that of someone else? He can't differentiate well enough to share the thought with Haworth.

Chapter Thirty

James, Fellside House, January 1921

'The girl is certain of it?' Shepherd asks.

'Entirely. I'd gone over there feeling sceptical, but she convinced me – of her certainty, at least. She genuinely believes that he's her brother.'

'And what do you think? Could he be?'

'I'm not sure,' James replies. He watches Shepherd pacing behind his desk. He knows this is not the answer Shepherd wants. 'I can't help but wonder whether she's just convinced herself.'

'Convinced herself *that* thoroughly? Is her state of mind such that she could genuinely believe a stranger to be her own flesh and blood?'

'It's a possibility, isn't it? It happens with shock. Why not with loss? I think she needs her brother back sufficiently that she may have forced her memory to respond falsely to Adam.'

'Was there anything in her demeanour to indicate that this might be volition rather than spontaneous reaction? Any hesitation? Any sense that she was reshaping her history to fit?'

James laughs. He nods when Shepherd lifts the whisky

bottle. 'Honestly, Alan, this thing is starting to test my sanity and my eyesight! I find myself picking at their faces, scrutinizing every crease and flinch. I crawl all over their eyes and want to take a magnifying glass to their mouths. I swear, I'm analysing them more than I've ever probed at poor Adam. I'm not sure it's healthy, all this cynical scrutiny!'

Shepherd clinks his glass against James'. 'I do understand what you mean, and I'm sorry about the interrogation. I just really hoped that one of them might fit. I suppose that I was wishing for an easy answer.'

James nods. 'And so was I. It's curious, though, this process; as I watch Adam interact with a wider group of people, I'm finding him increasingly difficult to read as well. There were times in the Vickers' house when I was certain he recognized things. There were connections being made and questions he was asking himself.'

'Connections? Such as?'

'He seemed to know things about that location that a stranger couldn't have been aware of. I mean, he responded to the landscape. He seemed to have some innate understanding of it. At certain moments that looked like familiarity.'

'But he's sensitive to that sort of thing, isn't he?'

James thinks about the noise of the wind over the water, Adam's eyes narrowing and the cry of geese that will come with the winter. There is something uncanny, something out-of-time about that place. James isn't sure that he hasn't brought some of that away with him too.

'Yes, he picks up on things that other men perhaps wouldn't register. He has a certain native insight and sharpened senses in some circumstances. I'm not sure that applied to Lucy Vickers' feelings, though.'

'He didn't upset her?'

'No, not that. It's more that he just didn't respond in the ways that she so obviously wanted him to. He didn't lean at all to meet her feelings.'

'You don't think it's a problem for Adam? You don't think that we're pushing him too much?'

'I think we need to tread carefully. He's so contained within himself when he's here, he's been calm and stable for the past few months, but it was different today. There were moments when he seemed vulnerable and fragile, like he was right back at the start.'

What had he seen in Adam's face as he looked at that painting? Why did James feel that the figure in the water might well be Adam himself? As James had looked at Adam's reflection in the glass of the painting, he had momentarily seemed anything but calm.

'When we were interviewing her, I noticed some pronounced differences in their accents. How do you account for that?' Shepherd asks.

'She said he was always softly spoken.'

Shepherd doesn't look convinced. 'There aren't many resemblances for us to hook on to, are there? The girl has such strong features and pronounced colouring.'

'I'd like to see the children and the other brother.'

'Yes. And you? How are you coping with all of this?'

'*Me?*' James looks up. The question surprises him. 'Why do you ask?'

'Just something Caitlin said.'

'Caitlin?'

'She said you'd been having some problems sleeping.'

Shepherd looks at him and James shifts uncomfortably. Is this how Adam feels when James tries to see what's going on behind his eyes? Is this how James makes the women feel? If it is, he is sorry for that. 'I'm overtired, that's all.'

'If I can get you anything to help – if you want anything prescribing, or want to talk . . .'

'I'm fine. It's nothing,' James lies.

Chapter Thirty-One

Lucy, High House, January 1921

'What are you playing at?' George asks, as he kicks his boots off and takes his chair by the fire.

'Playing at?'

She has been looking out for him, watching for him returning, wanting to tell him all about Ellis, but George has hardly acknowledged her since he's walked through the door. Cold air and tension seem to have followed him into the house. Lucy returns his question, but she doesn't look up. She doesn't cease with the scrubbing. Her brush continues to make soapy circles on the tabletop, but she finds herself holding her breath as she awaits his reply. Her back is aching, and the soap is stinging her hands, but she's been comforting herself with the memory of Ellis being in this room earlier today. A new calm had spread in her chest and she's caught herself humming a tune this afternoon, but now that George has walked in all that calm seems to have slipped away and there's something sharp in her chest instead.

'I saw him. I saw you. I watched you with that man.'

'You were here? Dear God, George!' The water splashes as she throws the brush at the pail. She wipes her hands on her apron as she straightens. 'Why didn't you make yourself known? I had to make excuses for you. It was embarrassing. Do you know what it looked like? It looked like you don't care.'

'I do care. I care about you. I care about what's going on in your head right now. Of course, I'd have made myself known had it been Ellis. But it's not him, is it?'

'What?' Lucy stares at George. Her chest feels tight now. 'You can't say that. You didn't see him close up. He's lost weight. His hair is darker than it used to be. But if you'd taken the trouble to meet him, if you'd seen his face, you'd have known him. I swear you would.'

'I saw enough. I remember what my own brother looks like. I know it's not him.'

He turns his head away from her and spreads the evening paper across his knees. It's a dismissal, as if he's drawing a line with this gesture, and as his face disappears behind the headlines, all the hope that she's gathered up today suddenly seems to be rushing out of the room.

'No,' Lucy says. As she pulls her hair away from her face, she smells the soap on her hands, and now her eyes are stinging too. She angles her face away because she doesn't want George to think that she's crying. She feels so frustrated, so exasperated, that she could cry, but she's not going to be dismissed. 'Why are you being so obstructive? So stupid? It's him! We've got him back. We ought to be going to the pub for bottles of beer tonight. We should be celebrating. Why are you being like this? Is it because he's not well? Is it that you don't want the burden? Because, I'll look after him – he doesn't have to be a problem for you.'

She would and she will. It's not as if he's coming home with a limb missing, or lungs that are rotten with gas. And he's not like Dora's cousin who now drinks all his wages, or Sarah's husband who gives her black eyes and no end of bother. He's not *that* damaged and she knows that he won't be *that* difficult. Ellis might be confused at the moment, but Lucy could see it as she looked at him: he is still the little brother who made daisy chains for her and picked up birds that had fallen out of their nests. She has to pick him up and look after him now.

'Jesus, Lucy! Can you hear yourself?' George leaves his newspaper by the fire and takes his chair at the table. 'Will you dry this off? Or do I have to eat my dinner amongst your soap suds?'

Lucy's thoughts leave wrens and daisy chains and good intentions, and she wants to beat her fists on George's chest then. She wants to pull his hair, and slap his face, and rub soap in his stupid eyes until they see. She has to fight the feeling down.

'Come with me to the hospital.'

'There's no point.'

'How can you say that? How can you not know him? You should have seen him in this room. He sat in his chair by the fire. He drank from his own mug. It was all back in place, like we've wished for, like we've hoped for. He knew his own painting!'

She replays the scene, and all the excitement and joy she'd felt at having Ellis in this room again comes back up to the surface. She had felt angry with him when she'd first been to the hospital; she'd felt like she'd been cheated out of something, that Ellis hadn't been playing fair, but having him here was different; things were back as they should be, as they could be again, and she'd felt a flush of optimism. Only now George seems determined to take that optimism away.

'I need you to help me with this,' she says. She dries the table and looks him in the eye as she leans towards him. 'We need to be on the same side. There's no way they'll let Ellis come home if you don't go along with it.'

'Play along with your charade, you mean?'

She takes the pie from the oven and puts it out without any ceremony, without any care to make it look nice on George's plate. Right now she feels that he doesn't deserve a nice plate. As she watches her older brother eat, silently, hurriedly, with his usual lack of appreciation or effort to make conversation, she feels resentful. Can she not ask this one kindness of him? Could he not make an effort for once? Does he feel no motivation to change the situation they're in? Will she be for ever stuck as his cook and his cleaner and mother to Ellis' children? Can he turn away his *own brother*?

'I bumped into Owen in town this week.' She knows that just saying his name is provocation, but she can't help herself. She'd like to prod George with her fork too. 'Ella has left him. Had you heard? She's gone. It's all over between them and she's moved down to Leeds to live with her sister.'

'Oh, Luce, don't go back there! I bet Owen didn't tell you why Ella left him?'

'You knew, then?'

'You can't think about starting again. You have to forget all of that now.'

Lucy still keeps a photograph of Owen under her mattress. A photograph from before the war, when it had seemed he might be her future, when she could still have a home, and a husband, and even children of her own.

'Forget it? And what do you mean by that?'

'Well, things have changed, haven't they? You're not seventeen any longer. You've got a family. You've got responsibilities.'

She wants to throw the rest of the pie at him for that.

'Responsibilities that you've seen fit to give me! I didn't want any of this. I didn't want to be here for the rest of my life. I don't want the stinking laundry. I don't want cooking and cleaning and having to tell Tom and Katie that he's not coming back.'

George pushes his chair back slowly and looks at her. 'It's just the way it is, isn't it? None of us wanted it to work out this way.'

Lucy wonders, has George ever really missed Ellis? He hardly ever says his name, always seems to divert away from the subject. But perhaps, she thinks, that's guilt. Does George ever ask himself if he ought to have gone in Ellis' place? She considers: if she had a choice, would she trade Ellis for George? As she watches him wiping bread around his plate, it's not too taxing a quandary.

'If he can come home, I'll take care of him and he'll get better. There's nothing physically wrong with him, and so he can bring in the wood and help with the cleaning. He can do all the heavy work. And when he meets the children, he might know them, mightn't he? Something in his brain might click and, even if it doesn't, he could learn to care for them, couldn't he? In time, he might even be up to finding a job again.'

'Will you listen to yourself?'

'Could you not for once just bloody well play the game?'

'The game? That's what this is, isn't it?'

'No! I didn't mean it like that.'

George rocks back in his chair. She wishes that he would stop looking at her that way, because she knows what he's going to say next, and he does.

'I'm worried, Lucy. I'm concerned about you. I think perhaps you ought to go and see Doctor Leach again.'

Doctor Leach had put her on pills after they'd had the letter that said *Missing, believed killed*. George had said that she'd been hysterical and needed something to calm her down. The pills did help her to sleep, but they also made her finger ends feel numb and everything came at her like words underwater. After a month, that numbness was worse than the hurt, and she'd pushed away the pills in George's outstretched palm.

'I've got a job to keep, a house to run and two children to feed and clothe. How am I meant to do that with a head full of fog?'

'Perhaps you need to stop this silliness, then? Perhaps you need to sort yourself out?'

'Silliness?'

'This pretending that some halfwit stranger is Ellis. Never mind pills, if Doctor Leach had seen you carrying on this afternoon, he'd be recommending you be put away.'

She laughs. She can't help it because it's so ridiculous, but she realizes that her laughter makes her sound unhinged. 'And when they've locked me up, you'll look after the children then, I suppose?'

'You've just got to pull yourself together.'

And it's the look on his face as he says it. Lucy doesn't want him to think that she's unravelling, but she's so very angry with him then. Just hours earlier she'd been standing here buttering bread for Ellis, watching him smile at the ticking of the clock and imagining how this could become their routine again. But now, because she'd like everything to go back to the way it was, George is talking about pills and putting her away. How is that right? How can she stand for that? Something seems to speed up in her blood as she watches George shaking his head. She has to ball her hands into tight fists to stop them from dashing his plate to the floor.

Chapter Thirty-Two

James

There's a lake in the wood of his nightmares now. It glistens like satin when he first sees it from afar, all slicked with moonlight, but then, as he approaches, the tattered trees double in terrible reflection all around its edges and it looks like the mouth of hell. James has been running, he is out of breath and when he gets to the edge of the water, the man who he has been following is well out into its depths. The figure is already up beyond his waist, and walking further out, his reflection glimmering and breaking on the surface of the water. He is too far out for James to see the details of his face – there are only fragments of familiarity and memory – but he knows that the man in the water is Nathaniel.

James stands at the edge of the lake and the light of the bombardment reflects in pulses of white light and black shadow. He can see that the water is dangerously full of debris, full of splintered trees and jagged metal and unfathomably deep, but he has to go in after Nathaniel. Rainbows of oil split on the surface as he steps into the water, and it comes over his boots with a sudden shock of cold. James moves forward, but it is all sharpness and softness and unstable, and he stumbles as his feet sink into depthless mud. Mist tatters and rolls over the water and it smells of sulphur.

'Wait for me!'

Ahead, ripples pool away from Nathaniel, stretch and echo to meet James' feet, and when he looks down, beyond his own pale reflection, he sees there are other men in the water. He hears himself gasp, he wants to get out of this water and run in the opposite direction, but he has to go on, and he has to look again. Bubbles of gas break the surface and there are bloated white faces down there, so misshapen that they are hardly faces at all, their eyes purple hollows and blue lips shrunk back. Weed and hair shifts in the water with the movement that James makes, and there are limbs that look like wax below, and swollen fingers that nudge against his feet. They all stir as he steps out further, and he wants to look up for Nathaniel, but he can't take his eyes away from the drowned men who are all around him and he is so afraid, so fully and painfully afraid, that he hears his own teeth chattering. Wind sighs over the water and somewhere the curlews are crying.

'Nathaniel!'

James stretches his arms out for balance and shuts his eyes as he continues onwards. He needs to keep moving towards Nathaniel, but he also doesn't want to see. He has to look, though, when he feels them circle his ankles. The hands stroke him at first, it might only be the movement of the water itself, but then it is no accident, no chance – the hands are pulling at his feet. James gasps and tries to step away. They are clutching and grabbing, as if they want to use him to surface; they need to grip on and clamber up him, and James feels himself being pulled down. He kicks at the hands that swarm over his legs, but the water is alive with them now. They writhe like eels, and James screams and swears because they are all around him. It is a frenzy then of tangling limbs. Of clutching fingers. Of grasping fingernails. Panic rushes through James' body as the white fingers twist and probe and climb him. He struggles and stumbles under the weight of their need and then he is going under.

They have gone when he dips under the surface. For a moment, it all springs away and there is space and silence in the milky blue water, but then their faces all push in again. In the glimmer of the liquid light he sees them all, all the men who he has lost. He knows them and does not know them, because they are distortions of once-familiar smiles, and gentle features, and kindly eyes. These are *his* men, the men who have followed his orders, who he has laughed with, and feared for, and mourned – and yet they're not those same men; these are his memories, or versions of them, and every worst moment that he meant to forget. Their lips are swollen, their eyes are from a fishmonger's slab, and then Nathaniel is there too, showing his teeth in a deathly, fleshy grin. James screams and the water rushes into his mouth.

He wakes with a gasp and Caitlin is there. Just for a second she is a drowned girl too and he wants to push her away, but then her features slide back into focus and she is sitting next to him with an empty bottle in her hand. He remembers a girl in a photograph then, long ago, side by side with Nathaniel on a swing, their twinned faces like mirror images, and James knows that, by tearing that picture down the middle, by leading Nathaniel away from Caitlin, he has brought all this sadness and complication into her life.

'You look like death,' says Caitlin's voice. 'I wish you'd come to bed. You look awful.'

It takes him a minute to surface, to once again know the

walls that surround him and the chair beneath him. 'I didn't want to wake you.'

'That didn't work out well then, did it?'

In the light of the lamp he can't tell quite what it is that flashes across Caitlin's eyes. Is it anger? Impatience? She stands with the bottle in her hands. 'I'm not sure that this is helping. Did Shepherd give it to you?'

'I couldn't sleep. I didn't drink it all.'

'Didn't you?'

'No, I promise.'

'It doesn't work, though, does it? You know that, don't you? Would you prescribe Adam a bottle of whisky per night?'

'Of course not. No, I know that. I only had a glass. I just wanted to be sure that I'd sleep.' His throat feels raw with it. The electric light is now too bright, so that he has to shade his eyes, but the nightmare is still there in the shadowed corners of the room. He wants to put his hands over his eyes, to sit quietly with his head in his hands, until he can work it away. But she's not going to let him.

'For how long did you mean to sleep? It's not making it better, James. Things aren't getting better.'

'I'm sorry.'

'Sorry?' She shakes her head and sits down next to him again. He hears the appeal in her voice then. 'It might help if you would talk. Isn't that what you tell everyone else? Release the repression, work it off and work it out? I've heard you say it to your patients: the worse thing is to keep it all in.'

She puts her hand over his and James can't help but think about the hands in the water. He knows that his hands are clammy. Sweat prickles on his top lip. His shirt is stuck to his chest and he knows that he needs to wash. He also knows that Caitlin wants to help, but at this moment he would rather be alone, to have the space to quietly work things out, and not to be seen trying to do so. 'There are some things that I'm not comfortable talking about,' he says.

'Really?' She is angry then. He feels her tense. She takes her hand from his and stands over him. 'For God's sake, James, I'm your wife! You've got to let me in. We're meant to get through this together. We're meant to work together. If you don't let this out, if you don't move on, how can we go on?'

She's right. Of course she's right. It's what they tell them all: that they have to share it, get it out, face up to it and find a way of living with the memories. He knows that if he keeps this in, it will destroy him, and his relationship with her, but how can he put those pictures in Caitlin's mind? He shakes his head.

'I feel like we're pulling apart,' she says. 'I no longer know how to speak to you. It's like we're talking in different languages and I'm so frightened of getting it wrong.'

'You're not. You never get it wrong.'

'I think it might have been a mistake to come here,' she goes on. 'I mean, it's filling you up with more of the same, and as long as we live here, I don't think the war will ever end.'

Is it true? Certainly it's all leaking into his dreams. 'Maybe we could take a break? We could get away for a week? You could go and see your mother for a few days?'

'That's not what I mean,' she says. She laughs, but there is no humour in her face. 'Perhaps we need to think again. Start again. Go somewhere completely different. Do something different.'

James thinks about Adam and the sense that it might be possible to reunite him with his name and his family, thinks about all he owes Shepherd for giving him this chance, and about the progress that he's making with the other men. 'I couldn't leave here now.'

'Then perhaps I should.'

It takes him aback. 'Please don't say that. You don't mean that, do you? Just tell me what I need to do.'

'Talk to me.'

James remembers Caitlin standing in a garden in Swaledale. He can smell the honeysuckle, and feel the sun on the back of his neck, and Nathaniel is there laughing. Caitlin's arm is through her brother's, her white hand links his, they sit in mirror image of one another, and this is their world and the sun is shining. But then James wants to make Caitlin smile; he needs to make her smile, and for her eyes to connect with his, and suddenly nothing else matters. And James can, and he does, and when she smiles just for him it is like the warmth of the sun on his skin.

But then it all breaks because Nathaniel wants to make James smile too. He will copy him, and shadow him, and follow him to war. Because James needs to be with Caitlin, he must also be with Nathaniel – but he will take Nathaniel away from Caitlin, and never be able to bring him back. That's where the mirror image breaks, where one half shatters, and leaves Caitlin looking into blackness; Nathaniel's gestures aren't there to echo hers now and their fingers can't link any longer. Seeing that, watching Caitlin struggle to come to terms with that loss, makes James feel like he's tightening his hand around shards of broken mirror. And, meanwhile, Nathaniel is still out there somewhere, left behind in that godawful wood, where he never should have been, where he never would have been were it not for James, with the wind and the rain and the sun whitening his bones.

How can James ever tell Caitlin that?

Chapter Thirty-Three

Celia, Churchyard Cottage, Ryedale, February 1921

As she takes her son's jacket out of the wardrobe, Celia can smell him. She puts her face to the fabric and closes her eyes. Robert is here in this room, squinting in the sunshine, smiling in his Sunday best. He looks down at her and puts his hand to her hair. It's the same touch, the same smell as that of the man she had met at the hospital. She never had any doubt. It is Robert. (Of course it's Robert!) How could they imagine that she wouldn't know her own son?

She brushes face powder from the fabric of the sleeve, chastises her own folly and carefully lays the jacket in the suitcase. He always looked so smart in it and he will again. Feeling a bulge in one of the pockets, she pulls out a pebble, a snail shell and a twist of silver paper. She smiles. It was always the same. How many acorns and pieces of flint has she accidentally laundered? As she looks around his room, at his bookcase lined with all the conkers and fossils and seed heads that he had brought home from walks, she is suddenly conscious of the size of the void that has dominated her life for the past four years, but she has never doubted him. She has listened out for his footsteps all that time and has known that they would eventually wind back home. She is struck by how lucky she is, amongst all those women at the hospital, to be the fortunate one, and she cries tears of joy into one of Robert's jumpers. It is fraying slightly at the cuff. She will fix it and knit him a new one. She will knit him so many new ones in the years ahead. What fortune to have that chance!

She puts socks and shirts into the suitcase. Will she soon be repacking it and bringing him home? Surely she'll be able to convince them that she can give him all the care he needs. From the pocket of a pair of trousers she takes a fold of paper and opens it out to find her own face drawn by Robert's hand. When she shows this to the doctors they will see how much he loves her. How much he needs her. They will let him come home now, won't they? How can they refuse that?

James

They watch Adam through the window. There's a camellia in the garden, covered in white flowers, and he's standing gazing up at it like a man witnessing a miracle. Beyond the vegetable patch, and the picket fence, there are yew trees and then graves. James thinks how strange it must be to live with that every day, to look out of the windows of the kitchen and the sitting room and the bedroom and to have that view. It would be the most forceful *memento mori*, he imagines, but Celia Dakers says that it is what she has always known. Looking at her, James considers that it perhaps makes her live life gratefully, rather than glumly. Could this be the view that Adam grew up with too? Was this the normality that he took in through the windows of his childhood bedroom?

'I've always just viewed it as an extension of the garden,' she says, 'and thought that I was lucky to have that. I love the shape of the yew trees and I plant a few more crocus bulbs around the old gravestones each year. It's all purple and gold in April. It is quite a thing to see.'

'Did Robert lose his father as a young boy?'

She nods. She looks down at her hands in her lap. 'He was four. It was sudden, a shock. We stuck together after that. It made us very close.'

'I can imagine.' It must have done, James thinks, with the gravestones all around them, never letting them forget. 'Is his father in the churchyard here?'

She shakes her head. It is a while before she speaks again. 'I'm afraid you misunderstand me, Doctor Haworth. My husband isn't dead,' she eventually says. 'My husband left us.'

'I'm sorry. I assumed that you'd been widowed.'

'Well, I was, in a way. I found myself putting on black clothes for a while – it seemed the natural thing to do – but then I decided to stop that. I took off my wedding ring and made the decision that I'd never wear black again. Patrick just walked out one day. There was no sign that it was coming. No clues. No rows. No proper explanation. I thought we were happy, but he wrote a letter telling me he wasn't, and he went out to work that morning and didn't come back.'

'Did you look for him?'

'Of course. I went to his office and I begged him, but he said it would kill him to come back. Can you imagine being told that? That was twenty years ago. I wrote to him when I received the news about Robert, but my letter was returned with a note saying he was no longer known at that address, that he hadn't been there for years. My husband might be dead, for all I know, but I've always been certain that Robert was alive. And my instinct was right, wasn't it?'

James is not sure how to reply. He feels that it's not fair to put a crack in Celia Dakers' fragile confidence.

'When my nephew died in France, my brother gifted the church a memorial window,' she goes on. 'They couldn't have his body back, but Arthur said that this was the next best thing – that they could look up at that coloured glass every Sunday and know that David was with God. It struck me, when Arthur said that, how certain he was that his son was dead, and how angry I was at God. But I knew that Robert wasn't dead. And I don't need to be angry at God any longer, do I?'

James shakes his head. He knows that he shouldn't build up this hope, but then how can he dash it down? There are palm crosses pinned all around the frame of the overmantel mirror, he sees. It is difficult to understand Celia Dakers' relationship with God; he could never lightly meet his own eyes in such a mirror. 'It must have been difficult for Robert to lose his father,' he says. 'Did he understand what was happening?'

'Yes, but young boys are resilient, aren't they? They bounce back. And there was so much else going on in his life. He was an out-of-doors boy; he liked playing in rivers and making dens and knowing the names of all the birds. His life was full. He laughed so much and had rosy cheeks.' She looks at James and smiles. 'I couldn't give over kissing his cheeks – oh, listen to me! Foolish old woman!' She looks at Adam in the garden and her face changes. 'But he's all black and white now. My poor boy. All the colour has drained out of him, hasn't it? I'm so frightened that he'll turn into his father. He's become the man in the photograph.'

'The photograph in the newspaper?'

'The one he sent from France, I mean.'

'From France? May I see?'

James watches in the mirror as she crosses to the dresser. It is a most unfeminine piece of furniture, he thinks – the black oak carved with pomegranates and grapes and Gothic masks – and he wonders if this was the taste of Robert Dakers' unhappy father. There is linen stacked inside, James sees, and from within its folds she pulls out a photograph.

'Here. He sent it with a letter. It came in the May of 1916. It's the last photograph of him that I had.'

'Thank you.'

James tilts the photograph to the light and sees a soldier sitting in a garden. He can make out a clematis flowering on the wall behind and there's a basket of cherries near his feet. He focuses in on the man's face. His eyes are obscured by the shadow of his cap, but his features are regular and the face shape is familiar. He looks up to see Adam stretch to pull a camellia flower towards his face. Could the man in the photograph really be Adam five years younger?

'He looks older now, doesn't he?' Celia says. Her fingers follow the pattern on the tablecloth. She sips at her tea.

'I'm sure we all do.' James can't help but wonder why she should want to hide this supposed last image of her son away amongst the bedspreads and tablecloths. Is there something about this photograph that she wanted to deny?

He can remember having a similar photograph taken in a garden in Bray-sur-Somme. Nathaniel had been there with him that day, and had asked James if he meant to send his photograph to Caitlin. He had then suggested that they have their photograph taken together, joking that it might be their last chance. He wonders if Caitlin has that photograph still. He can't recall ever having seen it. Is Nathaniel hidden somewhere amongst their bed linen and napkins too?

'It makes me realize how much time we've lost,' says Celia

Dakers. 'How precious these days are. How lucky I am to have found him again.'

The church bells ring. James nods, but says nothing. The right words won't come to his mind.

Adam

He stands under the camellia. This tree must be a century old, he thinks, probably more, and is quite magnificent. To see such a profusion of flower in February is like looking at an illustration in a fable. The flowers are purest white and might well have been pulled out of a magician's hat or from the pattern of a Chinese vase. Against the winter colours of the garden, this tree seems improbably exotic. Adam shuts his eyes, breathes in the delicate scent, listens to the clatter of the leaves and imagines an oriental forest shifting all around him. *Camellia japonica 'Alba Plena'*, he thinks, and smiles at the recollection of the name.

He steps out of the shadow of the tree and looks down the length of the garden. The laurel hedges are meticulously clipped and in the vegetable garden winter greens grow in orderly rows. The lines of kales and cabbages might well have been put in with a tape measure, and the soil in between is tidily tilled. There is not a weed in this garden, nor a plant out of place. He thinks about the walled garden, where his work is just beginning, where he has so much work left to do, and wishes that he could spend the rest of the day there rather than being watched by the woman in this house.

Adam walks down the garden and into what feels like memory. He watches a robin hop between the raspberry canes and is certain that he knows the taste of this fruit, and of the first peas that he will steal. He knows that she will scold when she finds his footprints and the empty pea pods, how his legs will sting, and the noise of the key turning in the lock of his bedroom door. What are these images? Are these memories his?

The garden fence is newly whitewashed. She has painted it again, as she does each spring, because this tidiness and this boundary must be seen. The wood is cut into points at the top, like a stockade, meant to keep things in. He knows that his hand will hurt when he levers himself over the fence, and how she will cry after him as he runs between the gravestones. She will scream that he has to come back. That he always has to come back. Adam can hear that voice, and see that expression on her face, but is the heartbeat that bangs in his ears his own?

He looks towards the house. He can tell that they are watching him, that his every move is being observed. She wants to keep him in because she cares, he knows that really, but it is a suffocating care. He has been put out here to play like a child, trapped in her polite, God-fearing good order. He reaches for a cigarette and throws the match amongst the lines of sage and parsley. Does this resentment, this urge to rebel, belong to him?

The scent of camellia flowers and wood smoke swirl around him and Adam blinks away the images. Within the walls of his own garden at Fellside he feels protected, and that he is in control, but the constriction of this space is like something pressing on his chest, and he just wants to go. He wants to bolt again. But then there is James Haworth's face in the window, looking out, and he trusts Haworth to take him away. To let him go back to his garden. He promised he wouldn't have to stay. He knows that Haworth's voice is the one that screams in the night and that he understands enough not to make him stay here.

James

Robert's room is all ready for him still, Celia says. It's always ready. 'Would you like to see?' she asks.

She invites Adam to take the stairs first. 'You know the way, don't you?' she prompts.

There are leaves in Adam's hair and mud on his boots. Following behind, James watches Adam's feet on the treads and his hesitation at the top of the stairs. Will he know which way to turn? Will his footsteps guide him to the correct door on the landing, or will Celia Dakers have to lead him? Her hand is on Adam's shoulder, and James is not sure how much she is steering him, how much pressure her fingertips are applying. At the top of the stairs, James sees that there are three doors, all closed. Adam puts his hand to the china doorknob of the middle door, and Celia smiles at James over her shoulder. The door opens, revealing a brass bedstead, a patchwork quilt and striped wallpaper. James wishes that he could also see the expression on Adam's face.

They follow him into the room. It is very much a boy's bedroom, in many respects; there are books about pirates and pioneers on the shelves, a wooden sailing boat and a map of the Empire on the wall. James tries to imagine the young man who slept in this room setting off to cross that map. There are also seashells and snail shells and fragments of birds' eggs lined along the edges of the bookcase. There are almost identical collections in his room at Fellside; it is very much like Adam, this detail. Robert Dakers would surely know the patterns of every square in that patchwork quilt, James considers; there must be memory stitched into every sprig and stripe. The calendar on the wall has kept this room in July 1915.

Adam's face is reflected in the tilt of the dressing-table mirror and James can see his eyes touring the room and dropping then to the bed. He watches as Adam sits down on the quilt, tests the springs, stretches out his legs and lies back on the pillows. He closes his eyes, as if he is the only person in this room.

James stands at Celia Dakers' side and they watch the breath in Adam's chest rising and falling. It is an odd sensation to look so closely, so directly, at another person like this. It feels voyeuristic to James to stand here, and not quite kind, but he somehow feels that he can't walk out of this room and leave Adam alone with Celia; and yet, if she truly is his mother, why shouldn't he? Why would that be wrong? After all, how many times must she have thought of her son in this room over the past five years? When she was told that Robert was believed killed, did she picture his dead body laid out on this bed? How many hours has she spent in this room willing him back, praying, making deals with her God? James watches the flutter behind Adam's closed eyes. To Celia it must be like looking down on her son's ghost.

'Adam?'

His eyes flick open. His feet shift position and the mud from his boots is now on the patchwork quilt. There's something about this carelessness, this thoughtlessness, that isn't like Adam, James thinks. He is more courteous, more sensitive than that. Adam wouldn't normally behave this way.

'It's a comfortable bed,' he says.

There's a photograph of a couple on the dressing table, a brass moneybox shaped like a Japanese pagoda and a hairbrush. James steps closer and sees Celia Dakers as a smiling bride, a camellia flower in her hair, presumably with her son's father, the other man who walked away. James looks at Celia and is struck by how time can write grief all over a person's face. He looks at the photograph face of the man who she married and tries to see Adam there. Could it be? James isn't certain enough to say. He takes the hairbrush in his hand and ripples through the soft bristles. There is not one hair there to prove that this is, or is not, the room in which Adam Galilee grew up.

Celia touches Adam's shoulder. 'I've packed a suitcase of clothes for you,' she says. When he doesn't respond, she looks to James. 'It is all right, isn't it? You don't mind? It's only that he looked like he was short of something warm.'

'Of course,' James replies. 'That's fine. It's very considerate of you.'

'Nonsense. How can a mother think of anything else?'

James looks at Adam. He is staring straight up at the ceiling and James can't read the expression on his face.

'Hopefully he'll unpack the suitcase, but then be repacking again soon enough,' she goes on. She smiles at Adam, but his eyes don't meet hers. 'Do you have any idea how long it might be, Doctor Haworth?'

'I can't say, in all honesty. There are other cases, other claims that we have to investigate.'

'False claims! Look at him; this is his room! This is his place, this is where he belongs. Can you honestly believe that a mother wouldn't know her own son?'

'I'm sorry,' says James. He watches as Adam stands up and walks out of the room. As he turns in the doorway something like panic fleetingly passes over his face.

Chapter Thirty-Four

Lucy, High House, February 1921

Tom is banging the bottom of a saucepan with a wooden spoon. Katie whoops delightedly at the noise this makes, and then takes up the colander and joins in, syncopating a rhythm on the corner of the kitchen table. Dora widens her eyes and Lucy screams for quiet.

'Dear God,' says Dora. 'How do you stand it?'

'It's not always like this.' Lucy shuts her eyes and leans her head back against the chair, breathing in the brief silence. 'Only six days a week.'

'Couldn't George take a turn? It does all seem to land on you, and don't you think they might benefit from a bit of paternal discipline?'

Lucy laughs. 'Paternal? I'm not sure George has paternal in him. He's only aware they're in the room when they're carrying on like this, and that's probably why they do it. He doesn't really talk to them, you know. It's as if looking them in the eye and hearing their voices would force him to face up to things that he doesn't want to hear and see. He only comes home after they've been put to bed. He'd rather work long hours than be here.'

'So the ferry runs round the clock these days, does it? And when I see him in the White Lion he's doing shifts there?'

'He's not very domestic.'

'Has he ever tried?'

Dora glances over at the children and makes a face. They're silently occupied under the kitchen table now, but Lucy knows that this quiet won't last. Dora isn't maternal, she's said it often enough (as if saying it will mean she never has to be); she wants nice clothes, to keep her waist and to go out at the weekend. Dora says she can't imagine being saddled with babies. How does she expect Lucy to reply to that? She hardly meant for it to work out this way.

'Perhaps George could have a crack at domesticity this Friday night? We're going out for a drink, me and the girls from Platts. It's my last day on Friday, you see?' Dora goes on. 'And, well, I wish you'd come too. I hardly ever get to see you these days.'

Dora winds her bracelet around her wrist. She's starting a new job on Monday, secretarial training, shorthand and typing. She seems to be sitting a little taller in her chair today and Lucy envies her that. Dora has painted her fingernails cherry-blossom pink, all ready to be tapping out a future on her typewriter, Lucy supposes. She looks down at her own hands and hates them.

'I'd love to, but I can't promise that I'll be able to get away. I will come if I can.'

Lucy knows, as she says it, that she won't. Dora knows that too, she can see. That's why she shakes her head.

'I saw Owen in the Lion last weekend. He asked about you. I told him that Ellis had turned up, and you should have seen his face. He was made up for you. Honestly, Luce, he looked so pleased for you to know that Ellis is back.'

'Did he?'

It's another reason why she won't go to the pub. She wishes

that she could see Owen and to talk to him, to tell him all about Ellis, and to catch up with his news, but it's all too complicated at the moment. She pulls her hands through her hair. She'd have washed it if she knew that Dora was going to call in. Dora has had her hair shingled, just like Gloria Swanson, and Lucy feels such a drudge.

'George told me that I'm not allowed to see Owen.'

'What?' Dora looks outraged on Lucy's behalf. 'What right does George have to tell you who you can and can't see?'

'His wages do keep us going.'

'But still!'

'Oh, don't. I lost my temper with him too last week and he told me that I was being hysterical. He said I ought to go and see Doctor Leach again.'

'What, so that he can put you back on those pills and you won't be able to get out of bed? Will George look after the children then?'

Lucy shrugs. Tom is now banging the pan on the table legs. They're both singing a song, but the words don't seem to make any sense.

'Hysterical?' Dora repeats. 'I think I might be certifiable if I had to spend more than half an hour in here.' She laughs, but then quickly apologizes. 'Sorry. I didn't think. I didn't mean anything by it.'

'Don't worry. You don't have to tiptoe around it.'

'How is Ellis?'

And that's just it: she's not sure. Lucy doesn't know how Ellis is because he gives so little away. He says so little now. There's an emptiness there in his eyes.

'Sometimes he looks at me and I swear he knows me, but then the next minute he's turned his back and I might as well not be there. I wondered if he was playing games at first, if he was having us all on, but then he'll come out with something so strange and I know that he's not at all right in the head. The doctor told me that he's working in a garden. He says that he wants to plant vegetables. Ellis was never interested in gardens.'

'George still won't go and see him?'

'And that's the worst of it. There were so many other people there, all these poor mad women who are convinced that he's their husband, or their son, and they're all talking to the doctors, trying to persuade them, you see?'

'How awful.'

'Isn't it? But it makes me worried, like I'm going to have to fight for Ellis. Occasionally I've felt that the doctors doubt me, that they might believe the other women more than me, and George never turning up has got to influence that, hasn't it? At the moment I don't feel like George and me are fighting on the same side.'

'And does George tell you why he won't go?'

'Because he thinks I'm daft. Because he says it's not him. He got a quick glance of Ellis when they came to the house and he made his mind up. George swears it's not Ellis. But he only ever got a glimpse of him as they were driving away in the car. He must think I'm mad, mustn't he? I'm bloody mad at *him* some days.'

'But wouldn't he want to know for definite? Doesn't he want to see Ellis up close and be sure?'

'He's too pig-headed. And I think he doesn't want to take on any more responsibility. He says Ellis would be a burden and that we haven't got the time or the money.'

'But he's your brother!'

'There are days when I despair of my brothers.' Katie approaches and puts her hand on the arm of Lucy's chair. 'Hello, little mouse.' The child looks at Dora under her eyelashes, all sudden shyness and suspicion. Lucy squeezes her hand and smiles. 'Aren't men silly, love?' Lucy says.

'You must want to shake him. You must want to shake the pair of them.'

'I got so mad with George last week that I threw a plate at him. Of course, he dodged and it hit the wall. I cried afterwards because it was one of Mother's – the willow pattern, you know? But Tom was screaming, and madam here was smearing jam on the cat, and George complained that his tea was cold. I just couldn't help myself. I snapped. I'm such a grumpy old dragon, aren't I?' She turns to Katie and makes a fire-breathing-dragon face. 'Uncle George looked a bit scared, didn't he?'

'You've got so much to cope with. I hope you told him that.'

'Like I said, apparently I'm hysterical.' Katie leans her head against Lucy's shoulder and she puts her arms around her. She looks at the girl's serious little face, so like her mother, and strokes her silky hair. 'But we're planning our escape, aren't we, poppet? We're going to run away and join the circus and become trapeze artists. We'll fly through the air in sparkly leotards, not give a fig for anything, and Uncle George will have to get his own tea.'

Dora grins. 'That sounds fun. I might tag along with you.'

'I do feel like I'm walking a high wire,' Lucy says. 'In all seriousness, some days it really seems as if I'm balancing on something very narrow. In truth, I'm frightened sometimes. I'm so high up and there's no safety net, and this sensation in my head is almost like vertigo. But I know deep down that I'm right, and I'm not some dizzy fool. I'm stronger than they think I am, and however difficult it is, however long it takes, I will make it to the other side. Won't I, Katie?'

'I believe you,' Dora says.

Lucy nods as she looks into the child's face. 'We're going to hold on tight, aren't we? And we're going to bring Daddy home.'

Chapter Thirty-Five

Adam, Ambleside, February 1921

The hoarfrost makes a silver filigree of the trees and the sky behind is burnished bronze. In the churchyard the yew trees are opening strange waxy blossoms and along the lane the bank is covered with snowdrops, their white lamps nodding slightly on the breeze. Adam and Caitlin pause to comment on the miniature ivy leaves, perfect and glossy as enamelwork, that are making their annual progress over the wall of the graveyard, and to listen to the lilting song of a mistle thrush in the elm.

'Do you hear it?'

They stand side by side in silence and Caitlin nods at him and smiles. Adam can see her breath on the frosty air. He watches her eyes widen and slide as she listens.

'They always sing in a minor key,' he tells her. 'They're one of the year's earliest songbirds, and they'll sing all through foul weather, but it's always a melancholy song, stopping and starting.'

'Isn't it? I wouldn't have known that. I would have just thought it was a blackbird.'

Adam likes to tell Caitlin things like this. He likes to share with her. She doesn't require him to talk, and he is glad of that, but he finds himself wanting to show her pine cones and seed heads and the shapes of birdsongs. She doesn't require him to remember, or expect him to be anyone he isn't. Caitlin doesn't impose any expectations on him. Just occasionally, Adam rather wishes that she expected more and that he could give it. He has spent the morning potting up overwintered geraniums for her windowsill, and now points out mosses and catkins and a skylark's song for her to appreciate. He is glad when she turns to him and smiles.

'Shall we do the circuit up through the wood?'

'I'd like that.'

The coltsfoot is bright in the hollows and young nettles, a vigorous green, are pushing their way up through the earth. The tassels of the hazel twist in the wind.

'I've worried about you this past month,' she says. 'You've looked unhappy. Are you wishing they hadn't started all this?'

'Perhaps.'

'Will you tell me why?'

Their side-by-side shadows stretch ahead on the lane, like a premonition of their future selves, and the gentleness in Caitlin's voice makes Adam want to tell her the truth. In exchange for Caitlin's kindness, for her company, for her caring enough to ask the question, he wants to be able to explain it to her.

'Everyone is so anxious for me to remember them,' he tells her. 'But I'm not sure that these memories are mine. It's like the clothes: I'm being given other men's shirts and jumpers to wear, and I understand that it's well meant, but I also know that these clothes have never once been on my back before. Am I meant to try to get used to that? To try to become what they want me to be? Try to ignore the fact that these things don't fit? How far will it go? Will I be asked to sleep in their beds next?'

'You shouldn't be expected to fit into any situation you're not comfortable with.'

'No? Even if those people really need it? Even if it takes away their sadness?'

'If they're sad, it's not up to you to make that better. That's not your responsibility, Adam. It's not fair on you. And it's not really solving it, is it? In the long term how can that be right for them? What happens if their sons and husbands come back one day?'

He laughs. 'They hit me?'

'Oh, Adam!'

'The problem is that I've no absolute certainty, though. What if perhaps I *am* the girl's brother or that woman's son?'

'Surely you'd feel it? Surely you'd know?'

He shrugs. 'I overheard Shepherd use the word "cauterized" when he was talking about me this week, like my nerves have been scorched out to stop the feeling. But it's not that I don't have feelings. Of course I do. I'd like to have people who care about me and to care about them, but I don't think that these are the right people.'

'You do have people who care about you. It might not be working out, but James and Alan started all of this precisely because they do care about you.'

'But they're getting frustrated by me now, aren't they? I can see it. There are things that I'd like to remember, I would, and I don't want to be uncooperative, but I don't think I can pick and choose my memories, and I feel I must've forgotten the bad parts for good reason.'

They turn off the lane and pick a path over the field towards the wood. The ruts left in the mud by a cart wheel are as solid as iron, the bubbles in the ice snap beneath his boots and mist clings in the cobwebs, gilding them now as the sun is rising. The winter wheat in the fields beyond is as freshly green as a streak of unmixed paint. Adam points to a kestrel above and they watch it turn on the wind. Rabbits are grazing at the edge of the wood and then are gone. Rooks rise on blue-black wings to circle and settle in the newly ploughed field. He looks at Caitlin, at the kind understanding that her face communicates, and wonders if James knows how lucky he is.

'Come on.'

They walk up and on through the trees. Light slices through the wood and Adam can hear the sheep back out on the fell again. The yellow powder released by the hazel catkins dazzles in the sunshine. Blown leaves spiral and the wood is ethereal in this light.

'You don't look happy either,' he says. 'Am I allowed to notice that?'

'Me?'

He nods.

'You're not meant to be the doctor!' Caitlin laughs.

'Sometimes you don't need a certificate. I mean, you look well today, you look perfect today, but sometimes I see your face at the window and you look so sad.'

'I'm worried about James. Things are difficult at the moment. They seem to be getting more difficult.'

'He's not sleeping. I can see that in his eyes.'

Her feet stop and she looks at him. He can see Caitlin measuring something in his face, deciding if she can trust him, but her eyes turn back to the path and she carries on. Acorns crunch beneath their feet, and it is the only noise, until a flock of starlings erupts from the branches above. It is a shock, a sudden crowd of clapping hands, and then an arrow streaking away. Caitlin turns to him, her gasp turning into a grin, and laughing then as her eyes meet his. But the moment is gone so quickly and she's walking on.

'James has some problems,' she finally says. 'He tries to hide it, but it's all there under the surface. Coming back here, coming to Fellside, hasn't been easy for him. It's not been an easy couple of years. He has terrible nightmares, you see, nightmares about the war, and I'm frightened that they're getting more regular, and worse.'

'I know. I guessed that.'

'You did?'

'I hear him sometimes.'

'God! He'd be mortified if he knew that. He thinks he can keep it quiet. I've told him he can't. I'm worried that it's starting to have an impact on his work too.'

'In what sense?'

Her foot rolls a stone on the ground. 'He's missed a couple of sessions with patients recently. He's not turned up. Alan found out and he's not best pleased.'

'All of this business with these women hasn't been easy for James either. I see that. These conversations are so awkward and he must be asking himself a lot of questions. He was probably tired and just forgot. If he's overtired, Shepherd will understand.'

She stops rolling the stone under her shoe and looks at him. 'Yes, probably. And you're right – I don't think he's exactly enjoying this process.'

'Does he tell you what he dreams about?'

'Things that happened to him in France. Things he says I'll never comprehend. But I wish he'd let me try.'

'Shepherd says that my brain shut down because I had experiences that I couldn't comprehend. Perhaps we have that in common, then?'

Caitlin smiles. It is a sad smile, Adam thinks, but he is glad to see her try.

She takes his hand as they clamber up the rocks and he knows then that Caitlin trusts him. He feels the grip of her fingers tightening around his as he pulls her up. It feels like a great compliment, a great gift, that trust – and Adam realizes that this is a new sensation. He grins at Caitlin's hand in his.

'Here.' She gives him one of her cigarettes and they sit on the rocks together and smoke. Windermere bounces back the blue of the sky and the view below is all shining serenity. The air is crisp and Adam feels contented to be here sharing secrets with Caitlin.

'Has James ever talked to you about Nathaniel?' she asks.

'Wasn't that your brother's name?'

'Yes.'

Adam watches her lips as she blows out smoke. She bats it away with her hand and he can tell that she is deciding whether to confide in him.

'James would never tell anyone, but Nat doted on him. James was two years older than us and he was handsome and clever, you see. Everybody loved him because he was beautiful and good and full of ambition. There was so much that he wanted to do with his life; he wanted to travel and he wanted to improve things for people; he genuinely did want to make a difference, and he wanted to share all of these things with me. All of that shone out of James, he glowed with it, and so, of course, Nat wanted to be around him too.'

'I can see that in him.'

'Can you?' she pauses. 'I'm glad you say that. I'm happy that you still can see it. We used to laugh at how Nat followed James around and how he copied him. If James wore flannels, so Nat would the next day. If he whistled a tune, Nat would have to learn the words. If James mentioned that he'd enjoyed a book, Nat would be quoting it the next week. I'm afraid that we all rather teased him.' She turns to Adam and smiles. 'We said that Nat would follow James to the ends of the earth – and he did, in a way. When the war started, and James got a commission, Nat had to join the same battalion.'

Adam nods. 'So James felt responsible for your brother going to war?'

'Yes. Sadly. And it didn't help that my mother stated just that. Nat was still nineteen when he left for France, and a young nineteen at that. He was a baby. He was a boy. My mother told James that he'd led Nat. Blunt as that.'

'And you?'

'Me?'

'Did you think that James influenced your brother?'

'Yes, of course. But not in any malign way. He didn't mean to.'

'Your brother died, didn't he?' he says, softly.

She nods. 'Nat was killed in 1916. James saw it. Only his body was never recovered. In the confusion of it all, they couldn't bring him back, and that has been a great regret to James. He felt that he let Nat down; as if he owed it to Nat, and to us, and he failed. I'm afraid that my mother hasn't been very helpful in deterring that sentiment. It's awkward.' She looks at Adam and he can see it on her face. 'James still wishes that he could find Nat's body. He still feels it's his duty to do that. Sometimes he talks about going back and looking for him, but how do you start? Where do you start? Do you know how many men have been buried with no name? It's an unachievable task, like some impossible trial from a Greek tragedy – but, meanwhile, James can't let it go. I know that he dreams about Nat. Sometimes he shouts his name in the night and then, when he wakes up, I can almost see Nat's face in his eyes. I worry that James isn't happy, and I don't know what I can do to help him. Sometimes I feel that because I look like Nat, I make it worse for him.'

Her eyes lift to watch the oak boughs strain in the wind. He hears her heels kick against the rocks.

'Nathaniel is a name without a body and I'm a body without a name,' Adam says. 'Do you think he links that? Is there a connection in James' mind?'

'I've asked myself the same questions and I think it's part of why you matter to him. But it's not the only reason that he cares about you.' She blows smoke and looks at Adam. 'Heavens, listen to me rattling on. Trying to analyse the analyst! I've said too much, haven't I? James would kill me. Christ, what would he think? You mustn't tell him that I told you. Will you promise? Will you keep that secret for me?'

He squeezes Caitlin's hand. 'It's our secret.'

Chapter Thirty-Six

Celia, Churchyard Cottage, February 1921

'I hate the thought of him being in an institution,' says Celia.

'Is it awful?' Stella asks.

'Oh, it's comfortable enough, and his doctors seem well-meaning, but there are walls around it, like a prison. When I think of how Robert was, how he'd take off down the lane and walk for miles each day, that must be terrible for him, mustn't it?'

'I can't imagine your Robert being in a place like that. Do you think he'll be well enough to come home, though? Does he seem himself? Could you cope with looking after him?'

'Of course! He's my Robert still. He's confused at the moment, that's all. He just needs to know that he's home, and loved, and everything else will fall back into place.'

'Does he know you, Celia?'

She hears the doubt in Stella's voice and wants to dismiss it, but she keeps going over the same question. He had seemed so strange when they brought him to the house last week, and yet surely she'd seen recognition in his eyes when he looked at the camellia in the garden and the books on his bedroom shelves? Wasn't it familiarity that she'd glimpsed there? But where had the familiarity been when he looked at her face? She wouldn't tell anyone, but she had cried after they left that afternoon. She'd gulped uncontrollable tears and beaten her fists on the kitchen table because she had seen the blankness in Robert's eyes as he lay on his bed. He might as well have been blind at that moment – but it was worse than blindness, because at least then he'd recognize her voice and respond to her touch. As they had parted at the garden gate, he had looked at her like he had never seen her before in his life. Half a bottle of brandy wouldn't take away the memory of that look. Her throat was raw and her hands had ached the next day.

She watches Stella across the table now, her fingers spinning the locket at her throat. Celia knows that the locket contains the plaited hair of Stella's three dead babies, so perhaps Stella has better reason to cry than she does, but she tilts her head and gives Celia a sympathetic smile.

'The doctors say there's a good chance that his memory will come back. These things take time, though.'

'And you have time.' Stella nods. As well as the empathy, Celia also sees pity on Stella's face. Celia doesn't want to give in to self-pity, but sometimes it's difficult not to. 'How will you go on at home? Will you need help? I believe that Margaret has a nurse come in every morning to help her with Philip.'

'But Philip's is a physical injury, isn't it? We'll manage. I'm sure we'll fall into a rhythm. I don't underestimate the task, but considering what we've been through, I'm so determined to make it work.'

In some ways a physical injury might be easier, Celia thinks. At least she'd know what it was, and how to deal with it, and there'd be medicines, and dressings, and treatments to make it right. This mental injury, if that's what it is, is so difficult to comprehend. There's something unknowable and undeterminable about it, and there doesn't really seem to be any established remedy. She doesn't know how far the strangeness in Robert's head extends, how it might express itself next or how long it will go on for. There's something daunting about not being able to measure the edges or the progress of it.

'Will he be able to leave the house?' Stella asks. 'If he goes out, will he remember his way home?'

Celia has given this thought. 'Not at first. I'll need to keep him in. But he always loved his books and he'll be able to go out in the garden. I'll watch him there. I know he'll be happy to be back in his own garden.'

Stella nods. She pushes her teacup away and stretches her hand out towards Celia's. 'You look tired, darling. It must be a worry for you. Are you sleeping?'

'Not well,' she admits. 'There's such an awful lot to think about. A lot to plan for. I keep making lists, only I can't cross anything off yet, and as soon as my head touches the pillow at night, all the things that I haven't written down start swarming my brain. I ought to keep a pen and paper by the bedside, but I always forget. I'll confess, I've started having a glass of something at bedtime, just to shut it down, to help me get off to sleep.'

Celia calls it her Medicine and reminds herself that it's only a temporary habit, a little comfort while she's going through this phase, and she won't let it become a problem again. She hopes the peppermints disguise the fact that she's had to have a dose of her Medicine this morning too.

'You must do what you have to,' says Stella, and Celia is glad of her understanding. 'What an awful lot of worry on your shoulders. But at least he's here. It will happen, won't it? It will be sorted out in time.'

Yes, in time, thinks Celia. Only, she has no idea how much time.

'I'm lucky really, aren't I?' she says.

'Yes, darling, you are.'

It is very quiet in the house after Stella leaves. Celia walks through the empty rooms and places Robert at the kitchen table, in the winged-back chair, there at his father's desk. Stella has suggested that she perhaps ought to try harder to trace Patrick and, although Celia had dismissed the idea, she has thought about her husband often in recent weeks. She hasn't really missed him for years (when he called her brittle and domineering that rather snuffed out any lingering fondness), but in recent days she has wished that there was someone here to help her through this. Someone to confide in. A person to whom she could say her concerns out loud and have some reassuring response. But then she doesn't know whether Patrick is alive or dead, and he never had much backbone, anyway. There have been times she has wondered if this weakness in Robert's brain might have come from his father.

She reaches for Robert's photograph and touches his face. For a long time she hadn't liked to look at this image, him in uniform, so obviously belonging to the army, because that's not what Robert is like. But now that he's coming home, now the uniform has gone and that period of them being apart is ending, she's put this photograph in a frame. There is a boundary to that version of her son, and it's all in the past tense now, isn't it? But what effect have the five years since this photograph had on him? She wonders: just how much has gone from his mind? It worries her, the blank expression that she'd seen on his face as he left last week. He's her Robert, her dear Robert, but she is worried that she no longer knows him.

Chapter Thirty-Seven

James, Flailcroft Farm, Calderdale, February 1921

It is a long, low farmhouse, with rows of weavers' windows. The land falls away at the gable end and James can see all across the valley. There are other farms in the folds of fields below, and then, at the bottom, a church spire, factory chimneys, terraces and the railway line.

'Please.' Anna Mason steps back, gestures for them to enter and watches as Adam passes through the door.

The porch smells of damp wood and dogs. It opens into a kitchen, where the flag floor is worn to a gloss by the passage of generations of feet. Adam's feet follow that path and James wonders if they know its texture.

'It's so very odd to see you back here,' Anna says and shakes her head. 'I almost feel I'm looking at your ghost.'

'Yes,' Adam replies.

James watches as Adam moves around this room, looking at the blue-and-white plates on the kitchen dresser, a sampler stitched with the name of an eighteenth-century schoolgirl, the patina on the back of a chair and the brass candlesticks on the mantle. Adam's fingers connect with all of these things. James tries to discern if there is any electricity in that touch, any spark of knowledge or recognition. Do these objects mean any more than the tea caddies in Lucy Vickers' house, or the quilt that Celia Dakers keeps on her son's bed? He also watches as Adam touches Anna Mason's hair. He hears her gasp as she turns towards him and sees their eyes taking in one another's face. It is the same intensity that was there when he approached her in the walled garden. Just for an instant James feels that Adam is on the edge of something; just for a moment he feels that he ought not to be in this room watching these two people connecting.

'Let me show you.'

Anna leads Adam by the elbow and points out objects that ought to be familiar to him. This is his grandfather's candle box, she says. His mother's Staffordshire dogs. His grandmother's brass scales. An embroidered cushion was a wedding gift from her sister. Their wedding, she emphasizes, *her* and *him*. Adam nods and looks at her like he's trying to figure this connection out. There's something similar, James thinks, in the way that Anna Mason looks back at him.

'Was this house always in your family?' James asks.

'On Mark's side. His grandparents came here. Before that it was owned by generations of Quaker families who were cotton and flannel weavers. Here, I have a photograph.'

She takes a framed image down from the wall. A young couple are standing in front of the house, she in a white dress and he in a waistcoat, with arms folded across his chest.

'They're Mark's parents – Joseph and Elizabeth.'

James looks at the photograph. The farm seems entirely unchanged. It has stood quite still. The passage of time has left so few marks. It is only the faces that change. Adam is there then at his elbow.

'I suppose you don't remember, do you?' she asks him.

Adam takes the photograph from James' hands and holds

it close to his face. James' eyes connect with Anna's in the moment of waiting.

'I don't know,' Adam eventually replies.

'It wasn't always a kind place to farm,' she says. 'It's not easy land. There was tuberculosis here in Joseph's day and swine fever. He had forty-six acres and twelve milkers and it was a hard life. The TB nearly broke him.'

'I can imagine.'

'It was always grazing land, but we were told that we had to plough it during the war and put in potatoes. Can you imagine?' Her eyes widen as she addresses the question to Adam. 'It broke the plough and nearly broke my spirits. It's never been arable, this land, and it didn't make sense. It was absolute donkey work, and to what end? I so wanted to tell you about all that,' she says to Adam. 'I wanted to write to you and ask for your help. I so needed you here then.'

James watches Adam nod.

'Where are my manners?' she says. 'I should make some tea, shouldn't I? We should go through to the front room. Will you put some more logs on the fire?' she asks Adam. 'It's right through there. You'll see where everything is.'

The fire has burned down to white embers and Adam must begin again, rolling paper into twists, laying the kindling and building the fire up. James sits down in an armchair and watches Adam work. While he lets his fire in Fellside burn out, and never seems to think to feed it, he sets this fire like he has been doing so all his life. Could it be? Is there some memory stored in his fingers and muscles? Does he know the idiosyncrasies of this chimney, how it draws and how the fire takes, and the texture of this wood in his hands?

As Anna comes into the room with the tea tray, Adam is striking the match. He turns towards her and smiles. There is something so domestic and comfortable about this quiet scene that, just briefly, it seems right. It seems to fit. But then Adam is looking around the room, like he's unsure where to sit. He seems to assess the well-worn armchair by the fire and rejects it in favour of an upright chair at the table. He glances back at the armchair like he's not sure whether to trust it.

'It's not so warm in here, is it?' she apologizes. 'Are you not too cold?'

James hears the tea tray shaking as Anna carries it into the room. All her strain, all her fear, seems to sing in that china rattle. She sets it down on the table in front of Adam, her eyes watching him, but the cups are upset then and James hears her intake of breath as they slide. A primrose-pattern teacup smashes onto the flagstones and she is crying as she bends to pick up the pieces.

'Please, let me help.' James rises from his chair. The china is in fragments all over the floor and he can see that there is a drop of blood on the piece in her palm. 'Is there a dustpan and brush in the kitchen? Please, I must help you.'

He takes the broken china from her hand and pushes his handkerchief into her palm. He holds her wrist, just for a moment, and blood blooms on the white linen. Adam watches as they leave the room.

'I'm sorry. I'm so nervous. What a fool. What a fuss,' she says, as he makes her hold her hand under water in the kitchen. A tear rolls down her cheek and she brushes it away.

'I'm a doctor. I thrive upon porcelain misadventure.'

Her eyelids lift for a moment, there is a twitch of a smile, but then her eyes skirt away. He looks down at her lowered eyelashes, her lips which look like they are about to speak but don't, her white lace shoulder and the red of her bloodied hand in his. As he looks at Anna's face he thinks about a repeated portrait. Adam has denied it, but is James entirely wrong to see some resemblance there? Surely it's the same woman's eyes? The same mouth? But then the portrait animates, Anna's eyes flick up and James realizes that he's been staring at her. He can feel her pulse as he holds a clean cloth to her palm.

'I understand,' he says. 'You're anxious. It's perfectly natural. This is a big day, isn't it?'

'It is.'

Adam is standing with his hands on the mantelpiece as they walk back into the sitting room, flexed between the Staffordshire dogs and the china cottages. James sees him watching them in the overmantel mirror. His eyes blink slowly, and James wonders why he experiences a fleeting sensation of guilt.

'I'll start again, shall I?' says Anna, as she places a new teacup and saucer down. 'Mark, will you?' She looks up at Adam and smiles.

He nods. James notices how he responds to the name and he does seem to be trying harder here than he did in either Lucy Vickers' or Celia Dakers' house. But she's trying so hard too, James sees. The neck of the teapot rattles against Adam's cup as she pours and his eyes don't leave hers. James wonders: is Adam figuring out the familiarity of her face too?

Adam puts his teacup down and walks around the walls of the room. The sitting room is handsome but humble. It has a threadbare gentility. The walls are painted sage green and lined with watercolours in ebony frames.

'They're Mark's mother's,' she tells James, watching the angle of his eyes. She balances her cup and saucer on her knee and it all looks like it might slide again. 'She was a great one for wandering the moors with a watercolour box in her pocket. Quite the Romantic spirit!'

The room smells of beeswax polish and potted hyacinths. Cushions and shawls are arranged to hide the patches on the sofa where the brocade has worn thin. A cranberry-coloured decanter is set out on a tray and the cut glass casts complicated shadows. Adam sits back down and looks untidy in Anna Mason's precise little sitting-room chair – too heavy, too male, too long in the limb – and James wonders how a farmer has ever comfortably sat amongst all this barley-sugar twist and sprig-pattern upholstery. How has a man with soil on his hands ever put one of those glasses to his lips? There are things here that may well fit, but also much that doesn't. James looks around and sees a collection of Bohemian paperweights on the mahogany writing desk and a cluster of framed photographs on the upright piano. 'Do you play?' James asks, wanting a reason to step towards the photographs.

'Badly. And it needs tuning. But Mark did. He has a sweet voice.' She looks at Adam and there is something suddenly shy in her smile.

James can't recall that Adam has ever approached the piano at Fellside. 'Would you like to try?' he asks.

They look on as Adam takes a place at the piano stool and lifts the lid, his fingers gently running along the murmuring keys. He sits with his fingers suspended over the keyboard then, and James doesn't know what to expect next. He looks at Anna. Her face is transfixed, but there is something else there; he can't tell if it's happiness or fear. The moments stretch as Adam sits with his fingers hovering; it is like in the cinema when the projection breaks down, James thinks, and a stuck image vibrates tensely on the screen. When it restarts, when Adam's fingers finally come down and connect, James hears Anna gasp.

It is a thing of strange wonder to listen to the notes of a nocturne being slowly released beneath Adam Galilee's dirty fingernails, the smoothest ripples of music flowing from his hands that dig in the banks and the hedgerows. It is like a magic trick, and as unsettling. The humble farmhouse parlour suddenly vibrates completely differently, the colours intensify and it all trembles with the sentiments of Chopin. There is something miraculous and profoundly moving about the moment – so pure, so unexpected – and when James turns to Anna again he sees her hands gripping the edge of the table and tears on her cheeks. Adam plays haltingly, sensitively, with such emotion and James has to shut his own eyes against tears.

But just as soon as the miracle is formed, it is shattered. James' eyes flash open and he starts at the noise of the piano lid slamming down. Framed photographs fall over, the stool hits the flagstones and Adam is running out of the room.

He looks at Anna and doesn't know what to say.

She stands. Her face is white. She shakes her head. 'He never played like that before,' she says. 'Nothing like that.'

James hears the noise of the porch door closing and runs after Adam. He sees him sprint around the end of the barn, leap up and over the wall, and then he is crossing the field behind the house. Sprinting like a startled hare. Like he is terrified. Sprinting like he needs to be away from this place.

'Adam! Wait for me!'

Anna

She watches them from the window. Mark rounds the end of the barn and is running up towards the moor. She can see the doctor running after him, but Mark's legs know the terrain better, and she knows that he'll get away. Does Mark mean to lose Haworth and to then come back? Will he come back tonight? And, if so, with what intention? The young doctor will not find him, she knows. Mark is familiar with every cranny and hollow of the moor. She remembers him running up and away over that path once before, only it was her crying after him that time. She hadn't been able to catch him either.

Anna turns from the window. The piano notes are still circling around the room. She had hoped that he would play, that the memory would still be in his fingers, but she had never expected him to play like that. Had he learnt it in France? It was a different man's music that had come from Mark's fingers today. Does she know this man? There is so much intensity when his eyes meet hers and yet she can't read him at all. Is he still angry? Is he trying to hide his anger? Or could he really have forgotten everything?

She had screamed at him, six years ago, as she watched him heading up and away over the moor. She had screamed that it wasn't true, that there was nothing to blame her for, that it was just baseless, spiteful gossip. She barely even knew the man that her name had been linked with, she didn't even know his name, but there had been such disappointment and hurt in Mark's eyes when he'd asked. He wasn't the sort of man who would hit her, but he'd looked so desperate that she'd briefly been afraid. She thinks of the slam of the piano lid and wonders if he is still that man. She doesn't know what the intensity in his eyes means today.

Anna can't see them now from the window. Is there really a chance that he might have forgotten what he accused her of? Could the look in his eyes today mean something else? Does he remember that, when he ran out that day, he didn't come back, and that it was the last time they had looked each other in the eye?

She gathers the teacups together. There is a swirl of tea leaves in the bottom of Mark's cup, but they tell her nothing. Did he remember that it was his mother's tea service? Was he angry that she had broken a cup?

Anna had watched him disappear over the moor in February 1915. She had discovered within days where he had gone, but it would be a full twelve months before he would write her a letter. He told her that he was in France. She could hear the awkwardness in his words, the tentativeness with which he'd formed his phrases. He apologized for leaving her with the responsibility of the farm, and hoped that she had found hands to help her. She had cursed him for that, for how insignificant his words had made that task sound, but she had written back to him, as he had asked. They would exchange letters three more times, before his officer replied to say that Mark had gone. When Anna read that news, she had remembered standing by this window and watching him retreat over the moors. She had known then that he would come back eventually. She knows that he will come back again.

James

He scrambles over the wall and falls clumsily on the other side. His chest feels tight as he follows up the hill. Whatever animal energy there is in Adam's muscles, James struggles to find it in his own. His shoes sink into the damp grass and his ankles twist in the unfamiliar terrain, but Adam is away. He's streaking towards the skyline and James' lungs are screaming.

Pasture turns to moor and crag, the muscles in James' legs make him groan, and then he realizes he has lost Adam. There's no sign of him. He stops and turns and takes in the landscape; there is a lapwing's cry, the smell of peat, the whisper of the wind, but otherwise there's nothing. He has gone. Adam has disappeared as absolutely and as suddenly as he first appeared. Has the sky taken him back up? Was he ever really here? Was he ever more than a product of James' own imagination?

He turns, listens to the wind and realizes that he can no longer see a single house. This landscape might have swallowed him and taken him back in time a thousand years. There are only his thoughts, the east wind and his own racing heartbeat. No one is looking at him. There are no questions. There's a sudden freedom in this isolation and he feels his breath slowing. James thinks about curling up in the hollow between the boulders, shutting his eyes and taking the rest of it away.

But then Adam's voice is there. James spins and sees him standing on the rock immediately above him. As if he has always been there. As if he has been watching James all of this time. For a moment, Adam is a monolith, he is a standing stone and a solid black silhouette against the sky, old and permanent as the landscape itself, and for the first time James feels something akin to fear as he looks at Adam. How can he know this man and what he is capable of? Is he knowable at all? But then his hands extend towards James and it is just Adam Galilee and his innocent curiosity again.

'It's a wren,' he says. '*Troglodytidae*.'

In the palm of his hands is a small, perfect nest, like something that has been carefully, lovingly woven, but inside there are only feathers and bloodied shell and white bird bones.

'They abandon them,' says Adam. 'It seems cruel, doesn't it? It seems barbaric. But it's nature. It's what they do. That's just the way of the world.'

Chapter Thirty-Eight

Caitlin, Fellside House, February 1921

Caitlin watches Adam through the gate of the walled garden. He is sitting perfectly still and at first she isn't sure whether he's awake. But then he shades his eyes with his hand and she sees the pencil between his fingers.

'May I join you in there?'

When he turns, she realizes that she has startled him; she briefly sees alarm on Adam's face, but then defensiveness is replaced by recognition, and he nods to her and smiles.

'Caitlin.'

Having seen that look on his face, she's now not sure that she ought to be breaking into his private space, and when the gate won't give to her hands, she wishes that she could retrace her footsteps and leave him to his thoughts. But he's walking towards her now, and his expression is mild, gentle Adam again.

'Is the gate locked? Have you magicked yourself in there somehow? Is it a trick, or did you scale the wall? Must I climb the wall too?'

'I wouldn't dream of making you do that. Although it might be amusing.' He suppresses a grin as he approaches. 'Hold on a moment.'

As Caitlin leans against the gate, she sees that Adam has been working on the walls again. James has told her that Adam has been taking out the old loose mortar and the new joints seem to pull the walls higher and inwards.

'I remember when we first came here, this garden was completely overgrown. It was a wilderness. The gate was rusted closed, so it was all sealed away, a little lost world, rather sad but very possibly enchanted. I don't know how long it had been like that. Alan told me that they used to have a full-time gardener before the war, but the walled garden looked as if it had been abandoned for decades.'

Adam nods. 'I had to take a pair of bolt cutters to the lock. It had rusted shut, but then having got through one portal, I had to fight my way through the roses. They'd gone quite feral and I'm not sure that they wanted to let me in. It was like a trial from some ancient myth, only I had a nice new sharp pair of secateurs instead of a sword. I don't think anyone had been in here for a long time.'

He bends down to roll a rock away from the gate. It's a large stone and Adam has to use both arms to turn it.

'But now you choose to shut yourself in?'

'Sometimes I like being by myself.'

Caitlin recalls how so many people have queued and clamoured for him over the past three months and can appreciate why he might want to barricade himself away. She also thinks of all these visits they're now making, and imagines poor Adam feeling so exposed as these women place him in their kitchens and parlours and gardens and try to make him fit.

'You don't mind that I join you? I honestly didn't mean to intrude. I'll leave you to your thoughts, if you want to be alone.'

'No, of course not. I'm always glad of your company.'

'Well, I'm complimented. Thank you.'

She can see from the stains on his knees, and the sweat on his shirt, that he's been working hard. There's dust in his hair and earth under his fingernails.

'James told me that you're fixing the old lime mortar.'

'Yes. The walls are in good condition, but some of the pointing has crumbled away. It's very old, this garden – certainly much older than the house. There must have been another house here before. I like the idea that houses and their residents have come and gone, but the cycle of the garden continues, don't you? The seasons eternally turning. I've found seashells and lumps of horsehair as I've taken the old mortar out. I even found a coin, but I couldn't make out the date on it. I guess that someone must have placed it there deliberately, so I put it back and sealed it in again with a new coin at its side. Maybe someone will find it again in a hundred years' time?'

She smiles. 'What a Romantic spirit you are!'

'I don't know about that. I'm undoing all this Romantic ruin, aren't I?'

'Alan tells me that you want to get the kitchen garden up and running again.'

'I think he likes the idea too. In his parents' day there were tomatoes and vines in the glasshouse, salad crops under the cold frames and pears on the walls. Those are evidently his childhood memories and I got the impression that he feels a bit sentimental about the tomatoes and the pears.'

As Caitlin watches Adam's eyes tour the walls, she can tell he's imagining it all, putting it all back as it might once have been, and she can also see that he'd like to make a long-term project of restoring it.

'Do you know how it looked before?'

'No, but I can work it out. So much of the structure is still here, you see, once you strip away the briars and the bindweed.'

'Will you show me?' she asks.

Though he has scythed back the worst of the weeds and brambles, it's still not easy to work their way around the garden. He's been turning the earth over and there are mounds and hollows where the vegetable beds have been and will be again. They step through groundsel, nettles and nightshade and he talks about herb beds and phloxes and delphiniums. She puts her hand to his shoulder as she stumbles, and he smiles as he catches her arm.

'For one thing, if I do some work in here, it'll be less precarious. The glasshouse will collapse entirely next winter if something isn't done.'

'It would be a big project to take on – years of a project.'

James and Alan seem to be so preoccupied with exploring alternate futures for Adam at present, and trying to make various histories fit, but when Caitlin looks at him she can see that he doesn't mean to be anywhere other than here. The previous evening James had been telling her how Adam had looked at the woman at the farm. He's convinced that there's something there, some link, some shared history, but as Caitlin watches Adam now, she's sure that he wants to make a future here.

'But I like to work,' he replies. 'I like to be busy. I like to tire myself out.'

'Yes, I understand that.'

'I mean to grow sweet peas. I will cut you bunches for the house this summer.'

'I'll look forward to that. Thank you.'

He shows her the old espaliered fruit trees and points out

the care that has been taken to train the branches in decades gone by. He's pruned the climbing roses back hard and says they'll regather their strength and come back better. The cold frames are all collapsed and shattered glass, but he tells her that he can make them right. Caitlin knows, as she listens to him talking, that he will revive it all with gentleness and patience and time.

'The greenhouse is a different matter, though. You can't go in there, Adam. It looks like a death trap.'

'Perhaps.' He shrugs.

'Why am I not convinced by that reply?'

Though they are blackened now, dahlias have flowered amongst the weeds, and here and there, kales and artichokes have seeded themselves, as they must have done year after year. They circuit around and return to the stone where Adam had been sitting.

'It's a sundial,' he says. 'Can you see? But it's toppled over. It can't tell the time any longer.'

She bends down and puts her fingers to the green copper of the dial. 'I wonder how long ago it fell. If the shadow hasn't been circulating around its dial, has that time really passed at all?'

Just for a second, in her imagination, she sees that shadow turn, and the spin of her wheel, and then everything seems to be going around too fast.

'Are you all right?' he asks.

'I'm sorry.' She looks back at Adam and sees the concern on his face. 'I'm tired, that's all. I've not been sleeping well.'

He nods. 'I can see that. I'd like to put it right,' he says.

'I'm sorry?'

'The sundial.'

He moves his papers aside, to let her sit.

'What were you drawing?'

'The thistles – the old seed heads.'

He passes her the sketchpad and she angles it to the light. 'That's so fine. It's exquisite. I did two years at art college, but I couldn't draw like that.'

'I look a lot. I like to look.'

'But it's more than just looking. You remind me of the John Ruskin sketches that I saw in an exhibition once. You have that precision. That care to get it right. You're very clever.'

He shakes his head. 'I can't even remember my own name. That's not very clever, is it?'

'But that's your illness, or injury, isn't it?'

'You can have it, if you want it.'

'The drawing? Really?'

'Yes.'

'Thank you. I'll put it in a frame.' He looks pleased but embarrassed at that, and she likes him for his awkward modesty. 'Harris is going home tomorrow. Has he told you? He's packing his suitcase this afternoon. He's going back to his family. Have none of these houses that you've visited with James felt like they might be your family home?'

'Not that I'm sufficiently sure of. This is the only home that I remember. I don't want to be anywhere else.'

'It can all stop, if you want it to. Nobody will make you leave here. You only have to tell James, you know.'

'Can it stop? Could it? I'm not so sure now. There are other people involved, aren't there? Some things feel like they've gone too far.'

'Too far?' she asks.

'The women. They're all making their cases, presenting their evidence. They're all having their audience, and I'm not sure that anyone is listening to me any longer.'

'I am. I always will. You can always talk to me. And James will listen to you too.'

'Will he? Are you sure?'

'Of course!'

He plaits a blade of grass between his fingers and she can see that Adam finds this conversation difficult.

'Two new men are coming in this week,' she tells him. 'Two new residents, I mean.'

'It's always changing over, isn't it? The faces at breakfast are always shifting. Sometimes I look up and it surprises me; occasionally I forget who is here and who has gone. I don't mind it, all the men coming through, the faces always changing, as long as they're civil and they're quiet in the night.'

'Yes,' Caitlin replies.

'That's why you're tired, isn't it? That's why there are shadows under your eyes. You're not sleeping because he's not sleeping.'

'Is it that obvious?'

'It is. And I pass your cellar window and you're not there working.'

'It keeps going wrong. I'm hopeless at the moment. Normally working makes me feel better, and I don't have any problem concentrating, but I can't get there now, I can't focus, and I'm so frustrated with myself.'

'You need to talk to James.'

'James needs to talk to me!'

'Physician, heal thyself? Would you like me to try to talk to him?'

'But that's the wrong way round, isn't it?'

'Not necessarily,' Adam replies.

Chapter Thirty-Nine

Celia, Churchyard Cottage, February 1921

'I thought I'd see how you are,' says Reverend Seabrook. Celia tells herself it's only his short-sightedness, but he does seem to be peering at her through his glasses. 'We missed you doing the flowers in church this week.'

'It's very kind of you to think of me, Vicar. There's been so much to do. I have to get the house ready for Robert, you see. I do want it all to be quite right.'

'Naturally, and I'm certain it will be. I suspect that Robert will be glad to be home, though, whether or not you've scrubbed the stairs and laundered the curtains.'

Celia is aware, at that, of what a state the house is in. What must he think of her? She's taken down the curtains to wash them and had been in the middle of waxing the bedroom floor when the doorbell rang. She did remember to take her apron off, but there's dust on her skirt and wax under her fingernails. She hasn't looked in a mirror, but she knows that she's hardly ready for company.

'I'm sorry. I'm rather in disarray, aren't I? You have to go through the upheaval before order reigns.' She smiles, though she suspects that Reverend Seabrook probably wouldn't know where to start with floor wax.

'Not at all. Please don't apologize. I can smell the beeswax and the brass polish. I'm sure that it's all going to glimmer like a new pin. Have they given you a date yet, Celia?'

No. And that's why she must fill her days with waxing and polishing and laundering, because the date is indefinite and the hands turn around the clock so slowly. She must keep on ironing and scrubbing and dusting into the corners, because that keeps the unwelcome questions out of her head.

'Not yet,' she replies. 'I'm going to visit him again at the weekend. All of the paperwork has to be absolutely shipshape, you understand?'

'As it should be. Only, I was wondering if you'd like me to drive over and visit him sometime? After all, your Robert and I always got along. We were never short of something to talk about, and it might be nice for him to see a familiar face, don't you think?' He turns to Robert's photograph face as he says that and smiles. 'Was that taken in France? I don't recall that I've seen it before?'

'No,' she says. 'I had it by my bedside.' Celia is sure that it's probably a double sin to lie to a vicar, but she isn't certain how to explain it otherwise, how she didn't like to look at him in uniform, all black and white, and so obviously far away. She thinks about Robert in the hospital now and he still feels far away. Should Reverend Seabrook see him like that? 'It's most kind of you, but they are a bit difficult about visitors. They don't encourage it. Some of the other patients are more poorly than Robert, you see, and they don't want them to be disturbed.'

'Perhaps if I wrote in advance? I wouldn't just turn up, of course. I'd explain my relationship with Robert, how I've known him all his life, and how it might be beneficial for him to see a familiar face.'

'I don't think so,' says Celia. She's not sure why it is that she feels so adamant about this, but she doesn't want Reverend Seabrook to be meddling, interfering, poking around and peering at Robert. 'They like to keep him calm. They're very particular about these things.'

'As you wish,' says the reverend, but she sees him looking at her from the sides of his glasses. 'I didn't mean to push.'

'I would offer you some tea, but I'm in such a frightful mess.'

'Of course. I'm sorry to have disturbed you, Celia. I didn't mean to intrude.'

'No, not at all! I'm the one who should apologize. I'll be there at church this Sunday.'

'And in the meantime – any time – if you wish to talk, you know where I am. You mustn't bottle up your worries. We're all friends and we're all on your side.'

As she shows the vicar to the door, there's a flutter in his hands that suggests he thinks her fragile and is perhaps a little nervous of upsetting her. Is that what they all believe? That she's delicate? Vulnerable? That she's maybe not thinking right? Not quite in her right mind? She can talk to God at home, she decides – he sees things for how they are, he knows what's going on – so she doesn't need to go to church and have them all looking at her that way.

Celia climbs the stairs and her legs feel tired. She's shifted all the furniture around in Robert's room, so that she can wax the floorboards, and it looks rather chaotic as she stands in the doorway. She hasn't taken anything out of the room, but the furniture is all at unfamiliar angles, and she supposes that's what it's like inside Robert's head at the moment. He'd seemed so terribly confused when she saw him last, talking about ordering flower seeds and fixing walls and wanting to plant a vegetable garden in the grounds of the hospital. She pushes the bed back into place. Surely if they'd let him come back here his mind would fall back into place more quickly?

Another woman had been leaving the hospital as Celia arrived, and she had worried about that on her way home. She'd told the doctor that she didn't like to see other women there; that it upset Robert; that it disturbed him. But the young doctor had still been talking about evaluations, and connections, and Robert needing to feel that he fits. Celia thinks about the doctor watching Robert in this room. Did he not see enough connections being made that day and Robert fitting back in to his place? Is that why those evaluations must carry on? Why other women must still be permitted to disturb him and put ideas in his head? For how much longer must it go on? How certain do they need to be?

She pictures Robert lying on his bed, and wishes that *she* could feel more certain.

Chapter Forty

James, Fellside House, March 1921

'She says that it's not natural for a family to be kept apart like this.' Shepherd looks up from the letter.

'None of us would disagree with that, apart from the fact that she can't actually prove she is his family.'

'She goes on to ask if she can have him.'

'*Have* him?' James looks up from the photograph of Ellis Vickers' wife. Lucy's handwriting fills the page that Shepherd is holding. It is crammed with her words, James sees. Her large, round letters leave no margins, so that at a desk's distance away this looks like a diatribe.

'If he can be transferred to her care,' Shepherd clarifies, 'be restored to the bosom of the family, as she puts it. She wants to be his guardian.'

'Does she comprehend what she'd be taking on?'

'His pension?'

'Alan! I don't think it's that cynical. I saw her face when she looked at him.'

'But they all look at him like that!'

Shepherd pushes the letter away. He straightens it on his desk, stretches his arms and walks towards the window. The sash frames a vista of wet hillside and trees swelling together with the wind. The room is pale and cold in the washed-out light. As he watches his reflection, James thinks that Shepherd looks tired. Is he finding this business difficult too? All the women's words seem to be circling around them, but there's so little back from Adam.

'I'm sorry,' Shepherd says. 'As Miss Vickers writes, Adam is a gentle man. He wouldn't be any threat to her or the children.'

'He's never met these children, though, has he? Or, at least, not as far as we're aware. Yes, he's much more stable than he was, and he's never displayed violent tendencies, but how well would he react to them? Is it fair to him to test that? Is it fair to them?'

'You don't think they are his children, do you?'

James shakes his head. 'I don't know. It's only gut instinct. But that's not to say that Miss Vickers doesn't genuinely believe Adam is their father.'

'She argues that his memory would return in the familiar surroundings of home.'

'But it may be some other man's home.'

Shepherd folds the letter back into its envelope. 'She suggests that the environment would be better for him than isolation in an asylum and, well, perhaps there's some reason in that. We can't absolutely deny it, can we?'

'I wouldn't disagree that a home environment would be better for Adam – but *his* home, not that of a well-meaning stranger. Eventually his relatives might appear, and if he's already been released to an imposter family—'

'Imposter? That's a bit strong.'

'But you recognize the potential dilemma?' James asks. 'The possible difficulty?'

'They can't all be right. They can't all be telling the truth.

But surely one must be. Three women can't really be so deluded, can they?' Shepherd turns away from the window. The rain is etching out striations of light across the glass.

'Or, maybe, Adam is all of these three men?'

'You mean he'd been living three lives under three separate names? Surely not! Can you imagine what hard work that would be? Think of the logistics! Think of the mileage! I reckon we're stretching possibility there.'

'Probably. Clutching at straws. Sorry.' James turns the photograph between his fingers. There is nothing but the girl's name, Phoebe Vickers, on the reverse. 'Doesn't it strike you as odd that Lucy Vickers can send us several photographs of her brother's wife, but she claims not to have a single image of him?'

'Yes. You're right. You're spot on. We need to find out more about Ellis Vickers. We need to dig a bit deeper. Someone must be able to tell us more about him. In the meantime, will you show the photograph to Adam?'

'I would like to see how he responds to it.'

Shepherd nods. 'So would I.'

James walks to the window and stands at Shepherd's side. A tray of glasses tinkles as he steps across the rug, making him sharply conscious of his own movement and weight and the way he places his feet. Sally is cradling the ginger cat in her arms down below and smiling at the parting clouds. Adam is pushing a wheelbarrow across the garden.

'He's wearing the coat again,' James says.

'The one that Dakers sent him?' Shepherd looks down and laughs. 'Does she realize that it makes him look like a rake?'

It's a frock coat with tails, and it makes Adam look like he has stepped out of the last century. Gathered about his waist with a length of rope, there is certainly something of the ragged dandy about Adam's new outdoor attire.

'A somewhat unsuccessful rake.' Though he has taken to wearing Robert Dakers' coat, James can't help but think that Adam looks as though he's wearing another man's clothes. 'Have you noticed that it's too big for him?'

'Didn't she observe that he's lost weight?'

'But he can't have shrunk, can he? It's too big for him on the shoulders and it's cut for a taller man.'

'Perhaps it wasn't his to start with? Perhaps it was always a hand-me-down?'

'We do have a lot of perhapses, don't we?' The sight of Adam in the coat reminds James of winters in France and how the men would take on the discarded layers of those who had gone before them. Whatever perhapses occlude Adam's past, James is sure that he must have been there, must have known that cold. 'No, it's the same with everything that she's sent in – all the sleeves and legs are too long. They're not his. It was terribly sad to watch him trying Robert Dakers' clothes on, because they so obviously don't fit him.'

'So, as far as you're concerned, that's it for Dakers?'

'It's not looking right, is it?' James says as he turns from the window. 'I told you that I've heard from Mason again, haven't I?'

'You said that she wants another visit.'

'She's asked for a longer stay. She thinks that if Adam sleeps a night in her house, if they can spend some time alone together, he might make a breakthrough.'

'There are things that she wants to say to him away from your prying ears? I don't think he should go alone. I'd raise no objection to a second visit, but I think you ought to go with him again. After all, he bolted last time, didn't he? What's to stop that happening again?'

'My thoughts entirely – but then, we're not his prison guards, are we?'

'We are here to look after his interests, though. He's still vulnerable. He might know how to prune roses and mix lime mortar, but could he fend for himself? If he ended up out there on his own again, would he take care of himself? There are ways in which he's practical, but in other respects he's an innocent.'

James nods. 'I do have to say: it's not just that we've invested time and effort in him; I've invested in him as a person too. I'm fond of him, I care about him, and I don't want this to go wrong for him. I'd like to make this right. I want him to be able to go on from here, to progress further, to know his name and his family, but I don't want us to make a mistake.'

'Quite. And what's your instinct as regards Mason's claim?'

'Both encounters have been emotionally charged. Much more so than any of the other claimants. There is some sort of electricity between them.'

'You make it sound like a romantic novel!'

'No, not like that. An energy, I mean. They responded to each other at some deeper level. There was some communication going on. At times, I felt slightly awkward being in the same room as them. And I'm struggling to get beyond the likeness between her and his drawings.'

'Maybe they should be allowed some time alone together?'

'With me listening at the keyhole?'

'But of course!'

'One thing that doesn't stack up, though, is Adam's voice. My father was from Calderdale. I know that area and that accent pretty well. I'm sure if there was some of that in Adam's voice, I would have noticed it.'

'Five years in different company?'

'But it never slips. Not when he's tired. Not when he was hypnotized.'

'I do wonder if Mrs Mason means to hypnotize him.'

'I'm sorry?'

'The plea for time alone. Could she mean to seduce him?'

James thinks of a bead of blood on Anna Mason's finger. Her bloodied finger put to her lips. He thinks of standing in Caitlin's mother's kitchen seven years ago, when she had cut herself with a knife, and how he had put Caitlin's red finger to his own mouth.

'I don't think we need that complication,' James replies.

The rain has passed and the sky is full of high scudding clouds. Adam is drawing the pine trees. They rock in the wind, showing their flexibility and strength, and his sketch is all wet light and movement. Adam's coat is soaked through, James sees. Droplets glisten on his shoulders, but he seems as rooted in the garden as the pine trees themselves.

'Were you out in the squall?' he asks.

'I didn't notice it.'

'Does the wind not keep blowing your paper away?' James asks.

Adam smiles. 'Yes, a couple of times, but it doesn't matter.'

It always intrigues James that Adam will spend hours working on a drawing, only to discard it. He finds Adam's sketches all around the house and in the garden. It is as if the finished drawings serve no purpose; it is the act of their creation and the observation that matters. It is only the drawings of the woman that he keeps. Her face covers the walls of Adam's room now, and James is sure that he's met her, but it's not the face of the woman whose photograph he presently carries in his pocket.

'I have something to show you,' he says.

'The wind takes away half of your voice,' Adam replies. His eyes don't lift from the paper. 'Yes?'

'Lucy Vickers has sent you a photograph. She says that the woman in this picture is your wife.'

He does look up then. 'My wife? Her brother's wife, you mean? Can I see it?'

James tells him that the girl in the photograph is called Phoebe. She is a pretty girl. Long curly hair. A shy smile. James watches as Adam brings the photograph close to his face.

'Do you remember her at all? Is her face familiar? Miss Vickers says you married her when you were eighteen.'

The tree trunks creak together in the wind. Adam spends a surprisingly long time looking at the image before he finally shakes his head.

'She died, didn't she?'

'I believe so.'

'That's terribly sad.'

'It is.'

'Am I allowed to keep the photograph?' he asks.

James looks at him. The expression in Adam's eyes is the same that was there when he'd been looking at the painting of the reservoir. Sorrowful. Pensive. Is it distress, even? 'I'll ask Miss Vickers,' he replies.

Chapter Forty-One

Adam, Fellside House, March 1921

The coltsfoot is yellowing the ditches now. The ivy creeps up the fallen walls anew and the daffodils are twisting open. The first green freshness is tinting the elder and it feels as though everything is pushing up from the ground beneath his feet. It's alive with it, writhing with it, Adam can almost hear it, and his blood quickens with the certainty that it will all come back again. In the fields around Anna Mason's house it had still been winter, permeated by the brown scent of the leaves breaking down into the ground, but three days on (can it be only three days?) he smells and feels the force of spring returning.

When he had first met Anna Mason in the walled garden there had been something about her that he recognized. He had needed to look at her closely in order to work out what that was, to breathe her in, to touch her hair and her skin. And occasionally, as he has watched her pupils dilate and felt the softness of her touch, he has felt pulled towards her too. But having observed her up close, knowing her voice, her gestures and the scent of her skin, he now understands that it is only a resemblance; there is just a slight something in her features and colouring that reminds him of another face. As he had looked at her three days ago, he had known that's all it was. Only an echo. A false echo. He had seen the need in her eyes, how she had been so desperate for him to acknowledge her, and he had pitied her for that, but he's not the person Anna Mason wants him to be.

Neither is he Lucy Vickers' brother. Adam knows that too, but he had felt a profound sadness as he'd looked at the photograph face of the woman Ellis Vickers was meant to have loved but had lost. He'd felt that grief when Haworth gave him the photograph, as if it was his own, but why was that? He'd cried last night (spontaneous, sincere and then uncontrollable tears), and asked his confused reflection where that feeling had come from. Was it sympathy or empathy? Has he too loved and lost? Is that what it was? Could it be that he's lost the woman who he sees in his dreams? Is that why her image persists and seems so important? But she'd been there that day in the wood, he is sure of it. Adam considers, and he knows that Haworth is wrong: she is real, she exists somewhere in this wood, and she isn't yet lost.

A song thrush lengthens its notes now; he doubles down under the hazels, and can taste the spring in the air. Adam takes in all the details of the new-made day; his eyes pick out the first celandines and ahead is a dazzle of white as the daisies push up crimson-tipped petals. The sycamore and horse chestnut are bursting with new glossy pink-green life and the rooks are busy building nests. Spiders' webs hold the last of the dew and glitter between the fragile filigree of the old year's leaves. The spring light seems to varnish everything this morning, quenching colour and giving it all a lustre. Husks from opening buds stick to his clothing and he breathes in the wood's secret vitality.

He knows Haworth believes that it's Anna Mason's face

in his drawings, but Adam has told him it's not. Haworth doesn't look convinced, though. Does he think that Adam is lying? How can he prove that he's not? He had seen Haworth looking at Anna Mason, trying to work it out, wanting to mirror her face against Adam's drawings, but there's a flaw in the mirror and it won't work. Why can't Haworth see that?

Haworth is determined to make it fit. Adam had felt angry with him three days ago, frustrated that he didn't seem to be listening. He knows that Haworth means well, that he wants Adam to have a home and a family and his own name, but he knows that none of these names – the Masons and Vickers and Dakers – are right. It doesn't fit. It's not a match.

The jays are starting to build nests overhead, cackling and circling, and he's sure that he's heard a nightingale. He doesn't know where that music came from three days ago when he put his fingers on the piano keys. Sometimes these things frighten him and that was why he'd run. He doesn't know what else is hidden away in his head, waiting to be unlocked, and what his hands are capable of. Sometimes the possibilities scare him. He sees the void open up again and he doesn't know what's there in the blackness. What else might he accidentally let out? He knows there are things that he mustn't remember.

Adam stretches out his arms, draws the forest air deep into his lungs, and is free and himself again. The sunlight through the glisteningly greening trees is like the glow of cathedral windows. He has thought about running if they keep on trying to make these women's stories fit, if he must be obliged to keep on drinking tea in over-heated rooms and filling the gaps in conversations that are not his own. It is better to be here, to sleep in the hollows and hedgerows, than to have to look into all these women's eyes and feel the tug of their memories, but he also wants to carry on working in the garden. He has such plans. It gives him such pleasure. Is Caitlin right – if he asked them, could it really all stop? He wishes that it could be so, but Adam has seen a look in Haworth's eyes that suggests he now can't stop.

There is the clap of a wood pigeon's wing ahead and he watches it flutter up through the brightening branches. The pollen from the hazel drifts and dazzles on the light and it is only then that he sees her. As Adam looks across the clearing, the face of the woman he sees in his sleep is there – the woman he draws, the real woman. When he blinks and, yes, she's still there, he realizes that he hasn't willed her into being. She is flesh and blood, breath and bone, both spirit and substance, and known. He takes a step closer to her and sees a shimmer of fear pass over her face. He holds his hands up like a gesture of surrender and hopes that she won't run.

He needs to speak to her, to ask her who she is, but he's so frightened of scaring her away. He feels that he must move slowly, calmly, smoothly around and keep his eyes connected to hers. Adam hopes that this connection, and all that it communicates, will stop her from bolting. He moves towards her as he would approach a deer, a fox or a hare.

Adam can hear and see the breath leaving her lips and quickening her chest. It seems a fragile thing, her breathing, like the pumping of a bird's heart under his fingers, and he is scared that he will make it stop. He can tell she is nervous, but her hands are still. They do not flit and fidget like the hands of the other women. Though she might flicker on the surface, inside he knows that she is composed in a way that none of the other women are. There is a peace and understanding underneath. There are no twitches or begging smiles. No flicks of hair or shows of teeth. Her eyes watch him, but they are not hungry like the others; instead, he sees knowledge and recognition and tenderness there. Hazel buds twist open at the sigh of her breath and jasmine twines at the touch of her fingertips. Wood anemones lift their heads in the space between him and her.

When she turns, he knows that she will let him follow. As she walks, he watches her black boots move through the ivy and the crane's bill and the dove's foot. There are buttons all up her boots and the dew glitters on her toes. Adam can hear the frogs down by the beck, the hedge sparrows, the blackbird and her breath. He doesn't dare to look at her face, but he feels that he has been walking by her side for ever.

Bracken fronds uncurl with the passage of their feet, and they step into glades where the grass is already trodden down and magic feels to be only just out of sight. The wood seems to stretch for ever today, and sometimes he is treading in her footsteps and sometimes she is walking in his shadow. She is neither following him, nor he her; it is simply the way that it seems to be and has always been.

She hasn't yet spoken to him, but when she does it is as if he has been hearing her soft, low voice all his life.

'You mustn't tell anyone that I was here,' she says. 'If they know that I've been here, they'll stop me from coming again.'

He nods. 'But there are others and they want to take me away from here.'

'I've seen them. But none of them will, because none of them are right.'

Adam turns towards her then and watches the shadows spin around her face. He sees his own face in the endless black of her pupils, and knows that his name and all his history are in there too. His fingers wind through hers and they lie down on a bed of sorrel and thyme and meadowsweet.

The blackbirds turn their wings, the rooks roost, the white owl cries as she hunts and the bats circle back. Dusk creeps down through the branches and in the distance someone is shouting Adam Galilee's name. He looks at her peaceful face and knows that he has woken so many mornings to that sight and the steady rhythm of her breathing. But will she be here tomorrow? When will he see her again?

'What?' She smiles as she opens her eyes.

'I need to know your name. I need to know who you are.'

He sits up and suddenly the need is urgent. This is what matters. This is the only thing that matters.

But she sighs as she rolls her head away. 'I'd give anything to be able to tell you that, and how it all fits together.'

'So tell me! Why can't you tell me?'

She's standing then, brushing leaves from her dress; the spell is breaking, and he can see that she's going to go.

'I can't.'

'Why?'

'Because I can't put it back the way it was.'

He can see the conflict on her face, that it's difficult for her, but this answer isn't enough. He hears the name Adam being called again and it's getting closer now. Fear flashes across her face.

'Please. Tell me. Stay. Talk to them. Tell them who you are and why we need to be together.'

She looks like she might cry now, but there's also frustration on her face. 'It's too late for that.'

'It can't be. I won't let it be. You need to speak. You need to explain it.'

He can hear someone coming through the wood. It's Haworth's voice, he thinks. Surely she can talk to Haworth and make him see that she's the one he's meant to be with?

'*Please.*'

Panic quickens his blood. He hears his name again and turns his back on her for only a second; the contact between their eyes breaks just for a moment, but he hears the gasp of her breath and when he looks back there is only a hare streaking away into the gathering dusk.

Chapter Forty-Two

Adam, Fellside House, March 1921

He had known that it was Haworth looking for him in the wood, that it was his voice, but Adam had needed some space to think. He'd cut back down by the riverside path and had left Haworth's voice there, calling, circling, echoing, going further into the wood. Adam knew that Haworth wouldn't like that, he could hear the fear in his calls, but Adam needed time to formulate his own questions, to make his own judgements, to decide what he must do next.

He is glad that Haworth didn't come up to his room last night, he needed that time alone, but he must speak with him this morning. Today he needs Haworth's help.

He eventually finds him in the sitting room. He can hear Haworth's voice, and Milner's, through the door, and though Adam feels a sense of urgency, he knows that Milner struggles to get his words out, and so he has to let him have his time. Adam sits on the floor on the far side of the door, and listens to Milner joining words up into sentences. He speaks so seldom, Adam is unfamiliar with his voice and he can't help but focus in on the anguish finding expression there. Milner is talking about his children, how he feels guilty about things that his children shouldn't have heard and shouldn't have seen (*Things children just shouldn't see*, Milner's voice emphasizes). It all suddenly seems to be pouring out of him, all that distress shaping itself into words and rushing out. Adam pities him, that he has kept all these painful words inside, but he's also starting to feel frustrated with Haworth because it's clear he's trying to rush him.

Adam listens to Haworth's voice and it's as if he's worked all of his questions out in advance, and he's not really taking in and responding to Milner's answers. He sounds like he's following a formula, and as the top of the hour approaches on the hall clock, he's not giving Milner enough space to speak. Haworth's voice is drawing conclusions and making summaries that don't quite correspond with what Milner has said. It's like Haworth decided on the outcome of this conversation before he even entered the room.

Adam feels sorry for Milner and all his hoarded-up, unheeded words. It seems such a shame. Such a waste. But Adam is also concerned by Haworth's voice because, although he is inclined to draw conclusions, he does at least normally listen. Adam thinks there might be something wrong with Haworth's voice this morning. He remembers his voice calling in the wood yesterday and hopes that it wasn't venturing further in there that has caused this strangeness in his tone.

But, thinking back to the wood, Adam also urgently needs to speak with Haworth. He can still see her up-close features; the recalled rhythm of her breath fills the hall now, and he can smell the scent of her skin on his.

When the door opens, Haworth seems to be ushering Milner out a little too quickly. Milner's face meets Adam's and he sees him roll his eyes. Adam wants to laugh at that momentarily, but it's really not funny and with the hurriedness Haworth seems to be displaying, Adam is worried that he won't have the time to listen to him either.

'Adam! I spent ages looking for you yesterday.'

Haworth's voice has changed now and it is clear that he wants to speak with him. All the flatness that Adam could hear through the door has gone and there's an eager lift there instead.

'I know. I heard you. But I was busy.'

'Busy?'

'I was walking. I met someone. I needed some time alone to work things out.'

They walk together down the corridor and Adam thinks that Haworth looks rather unkempt this morning. He hasn't shaved and he's got the same shirt on that he wore yesterday. As he follows Haworth into his office, Adam isn't certain that he can't smell whisky on his breath.

'And in your time alone you were contemplating . . . ?'

'Will you hypnotize me?'

Haworth looks surprised. He was about to sit down, but he stands behind his desk and braces his arms on the chair. 'Hypnotize you? But it didn't go so well last time, did it? You told Shepherd that you didn't want to do it again.'

'But I do now. It's different now. There's something that I need to remember.'

He feels Haworth's eyes moving over his face.

'*Need* to?'

'Yes.'

'It's really more Doctor Shepherd's speciality than mine. He'll be back this afternoon. Can it wait?'

'No. Please, will you to do it? I want you to do it this morning. You do know how to?'

'Well, yes, of course – but why the urgency?'

'Because I have to know her name.'

*

Haworth has made him recline on the couch, like Shepherd had done. As Adam laid down, he'd remembered his reluctance to do this last time. His fear. How he had felt forced by them. And hadn't those instincts been right? He feels frightened again. There's still a big part of him that doesn't want to do this. (What will he see? What will come back? What might accidentally slip out, rush out, stay?) But how can he wake up with the woman's face at his side again if he can't find her – and how can he find her without a name? Adam knows that he's meant to be there at her side, that that's where he always has been and where he must be again in the future, but he needs a name to make that happen.

Haworth's voice is trying to calm him. Adam can hear that. He's talking about a beach, about soft, warm sand and sunshine and the rhythm of the waves. He wants Adam to feel the sunshine on his face, to see the footsteps stretching away in the sand and to hear the gentle, reliable whisper of the waves. He is making it all sibilant and soothing, giving Adam the rhythm of the sea and the heat of the sun, but Adam doesn't know this place. He doesn't remember ever lying on a beach and the sound of the sea isn't taking the rush of questions out of his head. He shifts on the couch. His back is hurting. He rubs his eyes.

'Try to relax,' says Haworth. 'Concentrate on your breathing. Slow it down. Take deeper breaths. Feel the breath filling up your chest.'

Adam wants it to happen. He wills it to happen. He takes the deep breaths, but something else is fluttering in his chest. An image of khaki tents and sand dunes and a man putting a mask over his face. It's hot, and it smells of rubber inside the mask, and when Adam tries to draw his breath in, he can't. He sits up. He can feel his heart racing and sweat prickles on his scalp. He doesn't want to see any more of this scene. He doesn't want that to be in his head.

'I'm sorry. The beach thing doesn't work. I need to see her and hear her saying her name. Can you take me to somewhere where she'll be?'

He hears Haworth sigh. 'Try to calm down. I think you want it too much and I don't know that it's possible to go back and pick out a specific memory. It doesn't really work like that. Even if that memory is actually there.'

'Even if it's there? You mean you don't think it exists? You think I've made her up?'

'I don't know, Adam. I really don't. But, right now, I think you're trying too hard.'

Haworth sits forward in his chair. He puts his hands through his hair.

'Are you tired today?' Adam asks.

'Yes. The wind was noisy last night, wasn't it? I didn't sleep very well.'

'It was.' In truth, Adam can't recall that he heard the wind at all, but he had heard their voices, Haworth and Caitlin. Adam imagines that most of the people in the house must have heard their voices last night. And he had heard his own name in amongst the raised voices, his and hers, and Caitlin's brother's name there too. He hasn't worked out how they were linking the two, but he has seen Caitlin at her window this morning and she doesn't look happy either. Adam is sorry if something that he has done has made Caitlin sad.

'Why don't we take a break for a bit? Try to calm down. Get some air?' Haworth suggests and Adam can see that he needs it as much as he does. 'Doctor Shepherd will be back after lunch. It might be better if you had a session with him.

I'll talk with him, tell him what it is that you want to remember, and we'll all try together.'

Haworth doesn't look convinced, Adam thinks, and he isn't either. He can see that Haworth doesn't believe that the woman is real.

'All right. After lunch, then?'

'Yes. By the way, I've heard from Anna again. She'd like us to go back, make another visit. You'd be willing to, wouldn't you?'

'Anna Mason?'

'That's right. Don't you feel there might be a connection there? She's convinced and I'm not sure that she's wrong. Isn't it worth trying to explore that a little further?'

'What's the point?' Adam replies.

Chapter Forty-Three

Anna, Flailcroft Farm, March 1921

Each image must be full of potential connections, Anna thinks, as she cleans the glass of the photographs. Prompts. Provocations. Little sparks waiting to ignite. She places an old daguerreotype down on the bedside table. Mark's mother is a shyly smiling girl, her hair made up in ringlets, the image blurring mysteriously to black at the edges. Here Mark's father and his uncle, young men in their Sunday best, make proud faces in a photographer's studio. Mark himself, only a boy still (oh, sweet, beautiful boy!), lines up with his cousins in Whitsuntide whites. Surely, in each of these captured moments, there are triggers and links and routes back into memory. Anna imagines this amnesia as being like a pane of glass. If she can just make one crack in it, won't it all start to fall?

As she had watched Mark moving around the front room last week, she had been certain that he was close to making a connection. It was the way he had studied objects – how he put his finger to the brasses around the fire, the lustre-glazed teapot, his grandmother's rosewood candlesticks – and the way he had looked at her face. She had been sure that he was on the very edge of remembering. His eyes were moving all the time, as if he was searching, as if he was trying to piece things together, and she had felt such a weight of emotion with the connection of his eyes.

In a silver-framed photograph, they are a new bride and groom, him and her at the age of eighteen. Mark's father had died a few weeks earlier and he had taken on the responsibility of the farm. No longer a boy at leisure to roam the fields, instead he now had to sit over ledgers of figures and try to keep on balancing them out. Mark had found unexpected debts hidden away amongst his father's figures, sums owing, deadlines overdue, and so after those first few happy months, it had all become complicated. Anna looks closer at the photograph and tries to see if it was clouding over Mark's face even back then. There would be twelve months then of struggling to keep it going, of fighting to keep the farm, only for him to walk away from it. But she knows that she was the one who caused him to walk away.

Anna remembers the moment when Mark's face had briefly touched against hers in the walled garden. It had been like the first time, when they were seventeen and she had longed for his touch. He must have felt that electricity too, mustn't he? Surely he must have understood in that moment that there was something between them? As she had watched Mark moving around this house, it had been so difficult not to reach out and touch him. She had wanted to know the feeling of putting her hands through his hair once more, to kiss his fluttering eyelashes, to feel his breath on her neck again. That electricity had coursed through her for all the time that he had been in the house, but could they ever find a way back to their old intimacy? So much had changed between their first meeting and their parting; they had both changed and, maybe, in those last few weeks that they were together, she had thought about a stranger's touch.

She can't even remember the man's name – she might never even have known it – but he was a travelling salesman with a suitcase of buttons and ribbons. She had walked ten minutes along the canal path at his side, exchanged words that she now can't recall and taken a ribbon from his hand as he turned off the path. That was her crime. Her fingers had never even touched his. But then a sighting became a story, found its way to Mark's ears; there was the damning ribbon in her drawer, and suddenly he was looking at her like she had betrayed him.

She remembers a feeling of outrage, of injustice and abandonment on the day after Mark left. It was all out of proportion and so ridiculously silly. Had something been wrong in Mark's head even back then?

The framed images glimmer all around her. Mark's family surround her on the walls of this room, but she feels no guilt as she engages with their eyes, because, well, why should she? It is only occasionally that she doubts herself. If the stranger hadn't turned off the path, would she have carried on walking at his side, and what then? It had been easy to walk alongside him because he had laughed and complimented her, and she had laughed back. Perhaps if the preceding months had not been so difficult, if they hadn't been full of scrimping, and worrying, and Mark in a black mood, she never would have started to talk to that man.

She rewinds in her mind, spins back through all the cause and consequence, and knows that if the figures in the ledger had added up, the clouds wouldn't have come in, she would never have walked down a canal path with a stranger and Mark would never have walked away. She put that ribbon on the fire years ago. She would have scorched out the rest of it too, if she could. Anna has been married to her husband for eight years, but has lived with him for only two of those, one year of light, and one year of shadows. She has no idea what the next eight years will bring.

She remembers the hardship of that first year being on the farm on her own, the struggle to find hands to help, and to afford the price of feed, how she had cursed Mark and his presumptions; but her feelings had all changed when the letter came. When they told her that he might be gone, she had so needed that probability to be a miscalculation. She needed to have him back so desperately, and if there were chances of making that happen, she had to seize them.

It wasn't guilt that had made her search, it was nothing to do with easing her own conscience; she had kept on searching because of the feelings that came before, because of the year of light that came before the dark. She would never have stopped looking for him because she remembers a seventeen-year-old boy with soft brown eyes, a shy smile and a sketchbook full of her face, and however difficult the years ahead might be, she means to find him again. She's not entirely sure that the Mark she knows is there when she looks in his eyes now, but she will never stop looking and trying.

When she wrote to the hospital again, she had been concerned that the doctors might misinterpret her words. She has asked if Mark might stay the night, but it is only so that he might have more time and space to let the memories settle. After all, surely this was all about time? If he could spend twenty-four hours surrounded by familiar things, wasn't there a chance that he could fall back into that familiarity? Might he, if only for a moment, look up and feel the normality of it all? Yes, she has held the clean sheets to her chest and looked at her own bed – their bed – and thought about the possibility, but Anna knows that she needs to tread carefully. Small steps. She mustn't push. Steer maybe (certainly, she means to steer him away from some memories), but she mustn't push him.

And so she has prepared his parents' room. As she looks at the old brass bed, she realizes that this was probably the room in which Mark was conceived and born. It was probably the first sight that his eyes ever took in. There must be something powerful in that, surely? Somewhere within him there must still be knowledge of that. She has made the bed up with the best linen, with pillows stitched by his mother's hand and sheets purchased for their own wedding night. She had smiled to herself as she smoothed them out, laughed at herself for willing some enchantment into the cotton and the shape of the stitches. She wants Mark to remember, but she also wants him to shut his troubled eyes and to sleep.

She thinks of the strange melancholy music that had come from his fingers last week. It wasn't like him. She has never known Mark make music like that. When he had placed his fingers on the keyboard, she had expected a simple old tune, a folk song, or an easy, familiar singsong chain of notes. That was the music that they knew together – songs that were sung in the fields and in public houses. She doesn't know where this new music has come from, but it seems to fit with the new melancholy in Mark's eyes, as if it was the very expression of all of that sadness. For a moment, listening to that music, she had felt like she hardly knew the man to whom she has been married for eight years. Is this what the war has done to him? Or is it still her fault?

Anna looks around the room. It is so very odd to think that Mark will be sleeping in this bed tonight, one floor above her own room. That he will be back in this house again. His house. As she has imagined him, willed him, for so long. She is not sure that she will manage to sleep.

Chapter Forty-Four

James, Flailcroft Farm, March 1921

James watches as Adam's fingers push into the earth. He scratches up a handful of soil and then closes his fingers around it as he stands. When his hand releases, the earth is compressed into a lozenge incised with marks of his grip. There is something elemental and essentially Adam in this action; the earth in his hand says everything about him, James thinks, but then he is shaking it away and only traces are left in the creases of his hand. The earth picks out the lines in his palm, as if it is foretelling his future. As James watches Adam examining his hand, he isn't sure whether the earth is reading him, or him it.

What meaning does he see as he brings his hand close to his face? Adam seems to be inhaling the smell of it, breathing the scent of that earth into his lungs, appraising and perhaps looking for something familiar? But it startles James then to see the flick of Adam's tongue. It is such an unexpected action that James wonders for a moment if his own eyes are playing tricks. There is something both ancient and animal about this behaviour; it seems like an action full of meaning, ceremony and old understanding, but also simply primeval. Adam rubs his hands together and blows the dust away.

'This is poor land,' he says.

James turns and sees that Anna Mason is watching them from the porch. She is dressed all in white today and James wonders whether the bridal lace has meaning too. Does she mean to draw Adam's earth-creased fingers to her?

'I can see your father doing the very same thing,' she says to Adam. 'He always shook his head too.'

As she walks towards them, her face breaks into a smile. She looks calmer today, James thinks, and more positive. She also looks statuesque in her white dress.

'You're like a hawthorn in blossom,' Adam says.

James looks at him. He had been so awkward on the journey over, so obviously reluctant to come here, and generally taciturn. Since he'd tried to hypnotize him again – and failed once more – Adam has been uncharacteristically sullen, and James has dreaded how he will react to Anna Mason today. But surely, in Adam's idiosyncratic terms, this is a compliment? When James glances at Anna now he sees hesitation but also hope in her eyes.

'It smells so sweet, but the thorns are sharp,' Adam adds.

They sit around the parlour table and for long moments it seems that there is nothing between them but the ticking of the clock. James watches Anna's fingers tap in time on the tablecloth and the beat of it takes him back to Lucy Vickers' fireside, to more tea and more awkward passing of time. The clock seems to gasp before it strikes the hour.

'Did you have a good journey?'

'Yes, thank you,' James replies.

'Will you have more tea, Mark?'

Anna sits very stiff and still. Adam holds his cup out for her to fill, and then she watches him as she blows at the surface of her own tea. The set of her face is serene, it is the composed face of a woman in a portrait, but her eyes say something else. Her dark hair is sleekly set in waves and her hand often strays there. She must have had her hair styled for Adam's visit, James supposes. He wonders what thoughts had passed behind her eyes as she looked into the hairdresser's mirror. What conversation was exchanged beneath the flick of scissors? What emotion, what memories, does she seek to stir in Adam?

'The tea is as you like it?'

'Yes.'

'Good. You always had me make it strong. I'm glad your tastes haven't changed.'

James watches her green eyes moving over Adam's face and wonders how much they see there that is familiar. Does she intimately know the lines around his eyes, the shadow of his eyelashes, the angle of his cheekbones and the curve of his lips? Are these details as familiar to her as her own reflection? And, if they are, how can she calmly sit there a table's width away, her hands feeling only the texture of the tablecloth?

'I may take a walk,' James says. He looks at his watch and finds himself suddenly conscious of his own body language; he feels like an actor playing a part and flagging the meaning of his stage exit. 'I'll probably be back in half an hour or so.'

He is both surprised, and yet not surprised, when Adam scrapes his chair back and reaches for his jacket. James hesitates briefly; when he looks to Anna's eyes for confirmation, there are not quite the signals there that he expected to see. For a second he is not sure that he is doing the right thing, the safe thing, the wanted thing, but isn't this the risk that he must take? Didn't she, after all, want to take this risk?

'You stay here, Adam. Keep Anna company. I only want a breath of air. I'll return shortly.'

James looks back as he crosses the yard and catches their faces looking out at him; two faces framed in separate windows; two individual portraits with no obvious link. What looks, what words, must now pass between them? How will they begin? Where will they end? As he walks down the hill, he finds himself repeatedly glancing at his watch. He leans against a tree, lights a cigarette and keeps an eye on the house. However much he might have reassured Shepherd, he isn't convinced that Adam won't bolt again.

He breathes deeply, drawing the smoke down into his lungs, but there's no ease to be had from it today. All morning his thoughts have been returning to Caitlin and the expression on her face as he'd carried her suitcase out to the car. James had been glad to lift the case and feel its lightness, but he worries what conversations Caitlin and her mother might now be having, and what decision she might presently be making.

She had hardly spoken as he'd driven her over to the station, but he could see that she was asking herself questions. In turn, he asked himself: why was it so difficult to communicate? He knows that she's right – that he ought to have talked to her more, but it works both ways. Doesn't it? If they could only find a way of speaking to one another, and share their fears and worries, wouldn't that bring them together again? Because aren't their fears and worries two sides of the same coin? What unites them also divides them, but, surely, there has to be a way past that?

Caitlin had planted a light, dry kiss on his cheek as they had parted, and then her eyes had looked past him. Her gaze wouldn't meet his, as if she was frightened of giving something away. James had wanted to wait with her for the train, but she'd told him that she'd rather he got on with his work.

'When will you be back?' he'd asked.

'Next week.'

'Which day?'

'I don't know.'

The open-endedness worries him. It might be irrational, but he fears that Caitlin hasn't yet made up her mind as to whether she'll come back at all. Could it really be so? His only reassurance is the lightness of her suitcase, but, right now, that doesn't feel like enough.

For so long she has been asking him to talk, and as they had stood there outside the station, he had so wanted to say it all, to tell her everything, to share and then get past this impasse. But she had turned her back and walked on down the platform. James throws his cigarette away and kicks at the tree trunk now. Why hadn't he followed her? Why had he let her walk away?

Anna

'He seems a kind man, your doctor,' she says, not sure where else to start.

'He means well,' Mark replies.

He looks down at his cup and then glances at the window. She can see that he would have liked to follow the doctor out. Is he frightened of being here on his own with her? Does he really think she's full of thorns? Aren't hawthorn berries poisonous too? His murmured words had passed over her at first, she almost hadn't caught them, but then that last word – *sharp* – had startled her, and she can't help but keep returning to the image now and wondering exactly what Mark meant by it.

'I think your doctor would like you to be happy.'

'And then his job would be done.'

'He seems to genuinely care about you.'

'He wants it to be tidy.'

'Tidy?' she asks.

'All fitted back together again.'

'To have you fitted back into your previous life, you mean? And wouldn't that make you happy?'

'Only if I'm fitted back into the right life.'

There had been that crackle of connection between them on his first visit, she's sure of it, still some of that electricity from the garden, but it feels as though that spark has died today and something else has replaced it. Is it reluctance she sees as Mark's eyes shift? Is it resentment?

'You grew up in this house,' she tries. Though she feels like crying, she has to smile and she has to try.

'Did I?' He says it as if he's humouring her.

'Your parents lived here all their lives and your grandparents before them. A whole lifetime in one place – I think the furthest they ever ventured was Halifax! You once told me that you'd always come back here, but you wanted to see something of the world first. I hope that one day you'll be able to tell me what you've seen.'

'I don't know what I've seen.'

'No, of course not. Not now. I understand that. But one day maybe you will.' She can't read the expression on his face. 'It will always be your house. It will always be yours to come home to whenever you are ready.'

He stands, turns his back and walks towards the window. It feels like a rejection. Is it that he remembers feeling rejected by her? Is that memory still there? Even if he can't yet put it into words, does that sensation still linger in him? Does he really think her poisonous? She remembers the noise of the piano lid slamming down last week, the stretching discordant echo of the notes through this room, and the shock and fear she had felt in that moment. Why does she feel that way again? She watches his back and listens to the slow ticking of the clock.

James

He knocks at the front door when he returns, because it seems the appropriate thing to do, and then Adam's face is there on the other side of the door. For a moment it feels like this is his home, that Adam is the right person to be at this door. There is something both natural and proprietorial about the way that he steps back and beckons James in.

'Are you well?'

'Of course.'

Anna is spinning away from the mirror as James steps back into the sitting room. It surprises him, when she turns, to see that she had reddened her lips – but then, James asks himself: why should he question that? It's obvious that she wants to look attractive for Adam, and, he supposes, only natural. There is something about the lipstick, though – about the act of her marking out her mouth like that – that seems so obvious. Is it too much? Is she pushing it too far and too fast? Could she really mean to seduce Adam? James realizes that he is staring at Anna's sticky lipsticked mouth. Her eyes meet his, answer his, and then she quickly looks away again as if she is embarrassed.

'I'm sorry.' He steps back. He feels as if he has intruded, as if by catching her eye he has crossed some line.

'No. Please. Don't apologize. It just makes me feel a bit braver. Stupid, isn't it?'

'Not at all. We all have our armour.' He lowers his voice, conscious that Adam is only in the next room. 'Have I come back too soon? I can give you more time, if you'd like?'

'Not soon enough.' She laughs, but it's clearly an effort. 'We've forgotten how to talk. Wouldn't you think, after all this time, we'd have so much to talk about? I think he's angry with me.'

'Angry?'

'I'm not sure that he wants to be here. Is this a bad idea?'

'He's been difficult for the past few days – confused, imagining things.' James realizes that he is trying not to look at her new, bright lips, but with their lowered voices, they must lean closer. It doesn't feel right to be whispering about Adam when he's only there, on the other side of the kitchen door. 'It's not been an easy past few weeks. It might all have been a bit too much for him.'

'I understand,' she replies. 'I think I'm feeling confused too. I'm trying too hard, aren't I?' The red cupid bow of her mouth is printed on the handkerchief as she pulls it away from her face.

Adam

Adam leans against the kitchen dresser. He can hear Haworth talking to the woman in the next room and is glad that he has taken his place. Her watching eyes make him conscious of his every movement; there is something heavy about her gaze on his skin, and he feels lighter now that the wall is between them. She had rushed at him with so many words, but he had no idea what to say in return. He doesn't know how to meet her expectations.

'Are you all right?' Haworth stands in the doorway.

'Does she expect me to sleep in her bed?'

He sees the question working behind Haworth's eyes, as if he hadn't considered the possibility until now. How can he not understand that that is what she wants?

'No! I'm sure she wouldn't.'

'Only, I don't think I'd feel comfortable with that.'

'No, of course not. And she wouldn't expect it of you.'

'Are you sure?'

'I won't let you be put in that position, and I'm certain that's not what she intended. I will talk to her, if it'll reassure you – but, Adam, you mustn't worry about that.'

He hears her voice afterwards in the next room, Haworth speaking and then her laughter. He knows that Haworth wouldn't laugh at him, but would she? Is she? When Adam had met her the first couple of times there had been moments when he thought he might know her, when he had wondered if he had shared things with her, even a bed, but then she talks of people and places that are fictions to him, and he knows who his real wife is now, even if she doesn't have a name.

Anna Mason recalls speeches she claims he has made. Puts opinions in his mouth. Talks of emotions that he is meant to have experienced. When he'd turned away from her, he'd seen her put her hands to her eyes and he had known that there was frustration and anger and sadness there. Maybe even fear. But what can he say to make that better? What can he give her to fill the space that has been left by a different man? He wonders if she is perhaps mad.

Anna

She turns away from the mirror, away from the questions and the alarm in her own eyes. Though she's been married to him for eight years, Anna isn't sure that she knows the man who was sitting across the table from her minutes earlier. She certainly had no intention of taking him back into the marital bed tonight. Had Mark really expected that? Had he really asked that question?

When she'd written the letter to the hospital, she'd tried to make it clear that nothing of that sort was on her mind; she'd merely asked to spend a little more time with him, to let him spend a little more time in this house. Yes, she had idly thought of what a breakthrough might mean (would he put out his hand towards hers? Would he look at her as though he recognized her?), but the possibility had seemed sufficiently remote that she hadn't allowed herself to linger there. They would have to start all over again, she knew it. But he doesn't seem to want to know her today. Is it the case that he simply doesn't want to come back?

She had seen the embarrassment on James Haworth's face when he had walked back into the room and asked the question on Mark's behalf. She also heard some sort of doubt in Haworth's voice. Did he think that she looked the sort of woman who might take a near-stranger into her bed? She wipes the last of the lipstick away.

Adam

'Am I allowed to leave the house?'

Adam watches Haworth consider the question. 'Leave?'

'I won't go far. I promise. I'll sit on the wall. I'll only be there. You can watch me through the window, if you want.'

He is glad when Haworth nods. This house feels full of traps and he doesn't want to get caught. It's full of eyes that constantly watch him, and other people's memories in which she means to entangle him. He walks across the lane and leans against the green stone wall. The air is cold and sweet and he draws it down into his lungs. He sees Haworth glance out and Adam gestures to him. Much as he might want to run, he knows that Haworth will get in trouble if he goes. Adam remembers what Caitlin had told him when they'd sat together on the rocks, and the look that had passed over her face as she'd talked about Haworth's nightmares. He decides that Haworth is in enough trouble already at the moment. Adam doesn't mean to make it worse for him.

He hoists himself onto the wall and the old damp stone stains the palms of his hands green. He looks back across at the ancient oak tree that stretches its branches between the house and the lane. Its boughs are twisted by centuries of winds, the lines in the bark whorled like the swirl of a gale, a static expression of the weather in this valley, the very essence of the place. With the beseeching stretch of its branches, it might well be an antique king turned into wood, or a wizard. As Adam looks up at the oak tree, and watches the stir of its broad branches, he has a glimmer of once-upon-a-time sky through the shifting boughs and the noise of a girl laughing. Is that memory, or imagination, he wonders. Is it remembrance or a mistake? He would linger on the image if he could, but it is there only fleetingly.

He takes his pencil and pad from his pocket. His book opens on the face of the woman who he saw in the wood this week. Haworth thinks that the woman Adam draws is Anna

Mason, but can he not see that those are not her eyes? That is not her mouth. The woman who he records in pencil line is one who he knows so well – he is certain that somewhere inside, just beyond his grasp, he knows everything about her – but her name has presently gone along with his own. He wishes that he could remember her name, more than he wants to recall his own. At the moment her name is all that matters.

Adam's pencil traces the texture of the tree's trunk, the twist of its branches and the dazzle of the leaves against the light. Its shape is the breath of the north wind and the history of one hundred winters. In following these lines, in putting this form down on paper, there is something there that feels like repetition to Adam, like an echo. Could that be memory? He doesn't know the woman who lives in this house, he is sure of that, but he is certain at this moment that he has drawn this tree before. He also knows the howl of that dog.

James

Anna is in the yard at the back, tugging out brambles. She pulls at the long barbed lengths and they whip back at her. James wants to help her, wants to make her task lighter, but also thinks that this display might be for Adam, that it is his assistance and company that she seeks. James wants Adam to help her, to answer the call of her actions, but he's on the other side of the house. Has he deliberately put the building between himself and her? Does he want that barrier?

'May I help you?' James steps out into the yard. 'Isn't there a poem about a fugitive nymph getting all tangled up in briars?'

'I wouldn't know, but I have no intention of letting them tangle me up. Blasted things. I hate them. They mean to ensnare me. No sooner do I pull them out, than they're back again, faster than ever. I think that they mean to fasten me into the house.'

'Now that sounds like something from Brothers Grimm.'

She is wearing a man's overcoat (her husband's coat?) over her white dress. That white lace looks misplaced now, James thinks; it seems to flag the fact that she didn't expect the day to work out this way. The inappropriateness of her clothes also makes it clear that this is a display more than a serious endeavour, but the person who is meant to respond to this display isn't here. James takes a rake and hooks it around the high loops that tangle into and out of the hedge. The arching length comes away when he steps back, but springs at him as it falls.

'Why were such things put upon the earth?' he asks. 'My mother used to make bramble gin and that's probably the only justification for their existence.'

The barbs tangle and pluck at James' sleeves and for a moment he is back fighting his way through the wire in Trônes Wood and Nathaniel is there with cuts across his palms. The memory makes him want to put his hands over his face. It also takes him back to Caitlin's face as she turned away from him on the station platform earlier this morning.

'Thorns,' Anna says. 'I didn't imagine that, did I? He did say that?'

'Yes,' James replies. 'But don't assume that it was directed at you. It's his manner. He can be a bit odd sometimes and his observations don't always join up. He's not nasty, though. He never has been. That's not what he's like.'

'No? You'd think I'd know my own husband, wouldn't you? But that did throw me.'

'I can understand,' says James, and he does, but he's not

certain that he entirely comprehends the meaning of the comment himself.

'I used to go blackberry picking with my sister,' Anna says. James hears her take a breath, make an effort, force herself to refocus. 'My grandmother would give us a basket to take, but we always had to stop before the end of September because she said that Lucifer plunged down to earth and relieved himself all over the blackberries on Michaelmas Day. Can you imagine telling that to a small child?' She grins at James over the collar of her coat and it is a relief to see her smile. 'We used to look for him hiding in the hedge. Mind you, I'm not sure now that they aren't the devil's work.'

The backs of her hands are criss-crossed with cuts and there are thorns caught in her white lace cuffs. Blood beads on her thumb. He watches as she puts it to her mouth.

'Where is Mark?' she asks.

'He's sitting on the wall at the front.' James realizes that she must be short-sighted. Her eyes are hesitant until she takes a step closer to him. 'He's looking at the trees. He says that he wants to draw the oak tree.'

She nods. James sees that she would rather have Adam acting than looking, rather have him here, on this side of the building, joining her in her task. This isn't how she wanted this to work out. 'His father used to curse the drawing, you know. He called it idling, shirking work, and wasn't shy of telling him that. Mark would work when he had to, though. It's not that he didn't know how. He would graft until his shirt stuck to his back. I don't know how to begin to tell him that there's no longer any work to do.'

'In time,' James replies.

'That seems to be the answer to everything, doesn't it?'

She forks the brambles into a pile. James can see how they

have plucked at her white skirt. There is something sad about that, and he pities her, and wishes that Adam were here in his place.

'You don't look like a woman who knows how to plough. Certainly not in that dress.'

'Did I ever claim proficiency? Is that a comment on my bramble-murdering efficiency?'

He smiles. 'I wouldn't dare comment.'

'You know, it's not what I expected a lunatic asylum to be like,' she says, as she leans on the pitchfork. She draws a line in the dirt with the toe of her boot.

'A lunatic asylum? You mean Fellside? No, it's not that. It's not at all like that.' He wants her to understand. It's important she understands that's not what Adam is. 'We try to offer a place where men can rest and have support, if they want it, but no one is obliged to be there. Adam isn't a danger to himself or to anyone else. He's not been committed or confined. He's only there because we want to help him and he wants to help himself. We offer recuperation and re-education. Doctor Shepherd believes in the healing power of conversation and occupation – work and interest, that is – and of giving the men space. That more than anything: room to breathe and healing quietness.'

'But he is a lunatic now, isn't he? I mean he's still my husband, he looks out through my husband's eyes and speaks through his mouth, but it's as if someone else is living inside him. From a distance I recognize him, but up close, I don't know him at all.'

'He's still the person he once was. I wouldn't say there's any damage to his subconscious mind; I'd suggest that his character today is largely what it always has been, he's fundamentally the same person, with the same habits and opinions and passions.' As he looks at Anna, James wishes that he could see more agreement in her eyes. 'But we're only just starting to understand what shock and fear and exhaustion can do to a man's mind. Our understanding is that he suffered a trauma at some point, and that has caused parts of his brain to wilfully shut down – a survival mechanism, if you will. Parts of it are blocked, shut off, for his own protection, but it doesn't mean that he's not substantially the same man that he was before the war, and that his memory won't come back. The same experience can temporarily blind men, deafen them, cause them to forget how to speak, how to walk, how to control their muscles, but it comes back with time, just as Adam's recall probably will. There's no medicine to fix it, there's no quick solution, but I do believe that with time we can make great progress.'

'A trauma? I could understand how he might need to protect himself from an explosion, or something frightening, or shocking, but does he need to protect himself from me, from our marriage, from his home? Do you know what happened to him?'

'No. He hasn't spoken about it yet, and in all likelihood he has no memory of it. That was the cut-off point. We've tried hypnosis a couple of times, and it's often the case that we can dig deeper using this therapy, that a different part of the man's conscious will find expression, but we haven't had a breakthrough with Adam yet.'

'Hypnotism? Like a parlour game?'

'Like a scientific procedure. It's one of the oldest cures in the world, but one that we employ with great care and consideration. Please don't think that hypnotism is something we resort to lightly.'

'I'm sorry. I didn't mean to belittle your work. Mark doesn't object to being hypnotized?'

'A patient can't be hypnotized against their will. It's impossible. They have to participate materially in the process, apply the power of their concentration, give themselves over to it.' James hesitates. The first time, it was unsuccessful because Adam didn't engage sufficiently, he'd resisted, but the second time he wanted it too much. 'All success in these cases tends to be down to the willpower of the patient.'

'You mean he doesn't want to remember?'

'There are things that he wants to remember and others that he's evidently keen to forget.' James thinks that it wouldn't be fair to Anna to disclose the urgency with which Adam has recently wanted to remember the name of the woman in the wood. 'That's the singular thing about him: men in his situation are normally troubled by their inability to remember, it needles at them, it upsets them, but for the past couple of years Adam's seemed pretty well settled, really quite composed in the here and now, and the gaps in his past haven't nagged at him. Other amnesiacs that I've treated have felt more desire to find a way out.'

'You have treated others, then?'

'Yes, and seen them make a full recovery.'

'I'm sorry. I didn't mean to question your ability or experience. It's just that I was expecting someone with rather more grey hairs on his head.'

'We are taking care of him. Please be reassured of that. We do mean the best for him and I believe that we'll get there. We need to be patient, though. I don't want to push him.'

'I can tell you care about him. I can see it all over your face and I'm glad of that. He's lucky to have you and I'm grateful for it.'

James watches as she strikes a match and the brambles start to smoulder. Her short-sightedness sometimes gives her a misplaced intensity, he thinks. 'Adam's generally not unhappy as he is,' he says. 'He lives very much in the present tense and he's not troubled here, but I'd like him to have more, to be able to live more fully. I'm also very conscious that he has possibly left a gap in a family somewhere. For his sake, and their sake, I'd like to get to the point where we know his real name.'

'Mark Mason,' she replies.

Adam

He follows the sound. The howling is coming from the barn. As Adam stands with his ear pressed to the door, he watches Haworth talking with the woman. She forks at a fire and the smell of burning leaves drifts. Adam can't make out their words, but she doesn't look happy. Why can't she see that he's not the person who can take her unhappiness away? Her face changes as he walks towards her, a change as fundamental as a shift in the weather, and she smiles for him. It seems to be so easy to make her smile, she so obviously wants it to be that way, but it's another woman's face that Adam wants to see smiling.

James

'Can I let her out of the barn?' Adam asks.

Anna's eyes connect with James'. The look in her eyes suggests that she expects him to see significance in this. 'Yes.'

She places the bunch of keys in Adam's hand. Some of them are brown with age and some so big that they might well be the keys to a castle. They watch as Adam crosses the yard and, without hesitation, puts the right key in the barn door. James feels the touch of Anna's hand on his arm. 'Didn't I tell you?'

When the collie bursts out, it barks in circles around Adam. For a moment, James fears that it will attack him, but then Adam is sinking to his knees and rubbing his face against the dog's chest.

'Meg knows him,' Anna says. 'They don't forget, do they? She was always Mark's dog. He had her from a puppy. She still is his dog, isn't she? You can see that, can't you?'

As James crosses the yard he sees the tears on Adam's face and he realizes that he's never witnessed him crying before. Surely this is a breakthrough, then? When he looks up at James there is such intense joy and pain on his face.

'I think you've made a friend,' James says, but his words feel entirely inadequate. It must be more than that. Could it really be that there is a connection here?

Adam wipes his eyes on his sleeve and laughs then as the dog licks his face. 'She remembers me, doesn't she?'

Chapter Forty-Five

James, Flailcroft Farm, March 1921

The firelight flickers across the ceiling and they listen to the creak of Adam's feet on the floor above.

'You said he seemed reluctant to talk when I left you alone.'

Anna laughs as she turns and hands him the glass of whisky. 'Reluctant? It was more than reluctance! But then, perhaps I talked too much. Perhaps I made a bad start. I'm afraid that I couldn't stop talking. It was nerves, really. It all flooded out. I was so desperate to make conversation, to have him respond, but it was all one-sided. I couldn't tell if he was irritated or frightened of me. He walked away.'

'He left the room?'

'No, he just turned his back on me.' She curls her feet up under her on the armchair and pulls her cardigan over her shoulders. 'He stood by the window waiting for you to come back. It was like he didn't want to look at me. Is he scared of me, do you think? Is he angry? Has he said anything to you?'

'He seemed calm when I got back.'

'Did he? Would you say so? And that's just it! I can't read him. I'm having to guess all the time. Sometimes he barely seems to be in the same room as me. I feel like I'm a ghost in my own home, and now he's come back and just can't see me.

Or perhaps he doesn't want to see me? Do you understand? It's as if the shutters have come down and he's not letting anyone in.'

'It's self-protection to a degree,' James replies. 'He's wary. You must remember that he's had very little contact with other people for the past couple of years. He's unsure of himself, of his own boundaries, and of other people. It's difficult for him to know who to trust and how to be with people. But with time and patience and familiarity, I think that will change.'

'Will it? He was always an emotional man, you know; he could be nervous, moody, he reacted strongly to things, too strongly sometimes, but I can't read his moods now. We don't speak the same language any longer and I've no idea what's coming next. He looks like the man I married, but he's not the same.'

'As I said, you'll have to give it time.'

'Time again? So you keep on saying.' Adam's footsteps cross the ceiling and she looks up. 'He sounds like a trapped animal, doesn't he?'

Adam

The bedroom is up in the eaves and she has told him that it is where her husband's parents slept. There are photographs of these people all around the walls of this room. Has she put them in here to look at him? To find him out? Does she mean to force him to look at them? Adam is used to living in a room where he is surrounded by his own reflection, but none of these faces seem familiar. As he holds the candle out towards them, christenings and weddings and family picnics flicker. There is no glimmer of memory, though.

Adam walks around the room and he can hear them talking downstairs. The words are lost within the body of the house, he can't quite make them out, but he can pick out their tone and rhythm, and it is a call and reply. She laughs sometimes. Haworth sounds tired. Adam also hears the dog howling in the barn.

He opens the window and leans out. The night air is cool and sweet and scented with wood smoke. He looks down, but there is only darkness below. Is it too high to climb out? He has no sense of how far below the ground might be. He tests his muscles on the window sash, but the wood shifts under his weight. Will it hold him? Can he climb out and jump? He says the dog's name into the darkness and immediately the howling stops. He wishes that he could bring her to his bed.

James

'He's stopped pacing,' Anna says. The candle flame stretches and stirs the shadows around the ceiling. 'Do you think he'll sleep?'

'Probably. He used to have nightmares when he first came to Fellside, but he sleeps like a newborn baby these days. I think he's buried all the fragments of memory that provoked the nightmares fairly deeply. I wish I could sleep like him.'

'Are some memories buried deeper than others?' she asks.

'Sorry, I was over-simplifying. But he does seem to have tidily compartmentalized the memories that frighten him. It's impressive really. Quite remarkable. It's as though he's built high walls around his fears. But, unfortunately, that stops us getting at the parts that could help him too.'

'Like his name?'

'Precisely.'

'Perhaps, if he sleeps soundly, it's better that he does forget?'

'That's not fair on you, though, is it? To his family, I mean. To the future that he's presently denying himself.'

'Thank you for that. I have to say, you don't look like someone who sleeps well.' Her eyes meet with his and then she looks away. 'Forgive me. That's personal, isn't it? I shouldn't have said that.'

James smiles and shakes his head. Is it that apparent? 'No, you're right.'

'Will you be okay on the sofa?'

It is perfectly peaceful in this room. It smells of wood smoke. White logs smoulder and sigh on the fire and she has brought him piles of blankets and pillows. 'It's comfortable in here, thank you. You've been very hospitable.'

It is the first night that he has spent away from Fellside since he came back from France. The first night he has spent away from Caitlin. James thinks of her light kiss on his cheek and then her face turning away. He had kept glancing at her as he drove her to the station and had seen the tiredness showing around her eyes. The sleepless nights are taking their toll on her and he knows that her mother will see that too. What are they saying to one another this evening? Will Caitlin tell her mother everything? And what will she advise in reply? He imagines Caitlin back in her childhood bedroom and wonders if she will sleep tonight.

James doesn't think that he could sleep, but then he doesn't mean to, anyway. As he drove here, he decided that he'd keep himself awake tonight; he would read a book and smoke; he would smoke both packets of cigarettes if he had to; he wouldn't let the nightmares come to him here. He hates that Caitlin has seen him at his worst and he certainly can't let a relative stranger see him that way; not because of pride but because he feels so entirely vulnerable when he wakes with the nightmares, so totally lacking in control. What must Caitlin think of him? Has she told her mother about that? He must do something to break this cycle. The thought that Caitlin might be running out of patience scares him more than the nightmares.

'I'm glad that someone, at least, is comfortable,' Anna says. 'Mark was frightened that he'd be expected to sleep in the marital bed, wasn't he?' She puts her hands through her hair and all the set waves fall out. 'Oh God, it's hardly a good start, is it? It's hardly flattering that he was so obviously horrified at the prospect!'

James takes a mouthful of whisky. 'He hasn't known much female company for the past three years. You must remember that. The only woman he talks to with any regularity is my wife.'

'I'm sorry.' Anna brings her hands together in a prayer motion, but then clasps them in front of her smile. She arranges her hands like a woman in a portrait, James thinks. 'That was a silly thing to have said, wasn't it? Forgive me. No, of course, I never expected it. I only hoped that spending a little more time here, a little more time with me, might help him to remember some of the good memories from our past together. I see now that I might have been overly optimistic.'

'You might have to get to know each other all over again.'

'Mingling hands and stealing glances? What a pair we are. Poor Doctor Haworth, you must feel like a chaperone!'

He laughs. 'I've had more arduous tasks.'

'He has conversations with your wife, you say?'

'Yes. They get along. They always have. Caitlin is good at talking to people. She just has that instinctively; she always seems to come in at the right level, if you know what I mean? Adam's relaxed in Caitlin's company, so he talks quite fluidly with her. We live in the same house, so our lives are all tangled up together.'

Anna refills her glass and raises an eyebrow at him. 'In that place? Your poor wife lives in the lunatic asylum? How awful for her.'

He is glad to see the humour in Anna's eyes now, to see her mocking her own earlier misunderstanding. She has fine eyes, he considers, and at some point has studied how to use them to their best advantage, but they're clouding again now.

'You talked about a trauma earlier,' she says. 'You said Mark could have experienced something that knocked him out of kilter.'

'Yes, that's what we suspect.'

'Something happened to him in France, you believe?'

'He was still in military uniform when he was arrested; we don't think he'd been back in this country for long, so it's the obvious conclusion.'

She nods. 'I read about that. He was in Durham Cathedral, wasn't he?'

'Yes.'

'We were there once.' Anna looks down and swirls the whisky around her glass. James wonders what memories she sees there. 'After we were married, we had a week with my cousin up in Craster. It rained all the time. We had filthy weather, a real washout of a week, but we still walked for hours along the coast. We also went down to Durham on the train.'

'So Mark knew Durham?' He recalls Adam on the train, how he had stood up as the cathedral slipped from sight, how he had put his hands to the glass. They'd suspected that there must be some connection, some reason why he'd gone there in particular, but haven't yet been able to pin it down.

'Yes. We went to the cathedral. He loved the stillness and said it was full of history. I wanted to go to the market, I wanted to look around the town, but I couldn't get him out of the cathedral.'

'That's interesting.'

'Do you think he remembered that in some way? That there was some memory there? That it might have been a place of sanctuary?'

He looks at her long fingers against the whiteness of her dress and wonders if her husband fell in love with her hands. He imagines Mark Mason first seeing them, their hands linked in the rain. Adam Galilee's pencil putting their lines on paper. Adam's skin under the touch of her fingers. Only they are now all carelessly criss-crossed with scratches.

'There's a possibility.'

She nods. She drains her glass. He sees her mouth hesitate before she speaks again. There is indecision in the corners of her lips. Uncertainty flicks in her eyelashes, and her mouth starts to form words that her eyes don't yet sanction. 'There's another thing that I should tell you. When Mark left, in 1915, things were difficult between us. He didn't have to go. He was a farmer, you see? Reserved occupation and all of that; he wouldn't have been conscripted, but he chose to go, and some of that was my fault.'

James hears her sigh. She looks up. Her long, fine fingers drum on her empty glass as she continues. 'We'd had problems in our marriage. It hadn't all been easy. Mark inherited his father's debts along with the farm and he had to work hard to get out of that. We had a difficult year, but we were just getting straight, finally feeling that we might have a future to look forward to, when it all went wrong. There was a nasty lie put about and Mark heard it. The village has some sharp tongues in it, and they never let the truth get in the way of a good story. What I mean to say is, Mark heard a rumour that I'd been seeing someone else. It wasn't true. Obviously, it wasn't true! There was nothing to it. It was absolute nonsense. But we argued, he was upset, and that was when he went. Mark was emotional, he always was hot-headed, but afterwards I felt like I'd pushed him away, like it was my fault. Could that have done something to his state of mind? He was so attached to this land and I've always felt that leaving it must have been a big wrench. I mean a bigger loss than leaving me. It must have hurt him. Could that have damaged him in some way? Would you call that a trauma?'

'I don't know.' James looks into his glass. 'But I don't think you should link that with his current condition. It's most likely that Adam suffered a traumatic event while he was in uniform, that he went through something powerful and profoundly disturbing during the period he was overseas. Naturally, his personality and past experience would play a part in how he processed that event, but I don't think you should wind things back and seek out a reason to blame yourself.'

'Sometimes it's difficult not to blame yourself.'

'It is,' he says. 'I know.'

'Only, I wondered today: when he looked at me so coldly, when there seemed to be animosity there, could he remember that? Even if he can't recall the detail, can't bring back the precise whys and wherefores, could that *feeling* still be there? Is he still angry with me?'

'I can't say with certainty, but I don't sense that. He isn't a man who seems to carry any anger around and I didn't pick that up today.'

'Do you believe me?' she asks him, as she shares the last of the bottle out between them. Tears mat her eyelashes as she leans towards him. 'Do you believe that I'm telling the truth, that he is my husband?'

James considers. 'Yes,' he replies.

Chapter Forty-Six

Adam, Fellside House, March 1921

His seedlings are coming on under the cold frames. Three days ago he had felt such pleasure and optimism to see those tiny shoots looping up out of the earth, feeling all the promise that came with that. But today there are so many questions in Adam's head and he doesn't know what the spring will bring. He straightens and looks down the garden. He is restoring its lines, the box hedging and the square raised beds, bringing its structure back, but all the parallel paths that he has marked out look uncertain this morning.

He had walked up into the wood at dawn, hoping that he might see her again, because how else could he contact her? Without a name, all he has is chance and hope. He is so certain that she is real, that he hasn't imagined her, that he knows her face and her touch and her breath, but could it just be hope? Could it really just be wishful thinking? He knows that Haworth believes she exists only in his head and what can he say to prove him wrong? What proof does he have? His certainty had been so solid until yesterday, but then he had known the dog too, and it knew him, so what does that mean?

The crows had been calling as he walked through the wood and he had thought about their voices in the night,

Haworth and Anna Mason. He had heard them down below, the twinned rhythms of their voices all through the night. Their indistinguishable words were there, tantalizingly out of reach, every time he awoke, so that he felt surrounded by their questioning voices and had to pull the blanket over his head. He didn't want to hear them, didn't want to make out their words, but while they were there, he couldn't not listen.

When the dawn light had crept around the curtains, he had looked at the bedside clock. Had they talked all through the night? He had put the blanket around his shoulders and placed his bare feet lightly on the linoleum, knowing now where the boards gave and where they sighed. From the top of the stairs he could hear Haworth's voice saying Caitlin's name. Adam wasn't sure that Caitlin would want him to talk about her here, with this woman they hardly knew. He had crept back to the warmth of the bed again and wondered what this meant.

At Fellside, he can sometimes hear Haworth talking to Caitlin through the floors and the walls. He knows the vibration, the tone and rhythm of the duet of their voices, whether soft or raised, but Haworth had sounded different when he talked with Anna Mason. There was more rise and fall to his voice. He laughed more. It is not the voice that he speaks to Adam in either.

He had glanced over towards the house as he had picked his way back down the bank this morning and noticed that Caitlin's face wasn't there in the window. Is that what Haworth had to tell the other woman? That Caitlin would be going away? Adam hopes that she will come back and that Haworth does not mean to swap her for Anna Mason. He had pocketed a pink snail shell, a bronze curlicue of fern frond and a perfectly mathematical pine cone to leave for Caitlin for when she gets back.

When he had come down from the room yesterday morning, Haworth had been sitting with his head in his hands in Anna Mason's parlour, and he hadn't heard Adam cross the hall. He knew that she was up too because he'd heard the whistle of the kettle, but he was glad to find nothing more than her lipstick mark on a cup in the kitchen. Adam had taken the keys from the hook and held his breath as he pulled the door closed behind him.

The morning air was sharp and clean and the wet grass licked at his bare feet as he crossed to the barn. He heard the dog's chain shift inside, and turned the key as noiselessly as he was able, so that he didn't alarm her. He saw her get to her feet as he slipped around the door and locked it behind him. The rising sun pushed through the cracks in the blackness of the barn and it sparkled with movement in the air. The darkness smelled of hay and dog, and he had laid down beside her and curled into her back and listened to the resuming sighs of her sleep.

He digs the compost through now and imagines the lines of beets and cabbages and chard and carrots that he means to put in this spring. The climbing roses are sending out vigorous new shoots and he has planned where to put the rosemary and salvias, the hollyhocks, the phloxes and delphiniums. It all takes form in his imagination, takes shape; in his mind's eye the roses climb and wind and burst into scented blossom; it is orderly and beautiful and functional, and once more as it should be. But then he imagines a dog bounding between the borders and sniffing its way along the paths. What does that mean? If the dog is real – and if he genuinely has a connection with it – where does that place him? Does he get to have the future that he is planning here? Does he still get to walk in the woods and to hope that he might meet her there?

'I don't know whether to let her go with you,' Anna Mason had said as they readied to leave. She had looked at Adam and he had nodded; he didn't want to let go of the dog's collar, but Haworth had shaken his head. He had looked at Adam and told him that he was crying. Adam was surprised to put his hand to his face and find that Haworth was right. She would have let the dog go, Adam could see. He didn't understand why Haworth wouldn't agree to it.

'You will come back here again, won't you?' she said to him. Adam heard the appeal in her voice and didn't know how to answer. It didn't seem kind to say that he would come back for the dog.

Adam had shaken her hand as they left, and she had looked so hesitantly at her hand in his that he had wondered if that was right. Did she want more? Had he done the wrong thing? She had stepped back, as if she didn't know what to do next. Haworth had shaken her hand too, but she had smiled at him, as if he had judged the matter correctly. Had Anna Mason expected Adam to kiss her? Was he meant to embrace her? Was he meant to cry for her too? He had looked over his shoulder as the car pulled away and seen her standing on the lane with her hand raised. She stood like that, unmoving, until the curve of the hills drew a curtain across her.

Adam had expected that the journey back to Fellside would be full of questions, but it wasn't. He could see the fatigue around Haworth's eyes and something else there as well. Adam wasn't sure what that look was.

'You think it's her, don't you?' he had said to Haworth in the car. 'You think she's the one who is telling the truth.'

'We have to investigate them all,' Haworth replied. He glanced from the road to Adam. 'We have to look at all of their claims.'

'Will I have to sleep in all three houses?'

'No. I don't think so. It's just what Anna wanted. She thought it might help you.'

'Do you think she's the right one because of the dog?'

'There are other things too, but your response was spontaneous and strong, wasn't it?'

Adam hadn't known what to reply to that, worried about what his words might unintentionally imply, what traps they might spring.

'And when you've looked at all their claims, when you've investigated them all, what will happen then?'

'What do you want to happen?' Haworth had asked.

He considers now as he looks down the garden. He wants the companionship of the dog and to be able to lie at the side of the woman in the wood. But these are two separate lives and two different futures, and he can't stay here and have them both. Suddenly all the paths in the garden look like junctions.

He had so wanted to find the woman in the wood this morning. He wanted to speak with her and tell her that she had to say her name. He needs to tell her that, if she doesn't speak now, the others will come and claim him. It will happen because they'll trip him up and trap him. He needs her to speak up. She needs to speak now. She has to say her name.

But she hadn't been there in the wood this morning and he doesn't know if he will ever see her again. The walls of the garden are both a sanctuary and a prison now, and he doesn't know whether to lock himself in or to flee from it. Adam's hands tighten around the spade. He doesn't know quite what it is that makes him throw it at the glasshouse. The noise of the breaking glass is like the shock of a memory returning.

Chapter Forty-Seven

James, Fellside House, March 1921

'You're drawing her?'

Adam's pencil is moving quickly, as though he's intent on getting the image down before he forgets it. James sees that he has drawn the lines of a woman's figure, her face, dark hair, pale eyes and her hands over and over again. James looks at the drawings and thinks about watching Anna Mason the night before last. Surely it's her? And yet Adam so vehemently denies it. Is there a link between this denial and how cold Adam had been with her? Is he making himself reject her? Or could it really only be a likeness? James watches and observes that Adam is drawing both with urgency and care. These drawings are a love poem, James thinks.

'Are you drawing her because you want to remember her?'

'Yes.'

'Would you like to see her again?'

'Of course.'

'It's not her then, is it? I mean, it's not Anna Mason.'

'No. I've told you that already. It's the woman in the wood. I looked for her this morning, but she wasn't there.' His eyes don't lift from the page. It is like a meditation.

'The fairy?'

Adam looks up at him then. His pencil stops and he examines James' face. Does he think that James is mocking him? He can see that this is no laughing matter to Adam.

'Are you certain that you haven't imagined her? Could you perhaps have fallen asleep and dreamed that you'd seen her?'

'She's not a fucking daydream!'

Adam has never shouted before. He has never sworn.

'Adam, why does this make you feel angry?'

'Will you stop calling me Adam. I'm not called Adam. You know that's not my name.'

'I'm sorry. Would you take me to where you saw her?'

'He's drawing his fairy.'

'He hasn't seen her again?' Shepherd looks up.

'No, but not for want of trying.'

'Are you still convinced that it's all in his head?'

'I'm not sure,' James replies. 'There's definitely a likeness between the sketches and Anna Mason's face, but he so determinedly refuses it. He looks almost insulted when I say it, and that's prompted me to reconsider. I've been looking through his drawings this morning and I do start to wonder if I've willed myself to see a match.'

It would be so convenient if it was a perfect match, but having studied Adam's sketches closely, James has to concede that there are differences. The eyes of the woman in the drawings are paler and the cheekbones stronger. It's not the same mouth.

'Does this mean you're starting to believe in fairies?'

'Oh, for it to be that simple! I asked him to take me up into the wood to where he says he saw her last week.'

James hadn't been that far into the wood before. Amongst the dense trees, it was nighttime again. Adam had seemed entirely in his element there, but stepping over the fallen branches had taken James back to places he didn't mean to go.

'I take it there was no evidence that anyone had been up there?'

'Some slightly trampled grass in a clearing – he pointed at it and said that was where they'd laid down together – but I'd hardly call it conclusive evidence. It's six days ago, so it could have been animals, or, equally, Adam might have been there on his own. He could have fallen asleep and dreamed her.'

'Laid down together?' Shepherd raises an eyebrow and a smile. 'Right. I didn't know that part. He's shown no evidence of any sexual attraction to the other women, though, has he?'

'Absolutely none. I'd come to the conclusion that that part of him was shut down too. Anna Mason was obviously trying for him.' James recalls her lipstick smile in the mirror and her white fingers tapping on the glass. 'She was clearly making efforts, and she's an attractive woman, but it evidently wasn't doing anything for him. He was horrified by the thought that he might have to sleep in her bed. I felt sorry for her, if I'm honest.'

'He clearly only goes for the elvish folk.'

'Alan!' James smiles. 'We mustn't make fun of him. I made light of it with him earlier and he took offence. It's not like Adam to get angry. That's what made me hesitate.'

'Did Adam give you the impression that something occurred between him and his fairy queen? Did they just lie there amongst the daisies and hold hands, or was this sylvan love match consummated?'

James laughs. 'Mercy! You don't put a question like that to Adam! Can you imagine that he'd answer if I did ask?'

'No, you're right. But did he talk to this woman prior to their flattening the grass together? Do we know any more about her?'

'That was why he wanted to be hypnotized – he says she won't tell him anything. He asked her name, but she wouldn't say it. He called her his one-and-only-always wife this morning; only he doesn't know her name.'

'A somewhat unconventional relationship! I'm sorry that I wasn't here when he wanted to be hypnotized – not that I'd have been any more successful than you. It sounds as though he'd got himself rather worked up. Do you think he'd agree to it again?'

'I suspect the moment has passed.'

'This one-and-only-wife business does seem to rather nail the lid over our efforts, doesn't it?'

James watches Shepherd stoking the fire. The white embers collapse when he puts another log on. With the scent of it he is back in that room, the smell of whisky on her breath and the difficult intensity of that conversation.

'I don't know. Mason's case still nags at me. It wasn't so much how Adam acted there, but her manner towards him. Of all of the claimants her story is the most complete. It's not all convenient, hers evidently wasn't the most perfect of marriages, but in a way that adds to the plausibility of her claim. And it's the way that she acts towards him and looks at him.'

Was it wrong, James asks himself, that he had briefly wished that she would turn her eyes on him the same way that she looked at Adam? Had he made that too obvious to her? Had he confessed too much?

'But he didn't return those looks?'

'No, almost pointedly so. At times it seemed like he felt some antagonism, some resentment, towards her – and that would fit with her side of the story.'

'I suppose we have to consider the possibility that he might not want to go back to the life he had before. In those circumstances – if it all adds up, but he doesn't want it – we need to decide what we must do. Personally, I don't feel it would be right to force him into anything.'

'And her rights?'

'It's sad if it's true,' Shepherd reflects, 'but his wishes have to be our first priority.'

'Of course.'

James listens to the noise of a car on the drive, but it turns, and leaves again, and there's no sound of the front door opening. Last night, on the telephone, Caitlin had said that she'd come back today, only he'd heard such a lack of resolution in her voice. Her tone had been so flat. He hadn't been convinced that she really wanted to return at all. He is not sure what he will do if she doesn't come back.

'You said the dog also seemed to know him?' Shepherd asks.

'And Adam acted as if he knew it.'

'But dogs recognize people who like dogs.'

'It didn't like me! It showed me its teeth. But it's more than that – it's the way that Adam responded to it. He sobbed. And then, after he'd met the dog, he wouldn't be parted from it. He went and slept in the barn with it. I think it rather offended Anna that he'd curl up with the dog but he had such an obvious fear of her bed. He cried again when we left. He wanted to bring the dog back here with him and I think she would have let him.'

'Perhaps invite her and the dog back here again? I have to say that I'd like to see it for myself, and if he wants to keep the dog here, he can have it. It might help.'

'You wouldn't mind?'

'No, of course not – and I don't think it would upset anyone else.'

'I think it would make Adam happy.'

'Good.' Shepherd screws the top onto his pen as though the matter is settled. 'Miss Vickers has written again. It's the second letter this week. Do you think she supposes that she can batter us into submission by means of the postal service? Does she really imagine that if she writes regularly enough, we'll just shrug and dispatch Adam by return post? The poor girl must be spending all her free time writing letters. Any surplus income she has must go on stamps and stationery.'

'Does she mention the photograph of her brother's wife?'

'She says that Adam must keep it. She seems rather pleased that he wanted it. I suppose that's not surprising, though, is it? She probably chalks it up as a small victory.'

'I'm sure. Having seen him interacting with Mason, I can't help but feel that she's the claimant with the strongest case, but then he's put that photograph of Phoebe Vickers on his dressing table. I can't understand that. He flatly denies that he's Ellis Vickers, so why would he want to keep a photograph of the man's dead wife? Why would he want to look at it next to his own reflection?'

'Maybe he's not as certain as he makes out?'

James shakes his head. 'Could it be? You know, when we talked about the young woman dying, he looked genuinely moved.'

'Second-hand sensitivity? Sometimes Adam seems slightly lacking in empathy, but on other occasions those instincts are finely tuned, aren't they? Then again, he might regard the photograph as a curiosity, another interesting object to place between his fossils and flints. Or he could simply like her face?'

'It would make our lives easier if he was a bit more consistent, wouldn't it?'

'It would.' Shepherd sighs as he passes James a second

envelope. 'This simplifies things somewhat, though. It was in the post this morning too.'

James looks at the envelope. He turns it in his hands. 'From the war graves people?' For a minute, he thinks that it might be news of Nathaniel.

'Yes. It takes one hat out of the ring.'

Chapter Forty-Eight

James, Churchyard Cottage, April 1921

'You've had the letter already?' James asks. She had it in her hands when she came to the door. 'I'm sorry. I didn't realize. I hoped that I'd perhaps be able to tell you face to face.'

The envelope sits on the tabletop in between them now. Celia Dakers hasn't taken her eyes from it since James sat down. 'It came ten days ago,' she says. 'Of course, I knew what it was when it arrived, but I wasn't prepared to believe it.'

'Because you were certain he was still alive?'

'Because you brought him here eight weeks ago. Because he was out there in the garden. Because he was there lying on his own bed.'

'And now?' James thinks that she looks ten years older than the woman he met eight weeks ago. 'Do you believe it now?'

'Well, I have to believe it, don't I? It wasn't just what they told me in the letter, that it's there in black and white, it was the parcel that came with it. I knew then, when I held the things inside, that it was Robert after all, that I had lost him.'

'I am sorry,' James says. 'I did so want you to be right. I hoped that Adam might be your Robert.'

'I know that.' It's the first time that her eyes have met his today. 'I saw it on your face and I'm grateful for it.'

'They told you there will be a gravestone now?'

'Yes, and I'm allowed to choose an epitaph. I think I'll go there later in the year. I'd like to see his grave, to say goodbye, and to know for absolutely sure.'

James pictures Nathaniel's name on a grave. Would he know for absolutely sure, then? Would it help Caitlin to have that? Would it make her happier? Is she back at Fellside yet?

'You said they were able to send you some of Robert's personal effects?'

'Yes. Would you like to see?'

James remembers her producing a photograph from the dresser only a few weeks ago and the absolute certainty in her voice. Today, though, it is a wooden box. He thinks about the draughtsman's box that was also meant to link to Adam. Has it all been wishful thinking? So many promising boxes that are ultimately empty?

Inside the box there's a parcel, James sees, wrapped in linen cloth – the sort of cloth that is used to make a shroud, he thinks. Celia Dakers' hands tremble as she unwraps the fabric, and James reflects that it is difficult to comprehend the heights and depths of emotion that she must have experienced when this parcel arrived ten days ago. The treasures inside are humble and oddly familiar to James; they might well be his own once-upon-a-time possessions. Or Nathaniel's. The string on the dog tag is stiffly fused into the twists that it has held since Robert Dakers fell five years ago. The pay-book is stained with the colours of that earth, and warped with the damp of five winters. The leather wallet is stiff and mildewed and James thinks that it resembles something recovered from an archaeological dig; it might well be Viking or Roman. But Celia's fingers show him the tooled initials, and when she opens it their photograph is there inside. Five years have eaten at the image's edges and shadowed their faces, but James can still make them out. They are standing under the camellia tree in the garden of this house – a younger version of the woman across the table from him now and a boy who, for a moment, could have been Adam.

'He carried it with him,' she says. 'He had it with him when he died. I'm lucky to have it back, aren't I?'

'You are,' James agrees. With the smell of these objects that have been dug out from the earth, along with Robert Dakers' body, James is momentarily back in that place again, that familiar clay caking his own body and Nathaniel's up-close eyes asking too many questions. It is a force of effort to blink the memory away. Could that earth one day give Nathaniel back too?

'You sent Adam some of Robert's clothes,' he says. 'Would you like me to return them?'

It momentarily surprises James when she laughs, but he is glad to see that brightness in her face. He hadn't expected it to be there. Does she perhaps feel some sense of relief? Is there some comfort in finally knowing?

'No! Of course not. If Adam can make use of them, he must keep them. Far better that than they moulder away in a wardrobe, surely? If they keep the young man warm, that thought will give me some pleasure, and I know it's what Robert would want.'

'Thank you.' It strikes James that it's the first time she has said Adam's name. Though Celia smiles when she mentions him, there is something sad in the finality and completeness of that acknowledgement.

'Imagine a mother not knowing her own son! But, you see, when you brought him here, he *was* Robert. He had my son's face – but more than that: it was his voice. It was his manner. Robert was here in this house that day. That's the thought that nags at me, the thing that I can't understand. And I don't think I'll ever be able to explain that. You must think me quite foolish, Doctor Haworth.'

'Not at all. Grief and hope are powerful emotions. What we see is sometimes what we want to see.'

'Perhaps.' She looks at him as if she doubts him, as if she understands this better than he does. 'You know, my faith has wavered over the past five years. After you left that day, I cried for a week, but now, on reflection, it feels like a gift that I had him back, even if it was only for that one day. I have thanked God for that – even if that memory is as much as I will ever have.'

James nods. He remembers Adam in the bedroom above, his feet on the patchwork quilt and the expression on his face as he closed his eyes. There was something in Adam's behaviour that day that wasn't quite his own, that wasn't typical of him. Could he really have picked something of Robert Dakers up here?

'Do you think he would object if I were to come to see him again?'

'Adam?'

'Yes. I don't mean to make a nuisance of myself, but it would be a pleasure to spend some minutes in his company.'

For all of her new certainty and acceptance, there is something that still unsettles James. The face in the wallet photograph might well be that of a man who has been dead for the past five years, but it might also be Adam. James would like to see how she reacts to him another time. Will she still see her son in Adam's features, or was it just some passing mania? Why does he suddenly feel excluded from a conspiracy between Celia Dakers and Adam Galilee?

'Of course,' he replies.

Chapter Forty-Nine

Adam, Fellside House, April 1921

He sees her face at the garden gate. 'You're here.'

'Hello, Adam.'

'I worried that you wouldn't come back.'

He opens the gate for Caitlin. 'I did think about it.'

'James needs you back. He doesn't brush his hair, or change his clothes, when you're not here. That's not like him, is it? I've worried about him. I think he might have forgotten to wash too.'

She laughs, but it's a complicated laugh. 'I'd like to think that I'm more than the regulator of his personal hygiene.'

'He drinks more too. There are empty whisky bottles hidden behind his desk. That's to say, he *thinks* they're hidden.'

'I know about it, but it's difficult,' she says, and Adam sees it in her eyes. 'He thinks he needs it. He thinks it's helping him. It's part of the reason I went away.'

'I'm sad to know that.'

They walk together along the path. The pear trees are breaking bud and bees are buzzing around the comfrey and the cowslips. It ought to be an easy moment, but it isn't.

'I heard you rowing last week,' he says, 'before you went.

I probably shouldn't tell you that, but I suspect that everyone in the house heard too. If I don't tell you, someone else will.'

'Did you? Oh God! I lost my rag. I hope that Alan and Charlotte don't know.'

'I wouldn't discuss it with anyone else. I'm only saying it to you so that you know, so that you're aware that it's out there.'

'Thank you. You are a friend.'

He bends to twine tomato plants around their stakes. He's planted calendula in between, to keep away the whitefly, and he picks a flower and hands it to her now. 'When you were shouting, I heard my name.'

Caitlin turns away from him. For a minute, with the tension that he sees in her back, he thinks she's going to walk away, but then she's talking again.

'You can't not have noticed – I think James has got too wrapped up in your case. Alan has had to talk to him. He's rushing through his sessions with other patients and failing to turn up. He used to plan it all out in his desk diary, but I flicked through it last week, and there's nothing in there for the past month apart from the visits he's been making with you. He's not giving his other patients the care and the consideration that he ought to.'

'Is he spending too much time with me?'

'It's not your fault. It's not that you've asked for it, or that you demand any more of him, it's just that he's got too involved. He so wants to match you up with a name and fit you back into a family. And the more that he has these nightmares about Nathaniel being missing, the more he needs to slot you into a place. As if that would make up for Nat being lost – as if one would cancel out the other – only it won't, will it? I think he ought to take a break, I've told him that, but he won't have it. He does need to get it all sorted out in his head, though, to talk to people, to let it out, because right now it's all building up, which means there are going to be more nightmares, and rows, and empty whisky bottles.'

'I'm sorry. I didn't realize it was that bad.'

'You've no reason to be sorry, Adam. I came back on the condition that he talks to Alan. James needs help as much as the rest of you do. But he doesn't want to admit it.'

'He'll be better now you're back. He'll try harder.'

'Will he? I'd love to believe that, but I'm not sure.' She looks so sorrowful at that. 'Don't misunderstand me: I love my husband dearly, I admire him, I've adored him since the first day that we met, but he's not easy to live with right now. And I'm not certain that us being together is helping him. Perhaps the reverse. I thought last week that maybe he'd be better off without me, without the constant reminder of Nat.'

'He's not better without you.' Adam thinks about lying next to the woman in the woods and watching her sleeping face. Wouldn't his life be better if he saw her face every day? He has no doubt. 'I'm sure that when he looks at you, he doesn't just see your brother. I know that.'

Caitlin looks at him then, and it's difficult to hold her gaze because Adam sees so much complication and unhappiness there right now.

'Will you start work again?'

'I don't think I could. I'm not in the mood.'

Caitlin's hands move smoothly when she's working, there's something poetic in those fluid movements, Adam thinks, it is almost like watching a dance, but her fingers are all fast-moving spikes of tension this morning. She keeps clasping and unclasping her hands and it troubles him to see her so anxious. He bends to pick weeds from the path. Foxtail and clover are already finding their way up through the gravel. He doesn't need to pull them out now, but he has to disconnect his eyes from hers for a moment.

'How tidy you are these days,' she says as she looks around. 'How very orderly you are in here.'

'I'm not exactly feeling orderly.'

'How did it go with Mrs Mason?'

'Complicated. Like you say, James wants things to fit.'

Chapter Fifty

James, Fellside House, April 1921

He is relieved to see that her possessions are back in the bedroom. Her hairbrush and face powder on the dressing table. Her nightdress behind the door. The scent of her perfume. James stands in the doorway and thinks that it is as though Caitlin never left. Only she has not put her suitcase away, he notices. And there are more bottles of pills on the bedside table now. She says that the pills are to help her sleep, but James knows that he is the problem that disturbs Caitlin's dreams, and there is no pill to remedy that. Just occasionally he thinks that it would be better for Caitlin if he wasn't here.

When he steps back into the sitting room, she is there standing by the window. She stands so still that she might well have been there all this time.

'Alan missed you,' he says. He watches her half-reflection in the glass. 'He says that this house is much duller when you're not here.'

'Only Alan?'

'And Adam and Edward and Laurence and Jack. We had an odd number for cards last night.'

She nods. Her face – half oblique, half unreadable reflection – reminds him of the iterations of the woman's face all around Adam's room. If Caitlin hadn't come back, would he remember her so precisely? Would he recall every texture and shadow and flicker of expression? He knows that he would. He can't let her go away again.

'They've all missed you, but I have missed you more than any of them,' he tells her. 'I've missed you more than I thought I could. I'm adrift without you. I'm lost. I was terrified that you wouldn't come back.'

She finally turns towards him, but he still can't quite read her face. 'I did think about it,' she says. 'I was back in my old room at home and it was quiet. I slept so well, it was my own space, and for a few minutes when I woke up each morning, Nat might still have been there in the next room.'

'If you'll tell me how I can make it better, I'll do it. Anything. I want you to feel that this is your space. I want you to sleep, Caitlin. As I said on the telephone, I'll ask for help.'

'Will you? I want to believe you, but I've asked you so many times before. You say you'll do it now, but can I believe you?'

'But you've never left me before.'

She turns back to the window and he can see her eyes moving as she looks across the hillside. The white curtains frame a copper-coloured dusk. 'The leaves are coming back again. It's all greening up, isn't it? Spring is coming in and that ought to make us optimistic. I wish that I could feel optimistic.'

James watches her fingers leave the glass. The misted imprint of her hand remains. Her reflected eyes seem to be searching. He wonders if he is making her ill.

'I've thought, while you were away – we could rent a cottage in the village. I could just come here to work. I could talk to Shepherd. He could get in a nighttime caretaker. You don't need to live in this apartment. You don't need to be here all the time.'

'But you'd still be here, wouldn't you? You'd still bring it all home in your head. Besides, how could we afford to rent a house?'

'We could at least look into it. We could try.'

She shakes her head and he is struck by the depth of sadness he sees in her face. That sorrow has been there for the past five years, but it's more profound now. She looks like someone who has run out of hope, he thinks. He needs to change that.

'My mother says I have to try harder. I promised her that I would.' She laughs. 'You wouldn't expect her to be your champion, would you? But she was. I honestly think that she likes having the space at home and doesn't want me taking my room back!'

James knows that there are still framed photographs of Caitlin and Nathaniel on the dressing table in her childhood bedroom. There are still wax flowers and seashells and picture postcards that Nathaniel gave her. Had she felt better surrounded by all of that? When she met her own eye in her bedroom mirror, did she look more like herself with that framed all around her? Did feeling close to Nathaniel help her to sleep more soundly? Has he perhaps denied her the space to talk about her brother? There are so few mementoes of Nat in this apartment, he realizes. There's not one single photograph of him. How has he not noticed that before? Is that out of consideration for him? Is he denying her that too?

'I've been thinking about Nathaniel while you've been away,' he begins and then has to feel his way, the notion and the commitment forming as he puts one word in front of the next. 'Things are starting to surface now. They're digging around Trônes Wood. I've read about it. They're excavating graves. I could employ someone to look for Nathaniel. It would make it all different if we could find him, wouldn't it?'

He's not sure whether it's relief or fear that he sees in Caitlin's face. He is not sure which emotion it is that makes his chest flutter as she nods her head.

Chapter Fifty-One

Adam, Fellside House, April 1921

Adam watches Arthur digging. Arthur has fits and that means that he can't go out to work. Sometimes he swallows his tongue and wets himself and kicks his legs around on the floor, but Shepherd has given him a spade and told him to make a flower border. Shepherd says that if Arthur concentrates on his spadework, and waters his seedlings, and keeps down the weeds, he will stop swallowing his tongue. Adam puts his own tongue to the roof of his mouth as he watches Arthur dig; he can't quite figure out the mechanics of how a man might swallow his own tongue, but the digging does seem to be making it stop.

Shepherd tells Arthur to focus on the work that he is doing and to take deep breaths of air. Sometimes Adam helps Arthur with his weeding, and sees him pausing and taking those breaths, but Arthur likes to be in charge of his border and says that Adam ought to keep to his own garden. Arthur has been sent here by his family. He says they want to hide him, that they're embarrassed by him, and he thinks they'd like to lock him away here permanently. Adam thinks that he would happily stay here, remain in his own garden and never again find a family to embarrass. He keeps recalling what Caitlin said, about Haworth needing to give him a name, but he has decided that he doesn't want a name if that means leaving his garden behind and the chance of seeing the woman in the wood again. Can he not just carry on being Adam?

He's also been watching Haworth this morning. He comes into the garden, looking as though he has something urgent to share with Shepherd, but then turns on his heels; he has done it three times now. Adam can see from Haworth's face that he is troubled. Is he meant to be starting to talk with Shepherd today? He keeps throwing his cigarette away and Adam can hear him pacing behind the wall. Does Haworth too need to take deep breaths and perhaps try some spade-work? When he comes out onto the lawn for the fourth time, looking full of difficult indecision, Adam resolves that he will go and hand Haworth the pick, and ask if he will help him break up the soil – but then Shepherd has turned and it looks as though it's time for Haworth to start talking.

James

Shepherd leans on a spade. He often seems to be leaning on a spade as he watches Arthur working, but James has never yet seen Shepherd use the spade himself. It's a theatrical prop, James thinks. Shepherd's breath hangs around him in the bright, crisp morning air and he smiles at James as he walks across the garden.

'It's like a needlework circle inside.'

Sally has read a book about occupational therapy and so she now has them all embroidering tablecloths and cross-stitching samplers. The residents had found it briefly amusing to cross-stitch obscenities and swear words, until Sally had made them painstakingly unpick all of their miscreant stitches and replace them with Bible quotes.

'I don't think they dare disobey her,' says Shepherd, 'though I fear that it might get out of hand; she's talking about basketmaking next, and was wondering aloud if Caitlin might let them have an afternoon playing in her studio. Don't worry, I crushed the idea fast. I could just imagine Caitlin's face if Sally asked!' Shepherd widens his eyes. 'Adam's planting up his raised beds. Have you seen how well the walled garden is coming along?'

'Isn't it?' James replies. Adam is spending hours each day working in the garden now, and when he's not working, he's walking. James suspects that he's looking for the woman in the woods as he walks, and he worries that Adam doesn't eat enough to be doing such a lot of strenuous exercise. James watches Arthur stretch and look up at the sky. 'Though I suspect we might have something of a horticultural rivalry developing.'

Shepherd laughs. 'Let's hope it stays a friendly rivalry, eh? Adam has asked if we could order some glass. He wants to fix up the old greenhouse. You'd have no objection to him trying?'

What Shepherd calls the old greenhouse is little more than an overgrown slump of twisted metal and smashed glass. Shepherd has sentimental memories of his grandfather's tomatoes, but this task could take some time.

'No, of course not,' James replies. 'Did you see that Mrs Dakers was here earlier?'

'Adam didn't object to seeing her again?'

'No.' Passing the drawing-room door, James had heard Adam's voice mixing with that of Celia Dakers. The low, steady hum of their voices had sounded amiable. 'He actually seemed comfortable with her today.'

'Do you think that's because she no longer has a claim to pursue?' Shepherd asks.

James considers: is Adam prepared to spend time with Celia Dakers now because she can no longer take him away? Is it because she no longer needs him? But James doesn't think that's entirely the case – haven't they just changed their terms? Does some part of her still believe that Adam was Robert Dakers on that day in her house?

'Quite possibly.'

Adam is presently digging in trenches of potatoes and, James wonders, with all this planning planting schemes and fixing up glasshouses, is he thinking about making a permanent place for himself here? He would like Anna Mason to see Adam digging, to observe how she reacts to him occupied in this act, but isn't this work also another rejection of her and a life that might once have been his? She has written to James and asked if she can come to Fellside again with the dog. He hasn't mentioned the possibility to Adam yet. James isn't sure how he should reply.

Shepherd blows cigarette smoke away. 'It's good to see Caitlin back, eh? She looks well for her little holiday.'

'She does. I think her mother likes to cosset her when she gets her home.'

'We only spoke briefly yesterday, but she mentioned that there's something you want to discuss with me?'

James looks at Shepherd, trying to measure how much Caitlin has already said. 'There is.'

They walk back towards the house. 'I'm not sure I like the idea of being the patient,' James says.

'It's not that. I believe that it's actually quite common for a man working in our circumstances to pick up second-hand anxieties.'

'You make it sound like something contagious.'

'Perhaps it is to some degree.'

It is very odd to walk into Shepherd's office and to sit down on this side of the desk. James feels suddenly vulnerable. Is this how they all feel, then? He notices the faces in the flowers on the wallpaper behind the desk, wondering how he had never seen them before, and the scratches on the wall where the corner of Shepherd's chair habitually turns. How odd, how unsettling it is that that chair now turns towards him, that all of Shepherd's attention is suddenly focused on his face. James tries to look away, but the shelves to his left are warped with the weight of tomes on psychology and psychiatry and interpretation of dreams.

'I'd offer you a drink, but perhaps it's best to try without?'

James nods. He wonders if Caitlin has told Shepherd that part too. 'I'm not sure that I've ever needed a drink more!'

'Is it to do with your problems sleeping?'

'Yes.'

'Do you want to tell me what you dream about?'

'God! I do feel like a patient!' The walls of Shepherd's study are papered with William Morris pomegranates. The sharp intertwining leaves are momentarily a Gothic cage and a forest closing in. A postcard reproduction of *Jesus Light of the World* leans on the fireplace, but the man with the lantern offers James no enlightenment. Spokes of sun move over the waxed floor.

'If you're not careful, in the spirit of warming you up, I might feel obliged to share my dream about Aunt Pamela.' Shepherd looks over the top of his glasses.

'I've seen your aunt Pamela. Substantial lady? Somewhat fearsome?'

'Quite. The things my nocturnal imagination can make her do with a carpet slipper.'

James laughs. He runs his hands through his hair. 'Mercy!'

'When did it start? Have you been having these dreams since you got back?'

'Earlier than that. It started in 1917. I only had the dream occasionally at first, once every few weeks perhaps, and I assumed it was simply the strain of being out there. I was exhausted, you see. Absolutely shot. I'd had enough. So I told myself it was my subconscious flashing a red light, and I didn't linger on it for too long.'

Shepherd nods. The light glints on his spectacles. 'And since then? Now?'

'I assumed it would stop when I came home. I mean, I'm not under pressure any longer and time has gone by. It ought to recede really, shouldn't it?'

'But the opposite has happened?'

A vase of apple blossom drops silent petals. The oil heater throws out the smell of singeing dust. He sees Shepherd reach for his pad and pen. 'Do you need to make notes? Do I need a file?'

'No. I'm sorry. Habit.' Shepherd puts down the pen. 'So how often is it happening now?'

'Not every night, but often enough that it makes me want to stay awake. Maybe two or three times a week?'

'It could well be the environment here that's contributing. You're spending much of your day listening to other men's recall. It's not surprising if you're taking some of that away.'

'That's what Caitlin thinks. She's convinced that my work

is making it worse, that I ought to consider doing something else.'

'Which would be a great shame. It would be a great loss to us here. Alternatively, as you tell your patients, you could face up to the events that you revisit in your dreams and seek some resolution.'

He makes it sound so straightforward. So simple. So solvable. Is that how he sounds when he talks to Milner and Hartley and Adam? James thinks about saying it all out loud to Shepherd, telling him about Trônes Wood, how Nathaniel came to be wounded and how he let him down and lost him. How can saying it out loud resolve that?

'Are you frightened when you wake up?'

'Yes. It's almost physical.' He considers and corrects himself. 'It *is* physical. And sometimes I'm frightened that I'll hurt Caitlin. Of course, I wouldn't consciously, but I'm in such an idiotic funk. I feel as though my heart is going to leap out of my chest. But it's not the fear that's the worst of it; it's the feeling of guilt that comes with it – and that feeling is not just there at night. I walk around with it all the time now. It's colouring everything else. It's affecting my relationship with Caitlin. It's probably affecting my work.' He looks down, remembering the difficult conversation that he had with Shepherd recently. 'I'm sorry. I know it's affecting my work.'

'When you wake up, do you recall it all?'

'Much of it. Perhaps not all.'

'Would you like me to hypnotize you?'

'No.' The thought of it makes James panic. He's not ready to give up that control. There are things that he doesn't want Shepherd to hear him saying.

'Well, would you tell me about your dream?'

He knows that he should. He knows this is what Caitlin wants. He knows that until he says it out loud, this will all get worse, and things will get worse between them, but how can he honestly tell the whole of it? There's no way of making right what was done and Shepherd will only think less of him when he knows.

'Can we take this slowly?' James asks. 'Could I maybe start to tell you tomorrow?'

'*Mañana?*' Shepherd raises an eyebrow.

James' palms are sweating. He puts them to his trouser legs so that Shepherd won't see. 'I know,' he concedes.

Adam

The red girl takes Adam's hand and leads him out into the garden. She takes a crumpled bag of sweets from her pocket. The liquorice gums are all fused together, but she prises them apart with her red fingers and apologizes.

'Do you like them, Ellis?'

She always insists on calling him Ellis. He nods.

'Good. I'll bring them again, then.'

She's wearing a green knitted cap, the same colour as the gloves she has just removed. There are holes in her gloves, he sees. Adam suspects that money is tight.

'Would they pay you if you took me in?' he asks.

'What sort of a question is that?'

'I'm sorry.'

She looks at him as if she is angry, as if she wants to beat her fists on him.

'Is that why you think I'm here? Is that why I come? Could you honestly believe that I want to make money out of you?'

He looks at her intent grey eyes. He can see her teeth between her lips. 'No,' he replies.

'George says I should stop coming, that I should give up on you. He says you're not his brother and I'm only deluding myself. He says that you're a fantasy and I should save the train fare.'

It's an accusation, a challenge, the beliefs of this man called George. Adam feels as if he ought to defend himself, come back with an answer that equals out these doubts, but how can he? He tries to remember a brother, to place himself in a house full of sibling quarrels and the smell of laundry, but he can recall no childish spite, no hard words, or stings or bruises. There is only the silence of absence. As he watches Lucy Vickers' eyes, he wishes that he could give her one small glimmer of remembrance.

'I don't mind you visiting me here, if you want to.'

'Don't you?'

He can hear the doubt in her question and it echoes his own. He watches her. He can see her rolling a sweet on her tongue and a sentence that she's not quite certain how to form. She puts her hands to the lapels of his coat. 'Would you like me to bring the children next time too?'

'Your children?'

'*Your* children, Ellis!' She laughs oddly. 'Tom and Katie.'

'I don't have any children,' he tells her.

She turns away from him. He sees that this disappoints her, that it frustrates her, but he can recall no small red versions of himself.

'I'm not sure that this is a place to bring children,' he says.

'No, neither am I,' she replies.

James

He walks to the window. Down below, Milner is throwing stones at the garden wall, Hartley is planting his footprints in circles, making concentric rings in the wet grass, and over by the rhododendrons Adam is walking with Lucy Vickers. Or perhaps, James reconsiders, looking again at their body language, she is following him. 'Poor girl. She always seems rather downtrodden, doesn't she? I don't think it's the happiest home. I do sometimes wish that Adam would give a bit more of himself to them. He's happy enough to take bags of Pontefract cakes off Vickers, but I fear that he doesn't give much back. He doesn't make it easy for any of them, does he?'

'Not really,' Shepherd replies. 'But then why would he if he's certain that he doesn't know any of them? Why should he? It would be a bit of a stretch of his manners. Perhaps it's kinder of him not to string them along.'

'He's not really seemed to warm to any of them.'

'Maybe because they're all wrong.' Shepherd joins him at the window.

'Can they be? Can that many people be deluded? Can there be so much wishful thinking in the world?'

'Do you doubt it?' Shepherd asks. They watch Lucy Vickers mouthing words to Adam's back and it is as if he doesn't hear her. He seems almost oblivious to her presence. 'I do occasionally fear that we're dragging out her false hopes. If the brother is dead, which you must admit is likely the case, isn't she just postponing her grief?'

'We can't stop her coming here, though, can we?'

Shepherd shakes his head.

James considers. 'There's something else that I wanted to ask you: your contact with the war graves people, the chap that passed on the news about Robert Dakers, is there any chance that you'd be willing to put me in touch with him?'

'Of course. But why?'

'Resolution. Like you said. And perhaps a little wishful thinking.'

Chapter Fifty-Two

Adam, Fellside House, April 1921

'You look furtive,' Adam says. 'Are you hiding from him?'

Haworth's eyes slide towards his and Adam can see that he has startled him. 'Jesus, Adam! Where did you come from? You sneak like a cat sometimes.'

Haworth leans his head back against the wall. Adam can see fear and relief on his face, but he is glad when it breaks into laughter.

'I'm sorry. I didn't realize that you hadn't heard me.' He hasn't seen Haworth like this before and feels something shift in their relationship. 'I've been watching you. Are you frightened of him?'

'Of Shepherd? No, of course not! What a thing to say.'

Adam can see Shepherd leaning on his spade again as he watches Arthur working. Shepherd likes to tell Arthur what to do but never gets earth under his own fingernails. 'I'm a bit frightened of him sometimes,' he admits.

'Come here, will you?'

Haworth beckons Adam to stand next to him against the garden wall. He can tell that Haworth doesn't want to be seen. 'You don't want him to know you're here?'

'Not for the moment.'

'Have you fallen out?'

'God, what a lot of questions you ask!' Haworth fumbles for cigarettes, but smiles as he offers Adam the packet.

Adam is relieved to see that Haworth isn't angry with him, that they haven't fallen out. He doesn't like the way that Haworth's fingers tremble, though, as he works the lighter.

'Are you not well?'

'I'd be better if you'd stop asking questions.' They smoke together leaning against the wall. Haworth bats the smoke away with his hand. 'I feel like an errant schoolboy,' he laughs.

'Do you want to talk to me about it?' Adam asks.

James

James follows Adam up the bank. He climbs like a cat and seems to know every foothold and sturdy branch. James' inexpert hands pull away tufts of grass, and the smooth soles of his shoes skid, but he shadows Adam's movements, his footholds and handholds, and climbs higher.

'Is this the way you always come?'

'Most days.'

When James looks back he sees the house from a new angle. It seems to rise like a cliff from here, and he is pretty much opposite the window of his own sitting room. How strange it is to look in on his own life this way. How transparent it all is. He can see Sally beating a carpet, Letty dusting the piano top, Hartley and Milner crouched over a game of chess, and then Caitlin looking out. As James watches her pale face at the window, he's not sure whether to wave or to wish himself invisible. It's like looking into a doll's house from here and suddenly he understands what she means about the eyes on the hillside.

'Does anyone else come up here?'

'Up this path? Not that I know of.'

'Do you often see Caitlin?'

'Yes.' Adam smiles. 'She always seems to be looking out of the window.'

'Doesn't she?' James replies.

They climb up between juniper bushes and come out by a fallen wall. There are violets under the hedge and the blackthorn is full of white blossom. James gasps as a wood pigeon clatters out of the undergrowth and Adam's eyes are there then, looking straight into his own, seeing his alarm, questioning, measuring him. It all feels out of balance today.

'I saw you with Miss Vickers earlier,' James says, trying to get the balance back. 'I saw you out in the garden together. How did you get on?'

'She followed me around talking about people I don't know. She keeps giving me sweets, but I can't give her the responses that she wants.'

Adam's tongue is black from sucking on liquorice gums. It makes him look oddly sinister.

'Perhaps she's happy enough to spend time with you?'

Adam's eyes tell him this is a ridiculous notion. 'She brings me drawings done by other people's children and expects me to pin them up on my wall. Why would I want to do that? If I'm kind to her, if I pretend, I'll only make it worse, won't I? I mean, that's not really nice, is it?'

'I do see what you mean.'

Adam puts his hand out to stop their steps and they both crouch to watch a hare ahead. '*Lepus.* They're courting,' he whispers. The creature lifts its nose to the air, but is gone then with a flash of its tail. Adam turns towards James and smiles. 'You can hide up here if you want,' he says.

'Is this where you hide sometimes?'

'I used to. I don't hide any longer, though. Mostly I'm just walking. I like to look how it changes from day to day and I like to make myself feel tired.'

'So that you sleep?'

'Yes. You told me once that I should do that, but I did already know it.'

'Adam, are you looking for the woman?'

'I'm always looking for her. I want to see her again. I'm frightened that I won't. Would you like to see her too?'

'Yes.'

Adam nods. 'Do you want to hide from Shepherd?'

James laughs. 'Not really. Not quite, but he's been asking me lots of questions. Not as many as you, though.'

'I'm sorry. You looked as though you might want to talk.'

'No, it's me that should say sorry. I'm grateful for your concern and your interest.'

James considers: is he frightened of saying it to Shepherd? He is frightened that Shepherd will think him negligent and a coward, that he will think him disloyal and selfish and unprofessional. He knows that, if he says it out loud, Shepherd will think less of him. He can't say it to Caitlin for the same reason. Would Adam judge him, though? Would it matter if he were to tell Adam? James knows that he's terrible with secrets, but who does Adam tell his secrets to apart from him?

'You're fitter than me,' he says. 'You're more used to these paths. Could we perhaps sit down for a bit?'

'You want to tell me a secret, don't you?'

'Adam, I sometimes wonder if you are some sort of telepathist.'

'I can see it in your face.'

James looks at Adam's eyes moving over his own face and wonders how much he sees. When Adam talks about drawing, he tells James how he must look first. How he must *really* look. He says that he wants to look at things until he understands how they work. He does this before he even starts to put pencil to paper. James suspects that when Adam looks at him, he perhaps sees too much.

'The buds are opening up,' says Adam, as he sits down on a fallen tree trunk. 'You can almost hear them creaking. If you sit here long enough, you can actually watch them opening up. Is it about why you're not sleeping?'

James looks at him in surprise. 'You know that?'

'Of course. I hear you pacing about in the night. Sometimes I hear you screaming.'

'You do?' With the thought of it, James feels panic rise in his chest. How could he not have realized that? How could he have let it go this far? His hands are sweating and he feels slightly nauseous.

'You mustn't worry. You mustn't feel embarrassed. Milner screams too, and sometimes I wake up and I can hear Davies having conversations with himself. He talks far more in his sleep than he does when he's awake.'

'I do sometimes wonder if you ought to be doing my job,' James replies.

'I just watch. I just listen.' Adam shakes his head. 'But I am right, aren't I?'

'You are.' Sometimes when Adam looks at him, James thinks that he knows everything, that he can look inside his head and understands how it all fits together. There are times when it seems there is something uncanny about Adam and he might well have fallen to earth.

'Are you frightened in your sleep? Do you remember something that frightened you in the past?'

'Yes.' James watches Adam's fingers turning a pine cone; he studies it as if he can read that too, and James realizes that this rootless, friendless, uncanny man, who is every man and no man, is the person who he talks to most, and is possibly his best friend. He can't imagine even attempting to have this conversation with anyone else. 'It's the first time that I've told anyone this, and I'm not telling it well, am I?'

'You only have to tell me if you want to.'

'I want to. I'm just not sure where to start.'

'Is it about Nathaniel, then?'

He hears his own intake of breath. 'How can you know that? How can you know that name?' Has he screamed it? Has Caitlin heard that too?

Adam smiles. 'Don't worry. I can't read your mind. Caitlin has told me about her brother.'

'She did? When?'

'We've talked about him a few times. She first told me last year. I asked her why she looked sad and she told me that she misses him – and that his not being here makes you sad too.'

'She said that? I feel like I'm behind the game.' He wonders how much Caitlin has told Adam. How much has she told Shepherd? What extent of it does she know herself?

'Is your dream about when Nathaniel dies?'

'Yes. He keeps on dying in my head.'

'Do you feel bad about how he dies?'

'Yes.'

'Do you feel guilty?'

He nods.

'Should you feel guilty?'

Looking at Adam's face is like addressing his own

conscience. James knows that Adam won't make him feel better, but somehow he now needs Adam to judge him. 'Yes,' he admits.

Adam

'Does the wood not frighten you?' Haworth asks.

'No.'

'Not even when it's going dark?'

'Never.'

'You're lucky. I hate it here. I hate all woods. I think they're all malevolent. Caitlin says that she feels eyes looking in sometimes; that's how I feel in this place. Like there are eyes all around. Like there are bad things just out of sight.'

Adam wonders if Haworth has been drinking this morning. His breath smells sour and the back of his shirt is dark with sweat. 'No one is looking. No one is here. It's only you and me, and I won't look at you if you don't want me to.' He turns his shoulder to him, but hears Haworth laugh.

'Adam, turn back to me. Please. I want to tell you.'

Chapter Fifty-Three

James

In the flickering shell-light, the mud walls are bronze and permanent. The water is deep and it contracts in an icy grip around James' thighs, but the heavy stuff is flying above, and so they'll crouch down here for as long as they must. He looks around at the other men in the shell hole. Webb and Long are here, he sees, Milner and Laffin and Hartley. They shouldn't be here, James thinks – they don't belong together in this place – and yet this is where they have always been. The light shudders in the sky and James knows them only by the shapes of their bones and the eyes that they turn upon him. They look to him as their senior officer, he can tell, and he nods to them and they know that he will not put them in danger. It's only the sixth man who is not looking at him, but he doesn't need him to turn his face for James to know that the man in silhouette is Adam.

There is an almighty roar and eruption as the shell hits just ahead. The earth jolts as it slams down. It's a huge noise. Apocalyptic. For a moment it is all brilliant blinding white light, like a photographic negative, and in that timeless moment James sees all their terrified eyes angled upon him. The water leaps up and then comes down again. Earth falls in slow showers and breaks the surface. James can hear Milner's teeth chattering at his side. He can hear a prayer under Laffin's breath. But then there comes a quiet, as sudden and absolute as the cacophony that it follows.

The light continues to flash in the sky, but here it is a vacuum; there is no noise apart from the breath of each individual man. It is then, in that odd, impossible stillness, that Adam starts to talk. His hand stretches up, he leans over the top to pick a poppy from the edge of the shell hole and, as he turns, he adds it to the posy that he grips in his earth-ingrained fingers. He looks at it and smiles and holds this offering of greenery out. James can't help but smile too because Adam looks like a satisfied florist who might charge a city girl a shilling for a handful of hedgerow. But the solemnity of Adam's face doesn't let James smile for long.

Adam says the name of each plant before he offers it out, and they all reverently participate in his ceremony. James might have thought that they were his men, but he knows now that they are all Adam's. He extends the grey, feathery leaves of wormwood to Webb, to cleanse his body of choler, Adam says, and to purge the bitterness from his liver. James watches Webb's fingers obediently fix the greenery around the buttonhole of his top pocket. For Laffin, Adam chooses mallow, a flash of purple in the pyrotechnic light, to cool his hot agues and the temper that must make him lash out at those he loves most. For Hartley it is marjoram (James can smell its sweet peppery scent), for the sour humour in his stomach, to take the poison out and to give him appetite back. There is lavender for Long, to take the convulsions from his fingers, and the poppy he hands to Milner, so that he may find sleep.

Adam seems to consider for a moment. He looks at the posy left in his hands. It is drooping slightly now, and is a sorry offering, but he winds out the stems of lily of the valley. The flowers seem implausibly white, ethereal almost, they must be wax, but Adam puts the sprig to his nose and closes his eyes as he breathes it in. James thinks of a scent warming on Caitlin's neck and a bridal bouquet.

'For me?' he asks.

'For me,' Adam replies.

'For luck?'

'For memory.'

James watches as Adam's fingers push the stem into his top pocket. He looks up and his eyes connect with James' then. The bombardment is silently crashing all around and he sees the light strobe in the blackness of Adam's eyes.

'And mine?' James asks.

There is nothing left in Adam's hand but a sprig of woody stalk covered in dusky-green leaves. The water shifts soundlessly as Adam steps towards James and, though he can no longer hear the artillery falling, he feels the force of it deep in his diaphragm. He watches as Adam's black fingers fix the stalk to his chest. His face is all shadows, but James feels Adam's breath on his own cheek.

'Why do I feel like a marked man? Why do I feel like target practice?' he says as he looks down at the greenery on his chest.

'No, quite the opposite.'

'I don't know it. What is it?'

'But you know the scent of it, don't you?' Adam replies. '*Thymus serpyllum* for nervous disorders. Wild thyme for nightmares.'

Adam

The light flashes across the ceiling. Adam can feel the vibration of it and knows the storm is getting closer. He pulls the sheets back and walks to the window. The sash is rattling and the cold air is pushing in all around the edges. He puts his hand to the glass, meets his own black silhouette and watches the light strobing behind the hillside. He feels the hairs lift on his arm and wonders if Haworth is awake.

He has never seen Haworth look like that before. He is accustomed to Milner and Webb and Laffin with their trembling and tears, but he has never seen a man shake and cry that way. Has that been inside Haworth all of this time?

Adam hears the wind whistling under the roof tiles and imagines them lifting like a sail. Where will this house have drifted to by the morning? The storm lights the sky beyond the hillside and it all stands out in that strange, bright, colourless light. It is like a photograph of itself. Or a negative. This place, of which he knows every leaf and foothold, looks unfamiliar in the light of the storm. It is otherworldly suddenly. Unknowable. He sees the trees heave and the wood is transformed into a place of nightmares.

Haworth had told him about the wood that he revisits in his sleep. As Haworth had talked, Adam had pictured that place: its leper trees and splintering metal, the split trunks of mighty oaks, and the coiling brambles and the barbed wire. Adam could see from his face that Haworth had been terrified of that wood, but he had had to go back in there again and again, he said, and now he revisits it nightly. It is why he is frightened of woods, why he now dreads all woods. He had shaken his head at Adam as if he did not expect him to be able to understand.

Branches of lightning illuminate the sky and sear themselves onto Adam's retina, so that they are still there in his closed eyes after the sky has blackened again. He turns his back on the flickering hillside. The warmth has gone from his sheets now, but he wraps them around his feet. The light makes strange shapes of the roof beams, throws shadows at angles that he doesn't recognize, and for a moment he thinks about standing in Durham Cathedral and watching the trapped bird rising up the spire. Its wings clatter around his own ceiling and for an instant he knows and feels its fear. For a moment the room is full of the thrash of a bird's wings.

Haworth says that when he dreams about the wood he is not just frightened for himself but also for the men he is there with. It is his responsibility to look after them, he says, it is up to him to get them back. He is most frightened for Caitlin's brother, because he is young and scared and shouldn't be there. He wants to go home. He has told Haworth that he is only there because he wanted to be with him. Haworth is clearly worried about Nathaniel; he feels guilty and responsible for him; he is frightened that Nathaniel won't come out of the wood.

Adam can hear the thunder now. The sky has been signalling for a long time, but now the drum rolls are coming on too. When Haworth had talked about the noise of the big guns, he had said that it was like thunder and that he had felt it in his belly.

'But you must know that, at some level, mustn't you?' Haworth had said. 'You must have felt that? Something deep within you must recognize that sensation?'

He had felt like he was letting Haworth down when he had shaken his head.

The boy called Nathaniel is jumpy, Haworth says. He

doesn't seem to be in control of his own body and isn't acting like himself. When they have to run, and when they have to crouch down, this Nathaniel just keeps on steadily walking through the wood. Haworth wants to grab him, wants to pull him to the ground, because he is putting himself and all the rest of them in danger. He is angry at him. He is also scared for him.

The rain comes on in large drops and it sounds like shingle thrown against the glass. Each droplet on the window pane flashes with light, each one a microcosm of the storm. Beyond, on the hillside, the trees are lashing now. Out there the noise must be immense. The whole horizon is heaving. Adam thinks of how Haworth described the bombardment tearing into the wood. Is Haworth now looking out from his window below and remembering that?

When the bullets start to streak through the wood Haworth knows that one will hit Nathaniel. He says that he sees it before it happens, a phosphorescent streak straight through the trees, like an arc of intention. He is swearing at Nathaniel then and his blood is all over his hands. He is even more frightened now. He tries to pull Nathaniel onto his back, he wants to take him to where they can get help, but they have to keep on heading north up the wood and there is no help, only more danger there. Haworth says that when he takes the compass from his pocket the needle is spinning around.

The white light bounces around the mirrors and for a second Adam expects them all to explode. He braces for the crack and the leap of the glass, but when he looks again the mirrors have all switched back to black. How long will this storm take to pass over? It must be overhead now? The thunder makes the whole house vibrate. The windows rattle in their sashes, the roof tiles chatter and in the deep, lingering resonance he feels his own body throb too.

Haworth leaves Nathaniel in a hollow, a cradle of great thick tree roots. The white dressing is already turning red. Haworth promises that when they have got to the top of the wood, he will come back for him. He swears that he will. But it's hours before he can come back. Haworth spends all night walking through the wood, and it is full of dead and dying men, but his friend is no longer amongst them. He can't find him. He has lost him. He will never find him. Haworth says that everything changes at that point and he knows instantly that he has lost half of Caitlin too.

Adam won't recall whether it was the crack, or the blinding light that came first, but it hits the lightning conductor on the roof and for a moment he wonders if the house will rend apart. It is an almighty noise and the floor beneath his feet seems to heave. All the timbers and roof tiles are straining and creaking, as if they are debating whether to part company. But then there is stillness in the aftermath, and it is in those few silent seconds that Adam sees it; the shell hits just to his left, the man next to him is screaming, and it's no longer a second-hand scene from James' story, but his own memory.

James

'Did you sleep well?' Caitlin asks. 'You slept all through the storm.'

'The storm?'

'I thought it was going to lift the roof off at one point. It was like being in a small boat in the middle of a great angry ocean. Lots of trees have come down.'

'Good Lord, really? I went walking with Adam yesterday and he must have tired me out more than I realized. You know what he's like – I struggle to keep up. He was on real mountain-hare form. I didn't think I was that tired, though.'

'Perhaps you ought to do that more often?'

'Yes, perhaps I should,' James says.

'Did you also find time to talk to Shepherd yesterday?'

'A little.'

'And do you feel better for it?'

'Yes, you know, I do.'

Chapter Fifty-Four

James, Fellside House, April 1921

'You look well rested,' Shepherd says. 'You must be the only person within a five-mile radius who is. We had a couple of big trees come down last night, and I'll need to get someone in to look at the roof.'

'I haven't slept that heavily in years,' James replies.

'Did it help to have a talk yesterday?'

'Yes. I think so. Thank you.'

'Whenever you're ready to talk more, my door is always open.'

'I appreciate it. I rather talked myself out yesterday. I was dog-tired last night.'

'You must have been if that storm didn't wake you! On a canine note, isn't today the day that the charming Mrs Mason and dog are visiting us?'

'Yes – I haven't told Adam yet.'

'But you intend to?'

'I'm not sure. I worry that if I tell him she's coming, he'll run.'

'In that case, try to keep him in the house for the morning, perhaps?'

'Yes.'

*

James listens to Adam's pencil scratch on paper. The drawing is different today. Normally it's a detail of nature, or the face of the woman who he says he sees in the woods. This is the first time that James has seen Adam drawing male faces.

'Who are they?'

'I don't know. I think I was remembering the story you told me yesterday and imagining the men in your wood.'

James looks through the drawings. The figures are all in military uniform, but they're not just types; the men who Adam has drawn have individual characters, particular expressions, distinct eyes. They're all unshaven and, like Adam's this morning, their eyes look tired. Is this how he imagines the men in James' dream? Surely, with the detail and definition, it must be more than that? These men look as though they've been drawn from life. 'Do they have names? Do you think that they're faces that you might have known?'

He shakes his head. As well as the weariness, there is a terrible sadness in Adam's eyes this morning and James pities him. He looks as though he hasn't slept at all.

'I wanted to thank you for yesterday. I probably made rather a fool of myself, and you were very patient and generous.'

'Don't worry. I won't tell anyone.'

Yesterday seemed a significant day, Adam helped more than he probably knows, and James is sorry to have to make requests of him again today. He suspects that Adam will be reluctant to have another interview with Anna. James can see that he would prefer to be quietly left alone today. He doesn't seem at all in the mood for more conversations and questions.

'Listen, I have something to tell you. Anna Mason is coming here again today.'

'Why?' His eyes don't lift from the drawing.

'To see you.'

'She wants me to be her husband, doesn't she? I'm not. She's a madwoman.'

James recalls Anna calling Adam a lunatic. Watching the cleverness of his sketching fingers, the word seems so remotely inappropriate. 'She's bringing Meg with her. The dog? You remember the dog?'

He nods, but still won't look up.

'She says that Meg can stay here for a while, if you want to keep her. She thought that you might like that.'

'I'm not a child,' he says.

Does he treat Adam like a child? Perhaps he does sometimes. 'I'm sorry. I didn't mean to imply that. I just thought you might be pleased.'

'I wanted to walk today. I wanted to look at the trees that have come down. I wanted to go to the top of the wood.'

'And to look for the woman?'

'Yes. If she sees the Mason woman here, she might not come again. You promised me that I wouldn't have to do anything that I don't want to do.'

He feels he has let Adam down. 'Are you angry with me? Oh God, I'm so sorry if you feel harassed. I don't want you to feel pushed into anything.'

'I'm angry at myself for telling you about her. I shouldn't have taken you up into the woods. You might have scared her away.'

He can see it on Adam's face. There's something new there this morning. More than just anger. It looks more like despair now. Is he drawing these men because he's decided the woman won't come back? 'Perhaps she will be there tomorrow?'

'But she won't be, will she?'

Adam has been working on a drawing of an older man's face all the time that James has been in the room – dark eyes, a narrow nose, a thin-lipped mouth – putting down thoughtful, delicate pencil strokes, but he now crumples the paper in his hand. There is something petulant about the act. James can't help but feel that this demonstration is aimed at him.

'That's a shame. Were you not happy with it?'

'No.' His eyes shift around the pattern of the rug.

'Mrs Mason is coming at three. Will you be here?'

'Do I have a choice?'

'Of course, but . . .'

'I don't belong to her. I'm not her husband.'

'But were you once?'

Adam looks away.

'How is he? I thought he'd be excited to see Meg. He looked distraught when he had to leave her.'

Anna Mason is dressed in grey today and has the dog on a leash. It's clearly not used to being led, or she's not accustomed to leading it, and she laughs and curses as the dog leaps at the end of its restraint.

'He will be, I'm sure of it. He's just rather tired and irritable today. We had an almighty storm here last night and I don't think he slept.'

'Yes, I saw the trees down in the lane. Oh dear. I'm sorry if I've come on a bad day for him.'

James shakes his head. 'You've come a long way. It can't be helped. He has his ups and downs.'

'Has he talked about his visit to the farm at all? Has he talked about us? It seemed such a significant moment when he met Meg, didn't it? I have to admit that it's left me hopeful.'

James hesitates. 'He's a bit confused at the moment. As

you say, he felt he knew your dog. I think he's still trying to process all the facts.'

'I worried after your last visit that I perhaps pushed things too much. Too fast. I don't want him to feel under pressure. I can be patient.'

James smiles at her. 'I'm glad of that. I do think that we're progressing, though. I'm sure that he's getting flickers of memory again.'

'Flickers of memory?'

'Fragments of recall. Now and again, when we're talking, or in his drawings, he comes up with an image or a phrase.' James thinks of the face that Adam was drawing this morning. With the precision of the detail, with the care he was taking, it had to be more than a fiction pulled from his imagination. 'I don't know that it's properly coherent memory, but something's going on. He was experiencing similar events when he first came here, there were disjointed pieces of memory still there, but then he seemed to close it all up and suppress it entirely. It's difficult to get him to talk about it, but I think this might be a new phase. He'll have to face certain fears before he can unlock the rest, and that will be challenging, but I feel we might be heading in the right direction. My instinct is that this is progress, but we still need to have patience with him.'

'I've waited six years for him to come back,' Anna says. 'I can wait a little longer.'

She reaches out and squeezes James' hand, and he thinks about the smell of wood smoke and whisky, and a long night through which he might have talked too much. It seems a long time ago, that night. He feels he is perhaps a different person this morning.

'I must say, you're looking rather more chipper than last

time we met,' she says. 'You look as though you've caught up on a lot of lost sleep.'

Does she see it too, then? 'I am. I have. Thank you.'

They take tea in the drawing room while they wait for Adam to come down. Anna tours the walls, commenting on the family portraits and the collectors' cabinets.

'How lucky you are to live here,' she says.

'I recall that you pitied my wife for having to live in a lunatic asylum.'

'But I've never been allowed into these rooms before!' She laughs. 'It is all rather Gothic, though, isn't it?'

'The house belonged to Doctor Shepherd's aunt. It is all somewhat preserved in homage to her.'

'I thought I got a whiff of mausoleum.'

He hears the smile in her voice and watches as she walks around the room, taking in the panelling and plasterwork. Her finger points at the mermaids and peacocks in the ceiling frieze. She widens her eyes at the Indian swords and scimitars. The piano vibrates softly with the movement of her feet across the floorboards, and James remembers the strange music that Adam had brought into her house. There's a dreamlike quality to the memory of that moment, James thinks. Adam has never touched the piano here.

'The man who built the house imported sugar from the plantations in the West Indies,' he tells her. 'The design of this house is rather playful, whimsical in places, but I can never quite get away from how much human misery bought all this gilding and plasterwork.'

'What a thought!' Anna's eyes widen as she turns away again. James watches her face in the glass as her eyes move over the ammonites and cowrie shells and emus' eggs.

'Mark must love all of this, though. It's very him, this sort of thing. I've got a box full of flints and fragments of pottery, and bits of old brooch and belt buckle. He collected them when he was a boy. He would spend hours going over ploughed fields. In another life he might have ended up a dusty old archaeologist.'

'What we all might have been in another life.'

'Do you know, as a girl, I was drawn to the music hall? If it were not for my mother's notions of gentility, and meeting Mark, I might have ended up a grease-painted chorus girl.'

As James leans in to light her cigarette, he thinks of her lipsticked reflection in a mirror, looks at her laughing mouth and her eyes then sliding to the doorway. He turns and sees Caitlin there watching them.

'I heard the hilarity,' she says. 'I wondered what it was. I'm sorry. I really didn't mean to intrude.'

'No, come in,' he says. 'Do you want a cup of tea? Caitlin, this is Anna Mason. I've told you about her.'

'Of course.' She smiles rather formally, James thinks, as she shakes Anna's hand. 'How very nice to meet you.'

'And you. I've heard a lot about you,' Anna replies.

'Have you?'

'Will you join us?' James asks. 'We're waiting for Adam to come down.'

'No, honestly, I don't mean to disturb you. You might need to go and let Adam out, though. Sally caught him trying to slip out through the kitchen door earlier, so I think she's turned the key in his lock.'

'Oh God! I'm so sorry. That's awful,' says Anna, the unlit cigarette still between her fingers. 'He's locked in because he doesn't want to see me?'

'No! No, it's not like that. He was just having a bout of

wanderlust this morning. Caitlin, would you sit with Anna for a moment? I'll go and get Adam.'

James hears it start as he's climbing the stairs. The noise is unmistakably the shattering of glass. His first thought is that Adam has broken the window, that he's trying to climb out, but the sound of breaking glass just keeps on coming, and it is a terrible noise now. It is a barrage of sound, as if the room on the other side of the door is full of violence. He can hear Adam shouting, and glass splintering, and James is fearful as he reaches for the key. He doesn't know what to expect as he pushes the door, but the noise stops as it opens.

When he steps inside, Adam is standing in the centre of the room holding his wooden chair. Tears streak down his cheeks and blood is running down his arms. The floor is covered with shards of broken glass, a chaos of shattered reflection, and his red footprints. In this room that was once full of Adam Galilee's mirror image, the lights have all gone out and only the dull walls now answer back.

'What happened?'

Adam shakes his head. He rights the chair on the floor, sits and puts his head in his hands. There is blood all over his hands, and now his face.

'Dear God,' says James.

He walks towards Adam, puts a hand on his shoulder, and he can feel his body convulsing. His sobs are like the noise of a wounded animal. James kneels and puts his arms around him.

The only image in this room now is the woman's face. With the mirrors down, James is suddenly aware of the scale of it; she is there all around the room, in ink and pencil and charcoal – the expression of obsession. She looks out at James from every wall, her eyes surround him, and he wonders why he suddenly feels she has won. Is this what she has done to Adam? Has that obsession pushed him to this moment?

But, as he feels Adam's shaking shoulders, James knows that this is what he has done to him.

Chapter Fifty-Five

Adam, Fellside House, April 1921

'Has she gone?'

'Mrs Mason? Yes, she left some time ago. She was worried about you.'

Adam nods. She'd also looked scared. He is sorry if he scared her. Esther has bandaged his arms and his feet, telling him all the time that she'd been frightened when she heard the noise. Adam's cuts are angry, Esther says. She's asked him if he was angry. Was that why he did it? Adam had told her the truth: that he didn't know what it was, why he'd done it, only that he'd been scared too.

'I'm sorry if you felt we were putting you under pressure,' says Haworth. 'I didn't mean for it to be like that. And I'm sorry that you were locked in your room. That shouldn't have happened.'

'Don't blame yourself. I did it.'

'Was that what caused it – did you do it because you felt under pressure? Was it because Anna was here?'

'Not directly.'

Adam isn't sure that he can tell Haworth about the faces in the mirrors yet. He's not sure how to explain it. What it was. What it means. Where the faces came from. He only knows that he'd woken up and seen them, been surrounded by those faces and those scenes, and needed them to go away. If this is what remembering feels like, he wishes it could be as easily shattered as a mirror.

'Will you put the mirrors back?' he asks.

'Not if you don't want them.'

'No.'

'Perhaps just one so you can see to shave?' Haworth suggests.

'I'd rather have none.'

Adam looks down at his cut hands. Esther has put petroleum jelly on them and that seems to make the wounds look all the worse, and too much like the thing he'd seen in the mirror. His hands are throbbing now. He doesn't know how he'll do anything with them, how he'll work, how he'll draw.

'You'll need to make an effort to keep them clean for the next week,' Haworth says. 'I'll give you some cotton gloves. Put them on if you go out for a walk, and maybe it would be for the best if you don't try to draw for a few days. We don't want any infection getting in.'

Adam nods, but hasn't the infection already got in?

'I'm sorry,' Haworth goes on. 'I feel like I'm telling you to resist all of your natural instincts.'

'Don't worry,' he says. 'I'll be sensible.'

'Did you see something in the mirror?' Haworth asks. 'Did something frighten you?'

Adam has been waiting for the question, knowing it would come, but he's not sure how to reply. 'I'd fallen asleep.'

'Did you have a nightmare?'

'I don't know.' He would tell Haworth if he could, but he's not sure how to explain it. 'When I woke up I thought I could see faces in the mirrors.'

'Faces? Not your own face, you mean?'

'No.' If only it were just that.

'Are you sure? You could have been half asleep still.'

'I'm sure.'

'Did you see the men who you were drawing this morning?'

Had he? The faces that had appeared in his head this morning were fatigued men, exhausted men. They were tragic faces, but at least they were passive; frozen images, like photographs, they weren't really animate. But the men in the mirrors had been moving, they were closing in, and Adam had known that they meant him harm.

'Perhaps. Maybe. I don't know. But they were all looking at me.'

'How were they looking at you? Did you feel threatened?'

'I didn't think. I didn't reason. It wasn't like that. It was instinct. I needed to make them go away.'

'And when you broke the mirrors, did they go away?'

Have they gone away? Adam looks around the room. They're not here now, but he's not certain that they won't come back.

'Can you remember what they looked like?' Haworth prompts. 'Could you maybe draw them for me?'

'Can you give me a tablet to make me sleep?' Adam asks. 'Something to make me sleep, but not dream?'

James

'I think he's starting to remember things,' James tells Shepherd. 'He's started having nightmares again and parts of his memory are coming back with that.'

'And that's what prompted this incident?'

'He said he saw faces in the mirrors.' James turns away from the window, away from his own reflection. 'He was obviously terrified.'

'Your conclusion is that was the trigger – that, rather than Mason being here?'

'He was evidently anxious about her visit, I'm not saying that didn't contribute, but I get the impression it's more to do with the recollection of a fear coming back.'

'Is he remembering more than he's letting on?' Shepherd looks up from his notes. 'Would he submit to hypnosis again, do you think?'

'I'm not sure that he wants to engage with the memory. He asked me to give him a sedative.'

James could see it in Adam's face – that he didn't want to be forced to address whatever it was that he'd seen in the mirror. He didn't want to look it in the eye. James wasn't sorry to sedate him and he hopes that the sedative works. He can't force Adam to face up to that again. With the fear on Adam's face, he had remembered Nathaniel's face in the wood and that look in his eyes. He doesn't want Adam to have to go through that.

'How is his mood now?' Shepherd asks.

'Pretty bleak. Poor soul. He looks absolutely wrung out. I was relieved to give him something to help him sleep.'

'Mrs Mason looked somewhat distressed too.'

'Understandably, eh? She believes she's got her husband back, but now thinks he's a lunatic.'

Shepherd nods. 'This incident does have implications, doesn't it? It has consequences. We're going to have to think carefully about what we do next. I mean, what's to stop it being repeated? I'm not really sure that we should let him out for the time being.'

'You're not advocating locking him up?'

'No, of course not. But I'm not sure that he should travel again until things have stabilized. He's not ready to be released.'

'He's never been violent before, though, has he? It was a one-off, and it might not have happened if he hadn't been locked in his room. I don't think it's in him to hurt anyone else or himself.'

'But he's too vulnerable. I don't think that exposing him to risk would be fair to him or to anyone else. Do you?'

'No.' James shakes his head. He can't contend it. He thinks about the look on Anna Mason's face as Caitlin had led her away. He can't imagine that she would want to take Adam home any time soon.

'Anna Mason said something to Caitlin – that her husband was inclined to fits of temper and high emotion. I'd picked up something like that from her before. I suspect that he was maybe even inclined to self-harm, though she wasn't that explicit. She said that this behaviour was more typical of Mark Mason than the docile version of Adam she's met before.'

'So he's reverting to type?'

'She seems to think so.'

'And what do you think? Is it convenient for her to say that, does it just strengthen her case, or is it that his underlying personality is finally starting to show itself?'

'I don't know. I'm not sure. I'm inclined to believe that we fundamentally already know who Adam is. He was just terrified today. Genuinely. You should have seen his face when I opened the door. I haven't seen a man look like that since I was in France.'

'Do you think that's where he was mentally?'

James nods.

*

'How is he?' Caitlin asks.

'Sore. Upset. He was so scared when I went in there.'

She nods her head. 'Poor Adam. It's a step back, isn't it?'

'I've never seen him that distressed before. I feel terrifically sorry for him, but maybe it's the case that the blockage in his mind is resolving itself.'

'Resolving? As in, it's clearing? You think it's progress?'

She looks at him. He sees the judgement in Caitlin's eyes. 'I'm not sure that progress is quite the word, but in the long term, if he can address what happened to him, he can work through it and be well again.'

'Are you so sure? He looked far from well today.'

'He has to go back through those torments to get to the other side.' James thinks: isn't this, after all, what she has asked him to do? To talk about Nathaniel and let all of that go?

'You make it sound like Greek theatre. He's been so placid for the past couple of years, so comfortably contained within himself, but I saw a distraught young man this morning. I don't think it looked like progress.'

'But he can have more of a life.'

'Does he want more of a life?'

'If I'd not come back, if I'd lost my memory and was in an institution somewhere, wouldn't you want me to recover and come home?'

'If recovery would mean you being so wretchedly unhappy, if that's how you define it, I'm not sure I would.'

'Really?'

She nods. 'I know I'm not a doctor, but I'm not certain it's kind to him, bringing all these women here. He doesn't like it, he's told me, and they're all so needy, they're all so desperate for a face on which they can focus their own sorrow. I'm not saying that I don't pity them, but don't we have a duty to care for Adam's feelings first and foremost?'

He can't deny that the process has distressed Adam – he sees that now and he's sorry for it – but they were right to have tried, weren't they? 'If we found out that Nathaniel was still alive somewhere, but had lost his mind, would you want to visit him? Wouldn't you want to check and be sure that it really was him? Wouldn't you want to get him back?'

'Nathaniel? You can't keep equating Adam with Nat. You've got to break that link.'

Does he? He asks himself and he can't entirely deny it. It is part of why Adam matters to him. 'They're both lost.'

'In completely different circumstances!'

He can see that she's angry at him now. 'I suppose.'

'You *suppose*! Even if you manage to pin a name on Adam and install him happy-ever-after in the bosom of his rightful family, how does that bring Nat back?'

He sees her spread fingers tighten around her elbows. 'It doesn't. I know that. Of course it doesn't.' Is that how it appears? As if he's trying to balance out his own unfulfilled responsibility and feelings of guilt? 'I just want to help Adam. That's all I've ever wanted. And I wish I could bring Nathaniel back for you, but I can't.'

'But are you helping Adam? Really? He was so much more settled six months ago. Couldn't you have left him like that? If it's not hurting anybody, aren't some things better left broken?'

'It's not been a good few months, I know, but I do want to help him. We've only gone through all this because we care about him.'

'I know that. I'm sorry. I do understand that your intentions are good. But are you conscious of how many hours per day you're devoting to Adam? From the outside it looks like an obsession, James. You've crossed the line. You've made it personal. Have you forgotten that you've got other patients?'

'No, of course not. Did Shepherd say that to you? I know I've been spending a lot of time with Adam recently, but I felt we were close to making a breakthrough. I think there's a good chance that Adam could be Mark Mason. I wouldn't let her see him again if I didn't think there was some strong evidence.'

'But Adam doesn't believe that. What evidence have you got really? Adam thinks that she's mad. He also thinks she's been twisting you around her little finger, and having met her I'm not sure that I disagree. Isn't it just the case that you've fallen under her spell and so you want her to be right?'

'Under her spell? I feel sorry for her, but that's all. I'd like to help her and she's the most convincing candidate. There's nothing more to it than that. Yes, I find her amiable enough, but I'd far rather have her being amiable with Adam.'

'Amiable? Is that what it is? She told me how you talked all through the night, about how you shared all your problems, told her all about your dreams. I'm sure she was very sympathetic.'

'She told you that?'

'Yes, she was very forthcoming. Oh, was she not meant to? No, of course, I'm not meant to know about your dreams, am I? I wouldn't understand.'

He looks at Caitlin's eyes. How much has Anna told her? 'I didn't want to sleep that night. I'd kept having nightmares that week and didn't want it to happen again, so I tried to stay awake. She just ended up staying awake with me.'

'How considerate of her. What a splendid woman she is.

How terrifically *amiable*. Adam told me how she was with you. I was glad to see it for myself today.'

'I didn't realize that you and Adam had quite so many heart-to-hearts.' He doesn't mean it to sound as accusing as it comes out.

'Sometimes he feels he can't talk to you. He knows you won't be listening, that you're only going to push him in a particular direction.'

'He's the eyes on the hillside, you know.' James regrets saying it as soon as it is out. He wants to bite back his own words and the temper that made them come out.

'I'm sorry?'

'Adam. He's the one who looks in. He told me. He doesn't mean any harm by it, but he just likes to look at you through the window when he climbs up the hillside.'

'Adam? It's only Adam? But you've looked at me as if *I'm* mad! You knew it was Adam all along and you didn't think to tell me?'

'It didn't occur to me that it would be so important to you.' He doesn't mean it. Of course, he doesn't mean it. He knows how the feeling of being watched has increasingly unsettled her, and as she turns her back on him, he regrets that he sounds like he's dismissing her feelings. 'I shouldn't have said that. I'm sorry. I only realized recently that it was him. There's nothing sinister to it. It's only curiosity. I should have said something to you, though, shouldn't I? I wish that I had. Can you forgive me? *Please.* Caitlin?'

But she won't turn around.

'I heard you and Caitlin arguing. I hope I haven't caused problems for you,' Adam says.

He spreads his arms in apology, so that his shadow assumes

the form of a crucifixion and the show of his white bandaged wrists seems an exaggeration. It is slightly too much, all this bodily demonstration, James thinks.

'It's not you. It's not your fault. I've not spent enough time with Caitlin lately, that's all. There are things that we should have talked about, but we haven't. I should have made the time.'

'Will she leave again?'

The question surprises James. But should it? 'I do hope not. No, I don't want her to leave.' As he says it, James wonders if Adam could be right, though. He has never seen Caitlin so angry. And, worse than that, she seemed disappointed in him.

'You'll have to talk to her. You must make the time. You have to tell her that she mustn't go away.'

'I will.' Where was he meant to start, though? James stands with the sun in his eyes and wonders what to say. They had eaten breakfast in brittle silence that morning, neither of them knowing how and where to begin talking again. He could see that she had been crying. What could he say to stop her crying? 'Perhaps you can tell her too? She cares about you. She was worried about you yesterday.'

'But it needs to come from you.'

'Yes.' James nods. He knows Adam is right; still, as he looks at this man in his outlandish second-hand frock coat and white cotton gloves, it seems rather odd to be taking marital advice from him.

Adam has started work on the old greenhouse, sweeping all the fallen glass and leaves together and measuring where new panes must be fitted. The gutters of the greenhouse have rusted, the putty is crumbling away, and it seems the ivy is the only thing that's holding the building together. The glass sides sag ominously and the whole thing looks as if it might go at any moment. James is not at all sure that it's safe for Adam to be in here, but it is seemingly where he wants to be. As he watches Adam work amongst the piles of shattered glass, James thinks of him standing amongst the broken mirrors. He can't erase the image of Adam's face at that moment from his mind. But he is calmer today. He's a different man. Occupied in his task, he is back to being Adam Galilee again. Could Caitlin be right after all; isn't it better to leave him here like this, and not impose memory or relationships on him?

'Some of this is my fault,' Adam says, and nods at the broken panes.

'Pardon?'

'This place. The broken glass, I mean. I threw a spade at it a few weeks ago. Of course, nobody would have noticed, it was all so broken down already. Who would have spotted a few extra missing panes? But now that I'm going to fix it, I'll be conscious that I'm making amends. I do want to make it right.'

'You threw a spade at the greenhouse? Why?'

'Frustration. Confusion. It was after we'd got back from the second visit to Anna Mason's. I didn't know what was real and what wasn't, and where I was meant to be. I was torn. I was upset. But I shouldn't have broken something that's not mine – not this, or the mirrors in my room – and I should have told you about it too. I'm sorry.'

It's warm inside this glasshouse and full of a heady vegetable scent. The vines have formed a mesh, impenetrable as a thorny thicket, and Adam says that it will need to be cut right back. It will do it good; it's being cruel to be kind, he says. He will revive the vine. His fingers point to tight amber-green buds curling away from branches that look lifeless. James knows that if Adam is allowed to stay here, there will be no more broken glass.

'I've not been fair to you,' he says. 'I feel bad that you've felt pressured, if you've felt pushed into difficult situations, and I'm sorry if I've not listened to you enough.'

'We have both apologized to each other now,' says Adam. 'That means we are even.'

He draws a line in the dust with his broom as if to illustrate that the matter is closed.

James is not sure which of them is the ghost in the room, but they move around the apartment as though the other is invisible. There is an odd physics to it; like magnet poles pushing apart, they move through the same space, but always keeping that distance, always maintaining that resistance. Even their eyes can't meet.

Caitlin carries her teacup through from the kitchen as he is making up the fire. James hears the rattle of the spoon in her saucer, her chair being pulled out and her book placed on the table. It's because he feels her eyes on his back that he can't turn around, so he finds himself crouching over the kindling, staring into the lengthening flames. He finally has to stand because his legs ache. As he turns, he catches the angle of her gaze shifting to the window. The logs hiss and smoke sighs back down the chimney.

James walks to the window and braces his hands on the sash. Against the darkness of the trees, he can see the pale reflection of her face behind. He wants to tell her that the wisteria is coming out, that Arthur is feeding a stray cat in the garden below and that Sally and Letty are fighting the breeze as they peg out lines of sheets, but what use are such remarks? Why should she care what he sees?

Caitlin pushes back her chair and walks to the fireplace, stretching her fingers towards the flames. He can see that she is watching his back in the overmantel mirror. James recalls Adam's mirror face angled all around his attic room, but he thinks of Adam too much, she says. The window bounces back the shift in Caitlin's mirrored eyes and James realizes that the only connection they presently have is the words they have bounced off Adam.

She is a half-seen glimmer of grey fabric and soft, retreating footsteps on floorboards, and might well be an apparition, or a trick, or his own overactive imagination. Daylight moves around the walls, the shadows swing, and they move around each other in a silent dance, only James isn't sure of the next steps.

Hartley is teaching Milner how to foxtrot, and they laugh and swear, soldiers again, as they clash knees and step on one another's toes. After the heightened emotions of yesterday, there is a wilfully light-hearted mood in the house today. Shepherd croons along with the gramophone and conducts an invisible orchestra. Adam grins and beats the rhythm with his foot as he watches Hartley spin Corporal Milner. Were it not for Adam's bandaged arms, yesterday might have been a bad dream. Can they all forget and just begin again? Could they pretend that it didn't happen? James wishes it could be so easy and that he could take back the words he said to Caitlin.

Milner is wearing primula flowers in his buttonhole, James notices. He thinks about a dream and Adam's fingers holding out a posy of meaningful hedgerow greenery. He is talking about putting in raspberry canes and currant bushes now and has written off to nurseries for catalogues. Adam is making plans for four seasons ahead and James can't help but be struck by the permanence of his schemes. James knows that Shepherd will let him stay for as long as he wishes, but he can't presently imagine Adam ever leaving Fellside House. Should he write to Anna and warn her of that? He is not sure that he ought to write to Anna Mason ever again.

Adam has asked if he can have a sedative tonight, but he seems so much brighter now than he did yesterday. Remarkably so. Perhaps it is enough to know that he won't have to leave Fellside again for a while? Was that reassurance sufficient to stop the terrors? If that is the case, James is sorry to have subjected him to that anxiety.

Adam taps Hartley on the shoulder, breaks into the partnership and takes on the male role. Hartley makes a pantomime bluster of being affronted, and shakes a fist, but retires to a chair, laughing. Adam dances surprisingly lightly and smoothly, James observes, as if he is enjoying himself. He has never thought of Adam as a man who might have gone to dances, but he has evidently learned at some point in his life. With his raised eyebrows and mild smile, he has even put on the mask of a dancer. James imagines Anna Mason in Milner's place. Could she really have been Adam's partner? Was she the one who taught him the steps? Was it her lipsticked mouth that returned his smile? Did her long white fingers wind into his? How many other masks has Adam worn? James sometimes thinks that he understands the man in the greenhouse in his eccentric coat, but does he really know Adam that well at all?

Shepherd sits down next to James. He is glowing slightly from the effort of conducting and wafts at his face with a white handkerchief. He smiles at James and pats his shoulder.

'Have you noticed how he can dance? Look at his feet! I didn't think he had that in him.'

'He can steer his way around a dance floor rather more

elegantly than I can. I'm not sure why it surprises me. Perhaps it's just that it doesn't go with the earthy fingernails and tree climbing?'

'But shouldn't it? He's quite a complicated character.'

'I realize that more every day.'

'I've realized one thing that he's not today,' Shepherd says.

'And that is?'

'Ellis Vickers.'

James turns towards Shepherd. He leans towards him to cut out the blare of the gramophone. 'You've found something out? How so?'

'I called a favour in from Fairclough and asked him to do some digging in the records. Vickers was demobbed in January 1919. He disembarked at Southampton. He might be missing as far as his family is concerned, but the military authorities would beg to differ.'

'But Adam was already here in January 1919, wasn't he? So, it's conclusive? There's no case there at all?'

'Fairclough managed to pull up Vickers' enlistment papers as well. There are distinct differences in appearance: Vickers was three inches shorter than Adam, for a start. He's hardly likely to have had a growth spurt in his mid-twenties, is he?'

'So that settles the matter. That rules him out.'

'That, the absence of a tattoo and the fact that the colouring is all wrong. Vickers has auburn hair, same as his sister.'

'So it's not even that they look alike? How could she have imagined it? Did she believe it – or is this something more sinister?'

'I don't know. She seemed so entirely sincere, didn't she?'

James thinks about Adam looking out at the water and looking into the painting. He had been so certain that Adam felt something in that place. Had he got that wrong too?

'I'm starting to wonder whether I'm much of a judge of character at all. Could she know that her brother is alive? Do we have a responsibility to let her know?'

'I don't know about responsibility, but I have to say that I'm curious. Aren't you?'

Chapter Fifty-Six

James, High House, April 1921

In the mist, the house looks like a lighthouse. As James walks towards it, he now wishes that he had written first. He's uncertain how to begin this conversation. What will her reaction be? Does she know her brother is alive elsewhere? Has she always known? Does she just want a father for the children and an army pension? Was it nothing but a cynical gamble?

James looks up and an arrow of geese flies crying overhead. They are Canada geese, as Adam said they would be. Could that simply be a likelihood, an informed probability, that he calculated correctly, or has Adam been here before? It is somehow difficult to believe that he hasn't.

'Doctor Haworth?' He can see the surprise on her face as she opens the door. Her hands straighten her apron, smooth her hair. 'Is everything all right? Ellis isn't unwell, is he?'

It looks like genuine concern on her face. Is she an accomplished actress, or has she convinced herself? James can hear children's voices from beyond the door.

'May I come in?'

There are two small, red children in the kitchen, cutting out gingerbread men. They look up at James with staring, but uncommunicative eyes. There is much about this place that is too like a fairy story, James thinks. The room smells of a newly struck match and treacle and ginger.

'This is Tom and Katie,' she says. 'Ellis' children. Will you shake Doctor Haworth's hand, Tom?'

The small boy's hand feels shapeless in James' own. He looks down at his frowning face and sees nothing of Adam in the boy's features. The children both have Lucy's colouring and sharpness, as Ellis must too. They might well be her own children.

'Is Father coming home today?' the boy asks him.

'Not today,' James replies.

The girl slowly licks a spoon as she eyes him. There is something unnerving about these gingerbread-coloured children who watch him with unblinking eyes.

'I'll put the biscuits in the oven. Katie, don't wipe your hands on your pinafore. Why don't you put your coats on and go and look for ghosts in the barns?'

'Look for ghosts?' James laughs. 'You and your brothers did that too as children, didn't you?' He watches them run for the door and hears them squealing out in the yard. It sounds like a rough game.

'You think my childrearing is a bit unconventional, don't you? It's what they enjoy doing, though.' She shrugs. 'Yes. It's what we did.' Her smiling face is suddenly serious. 'But you're not here to play games with the children, are you?'

He watches as she counts out spoonfuls of tea leaves. There is a picture of Durham Cathedral on the tea caddy, James notices. Is he now seeing false clues? Is he picking out patterns that aren't there? Has he been misreading the signs all along?

'I've got some information about your brother,' he says. It seems kinder to say it directly, not to dance around it, and he wonders if this is why Adam has always been so spare with the women.

'About Ellis? Yes?'

'A friend with contacts managed to pull out some records.'

'Go on.' Her hand hovers with the teaspoon. Her face is inscrutable.

'Ellis was only missing temporarily. He was injured, as you know, but when he was discharged from hospital, he was transferred to the Labour Corps. He saw out the rest of the war there. He was demobbed at the start of 1919.'

'And then he came to your hospital.'

'I'm sorry, Miss Vickers. I don't know where your brother is, but he's definitely not with us.'

'He's run away again, you mean?'

He watches her stir the tea. Is she determined to misread him? 'I'm afraid you misunderstand me. He's never been with us. Your brother has never been at Fellside House.'

'But how can you say that?' She laughs. She punctuates her sentence with a wave of the teaspoon. 'You brought him here.'

'We don't yet know who that man is, but we know now that he's not your brother.'

'That's ridiculous! What a thing to say. Of course he is!'

'Miss Vickers, the patient we call Adam Galilee has been with us since November 1918. According to the records, your brother was still in Belgium at that time. It's impossible. It can't be the same person.'

'The records are wrong, then. Do you imagine that I don't know my own brother?' She sits down opposite James. Her actions are slow, calm, measured; her eyes communicate anything but that. 'You brought him to this house. He sat at this table. He drank from his own cup. You saw how at home he was here.'

'I'm sorry, but that cannot be the case. Papers show that

your brother disembarked at Southampton in January 1919. He can't have been getting off a boat in Hampshire and in Westmorland at the same time.'

'Then the man on the boat is an imposter. You read about it. It happens. He must have had Ellis' papers. He could have stolen Ellis' identity.'

'I can't deny that's possible, but we decided to check your brother's enlistment papers too. The physical description doesn't match.'

She shakes her head. She looks at James as if he is a fool. 'He is Ellis. The man who you brought here is my brother. I don't care who this other person is. The man in your hospital is Ellis.'

James is suddenly aware of the smell of burning gingerbread. The stewing tea steams between them. He can see that whatever he says won't convince her that she could be in error, and her cast-iron conviction makes him question himself. He had walked into this room with such certainty, he had no doubt, but Lucy's refusal to believe him cracks his resolve.

'Is it that you need help with looking after the children? Some practical assistance? Some extra money?'

'No! Is that what you think I am? Do you think I'm a fraud? That this is a scheme? Do you imagine I want his pension?'

James had considered the possibility on the journey here, but now he feels ungallant for having thought it. 'I didn't mean to offend you.'

'Well, you have! If you could see that I was a wealthier woman, you wouldn't have even poked around in the paperwork, would you? Was I meant to slip some money under the table to you?'

'We've investigated all the cases. We've tried to be impartial.'

'Have you? I bet you've investigated some more than others.'

Is she right? On reflection, they've done little work on Mark Mason. Shouldn't they have pursued a copy of his enlistment documents too? Do his colours and measurements fit?

'I'm sorry,' says James, not sure what else to say as he looks at the earnest face of the woman in front of him. 'I know it's not what you wanted to hear.'

'Wanted to hear? I can't believe my ears.'

Her fingers straighten a teaspoon on the tabletop. James notices that she repeatedly does this, as if this alignment, the orderliness of this small detail, is vital to her.

'But, you see, it opens a window for you. It's not all bad news. Your brother is alive.'

'I know he's bloody well alive!' She scrapes her chair away and turns her back on him. The teaspoon rattles into the sink. 'What is the point in you being here?' she says. She swears as she takes the tin from the oven. It clatters onto the table, James can feel the heat coming off it, and the gingerbread men are so many smoking silhouettes. A bitter smell fills the room and he knows that Lucy wants him to go.

'I am truly sorry,' James says as he buttons his coat. He can see the tension in her back. 'You should speak to the police. Register him as a missing person. For all you know, he might not be far away. You haven't lost Ellis. You can get your brother back.'

'I've already got him back and you can't stop me from seeing him,' she says as she turns.

The ambulance is there as James pulls in to the drive. His first thought is Caitlin and how unhappy she had looked as he left. His second thought is Adam.

He leaves the car door open and runs. Shepherd is standing on the steps with his arms folded.

'Alan? What is it? What's happened?'

He turns towards James and shakes his head.

Chapter Fifty-Seven

James, Ambleside, April 1921

The congregation looks pitifully small when they move into the church, just the eight of them from Fellside and Milner's family, and there seem to be an awful lot of empty pews behind. As James watches Sylvia Milner's shoulders in the row ahead, he wonders if she's angry at him. Does she feel let down? Does she think they have failed her? He recalls the difficult conversation that he had with Shepherd two weeks ago and the implication that he might not have been devoting enough time to Milner. Is Sylvia Milner aware of that too?

'It's Milner,' Shepherd had said on the steps. It wasn't the name that James was braced for. It wasn't what he had expected. After all, hadn't they been making progress? If James had thought that Milner needed more attention, he would have given it, but wasn't he getting better? Talking more? Talking about future plans? His last image of Milner's face is lit with laughter as he foxtrots around the sitting room with Adam. Why, just twenty-four hours later, had he decided to take his own life? Sylvia Milner has asked that same question. James doesn't have an answer.

'What's got into this house?' he had said to Shepherd. Within two days they've had two traumas. And one must have contributed to the second. How could it not? James knows that he has played a part in the process that ended with Milner tying his dressing-gown cord around the beam in his bedroom.

They sing 'Abide With Me' and James watches the family in front huddle together. Mrs Milner puts her arms around her children's shoulders, as if she means to brace them together, and to shelter them. Does she feel some guilt too, James wonders. After all, it was at her injunction that Milner was transferred to Fellside. She had wanted her husband to get help because he had kicked her. James can still bring to mind the photographs of the bruises on her ribs. But she had said that her husband wasn't in his right mind, and they could hardly deny her that. She had talked about him as if he was possessed by something other than his own personality. This behaviour had been going on for some time, James suspected, but when Milner had taken his belt off to his children too, a line was seemingly crossed. She had told James that this temper was never there before her husband went away. He had brought that back, like a wound, from the war. Like a lesion that wouldn't heal, couldn't it be treated too?

James had felt uncomfortable at first, trying to empathize and sympathize with a man who could do that. It is the first case of that kind that he has been required to deal with, and he can't imagine circumstances in which he would ever raise a fist to Caitlin. But then, he supposes, we are all flawed, aren't we? And aren't there other kinds of cruelty and neglect? Milner didn't want to be that man, he desperately didn't, he wanted that part of his personality cutting out, and assisting with that had seemed the right thing to do. And James had thought they were getting there. He had thought that Milner had faced up to all those memories of limitless violence, and that trigger in his own temper, and was putting all of that behind him. Had he been so wrong? Has he really been neglectful of his responsibilities?

'"The Lord is my shepherd,"' they repeat. '"I shall not want."'

Milner had talked, under hypnosis, about a trench raid that had gone wrong, about hand-to-hand fighting and savage bloodshed. It had shocked him to see bodies being broken that way, and then to know that he too could cut and cleave and crush, and it had broken something in his brain, he said. Rules had been broken. Boundaries had been crossed. Whenever he looked at his own hands now, he saw what they had done, what they were capable of doing, and sometimes he couldn't control them. It was as if his hands were *possessed* by something beyond his own volition. It was the word that he had chosen and seemingly passed on to his wife. Had that been true when he had tied up the cord too?

'"He maketh me to lie down in green pastures,"' James repeats. '"He leadeth me beside the still waters."'

Sally had been the one to find Milner. They had come running when they heard her screams, and they had all seen him, but it was already too late. Hartley had helped Shepherd to bring him down. Adam told James how Hartley had sobbed.

There are no old comrades here in the church today, or friends from before the war, which seems to imply that the life being marked was one of isolation. Was Milner lonely? Were there friends from before who he had missed? Did his subsequent behaviour sever those friendships? Will all the Fellside men one day be buried like this? They are all in overcoats, in black and grey and brown, but the sun slants through the church windows and washes them over in red and gold and ecclesiastical blue. James looks down at his own hands around the prayer book and the page glows purple. He turns his fingers, strange to him suddenly in the stained-glass light, and looks up to see Adam's observing smile.

'"Surely goodness and mercy shall follow me all the days of my life,"' they echo, '"and I will dwell in the house of the Lord for ever."'

James looks at Sylvia Milner and wonders what she will do now. Does she feel some sense of relief that she is no longer tied to a husband with a hair-trigger temper? Is it a mercy? Was it a kindness on her husband's part? Given the progress Milner was making, he might well have gone home within the next couple of months, but could she ever have felt entirely calm in her husband's presence again? Surely it would always have been there, that fear, that possibility. Wouldn't she always have been afraid for her children?

Milner's children are younger than James had supposed them to be, and he wonders how much they actually know. What have they experienced? What have they witnessed? They could not have been more than babies before the war, so is that damaged version of Milner the only father that they have ever known? James hasn't seen the children before, and wouldn't have picked them out as Milner's; there is no particular family resemblance there. Their wide uncommunicative eyes remind him of Lucy Vickers' children. What things children must witness these days.

James can hear Hartley's sobs in the pew behind, his groans, and it is terrible to hear a man cry that way. James knows that this incident will put them all back. Why couldn't Milner have talked to someone that morning? Why couldn't he have reached out? Yes, James had gone to see Lucy Vickers, but Shepherd had been there. Could Milner not have knocked on his door? If James had been there, would it have made a difference? Is it his fault?

They sing, '"Peace, perfect peace, in this dark world of sin. The blood of Jesus whispers peace within."'

James hears the sigh of Adam's breath at his side and is taken back to an image of a posy in his hands and a poppy held out to Milner. In the flickering light of his recall, James sees Adam's fingers winding the stem of the poppy into Milner's buttonhole and his voice whispers, 'To help you sleep.' In that odd wavering shell-light James had watched the shadows moving over Milner's face, and hadn't he seen a smile there? As Caitlin said, has James spent too long thinking of Adam? He remembers rushing through Milner's last sessions. Had he slowed down, had he listened, might they not be here now? There are paper poppies in the wreath on his coffin.

'"It is enough,"' they sing, '"earth's struggles soon shall cease, and Jesus call us to heaven's perfect peace."'

With every noise in the church James looks around. Caitlin had said that she would meet him at the gates at three. It is not like her to be late. It is unlike her not to make the effort to be here. Her black dress had been hanging on the back of the bedroom door as James left. She has not worn it since the memorial service for Nathaniel. As she pulled it out of the wardrobe, she must have recalled that day, James supposes.

She had asked him to address the congregation, because he was the last person to have seen Nathaniel alive, but when he had looked down and seen her parents' faces, he had recognized something that looked like accusation. James remembers how his notes had trembled in his hands, and how all their eyes had been on him. How hollow, how inadequate his words had seemed, and how difficult it was to get them out. He can still picture Caitlin's mother's face and knows that she will never forgive him. Did they talk about that when Caitlin went to stay with her mother? Has Caitlin ever really forgiven him too?

There is no eulogy for Milner, no friends to offer kind recollection, or family members to share reminiscence. Shepherd had offered to say a few words, but Sylvia Milner had said that she would rather have a simple service. Just words from the Bible. Some hymns. Only the vicar's voice. Was she scared of what Shepherd might say out loud?

How very plain and simple it seems, and it is over so fast. They step out into the spring sunshine and it hardly feels like they've spent enough time in the shadows.

'Will he have to be buried outside the churchyard?' Adam asks.

James looks at him. There is only an innocent curiosity on his face. Something that reminds him of the Vickers children who spend their days looking for ghosts. 'No, of course not.'

It is a plain pine coffin, marked with his name and dates. James is surprised to see that Milner was only twenty-eight. He would have put him twenty years older. Sylvia Milner throws a handful of soil in and it skitters on the lid of the coffin. The little boy has evidently been told to do likewise, but he stares at the earth in his hand as if he has forgotten what he must do with it. The gesture reminds James of Adam at Anna Mason's farm, and of the certainty he had felt then that Adam had not entirely forgotten that place. It is only with his mother's prompting that the boy lets go of the earth. His eyelashes lift and he looks directly at James. What knowledge and feeling is there in that look? Has his mother told him who James is?

The only tears at the graveside are Hartley's. James feels sad that no tears wet the cheeks of Milner's wife or his children.

Is that damage done, James considers, or stoicism? It looks more like hurt than strength.

The words *A Soldier of the Great War* will be cut into Milner's gravestone. James supposes that is what Milner has been, and always will be now, but he wonders why his wife has chosen those particular words, which imply he belonged more to the war than to his family. The gravestone will be that of a soldier rather than of a father and a husband. Did she feel she'd already lost her husband? Perhaps she chooses to blame the war.

Adam

'The blackbirds are nesting,' he says. He touches Haworth's elbow and points. He wants to distract him, give him hope, because he looks so bleak today. 'The bluebells will be out in the wood within a week. Perhaps you might take Caitlin and show her?'

'Yes.'

There are crocuses and daffodils around the old tombstones and all the cemetery is purple and gold in the spring sunshine. They walk between the graves, between the *dearly beloved* and the *sadly departed*, and there are violets and wood sorrel at the shaded edges of the churchyard.

'The seasons turn,' he says. 'The world goes round and it all goes on. We should open our eyes, take it in, enjoy it all while we can, shouldn't we?'

'You're right,' Haworth replies. He lights a cigarette and turns amongst the old headstones. 'How wise you are.' But he doesn't sound as though he really means it.

Adam kneels and puts his fingers to a leaning stone. The

sentiments and dates are crumbling away. 'I can't read most of them. The wind and the rain are rounding the letters off, softening the angles. It gives the impression that they have all died quietly in their beds, doesn't it? These words couldn't possibly say anything violent or strange. One day, no one will know who is here.'

'Quite possibly.'

Haworth exhales smoke. Adam can feel the tension coming off him.

'Caitlin was meant to be here, wasn't she?' he asks.

'She said she would be.'

Adam had seen Caitlin the morning after Milner died, her red eyes and all the light gone out of her face. They had sat quietly together in the garden, she had squeezed his hand before she silently walked away, and he had known that this was about much more than Milner's death. Adam has heard no voices in the apartment down below since and James says that Caitlin's silence is breaking his heart. He says that he wishes Caitlin would talk, that she would tell him how she's feeling, but it's as if she has no words left. James says that he would rather have her scream. He doesn't know what Caitlin's thoughtful silence means, but Adam can see that he is frightened by it. It's there on his face today, that fear, and Adam worries that something is breaking.

'Perhaps she didn't feel well?' Shepherd suggests as he approaches. They stand together and watch Haworth looking up and down the road. Adam's eye catches Shepherd's. 'Perhaps she didn't feel up to it?'

Haworth nods. 'She doesn't like funerals.'

Adam hopes, for Haworth's sake, that it's only that.

'I've asked the family back to the house,' Shepherd says, 'but Sylvia wants to get the children home.'

'I could understand if they didn't want to come back to Fellside,' Haworth replies.

Adam can understand it too. He had watched as Sally and Letty and Esther folded all of Milner's clothes into a suitcase. They had cried as they smoothed the creases from Milner's shirts and Adam hadn't known what to say. That suitcase is the only thing in Milner's room now. Adam wonders how long it will stay there. Will anyone come and take it away? Will anyone want it? He's not sure that anyone will want to stay in that room again. It is difficult enough just to walk past the door.

James

Sylvia Milner shakes James' hand as they leave, and he remembers the bruises that he once saw around her wrist. The touch of her black leather glove is cold, and she withdraws her hand quickly. Her smile is complicated and fleeting, but her blue eyes hold his gaze and it feels like a challenge. He suspects that she is angry at all of them, and will be glad to be gone. As he watches her black hand close the lychgate, he considers what life she will now return to. He hopes that, like Adam, she can find a way to blank out memories and make a future in which the war leaves no echoes.

He follows Shepherd's car back to the house and Adam sits at his side pointing at cowslips and talking about hawk moths and house martins. How lucky he is, James thinks, that these are his concerns and his memories. At this moment, he wishes, for Adam's sake, that he will never remember.

Back at the house, Sally hands around a tray of teacups and Shepherd opens a bottle of rum. James had promised Caitlin that he wouldn't have another drink, but it is companionable that they all take a tot in their tea, and there is that post-mourning collective sense of relief. They pull chairs up to the fire in the sitting room and take turns to toast teacakes with a fork. As the lights are lit, and the conversation gets louder and further away from the events of the day, he keeps looking up, expecting to see Caitlin's shape in the doorway.

'Will you excuse me? I'd love to get out of this suit,' he says.

The apartment is in darkness when he pushes open the door. Is she still sitting in the shadows looking at her black dress? He flicks the light switch and it is all as it was, but all different.

'Caitlin?'

The dress is still there on the back of the bedroom door, looming like Caitlin's ghost, but as he looks around the room he realizes that other things are not there. The dressing-table mirror returns the dazzle of his own confused reflection as he looks for her hairbrush and perfume and face powder, and finds only absences. He catches his own movement in the reflection of the window, but his is the only movement here, and in the picture that the window frames, he sees only his own possessions.

'Caitlin!'

The breath that he hears is only the wind through the trees, the knocking only the branches on the roof and the approaching footsteps are only the water in the pipes. When he opens the empty wardrobe, he knows she is not coming back.

Chapter Fifty-Eight

Caitlin, Oxenholme, April 1921

The headlights of the taxicab pick out the shapes of hedgerows and blurs of stone walls, the dazzle of reflection in a rabbit's eyes and the silhouette of a fox scuttling across the road ahead. The beams cut through the all-around blackness, so that Caitlin feels she is plunging into a tunnel of light. She doesn't like the man driving so fast, particularly since he keeps fidgeting with his cigarettes, but then she also wants to get to the station before the last train. She holds on to her seat and feels as if she's falling.

It isn't that she has planned this. It's not like that. She didn't wake up this morning knowing that the day would end this way. When she had come back from her mother's last week, she had meant to make it work, to try to be patient, try to be understanding, but for the past few days it has felt as though everything was spiralling away from her good intentions. And then this morning, he had said Nat's name.

She thinks of James returning to the apartment. Is he there yet? Does he know now? Will he try to follow her? Will he be all right? She shakes her head at the last question. Of course, he won't be all right. She should have written him a letter at least. He deserved to know her reasons. But then, how could she put them down on paper? That would require her thoughts to be rational, logical, watertight, to shape into one half of an argument, but it isn't like that. She is running away from trying to explain, and she knows that isn't fair to James. Right now, though, it also feels it's the best thing for both of them.

They had clung together the night after Milner died and had needed one another then. They couldn't have been closer in those first few hours after the shock, but she had seen the guilt on James' face the next day, and what could she say to make that go away? He'd had the nightmare again the following night and she'd understood that it was all linked. The car's brakes squeal on a bend and she braces her hand against the door. If this is for the best, why does she feel she is fleeing the scene of a crime?

It had been another disturbed night and then there had been his face this morning. When she'd opened her eyes in the early hours, she had seen the flash of raw panic contorting James' features into a face she hardly knew, and then he had said it – he had called her by her brother's name. He had looked into her eyes as he spoke, his voice breaking, desperate, cracking with sadness, but entirely distinguishable.

'Nathaniel.'

It had lasted only for a moment – the intensity of that look, the name there between them – and then he was blinking, apologizing, not entirely certain of what he'd done, still in the blurred boundary between dream and reality. It had shocked her, she hadn't been sure what he might do next, but what had frightened her most was that when she'd looked into the black of James' eyes, she'd also recognized Nathaniel's face reflected there.

Does James even remember saying it? He'd been quiet this

morning and they hadn't talked about it. But it's done now. It's out. It's been said. She won't forget how he looked at her then, and she knows now that it's true – that her face is the trigger for his nightmares. While they are together, while her face is the last thing that he sees at night, how can James stop reliving that scene? And how can she move on from losing Nat when the man at her side must go back there every night?

She'd splashed cold water on her face and looked at herself in the bathroom mirror. Had she imagined it? Had she misheard? No, she knew that she hadn't.

'What now?' she'd asked her reflection.

Her mirror face told her that she had to keep on trying.

She has spent the day repeating that mantra: *Try, try, I have to try.* She loves him. They simply have to work through it. There has to be a way. But then she'd stepped into that dress, and, in the mirror, she'd been the girl from her brother's memorial service. It was five years ago, she's not a girl any longer, and yet Caitlin feels she's hardly had chance to mourn him, and so it could still be yesterday. She can't let go yet. There hasn't been space for it. There hasn't been space for her to be angry. Barely space to cry. She hasn't been able to ask questions.

Her head is full of so many questions, but how can she say them out loud to the one person who might be able to answer them? Every question would be like pushing a pin into James' skin. And so, while Nat is still there at the edges of her reflection, that's all she gets to see. Though she longs to hear his voice, she can't. Nor can she touch him, or see his smile. She wishes that he would step out from behind her, but he won't. That sense of his presence, his eyes watching, isn't a comfort any longer because she knows that he's not at peace. She remembers a William Blake watercolour of souls suspended in limbo, and while she doesn't like to think that Nat might be caught in that restless churn, on the nights when James screams, it feels as though they are all stuck in that in-between place. For his sake, for her sake, don't they have to break out of that?

She sees the station sign flash in the headlights.

'Would you like me to wait, miss?'

'Don't worry. Thank you. It's due in ten minutes.'

'Do you need a hand with your suitcase?'

'No, it's quite all right.'

She has only taken one small suitcase and Lord knows what she's put in it. She had grabbed handfuls of clothes from the wardrobe in her panic and swept the bottles off the dressing table. She only has the pair of shoes that she's wearing, she's left all her jewellery behind and she doesn't even have a photograph of James. (*Oh, dear God, his face!* She thinks about a boy who had once looked down on her in a London park and the tortured face of the man at her side this morning. How has it come to this?) But if she was going to go, she had to do it before he came back. If she'd had to explain it, if she'd had to say it to James' face, she wouldn't have been able to leave.

The evening air is cool and Caitlin wishes that she'd brought a coat. She pulls her jumper around her and leans her head back against the wall. The station master touches his hat to her, and she feels awkward and embarrassed, standing here in not enough clothing and tears on her cheeks. She feels so obviously (ridiculously!) like a woman who is running away from something. The moonlit railway tracks taper away.

What will her mother say when she turns up on her doorstep again? Last week, she'd told her that she needed to try harder, that a failed marriage was a failure of character, and she must make more of an effort. But on the day she had last worn that black dress, the day of Nat's memorial service, her mother had said that he would still be alive if it wasn't for James.

As Caitlin had looked at herself in the mirror this afternoon, she'd reheard those words. She knows that it's not true – at least not in the sense that her mother had meant – but she also knows that James had heard those words too. If he can't forget that, if he can't let Nat go, what will happen to him? Will he drink himself into hospital? Or, like Milner, in a moment's desperation, will he do something terrible too? She loves him enough that she doesn't want it to end that way. But how can he ever forgive himself when he sees Nat in her face every day?

As she hears the whistle of the train, Caitlin tells herself again that this is the right thing to do. Only, it feels so very wrong.

Chapter Fifty-Nine

James, Fellside House, April 1921

James follows Adam's path and climbs up through the wood. Just as he said, all the bluebells are out, shimmering under the shadow of the trees and as far as James can see, and he breathes their cool scent. He doesn't want to walk through the bluebells, to step on them, they are too fleeting and precious for that, but he can't seem to avoid it. His footsteps mark out his own path and the hems of his trousers are wet.

He has not slept again. He spent the night going over the words that he should have said, but didn't, rehearsing all the lines that might have made a difference, had he found the courage to say them. He has thought about writing to Caitlin, or going to her mother's house (because that's surely where she must be), but he knows that it's too late for those words now. He wishes that she could have told him exactly why she left, that he could have heard her words and had the chance to reply, but hasn't she already said it all before? He should have tried harder to listen. If they'd talked, would it have made a difference? Could he have changed and made her stay?

He turns in the blue-green dappled, enchanted light and realizes that Caitlin has never been up here. There have been three springs of bluebells since they moved to Fellside, and he can't think why he never made the time to show Caitlin this. An imagined version of her runs ahead through the blue haze and turns and laughs as she goes. How could he have missed that chance? Why did he not take her hand and bring her here? Why did he never pick her a bunch of bluebells? The sunlight breaks through the trees and glitters in the dew and it is a morning fit for a watercolour or a poem. James feels he has missed so many chances.

He climbs out of the wood and up onto the rocks. The gradient pulls on the back of his legs and he feels the effort of it in his chest, but something is drawing him higher. He skirts the stone wall and then, through the break in the trees, the lake is there below. Windermere is a mirror this morning and gives back the blue of the sky. Three years ago they had taken a boat out onto the water, and it had felt as if their life was finally beginning. Could it be over so soon? It all seems too brief, too complicated, too far removed from the life he had wanted to make for her. James sits on the bench for a moment. He can hear his heart pumping when he shuts his eyes, feels his blood moving fast through his body and he wonders how it still can.

His feet follow the rocks, finding the footholds out onto the crag. The stones thrust skyward here, they shout their own twisted geology, and he has to use his hands to pull himself up. He scrambles up the naked rock and when he turns it all falls away below him. The wind tugs at his hair and billows his shirt. He breathes in the morning air and he can see Coniston Fells and the spire of the church at the bottom, where they left Milner last week. All the valley opens up below this ridge and it is like looking down on a map. It all makes sense from up here, everything is put in place, but so much is still senseless.

He tries to make a list of reasons not to step off the rocks.

1923

Chapter Sixty

Adam, Fellside House, May 1923

Adam stands under the apple tree and the wind-blown blossom flickers around him. To stand here, in that pink-white glimmer, is delightful. He had pruned the trees hard in the autumn, and though the firewood burned sweetly, he had worried that he had cut back too far. His answer is this blizzard of blossom, and he feels as much relief as pleasure.

His boots are heavy with earth. He has just heeled in the new damson saplings amongst the twisted trunks of their ancestors. When he had cleared out the orchard, there were so many ancient stumps. Shepherd had told him they were once sent to Manchester to make purple dye, but Adam put the fruit to better use making damson gin with Charlotte Shepherd last autumn, and jam with skins that rolled and stuck pleasurably to his teeth. The damsons came to Britain with the Crusaders, Shepherd said, brought all the way from Damascus, and, since they have been here for so long, and have travelled so far, it seems the right thing to perpetuate that. Adam has underplanted with wild flower seed and the bees are busy now in the cowslips and yellow rattle and corn cockle. There is scarlet pimpernel coming through this year, moon daisies and field poppies.

In the dazzle of the white blossom, Adam thinks about

standing under the camellia in Celia Dakers' garden two years ago, those flowers that had looked like miracles on a February day, before the walls had closed in and they had taken him to that bedroom where everything was familiar, but not. When Celia visits now, she talks to him as if she believes he's her son's ghost. She tells him that he's dead, that he's been dead for seven years, but she evidently still thinks that he needs feeding and clothing. Celia brings him apple pies, though they have a glut of their own fruit at Fellside, and the cake with cinnamon that Robert liked. He tries to be Robert again for her in those moments, because he can see that it eases her heart, and he nods as she tells him how she keeps his bedroom exactly as he left it.

Sometimes, as Adam talks with Celia, he thinks about his own mother and who she might have been. Is she alive? Does she know that he's alive? Or perhaps Celia is right and he is a ghost. Either way, dead or alive, he can't bring himself to tell Celia that he can't abide cinnamon.

He sees a movement and steps out beyond the blossom. He doesn't like to set traps for the rabbits, though they're taking the peas and the broad beans, but he shouts when he sees them and is happy to watch them scarper. It's not the rabbits this time, though; it's a man, walking towards the house, with greying hair in a grey coat. Just for a minute he is the ghost of someone Adam once knew. He rubs his eyes and when he looks again James Haworth's shadow has gone.

James

'So much is different,' says James as he turns in the middle of the sitting room. 'It's like seeing an old friend in unfamiliar clothing.'

'Good.' Shepherd grins. 'I'm glad you say that. It's our home now.'

'I didn't know that you'd sold Loughrigg. I went there first and found it all shuttered up.'

With the windows boarded over, it had looked like a frontispiece in a Gothic horror story, and James had remembered how Caitlin once called it Wuthering Heights.

'It looks terribly sad now, doesn't it? It finally sold this spring and it's going to be split up into apartments. It was a wrench to leave it and to know that was going to be its fate, but it got too big for us. We closed down one room after another, and eventually we realized that we were only living in a fraction of it, but paying for the upkeep of all the rest. We were sitting at the far ends of a great long dining table, yards of mahogany between us, and I couldn't hear what Charlotte was saying any longer. When your gravy has gone cold before you've hiked the length of the table to reach it, it's time to think again, isn't it? It didn't make sense to keep both houses on.'

'It's strange to see all the furniture from there in here. There are stuffed stoats where the scrimshaw and ostrich eggs ought to be. It rather messes with my memory.'

'Aunt Cecily's collections have been confined to the old servants' bedrooms. I'm expecting the haunting to be malevolent and to commence any day.'

James looks around this once-familiar room. The shelves and ceiling seem to sag more, the upholstery looks more slumped and the pattern is wearing from the rug. It is startling to see the passage of time, the dimensions of his own absence, so clearly marked out. 'And everyone has gone? You and Charlotte are here on your own now?'

'Hartley and Long left in 1921. Webb and Laffin went last

year. I still hear from them all, which is nice, isn't it? They all take the trouble to write letters. Everyone is muddling along. They'll all get there. They'll all be all right.'

'I'm glad to know that. And Adam?'

Shepherd laughs. 'I don't think that Adam will ever leave. He's a fixture. He'll still be here when I'm six foot under. We'll get rid of the wet rot and the woodworm before we get rid of Adam. He's still up there in his attic, surrounded by the face of his fairy. Have you seen what he's done with the garden?'

'And he's well?'

'In his way. He keeps himself to himself, as he always did, but he's contented enough in his own company. I have a suspicion that some of his memory has come back, but he's not keen to talk about it. Sometimes I look out of the window and see him down in the walled garden and he's just standing there, quite still, for a long time. He might well be a statue in the garden. I know that he's thinking in those moments and I'm certain he's remembering. I'd be interested to hear if you get that sense too. I do wish he'd talk, that he felt inclined to share, I think it would be good for him, but I don't want to push him if he's uncomfortable. He puts so much mental and physical effort into his work and it's apparent that that's where he wants to keep his focus. The garden is all very orderly now, you'll see, and he evidently derives satisfaction from that. He's made straight lines in what was a wilderness. It's obviously therapeutic.'

'Bringing control to chaos? I'd like to imagine that mirrors his mental state. We exchanged letters with some regularity at first, but it's been a few months now. Has he seen the woman in the woods again?'

'Yes, several times, I think. Adam and the fairy folk now

seem to have an arrangement. He doesn't tell me too much, if I'm honest with you, James, because he thinks that I don't believe him. I really shouldn't call her the fairy.' Shepherd smiles. 'He has no sense of humour where she's concerned. It is curious, though – you must have a look – in his drawings she's ageing. There's definitely an evolution. Don't you think that's interesting? Whereas Adam himself never seems to get a day older.'

'I've never been entirely certain that he didn't actually fall out of the sky. He hasn't asked to be hypnotized again?'

'No, and I don't think he will. However he rationalizes it all, I think he's achieved some sort of truce and balance. As far as I'm aware, he's not had a nightmare for a long time, and his relationship with the woman, whether she exists entirely in his imagination or not, seems to put a smile on his face. I do wish that he'd invite her in for tea, though.'

'Does he ever get visitors?'

'Yes. Regularly. It's the same faces. They all still come. Dakers brings him clothes and books and cakes, Vickers follows him around the garden telling him off, and Mason just sits and looks at him. We've never got any further, but he tolerates them now and they seem to get something out of it.'

'Celia Dakers still insists on coming?'

'They talk about gardening together and exchange cuttings and envelopes of seeds. Adam has told me that he worries about her; she's not as smartly dressed as she used to be, and he says he smells alcohol on her breath sometimes. She seems to be unravelling around the edges. He says she talks to him like he's her son's ghost.'

'That's sad. I did wonder how she explained it to herself. Amazing how realities can be bent to fit, isn't it? Vickers' brother never came back, then?'

'Not that she's informed us. She's brought the children in a couple of times. Adam was kind enough with them, he played along and obviously didn't want to distress them, but I didn't see any connection.'

'And Anna Mason?'

'I get the impression that her life stands still. Visiting Adam doesn't appear to make her particularly happy, but she seems to feel she needs to come. It's a form of vigil, I suppose, and I do pity the poor woman, but what more can we do?' Shepherd shakes his head.

James thinks about how he had been so determined to make one of these alternate realities fit, how important that had seemed to him two years ago. To find a balance in his own mind, he would have transferred Adam to the care of a woman who had an overwhelming need, but no real shared history with him. James would have given him a false name and what would his life have been like then? He can now see how illogical it all was, how irrational and wrong, but there'd been a time when instinct told him that fitting Adam to a history and a name would make Nathaniel's absence less weighty. Like some cosmic algebra equalling out – of course, it made no sense, he thinks now. Being back here again, he rather pities his younger self, his twisted logic and the insistent voices of his demons.

Caitlin was right all along – he should have spoken to her and to Shepherd sooner, asked for help, admitted that he was suffering as much as his patients. But perhaps, ultimately, he needed to go back to the wood and to realize that Nathaniel wasn't still there waiting for him? Perhaps it had to be that way, it had to run its course, and completing the journey was the only way he could have addressed and silenced those irrational instincts? He wishes he hadn't lost so much in the course of that journey, though.

'Anyway, enough of us; how is France?' Shepherd asks.

'Hard work. Testing work. There's still so much to do, it doesn't feel like it will ever be finished, but there is some fulfilment in getting it done.'

'Still no sign of Caitlin's brother, I take it? You've never found anything?'

'Nothing. The graves in the wood have all been relocated now and we've combed through it, but there were so many bodies that we couldn't identify, so very many men who could have been Nathaniel. If I'm honest, I don't think I will ever find him.'

'And how do you feel about that? Do you have any sense of closure? Having done this, how is your peace of mind?'

'I've tried my best, I know that we've done a thorough job, and there is some peace in that, some sense of resolution. Realizing how many other men will never have their name on a gravestone, I can accept that Nathaniel's situation is by no means exceptional. If I failed him, then tens of thousands of other men have been failed too.'

'So you've forgiven yourself?'

James considers Shepherd's words for a moment. 'Having been into that wood again, having once more walked over that terrain, I've accepted that on that day I couldn't have done anything differently. I just couldn't have got his body out. And so many other men died and were lost that day. I can't feel guilty for all of them, and I couldn't have changed the outcome for any of them. Over the past eighteen months, I've done everything I can. So, I suppose, there are fewer question marks now, fewer what-ifs to nag at me in the night, and yes, less on my conscience. You wouldn't believe the things that we see day to day, but I sleep better now.'

He couldn't share with anyone what he's seen over the past

eighteen months. Only the men who have been in the wood will ever know that, and they will never speak of it. In some respects, the exhumations had been worse than the experience of being there in 1916, but now there are white graves and roses and a green lawn. That's all James would want anyone coming after to know; they don't need to understand what it was like. And, oddly, in being part of that cover-up, there is some satisfaction. It's fatigue mostly that makes James sleep, the sheer weariness of his muscles and mind at the end of the day, but there's also a strange comfort in turning it all into clipped grass and parallel stones. Nathaniel might not be buried with a name on his gravestone, but he probably is under the lawns and roses now, and James no longer sees his face in his dreams.

'You said in your letter that you were coming back to see a solicitor?'

'To sign papers. Caitlin is getting married again, so we needed to finalize everything.'

'Really? I'm so sorry to hear that. I often think of her.'

He looks sorry and James is grateful for that. He knows that Shepherd was always fond of Caitlin and did want it all to work out. 'She writes to me and says she's happy. She deserves to be happy. I can't deny her that, can I?'

'No, of course not, but I'm sad to know it. I talked to her when she came back to pick up her things. Helping her to carry her suitcases out was one of the most horrible tasks I've ever had to do. I often go back over it all and ask myself if I didn't make it impossible for you both.'

'By bringing us here?'

'Yes. I mean, it wasn't the easiest start to your life together, was it? It was a huge thing to ask of a young woman.'

James shakes his head. 'You gave me a job. I don't know

what I'd have done otherwise – and you gave Caitlin her studio space. She started working again last year. She rented a workshop in Richmond and she's been making a success of it. And it might well have worked out for us here. I can only blame myself for the fact that it didn't.'

'I hope you haven't blamed yourself too much?'

'Perhaps. For a while.'

James thinks about the day he'd nearly stepped off the rocks. There hadn't been enough reasons *not* to let go, and he did blame himself, but then Adam's voice had been calling from the wood and, with that, James knew he was still needed. There were actions he had to take in order to ensure that Adam could stay at Fellside, and he'd felt a sudden urgency that he must secure his future here. And, at that moment, he also knew that he had to go and look for Nathaniel. He has written to Caitlin from France and has shared the search for her brother with her. He has also told her all about the day Nathaniel died, has finally given that to her in all its terrible detail, because she needed to know it too in order to let go. It is difficult knowledge, and the pieces don't fit together perfectly, but James hopes that the questions no longer torment her, and that she now has some sense of Nathaniel being laid to rest.

'Caitlin and I keep in touch,' he tells Shepherd. 'We exchange letters from time to time and, strangely enough, I think we understand each other better now. Sometimes it's easier to put words down on paper than to speak, isn't it? And there are some things that you can only really say from a distance. We've both been completely honest, and it's as if we finally truly know each other, totally candidly, though we've been four hundred miles apart. We'll stay in touch and we'll always be friends, we'll always have a special understanding, because we've been through so much together. The only trouble is, I have to admit, I still find myself looking at her envelopes when they arrive and hoping that, for once, they might contain more than friendship. More fool me, eh? But over the past few months, her letters have been full of a man called Charles, how he makes her happy, how they're making plans, and so I have to stop hoping.'

'I am sorry, James. So you'll go back to France again afterwards?'

'Yes.'

'I know that you feel your employment there is worthwhile, that you're making good, but do you not miss the work that you trained for?'

'I'm not convinced that I ever made much difference here.'

He hears Shepherd's hand strike the table.

'Really? Dear God, James! I'm sincerely sorry if you think that. It simply isn't true. I'd have you back here tomorrow. I know there were problems at the end, but you were ill too, and I ought to have recognized that sooner. I should show you some of the letters I've had. You should see what they say. How their lives have changed. How you made it possible for their lives to go on. Can you truly think that you didn't make a difference? Seriously? You should go and talk to Adam for a start.'

'Hell's bells, is it really the same place?'

Adam is standing in the old walled garden leaning on a spade. He turns as James approaches, and for a moment it all spins back five years. When James looks in the mirror he sees grey flashes around his reflection now, and new fine lines around his eyes, but Adam looks not a day older. His face is still that of the man James met in Durham gaol in November

1918. Can five years really have gone by and all of that leave no mark? But, as Adam's smile stretches, James sees how much he has changed. The calmness, the stillness, has extended and there's a confidence there now too. Adam smiles like a man who is sure of his place in the world.

'I've worked hard while you've been away.'

He spreads his arms towards the stone walls where the pears are sweetening in the sun. His posture is all beneficence and he grins then as he pulls James into a hug.

'I can't believe how well you look. You look ridiculously well. I'm not certain that you haven't got younger.'

'You look older,' Adam replies. 'It is your face, the face that I know and have missed seeing, but somehow softened, like a statue that has stood out in a garden for a long time and known all weathers.'

'I don't think that's a compliment, is it?' James laughs.

'Your hair has changed colour. You're going grey. You look like a chalk drawing of yourself, but you also look like you've remembered how to sleep.'

'You're right. I have.'

They walk around the garden and Adam points out the espaliered pears and raised salad beds and blackcurrant bushes. There are rows of broad beans and lettuces and the scent of sweet peas, and he stands smiling with a watering can. The glass in the greenhouse has all been replaced and, beyond the orderly reflection of the garden, James can see tomatoes climbing inside. He also sees Adam's reflection in the glass and remembers his face in a circle of mirrors. He might not have aged, but his demeanour is different now and the tension has gone. James asks himself: how much of that tension did he create in trying to make Adam fit into gaps that weren't right? James still feels it was his fault that the mirrors broke, but looking at Adam now, he sees contentment on his face and how well he fits here in his garden. This is where he is meant to be.

'Is this your Garden of Eden? Your earthly paradise?' he asks.

Adam picks a marigold and hands it to James with a magician's flourish. 'Something like that.'

'But still no Eve there under the apple tree?'

'Only in passing. But there are no hissing serpents either.'

Adam smiles and James thinks about what Shepherd said about his memory. James also gets a sense that gaps have filled. Adam's speech is more fluid than it once was. That staccato in his attention has eased. James doesn't like to ask him if he has remembered, but something has certainly changed.

'I was glad of your letters,' Adam says. 'I looked forward to them. I miss your company.'

'I'm sorry. It's been a while, hasn't it? I will write again, more often if you wish it, on condition that you reply. I liked to get your drawings, but you should have drawn all of this for me. I had no idea that you'd done so much work.'

'All the digging leaves less time for drawing, but I get a sense of satisfaction when I look at it now. I feel that I'll leave something behind, that I've achieved something, and I don't need to walk so far any longer. When I have worked here all day, I'm ready to sleep.'

'Yes, I've learned that too,' James replies.

Adam has made a proper pathway up the hillside and they walk up between the rhododendrons, surrounded by tones of impossible pink and the clatter of leather green leaves.

Adam laughs. 'I can't believe that you've been working with a spade. You didn't know a daffodil from a leek!'

'Which is why they mostly have me working with a

typewriter. You should come out and visit, though. You'd be interested to see. They're putting in plants that will be familiar to visitors – roses and saxifrage and heathers. They want the cemeteries to resemble manicured English gardens.'

'Nothing out of place but the number of gravestones?'

'Regrettably.'

The elders are a froth of white blossom and the dog roses are just breaking bud. There are foxgloves in the wood now, wild strawberries and a grave. Planted around with lily of the valley, it looks like a child's burial place.

'Who is it?'

'Meg.'

It takes James a moment to remember. 'Anna Mason's dog?'

'Yes. She did come here in the end. I had her here for eighteen months.'

James puts his hand to Adam's shoulder. He can see that the sharing of this information brings back a sadness that's still close to the surface.

'I'm glad to know that. You were happy to have her here?'

'I was.'

'And Anna still visits you?'

'From time to time.'

'I'm sorry that I tried to push you.'

Adam shakes his head. 'You meant well. Your intentions were good. I know that.'

'But I got it all out of perspective. I cornered you. For my own confused reasons, I tried to force you into something that wasn't right.'

Adam smiles as he takes James' hand. 'I understand and there's nothing to apologize for. I'm an expert in confusion. I'm a textbook model – quite literally! And I'm not sure that

I could really define perspective. But you told me once, long ago, that you would be my friend, and you always have been.'

It's strange to step back into this room again. For a moment James expects the floor to be all fragments of reflection and Adam's bloodied footprints, but there are just the scrubbed blond boards and his Afghan rug worn thinner. The room is tidier than James remembers it, as Adam's state of mind seems to be too, and it is brighter. When James had left, the walls had been covered with his drawings in black and white, but now the room vibrates with colour. James turns and marvels at it.

'All this is you?'

'Mrs Shepherd bought me a set of oil paints the Christmas after you left. They have been very kind to me. I'm learning all the time, all the tricks and cheats and practicalities, and I'm enjoying it.'

'So I can see. You astonish me. It's like standing in an altar, a room full of miracles.'

Though they have jumped from ink line to vibrant colour – and that seems to indicate so much about his mental well-being – Adam's subjects are the same; he paints details of nature (an oak leaf here, a swallow's wing there, a study of wood anemones and the feathers of a kingfisher), and still the woman's face is everywhere.

'I didn't know that was the colour of her hair.' James is reminded of Millais and Rossetti, of walking through Manchester Art Gallery with Caitlin a lifetime ago. 'I had no idea that I was living a floor below a Pre-Raphaelite.'

The largest painting is like an altarpiece. It is a meditation and a work of devotion. James recognizes the woman's face instantly, it has always been the same, but Shepherd is right: she is a woman, rather than a girl now. Her hair stands out like a halo, so that she seems as if she's been projected out of the dark trees behind. James can see the details of the embroidery on her white dress, so finely are these stitches picked out in paint. Her bodice is a constellation of silk stars and ivy leaves wind up her skirt. Though her dress might be that of a priestess, her bare feet are visible in the billows of the hem. James can see how the dew is wetting her toes as she steps through the cowslips and bluebells. She is an ideal, but she's also sufficiently real that James feels sorry that he ever doubted her existence.

'She's beautiful,' he says.

'Isn't she?' Adam replies.

'And do you still see her?'

'Yes. Not often enough. Every time I find her in the wood it feels like witnessing a miracle. It's special – beyond special, but I wish she'd stay, that she could just reliably be here every day. I'd like her to be my normality. I'd rather have that than miracles.'

'I can see that in the way that you've painted her. I understand.'

It's then that James notices the bowl on the chest of drawers below. If the painting is an altarpiece, this is a chalice.

'It's one of Caitlin's, isn't it?' He glances back and his eyes meet Adam's. 'Do you mind?' James takes the bowl in his hands and turns it, and it's like stretching a hand back through the years. 'I don't think I've seen it before. Did she make it for you?'

'We made it together. I threw it. She showed me how. She decorated and fired it for me.'

Adam takes the bowl from James' hands, and as he runs his fingers over the pattern of the glaze, James can see that he too is reaching back to a memory.

'I miss Caitlin,' Adam says.

'Yes,' James replies. 'I miss her terribly too.'

The stained-glass roses are still twining together in the fanlight over the door and the nightingale endlessly sings. James pushes the door, flicks on the electric light and two years spin back. For three years these rooms had been their home, only it couldn't be a home without her. He walks around the apartment, putting on lights, and rooms of sheeted furniture flicker into bright existence. They had laughed about this house being full of ghosts at one time. After all, what were wraiths and phantoms when they were living in a house filled with psychiatric cases? In the bare electric light, and with the echo of James' own footsteps, the apartment seems both hollow and full of their own ghosts. The boxes of books, the scratches on the backs of the chairs, the chipped plate that she bought in a junkshop in York, all these things are suddenly memorials, and James needs to touch them to be certain that they once were real, and his and hers.

Looking at the picture hooks on the walls, he remembers the etchings and watercolours that Caitlin had chosen for their first home together. He wonders if she has them still, and if they will soon be mounted on the walls of a different hall as a new life starts. She has left the pictures in the sitting room. They never knew the names of the sitters in these portraits, they are all as eternally anonymous as Adam, but Caitlin had picked them out in a Swaledale auction for their kind features and colours. James can still see her walking around the salesroom, putting her fingers to frames and giving names to strangers. Was it foolish to ever think that this auction-bought ancestry, this borrowed family, could stay together? The fireplace is still full of white wood ash and the room smells of the cold hearth and geraniums. The plants have scrabbled all up the shuttered windows searching for light, but have failed and died and desiccated. The yellow leaves flake in James' hand and, in that peppery, herbal, green scent, Caitlin is there. It will always be her smell. It will always summon her back for him. As he pauses in the doorway, he notices the dint in the plaster where she had once, mid-argument, thrown back the door and broken the china handle. She had finally cried at that and held the fragments out towards him.

'Why can't you just talk to me?' she had asked.

He would give anything to be able to talk to her now. The wind sighs in the chimney and wood ash stirs softly in the grate.

The wallpaper has started to peel in the kitchen, which Caitlin always said was damp. Where the paper curls, he can see another pattern below, and in it the shapes and colours of other lives that have played out in this room. There is a dead centipede in the sink, and the cupboard doors, which had never closed properly, are all stuck ajar. He leans against the dresser and watches the ghosts of his and Caitlin's movements around this room. Their paths and habits are all still in here, in the thinning pile on the rug, and the varnish on the floorboards, and the wear on the paint where she leaned against the sink. She is here with him in this room in friction and scratches and echo. Only Caitlin is not a ghost, and no rituals, no candles or incantations, will summon her back today.

Had they really spent so long passing each other on the same staircase, listening to the tick of the same clock, turning the same door handle? How could it no longer be so? He hears the wind in the chimney and remembers that noise had always been there, reliable as an echo and, with it, her voice. How can her voice no longer be there in the next room? How can that constant have ceased to be? He meets his own reflection in a dark mirror.

As James walks into the bedroom, he half expects her black dress to be suspended there. Does she still have it, he wonders, does she pretty it up now with beads and brooches when she goes out to dinner, or had she left it behind on the day she walked out because she couldn't bear the thought of putting it on ever again? Had that dress finally brought it all home and been too much? Perhaps she has burned it. There is nothing in the wardrobe but the clatter of coat hangers.

He hears the trickle of her pearls, returning to the glass bowl on the dressing table, but he knows, before he turns, that it is only in his mind and memory. There are photographs, of him and her together, pushed into the frame of her dressing-table mirror. James is sorry that Caitlin didn't see fit to take them with her. Was it because the face behind the camera was Nathaniel's, because the wallpaper pattern in the background is that of Nathaniel's childhood bedroom? Can Caitlin still picture that instant, as he can? The three of them had walked down to the river afterwards and James had noticed how Nathaniel always seemed to be watching him. He had met Nathaniel's shy smile and returned it, but should he have looked away instead? Would Nathaniel still be with Caitlin now if James had not looked him in the eye? Could the trajectory of their lives have been completely different?

James remembers how he'd looked at Nathaniel's face in France, animated in turn with excitement and amusement and terror, and had always seen Caitlin there. And then, ever afterwards, when he looked at Caitlin, so Nathaniel was in her face too. He wonders if things would be different now if he had brought Nathaniel back and given Caitlin a grave to mourn at. Would she still want him to sign divorce papers?

But James has spent the past eighteen months looking for Nathaniel, and knows now that he will never find him – and, however much he might wish it, things can't be different. Caitlin is going to marry a man called Charles this autumn, a man James has never met, who will probably never recognize Nathaniel in her face. James hates this reality, he hates having to accept it, but he hopes this marriage is a sign that Caitlin has forgotten her sadness.

In the squares of the patchwork quilt on the bed he sees the stripe of a cut-down dressing gown, the embroidery of a summer blouse and the sprig of the dress that she was wearing on the day they first met. There are fingerprints tarnished into the finial of the brass bed post and James doesn't need to put his own fingers to them to know that they are hers. They will always be here, decades after she is not.

'Do you think you'll come back?' Adam asks.

'England? Here? Fellside?' Adam nods and James tries to imagine himself living in the apartment again. With all the memories that fill this house, he doesn't think he ever could. 'No. I have no family in this country any longer, and there's so much work to do over there. I have a lifetime of work. I can't presently see it ever ending.'

'Perhaps I might visit you one day? Perhaps I might come over to France?'

'Would you? I'd like that. I would like that very much.' James considers what motives Adam might have, beyond friendship, for making that journey now. He is not sure that he ought to ask, but somehow he can't not. 'Have you remembered anything of France? Do you have any recall of the war now?'

Adam looks down at his earth-ingrained hands. James can

see that the question is not a straightforward one. 'Sometimes, when I wake up, I know I've dreamed about it and there are fragments still there, but I can't piece it together. It's always just out of reach. But I don't particularly want to reach out and drag it back. I know that it's there, that all of that is in my memory, but I don't particularly want to straighten it out and look at it up close. I'm sorry if that's wrong of me.'

'Sorry?' James shakes his head. 'I used to think that it was necessary to address it, to face up to it, to look your demons right in the eye before you can banish them, but I'm not entirely sure any longer. I don't know. Perhaps, if you keep it out of reach, that's for the best.' Over the past two years James has realized that he was spending too much time looking his demons in the eye, and that was twisting his perspective on everything else. He did need to find some closure, some acceptance, to answer his own questions, but he has come to understand, in recent months, that it doesn't do to focus too long on the unanswerable questions. He is not sure that he has achieved peace of mind yet, but the nightmares return with less regularity. He feels he's learning how to forget. 'I don't think you should force yourself to look. Perhaps you were wiser than me all along.'

'I'm not wise.' Adam reaches with his secateurs and cuts a stem of lilac. 'For your buttonhole on your way back,' he says to James.

'Does it have a meaning?' he asks.

Adam laughs. 'Only that I mean you to remember this old friend.'

'How could I forget you?'

They walk on through the garden and the smell of lilacs. 'You are wrong, though, you know,' Adam says. 'You do have family here: you have me. You are the only family that I have.'

James looks at this odd man, in his outlandish hand-me-down coat, who paints fairies, has pockets full of seed packets, and who might well have dropped from the sky, and realizes that he is right: Adam Galilee is the closest thing that he has to family.

'I will see you again, won't I?' Adam asks.

'Of course,' James replies.

1925

Chapter Sixty-One

Adam, Fellside House, October 1925

The noise rocks him out of his dream. The whole house seems to shudder and recoil with it. For a moment Adam isn't sure whether he's still dreaming, but the roar of it goes on, he can smell something burning, and then there is a crash of glass smashing. He runs to the window and all the garden is lit up, the walls flash in this strange, bright, flickering light and devilish shadows leap. Smoke is rolling across the lawn and he hears things shattering below. The noise is terrific. When he opens his window, the curtains lift and instantly start to darken. Sparks are flying up. The whole house looks to be ablaze below.

When Adam opens the door of his room he feels the blast of the heat. The fire is already on the staircase, creeping and blistering its way up the banister, and the air seems to draw it up. He shuts the door and pushes a chair against it, as if this is an intruder he might keep out.

Adam has swallowed the smoke and he doubles up coughing. He can feel the heat of it on his face. Instinct pulls him back to his bed, to the tangle of his sheets. He knows now that it is coming to get him, and he has nothing to fight it with but the water in his washbasin. His room is full of extraordinary light.

He hears another window go. It is consuming the house below. Are Shepherd and Charlotte still down there in their beds? He has heard no voices. Have they got out? Have they called the fire brigade? Will they be coming for him? He goes back to the window. He sees only leaping flame, falling ash and broken glass on the ground below. Strange shadows animate the walls of the garden.

It's crackling on the landing now and the smoke is pushing its way up through the floorboards. Adam throws the wash-basin of water at the white light that's flickering under the door, but the hiss that it makes is derisory. It's as though the devil himself is outside the door now.

There is an almighty crack somewhere below, like a ceiling is collapsing, and the smoke rising from the floor billows. Adam knows that the fire has won. A ribbon of flame skips along the rug. There is something imp-like about this dainty, skipping incursion, delicate but malign, Adam thinks, but then the devil is roaring into the room and the curtains are billowing in flame. He retreats to the window, but the paintwork is rising and running liquid. He watches, through the smoke and the peculiar red light, as his paintings start to blister. They are releasing the smell of turpentine and linseed oil and he is back at the moment of their creation. The light wavers over the lady of the woods and she is under the canopy of the trees again, the air stirring her hair and her cloak borne away on the wind. He wants her to gasp and to run, as she did then, but the bluebells on which she walks are starting to blacken. His door splinters and the flame pushes through.

The paintwork on the windowsill burns his fingers when he first touches it and he pulls them away quickly. Adam bundles his coat around his hands to push the sash up. The flames are roaring up outside. It is hotter than in the room, but he knows that he has to get out. As he climbs up onto the window ledge he can hear his own heart hammering above the crack and growl of the fire below. He takes one last look back at the lady, but her face has thundered into flame, and in that moment of ultimate fear, it all hurtles back and joins up. Adam is in Delville Wood again, screaming and running for his life. He tears through empty streets in Arras, with the ruin all around. Rain and tears pour down his face as he looks up at the sky from a shell hole north of Ypres, and his whole body trembles as the barrage comes down. All the adrenaline and fear and pain and loss rushes back, and rushes past, and then he remembers what came before and, in that very moment when he lets go, he wants to hold on to it all again. He screams Eleanor's name as his feet leave the ledge.

TELEGRAM

JAMES

HOPE THIS FINDS YOU. SOMETHING AWFUL HAS HAPPENED AT FELLSIDE. ARE YOU ABLE TO COME BACK? I HOPE SO.

PLEASE COME.
CAITLIN

Chapter Sixty-Two

James, Ellerton House, Richmond, October 1925

He'd set off as soon as he got her telegram. He'd assumed that it must be Shepherd, that he must be ill, or worse – after all, hadn't James been struck by how much older he looked when he last went back? And hasn't Adam remarked in his letters how he seems to be slowing down? James did want to be there, if it was true. He had meant to go straight there, to drive directly up to Ambleside, but somehow he has found himself carrying on north, and he's standing on the doorstep of Caitlin's mother's house now and experiencing the strangest sensations.

Those are Caitlin's footsteps, he knows, approaching the other side of the door. It is her voice in the hallway. It's her face then.

'James.'

Though he has spent the journey imagining this moment, he finds that he's not ready for her face and her embrace; for the smell of her hair and the touch of her fingertips on the back of his neck; he is not ready for any of it and struggles to keep on being the man that he's now required to be. He wants to put his arms around her, as hers are around him, but he has to keep his hand on the railings. He is not ready for the sound of her voice in his ear and then to see her tears.

'I didn't know what to do,' Caitlin says as she finally steps back. 'I heard the news and I thought I ought to let you know. I didn't want you to see it in a newspaper, and who else was going to tell you? After I sent the telegram, I wondered if I'd done the wrong thing, but I'm so glad you're here.'

'How has it been four years?' he asks as he looks at her. It's not what he meant to say, what he ought to say, but the words just fall out.

He follows her through to the sitting room and remembers first coming into this house twelve years ago. They're still there in the painting over the fireplace, Caitlin and Nathaniel, their mirror-image faces, in oil paint at seventeen years old. The portrait had just been hung the first time that James had stepped into this room and they had been sat there together on the sofa laughing at it. Their twinned hands linking. Their twinned mouths smiling. But today there is only Caitlin on the sofa and there are tears in her eyes. James doesn't know whether he's meant to sit next to her, whether he's still allowed to put a hand to hers. He wants to hold her when he sees her tears, and how difficult it is not to do that, how hard to accept that this is now another man's role, that she's another man's wife. He feels so terribly torn, and awkward, and how sharp the stab of this regret.

'Your mother's not here today?' he asks.

'Aren't you fortunate, eh? She's in Scarborough. She's taking gulps of restorative sea air with Aunt Maud.'

'Will you pass on my regards? Do tell her that I'm sorry to have missed her.'

'Oh, James, you liar!' He is glad when, at last, she smiles.

'The telegram was sent from Richmond. I noticed that. That's why I came here. Only, I wasn't sure why you'd be back here. I thought you'd moved south. I thought you were setting up home in Herefordshire after the wedding. Are you having a few days with your mother?'

'I never left in the end.'

'But Charles—'

'Have you been to Fellside yet?'

'No, I came here first. I've been on the road for twelve hours. I'll get some sleep tonight and drive over tomorrow morning.'

She nods. 'You must. You can stay here tonight. I'll get Mary to make a room up, but you should go there tomorrow.'

'It's Alan, isn't it?'

He had thought about it for those twelve hours on the road, has played through all the likely scenarios. He knows, if the news is the worst, that he will need to be there for Charlotte; that he must support her, as they supported him when he needed it. He will have to be there for Adam too. He has asked himself: what will happen to Adam now? James can't imagine him being anywhere other than Fellside, leaving his garden, but surely Charlotte won't want to stay there on her own? If Alan has passed away, Adam must now be James' responsibility. James has thought, over recent months, that he might finally be ready to come back to England. If Adam needs his protection and his friendship, he must come back and he will.

'You hadn't heard, then? You didn't see it in the newspapers?' Catlin asks.

'I don't know what you're talking about.'

'There was a fire, James. There's nothing left of Fellside. It's all gone.'

She pours herself a brandy while he reads the newspaper article. He can feel that her eyes keep glancing back at him.

'Do you want one?' she asks. 'I'd understand if you needed one.'

He shakes his head. 'I haven't for a while. You were right. It didn't help.'

It's the truth, but as the paragraphs blur, he wishes that he could.

'That's how I found out – I happened to spot the piece about their funeral in the paper on Monday. I didn't know what to do; whether I ought to get the train and go over there myself; whether I should try to get in touch with Alan's family. But I was certain that you'd want to know. They think it was a lightning strike,' Caitlin says, as she sits down next to him on the sofa. 'Only, it's not meant to strike in the same place twice, is it? I know you don't remember anything of the storm we had in 1921, but it hit the lightning conductor that night, and I can still remember how frightening that was. I can't stop thinking about Alan and Charlotte and how terrifying it must have been for them. I mean, they'd know what was happening, wouldn't they? It wouldn't be instant. I can't sleep at the moment because I keep imagining them trying to get out of the burning house. I see the corridors and stairwells and doors and keep imagining it all bursting into flame, all the curtains and carpets going up, and them being stuck in there and not able to get out.'

James can see it around her eyes. He also sees how the glass trembles as it approaches her lips. He puts his arm around her then, whether he's allowed to or not. He feels the sorrow of her tears as she turns her head to his chest and he's thankful to be able to comfort her at this moment. But those images are also in his head now and he needs to know about Adam.

'The article only mentions Alan and Charlotte.' He pushes the newspaper away. 'No one else. There's only their names.'

There is brief mention of the house's history, how it had been a hospital during the last war, and then a convalescent institution in the years following. It also mentions the living unknown soldier, and how, despite efforts, he had never been identified. There is no mention, though, that Adam might have been in the house at the time of the fire. But, James reasons, how could he not have been there?

'You mean where was Adam that night?'

'Yes.'

'I keep asking myself the same question. And I don't know the answer.'

Chapter Sixty-Three

James, Ambleside, October 1925

Alan and Charlotte Shepherd are buried in the graveyard of Holy Trinity, a few yards from Peter Milner. The old graves around are furred with moss and stained orange with lichen, but their shared gravestone is new-cut white stone. He should have been here for the funeral, James thinks, he should have been there to pay his respects and give his thanks. He remembers how difficult it had been when he first came back from France, how he had struggled in those early weeks and wondered if he could ever go back to a normal job again, but then Shepherd had given him a chance. Had he ever actually thanked him for that? James wishes now that he could rewind and say those words. He hopes that the newspaper report is right, and that the fire took the house fast. He is horrified by the thought of them being trapped inside the burning building and hates that those images are in Caitlin's head.

Milner's gravestone has some patina of age now. James cannot believe that it is nearly four years since they stood around his coffin. Is it really that long since Caitlin left? But the lichen on Milner's grave confirms it to be the case. He thinks of standing here with Adam, him pointing at the magpies and the cowslips, and talking about bluebells. But where is Adam? How could he not have been in the house? How can no one have accounted for him?

James walks through the churchyard. He'd felt unsettled after his last visit, and for the past year, he has kept thinking about returning to England and coming back up to Fellside to visit. He wishes that he had talked with Alan one more time, feels he might have done something more, and yet how could anyone prevent a lightning strike? He asks himself, what more could he have done? There is no rational reason for him to feel guilty, he knows, and yet he has a sense of unfulfilled responsibility and so many words that were left unsaid.

'I should have told you how grateful I am,' he says to Alan and Charlotte's gravestone.

As James stands and turns, he spots another new white headstone between the old graves and then, as he walks towards it, the name Robert Dakers comes into focus. It is some moments before he makes the connection.

'The fire at Fellside?' The curate looks up from his papers. 'Yes. We could see the flames from the village. It went up really fast. By the time the fire brigade arrived, it had well and truly taken hold. It was a lightning strike, they said – an Act of God. That's how they worded it on the official reports, although I'm never entirely sure that I like that phrase. Personally, I'd rather blame magnetic charges and the movements of clouds.'

James nods. 'And there was nobody else in the house at the time? No one else got out?'

'The girl who worked for them had gone home for the night. I remember that. She cried terribly at the funeral. Everyone was very fond of Doctor Shepherd. He was well respected and well liked. His death is a loss to the community. And then there was the young man.'

'The young man?'

'The young chap who was lodging with them. The inspector said that he jumped from the roof.'

'Do you know his name?'

'Dakers. Robert, I think it was. There was some confusion as to his name, but then his mother came forward. They hadn't known what to put on the paperwork. She only turned up the day before the funeral.'

'Celia Dakers?'

'Yes, that was the lady's name.'

James stands in front of the grave that bears the name and dates of a fiction. He somehow can't believe that Adam is lying in this grave, and yet, who else can it be? In putting her son's name on this headstone, did Celia Dakers finally feel that she'd put him to rest? Did she then genuinely continue to believe that Adam was her son? But she couldn't have been right, could she? James pushes aside yellowing roses to see the epitaph. The crisply new letters read: *Forgive, o Lord, a Mother's wish that Death had spared her Son.* There is so much meaning and resonance in those simple words, James considers – but who, apart from him and her, would really know it? He imagines Celia Dakers looking her God in the eye and making a final deal.

The curate had said that the story had been widely reported in the newspapers and so the church had been full. It was a big funeral – symbolic, he said – and there were many families there who had lost men in the war. Is there a possibility that Adam's real family might have been there amongst those faces? Were Anna Mason and Lucy Vickers there that day too?

And, if so, how do they feel about the name on this gravestone? He remembers the sadness of the empty church on the day that Milner was buried, and Adam's voice and breath at his side. He remembers Adam turning amongst these same gravestones and saying, 'One day no one will know who is here.' It seems suddenly prescient.

He had so wanted to give Adam a name – his real name. It mattered that he was reunited with it, because how could he fully be himself without it? And, with a name, there comes a family, a history and a home. There'd been a time when he wondered if Adam might be Robert Dakers, but surely it couldn't be true? Didn't Celia already have a grave for her son? Surely this name is a lie, then? James thinks about all the men in the cemetery in Guillemont who have been buried under the words *A Soldier of the Great War Known Unto God*, so that even the unidentifiable casualties, some of them mere fragments of men, might be remembered as something more than statistics. As they have erected these headstones, each has felt slightly like a failure (of record-keeping, of care, of respect for flesh and blood and family), but they are less of a falsehood than the name on this grave.

The curate told James that the man's identity had been confirmed by the initials on the label in his coat. James knows that coat. He can picture it. He knows that label, stitched in by Robert Dakers' mother. It's unlikely that anyone else was wearing Adam's coat. James tells himself that, though he doesn't want to believe it. Can this really be Adam Galilee's final resting place? Once upon a time, he had joked that Adam might well have fallen out of the clouds, but could death really have flashed out of the night sky and put him in this ground? There are no flowers planted around the grave. There ought to be lily of the valley and wood anemones, so how can this be Adam's grave? It can't be right, can it? James curls on the grass and cries. He can't quite believe that Adam Galilee has left this world and that he must still be in it.

Chapter Sixty-Four

James, Fellside House, October 1925

The sight of it takes him back to Ypres in the final winter of the war and his feet stepping amongst the splintered Madonnas and the broken ribs of a church roof. There is a great expanse of blackened stone, smashed slate, charred roof beam and twisted metal, but James can't believe that this is all that is left of Fellside House, that it can have come to this. He crouches down on his knees, turns a piece of charred crockery in his hand, rubs the smoke away and recognizes the pattern of Charlotte Shepherd's coffee service.

He thinks of the storm clouds shifting, the pressure gathering, building, rolling in and the glint of the wet slate roof down below. Did they feel the storm approaching? Did Adam hear the thunder coming? Was there a shock as the lightning bolt connected? Did the ceiling lights swing and the mirrors all shift on the walls? Did the sherry glasses sing on their tray, and was there a moment when shock stopped the clocks, or did it all just instantly ignite? James imagines all the stuffed game birds taking flight in the flames, the collectors' cabinets bursting, the rows of birds' eggs blackening and all the family photographs going up. He thinks of their apartment, of the photographs of him and Caitlin together that had still been tucked in around the dressing-table mirror, her reflection in the twilight windows and her fingerprints on the brass bedstead. James looks at the wet, black ruin and understands the magnitude of that phrase: 'Act of God'.

He walks around the ruins. It has rained overnight and the charred wood glitters horribly. Is Caitlin's brass bedstead in there somewhere? Are fragments of her patchwork quilt there, and the overmantel mirror in which he had watched her during those last awful days? Is Adam's painting of the lady in the wood amongst this debris? Can all the beams of Adam's rooftop eyrie really have come down? He half suspects that, if Adam jumped, he might fly. Does he have to be dead? Could he not have gone back to where he came from?

All the perspective is different now that the house has been levelled. James thinks of Caitlin's eyes looking out at the facing hillside, but today that wall of trees seems to be closer and to loom above him, belittling the slumped ruin of the house. The trees on the nearside have been scorched by the fire, but the garden behind is still tidy. With its orderly lines maintained, it looks oblivious to the fate of the house. James can see that it has recently been dug over; the flower beds are turning to their autumn tints, but they appear to be tended, and no weeds grow between the neat lines of cabbages and chard. He can still make out Adam's path up the hillside. Could he not have gone back into the woods and still be walking that path yet?

But it is hope against hope, isn't it? It is wishful thinking and he is once again seeing signs where there are none. James feels such a sense of desolation as he looks at the ruin of Fellside House. It's an image from nightmares. He will plant bulbs around Adam's grave in the spring, and feel like he is making the right gesture, he will visit his grave and will talk to him, but there is no consolation to be found here. To stand here is just a torture. He is glad that Caitlin hasn't seen it.

It is only as he makes his mind up to go, and turns away from the ruin, that he catches sight of the woman. She is some yards behind him, so obviously watching him, and there is something about the way that she is standing there that seems significant. Something about the way she stands is familiar. Something about the shape of her face. Is it Anna Mason? It is four years since James has last seen her. But he knows that he recognizes this woman. He also knows, as he takes a step towards her, that she is going to run.

'Please! Don't go. I only want to talk to you.'

James can see the hesitation on her face as he quickens his steps. She looks around as if she is thinking of fleeing into the wood, and it is at that moment, with that glance, that he suddenly knows exactly who she is.

'I'm James.'

They are walking through the walled garden. Dahlias are still flowering, in colours of implausible richness, between the lines of winter greens. He notices the filled watering can and the discarded gloves. Could it really be that Adam is still here?

'I know. I know who you are. He told me all about you.'

James doesn't dare to look at her for too long. He doesn't want to stare, but he is certain that it must be her, and it is like seeing a statue come to life. From a distance she might have been mistaken for Anna Mason. Had Adam seen that too? But, up close, her hair is lighter, her features finer, her eyes paler and somehow ethereal. There is something determined about her profile, noble almost. Painted with a cape of ivy and a crown of frosted hazel twigs, she might well be the queen of the woods, but James sees the mud on her boots, the soil down her cracked fingernails and the shadows under her eyes – and he knows that she is mortal and more than a figment of Adam's imagination.

'I think I know who you are too.'

She turns towards him then, her eyes finally meet his, and James understands in that moment why Adam drew her a thousand times. All those iterations flicker through, in pencil, and ink, and paint, and he realizes that he has known the face of this woman for seven years. He knows this woman's face almost as well as he knows Caitlin's. Her expressions, her attitudes, her angles are as familiar to him as the memory of Adam's face reflected all around that room. Her eyebrows lift as she asks the question. 'Do you?'

'Well, yes and no. I've seen your face so many times, but I have no idea of who you really are, how it all fits, and I've never heard your name.'

She nods. 'He kept asking me to tell him my name. I wish I could have told him.'

They walk between the damson trees and white moths flicker in the shadows. The last of the fruit has fallen and the leaves are yellowing, but these trees are six foot high now. Was it only two years ago that James had watched Adam heeling in the saplings? It seems like both yesterday and decades ago.

'You came to see him, didn't you?' he asks.

'Yes.' She flickers between being the ethereal queen in Adam's painting and a flesh-and-blood woman in a man's overcoat and mud-caked boots. She pulls a strand of hair away from her face and narrows her pale eyes as she considers James' question. 'I came here as often as I could, but I couldn't just walk up to the door and announce myself, and I didn't want to be here so often that I disturbed him.'

'Did he know you?'

'In ways. No, he never remembered my name, or how we'd met before, but there are other ways of recognizing and understanding another person, aren't there?'

'There are.' There are fine freckles across the bridge of her nose. He remembers seeing that in Adam's painting, when he had leaned in close. Her dark eyelashes blink long shadows, making the green of her eyes all the more startling. He both envies and pities Adam for being so close to, and so far away from, this woman. He thinks about Adam putting this woman's eyes down on paper, delicately, thoughtfully, how it had been an act of adoration, and remembers how Caitlin's eyes had lifted and met his two days ago. 'Were you his wife?'

'Yes. A very long time ago. I'm Eleanor.'

They climb up Adam's path and James sees how she places her feet in his footholds. He has the feeling that she has been here the whole time, walking these paths, watching for seven years, only just out of sight. He turns and looks where the house once was, where a window once framed Caitlin's face; there is only the other side of the valley there now, the church spire newly visible, like an exclamation mark, and the black ruin down below. He wonders, as he watches the woman climb so sure-footedly ahead of him, whether she was the eyes in the hillside too. Was it perhaps not just Adam looking in at Caitlin?

'We married before the war,' she tells James as they walk through the fallen leaves. 'We were well-matched and knew perfect contentment in each other's company; we were our own world and needed nothing else, but then he had to go.'

The smell of the turned leaves is sweet and smoky, like foreign cigarettes. The oaks are yellow ochre today and the elms raw sienna. It is umber, madder and vermilion and as if Adam's brush is playing with the light, but then James pictures those canvases blistering to black, and the maples are the colours of flame. 'He was conscripted?'

She nods. 'He didn't want to go. He loved his home and his garden, his place in the world and the knowledge in his hands. He didn't go voluntarily; he was sent. He wanted to stay at his work, he didn't believe in the war, but what choice was there? Eighteen months on, he was reported missing, believed killed, and I believed it; I felt his absence as surely as I'd know if I lost a limb. I grieved. Something inside me broke. That was until I saw his photograph in the newspaper. I'm not certain which hurt my heart more, losing him or finding him again and not being able to come forward. I watched all the other women coming. I was there on that day. I had to watch them all queuing to claim he was someone else, and I wanted to scream; I wanted to scream the truth, and come and get him and bring him home, but I couldn't.'

'Adam told me you were here that day, but I wasn't sure whether to believe him or not.'

'And I've been here on many days since. I came as regularly as I was able.'

'We were never sure whether he imagined you. We thought we had a fairy living in the wood.'

She laughs. There are gaps in her teeth and James likes her laughter all the more for that. She has stepped out of Adam's portrait, and yet the light in her face is something other than the gloss of oil paint. She is an unlike likeness of a face in a painting and fascinatingly so. While the woman in Adam's painting is under-painted in dark, rich colours, the woman in front of James seems to glow with an underneath brightness.

She looks down at her oversized overcoat. 'I don't feel much like a fairy.'

'But why didn't you come forward? How could you not? What was to stop you from taking him home?'

'Because I'd been a fool.' All the light suddenly goes from her face. She looks away and wipes her eyes on her sleeve. 'Because I made so many mistakes and it was too late to make it right.'

They walk on and follow the path back down to the beck. Amber reflections tremble and fragment on the water and the streak of a kingfisher's wing is electric blue. The willows dip chrome yellow leaves and emerald green weed stirs beneath and shows the direction of the flow. Eleanor skims a stone and it skips one, two, three times across the water. For a moment, Adam is by his side again, and James looks at her and smiles.

'In 1917, when they told me he'd died, I felt as if something in me cracked,' she says. 'I didn't want to leave the house any longer. I didn't want to get out of bed. My mother despaired for me. She said it was too much, that I was going to ruin my health. My father kept calling a doctor, but what use was that? I had no reason to go on.'

James nods, recalling the first few days after Caitlin left, and how he had very nearly stepped off the rocks.

'At my lowest ebb, I was grateful for a friend's kindness and to feel I could be of some use,' she goes on. 'Sidney had lived next door to me all my life, we'd been like brother and sister, and when he told me that he wanted to take care of me, I accepted his kindness. He'd come home invalided out, and he needed someone to help him too, to look after him, so we agreed to take care of each other. I knew my husband was dead, that I was finished as a wife – as a true wife, I mean – but perhaps I could be useful to another person. I finally agreed to marry Sidney in the spring of 1920. Six months after that, I saw the picture in the newspaper.'

'So you couldn't come forward.'

'I read stories in the newspapers about women in the same circumstances finding themselves in court accused of bigamy. Can you imagine? I dreaded anyone finding out; I particularly dreaded Sidney finding out. But, anyway, when I came here and met him, I understood that he no longer knew who I was. That broke my heart all over again, but I realized what had happened to him, and that he needed to be here and to have your help. I kept all the newspaper clippings about him, and I got the train up here as often as I could. Sidney never knew. He had no idea. He thought I had a friend in Carlisle with a frail constitution.' She laughs, but it lasts only seconds. 'He never found out and then it was all too late.'

'Too late?'

'Sidney passed away a couple of months ago. He'd been treated for gas inhalation during the war and never really recovered from that. Please don't misunderstand me, Sidney was very dear to me and I was sorry to lose him. But now I had a choice and a chance. Was it time to speak? To finally tell him my name, who I was and what we'd been to each other? I came here six weeks ago, and I'd decided that I'd do it, that I'd say it, but Samuel didn't come into the wood that day. I stood on the hillside, and I could see him working in the walled garden. For so long I'd wanted to tell him, only now it was much more difficult than I'd thought it would be. I was too frightened to step out of the trees and so it never happened. My courage failed me and that was the last time.'

'Samuel?'

'Yes, of course, you don't know, do you? My husband's name was Samuel.'

The past tense strikes him, the knowledge passes from her eyes to his, and with that the small, desperate, illogical glimmer of hope that he's been clinging on to flickers out. 'Was?'

'I have cried until I can't cry any longer. I don't think there is a tear left in my body.'

He looks at her, the shadows under her eyelashes, and he believes her. She had sat quietly while James cried and there is a companionable comfort in her stillness. She finally puts a hand to his arm.

'I hoped it wasn't so,' James says. 'I hoped that I'd added two and two and made five. I had a notion that Adam was indestructible. Isn't that silly? I half believed that he wasn't quite mortal, that he didn't conform to normal rules and perhaps existed outside of time.'

Eleanor smiles, and it is a quiet, calm, understanding smile. 'I wish you were right.'

'They told me that he jumped.'

She nods. 'Isn't it a pity that he didn't fly?'

They walk back through Samuel Fairleigh's garden. James is still getting used to the name. He thinks that he will for ever be Adam in his head. He can't accustom himself to the fact that Adam is gone.

'Will you tell me about Samuel Fairleigh?' he asks her. 'I'd love to know who he was.'

'I think you knew him better than anybody.'

He feels her eyes moving over his face and he knows that she is reading his lines and shadows. It reminds James of how it felt when Adam looked at him – feeling that Adam might be looking through him and seeing something deeper. It also reminds him of how men look at each other in moments of fear and imminent danger; there is something heightened about that look and that understanding, some profound sense of sharing the moment, of closeness and linking fate.

'But what was his life like before the war?' he goes on. 'What did he do?'

As Eleanor walks through the garden, she collects seeds in twists of paper and smiles as she stores them away in her pockets. It is like something passing from Adam's hand – Samuel Fairleigh's hand – to hers, James thinks.

'Before the war? He was a gardener. What else! He started at Scowcroft Hall as a fourteen-year-old and worked his way up to second gardener. He looked after the peach houses and vines and the rockeries, and he was proud of what he could do. He knew all the Latin names, and liked to recite them for me, how to prune and propagate, and he had such wonderfully clever hands, and care and patience. All that part of him never went away, you see. That never left him. That is who he was.'

'Of course. It makes perfect sense.'

'I'm glad you say that. I feared that the army might obliterate him,' she says. 'That it might change him, I mean, that all that I loved about him might be processed out of him. His singularity. His contrariness. His passions. I worried that he might come back a different man. But he didn't.'

'No?'

'No. Absolutely not. He might not have remembered his name, or mine, but he was still emphatically Samuel, and I was so glad of that. He never stopped being the man I loved. That was a marvel to me.'

'Glad?' James marvels at her. There is something heroic about Eleanor in this instant.

'Yes. I have some photographs of him in the garden at Scowcroft Hall,' she says. She smiles as she recalls, and James likes to see her face light up as she talks about her husband. 'He was so happy in his work there, and he was again here. He loved this place, and the woods, and the garden he'd created. He told me that, and he told me about your friendship. I'll bring the photographs for you next time.'

'Next time? Yes.'

'I'm going to plant an apple tree for him. He would like that, wouldn't he? My only regret is that I never told him who I was and what I felt for him. I could sometimes see that he was tortured by trying to piece it all together, and I wish now that I'd found the courage and the occasion to speak. Samuel was the one person who I have loved in my life, who I will ever love, and I should have said that to him. I hope he understood it. It's all gone so quickly, I realize now, and if people matter to us, we should tell them, don't you think?'

James looks at Eleanor Fairleigh, her dark hair shifting around her shoulders, and she is Adam's queen of the woods, and she is right.

Chapter Sixty-Five

James, Ambleside, October 1925

There's a letter waiting for him when he gets back to the hotel. Caitlin's handwriting. As James turns the envelope between his hands, he hears Eleanor's voice talking about missed chances and regrets and finding the courage. He also thinks of Caitlin's face when he had said Charles' name. She had changed the subject and had not let James go back there. Is it really too late to hope? He wishes he could tell her that he's not the same person that she walked away from four years ago, that he's straightened things out, worked out his priorities and that he knows she's the only woman he'll ever love. But could she understand that? Can he say that? Could there still be a chance?

He reads her words as he climbs the stairs. She wants to know if he's all right and what he has discovered about Adam. James can tell, as he reads her lines, that she is expecting the worst. That she'd guessed the truth already. That she felt it. And really that was why she'd sent the telegram and was part of the reason for her tears.

I wish I was there with you. I am so worried about you, she writes.

He is glad that she hasn't seen Fellside brought down, and stood by Adam's misnamed grave, but he wishes that she was here now, and that she'd heard how Eleanor talked about Adam.

I have missed Adam for the past few years – his friendship, his gentleness, the way that he always listened, and his charming, ethereal oddness. I have wanted to go back and see him, but having left Fellside, I've never really felt I had that right. I've been thinking about Adam today and I've also been thinking about you. I have missed you too. I realized quite how much yesterday.

James is racing through her words now, skipping and circling back through her sentences. He sits down on the stairs.

I do have regrets, she writes. *I wish I'd been braver, stronger, more understanding, that I could have stood back and blinked hard at my priorities and understood that I needed to let Nat go. It's taken time to do that, though. I have mourned him for the past four years. I felt I needed space to mourn. But I have been selfish in my grief, I have indulged myself in it, and now I am sorry for that, because while I have been busy digging holes for myself, I have hurt you.*

In James' memory he is walking through Fellside again two years ago, through the rooms of their apartment, so full of her and so terribly empty. He had felt such regret as he stepped through the shadows and memories. He had remembered the two of them moving around one another, watching one another, but unable to find the words to connect. He recalls the confusion in his thoughts and the conflict in his feelings. That failure of words is a regret. The page in his hands is now full of words that seem to want to connect with him again. James takes a breath, and he knows that he is stronger, steadier, more sure of his priorities than he was four years ago, and he is ready for her words.

You kept saying Charles' name yesterday, she goes on. *I didn't know how to reply and so I avoided the question. I have thought about writing to you several times over the past year, but you have a new life now, and what right do I have to attempt to reclaim a place within that? Why should you care? But, to answer your question, it didn't happen with Charles. I called it all off because I realized that I didn't really love him. I didn't feel for him the way I felt for you, and that didn't seem to be fair to him. It was such a difficult decision to make. I hated letting him down. But, in making that decision, I realized just how much I had lost and how intense my feelings had been for you.*

James looks up from the letter and Caitlin's and Eleanor's words weave together. He rubs his hands over his eyes and thinks about the space that Adam has left. Questions that have stretched for seven years have been answered today, and yet there isn't quite a sense of resolution because, at this moment, he misses Adam too much. James sees him standing in his attic room, running his fingers over the bowl that he and Caitlin had made together and saying how much he missed her. There had been such perfect understanding between them in that moment. There are so many things that James wants to say to Adam now: to tell him how much he misses his friendship, his understanding and his clear-eyed observation. He would like to tell Adam what he means to do next, to say it out loud, and hear his affirmation.

I might be wrong, Caitlin writes, *I hope I am wrong, but I fear that we have lost Adam, and I know how much that will hurt you too, what a large space his absence will leave in your life. I will never be able to fill that gap, but if you need someone to talk to in the months ahead, someone to remember with, and cry with, I am here. I'd like to talk again. You looked well when you turned up on the doorstep yesterday, you look as though you've remembered how to sleep, and I was so glad to see that. I hope that losing Adam won't set you back. I know that I failed you once before, but I'm here for you now and I always will be. I will miss Adam too, but most of all I miss you.*

James stands in the stairwell and watches the clouds rolling over the fells. He can make out the spire of Holy Trinity between the trees, and thinks of Adam's grave there in the churchyard, and Alan and Charlotte, their voices now all silenced. He thinks of Eleanor's voice as she had talked about missing her husband earlier today, the regret, and sincerity, and certainty that he'd heard there. There is writing paper in his hotel room. His words rush onto the page.

Chapter Sixty-Six

Anna, Flailcroft Farm, October 1925

She lifts the photographs down from the walls, wrapping them in newspaper, one by one, and placing them in the box, all the while thinking of that day, five years ago, when his face had suddenly reappeared in newsprint. Anna means to whitewash the walls tomorrow, before Lena's furniture arrives at the weekend. It will be like a blank canvas then, and her sister will be able to make this room her own. Anna looks forward to hearing Lena's footsteps on the floor above and having her voice in the house. There is a reassuring familiarity in being surrounded by the mementoes of Mark's family, but she will also be glad to see her sister's boxes coming in.

Last weekend Lena had asked if she meant to contact Jack Giddings again and restart the search for Mark, but Anna had shaken her head. She knows where Mark is, even if his grave has another man's name on it, and she has begun to mourn him over the past month. There will be months more of this hurt ahead, she knows that, but there is also a new stillness in her chest. It's the truth. She has no doubt. She just has to learn to live with that truth now. Lena had held her hand at the funeral, had gripped on tight, and Anna will be glad to cling on to her again over the months to come.

They have planned together over the past few weekends, chosen new curtains, measured up for where Lena's furniture will fit, and cooked forgotten (now remembered) recipes together from their mother's notebook. Lena had even played the piano one night, when they'd had a bottle of beer too many. Anna had felt frightened as she heard the first few notes – she hasn't touched the piano since that day, almost fearing that it could be possessed and that strange music might come out again – but under Lena's fingers it had only made faltering Sunday-school tunes and music-hall choruses, and it had felt like something had been exorcized.

As she takes down the last photograph from the wall, and looks around the room, Anna thinks about Mark sleeping in here four years ago. She hadn't changed the sheets since that night, but she has stripped the bed back to the mattress today and watched the dust fly up. That had felt like something significant too. Sometimes, when the weather changes, the ceiling of her bedroom creaks, and she imagines that it is his footsteps pacing the floor above. But Lena will be here on Saturday, and when she hears noises in the night again, Anna will know that it is only her sister stirring and that Mark is sleeping peacefully in his grave.

She has wrapped his mother's vases, and candlesticks, and china dogs, and has stored everything carefully away. The rugs are rolled, and the mattress turned, and it is all ready for Lena now. Anna doesn't mean to part with Mark's history, it is all boxed away under the eaves, but it feels as though a new chapter is beginning today and the light in the house seems to have changed.

He will always be here, he will always be part of this house, and the land around it will for ever be his, but Anna feels she has let him go now, and has decided how she wishes to remember him; the last five years have not been easy, but amongst the days of confusion, and talking at cross purposes, there have been moments when their eyes have connected once more, when there has been unspoken understanding between them, and there were smiles that she means not to forget. She recalls every minute of the day when she first found him again in the walled garden, and that second when they'd touched. She is sure, she is certain, that he did know her then, and she will always have that.

Lucy, High House

George pushes the newspaper across the table.

'Look,' he says and points. 'Please, Luce. Look at the Notices column.'

She's not in the mood for gossip or going out, for other people's good news or bad news, or another of George's get-rich-quick schemes, but his expression is so serious that Lucy can't not look. She follows the lines down with her finger, and in between the baptisms and *in memoriams*, there is a Missing Person notice and her brother's name underneath it. Her eyes rise to George's suddenly earnest face, and she feels both angry and sorry.

'But why? Why would you do that? We know where he is.'

'Do we? Honestly, Lucy, do we really?'

'I went to the funeral. I saw his grave.'

'It's not his grave, though, is it? You told me that yourself. It's not his name on the stone.'

'Only because they all lied. Only because you wouldn't let me talk to the police.'

'But it never was him, was it?'

He's looking at her as if she's stupid, but also as if he pities her. 'It was!'

'Lucy, that man, whoever the poor sod was, is dead. But Ellis is still out there somewhere. It's right what they told us. He could be nearby for all we know. He might be in another hospital, or in a prison cell, or sleeping on the streets, but he is alive. You can still have him back. We can find him and tell him that he must come back.'

She so wants to believe it might be true, but how could it be? George reaches his hand out towards hers and squeezes. Kindness crinkles the corners of his eyes, she sees how much he means it, and it's difficult not to cry then.

'And I was thinking,' he goes on, 'I could start looking after the children at the weekends, so that you can have some time off, some time to yourself. I know you get tired and I shouldn't have heaped all of this on your shoulders. It's time that I took some of it on. I've not been very fair to you. I should have taken more of it on years ago.'

'Is that an apology?'

'Something of the sort.'

'Why now?'

'Because I saw your face when you came back from that man's funeral.'

'Ellis.' Lucy looks down at the name in the newspaper.

'And I wanted to say to you – all that business with Owen, the year before last, I'm sorry about that too. I shouldn't have spoken to you like that. It's not up to me to tell you who you can and can't see, is it? I do want you to be happy, Luce.'

She takes a breath. 'I haven't spoken to Owen in months, probably over a year, but I did see him again last week, actually. I saw him from across the street. He looked like he'd been drinking all day and he could hardly stand up. I watched him and I was glad that he didn't see me. If he'd looked towards me, I think I might have walked in the opposite direction. Doesn't that sound awful? Isn't that wicked of me? But he's been that way since he came back from France, Ella told me. He drinks every penny he earns and he keeps getting into fights. I wouldn't know how to make that right.'

George nods but says nothing.

'Did you know that?' she asks. 'Were you aware of that all this time? Was that why you said what you did?'

'I'd heard. I didn't want him to let you down again. I know I spoke out of turn, but I only wanted to look after you.'

'I feel sorry for him,' Lucy says, 'desperately sorry. It's tragic, isn't it? As a friend, I want to do something to help him. But I don't want my life to be like that. As I watched him last week, I realized that I could have been the woman who he comes home to, the one who has to pick up the pieces. I don't want to be that person. I'm glad that you didn't let me go back to him. I'm grateful you said what you did.'

'Is that a grudging thank you?'

'Something of the sort.' She nods as she echoes his words.

'I've paid for this advert today and tomorrow,' George says. 'And I'll keep on putting it in as long as I can afford to. Ellis is out there and one day it might get to him. I know it's a long shot, that it might take time and, yes, we'll need a bit of luck, but sometimes miracles happen, don't they?'

Lucy thinks about Ellis standing in the walled garden, his eyes not quite connecting with hers, that gravestone with another man's name on it and his handwriting letters making the words *Forget Me Not*. She's not forgotten. She'll never forget. And she knows, as she looks into his eyes, that George won't forget either.

'Yes. Sometimes,' she concedes.

Celia, Ambleside

It is very strange to dig in the earth around his grave. She places the bulbs in tidy holes and tells Robert that she doesn't mean to disturb him. Celia plants crocus and grape hyacinths now, and snowdrops to see the spring in. When the flowers have faded, she'll bring forget-me-nots and he'll have those for the whole summer. '*Crocus vernus. Muscari. Galanthus. Myosotis,*' she recites, and the words are like a poem for her son.

When Robert was a boy he used to help her to plant bulbs in the churchyard at home, and then in April they'd look out of his bedroom window and see the reward for their hard work, all purple and gold around the old graves. They had felt pleased at that, because wasn't it a nice thing to do, to show that the dead were still cared for and remembered? They would talk together, as they dug in the bulbs, and Robert would read the words on the old gravestones aloud, all the names and the dates and the archaic epitaphs. He liked to remember the names of the people in the graves, it seemed important to him, and he would call each headstone by its Christian name, so that they were Matilda, Maud and Augustus, Silas, Tabitha and Elizabeth-Anne. She had smiled at her boy for that. She smiles at him again.

Celia likes to sit here by Robert's grave and to talk to him. Some days she stays until the evening, until it is dark, and when she says his name into the blackness, she's quite certain that he can hear her.

Her knees hurt now, but that's not what matters. She stands back and thanks God again for letting her have him back. The sun is glowing in the church windows this afternoon, and as her eyes lift she watches a pair of swallows, turning, tumbling together on a current of air. They flit and fall and soar, over the church roof and away.

Chapter Sixty-Seven

Caitlin, Richmond, October 1925

Caitlin watches a flight of swallows streak across the tattered tops of the castle walls. They are late to leave this year, she thinks, and must be on their way south soon. She imagines their aerial progress, arrowing down to France, over old battlefields and new cemeteries, through Spain and into Morocco, seeing the driest deserts and the greenest forests below, down, down, all the length of Africa, to circle the rooftops of Cape Colony, half a world away. She turns and takes the path into the wood and, though it is October, blue sky glitters through the branches above. She steps over fallen boughs and knows the leaves of ash, oak, beech and lime, now turning to their autumn colours, and can hear Adam's voice at her side.

In his letter James says that he can't believe that Adam is gone, he's struggling to accept that it can be so, and as she remembers Adam's voice, the animation of his eyes and his hands, and the vitality that always seemed to rush through his veins when he took her into the woods and the walled garden, she understands exactly what James means. But Adam is alive in the knowledge that he has given her, in the shapes of the leaves and the songs of the birds, and she hopes that, with time, James will see that too.

She is worried about him, though. As she had begun to read his letter, she had wanted to get the train and go there and be with him, but he says that he wouldn't want her to see Fellside now, or rather what is left of it. It is too sad, James says, and he wants to spare her that. But, as she had read that line, she had so desperately wanted to take away his sadness.

Her route is lined with hazel and holly and sunlight shifts on the path ahead. She can't walk down to the river without remembering taking this same path with Nat, their teenage footsteps rushing on the incline and their voices echoing through the wood – and then the day they had taken James down to the river too. Caitlin can still picture him walking backwards ahead of them, the dappled light moving over his face, his eyes shifting from her to Nat, and laughing. How could the wood have become a nightmare place for James? How could the boy walking backwards with the sun in his eyes have become the man who screamed in the night and looked at the shadows in the corners of the room as if they might contain terrors? But then, James has told her about that awful wood in his letters, about bringing all the bodies out, and she thinks that maybe she now understands some of how that change happened. She hears the rooks and jackdaws in the trees beyond and somewhere the screech of a white owl.

Something has changed again, though. She'd seen it in his face when he was here last week. James will never be that boy again, none of them will ever be that innocent again, but some of the light has come back into his eyes. The path opens out to the meadow and she skirts along the south fringe of the wood. She startles a rabbit and suddenly the field ahead is full of white tails bobbing away. Though she wishes she was sharing the sight, she can't not smile. She follows across the field, and with the sun on her back it feels like midsummer again.

Caitlin stands on the footbridge and the river glimmers mercury, copper and gold below. The briefest flicker of blue might be the wing of a kingfisher or her imagination. She remembers Nat and James dropping sticks from the bridge, making it a race to see whose would emerge first from the far side – and then those times when she had seen James and Adam playing the same game on Clappersgate bridge. How many echoes. How many absences. She imagines James standing on the bridge again now and how lonely that picture seems.

The path becomes a holloway as she descends towards the riverbank, the branches weaving together above, a funnel of dark and light ahead. The three of them had joined hands that day as they had plunged down the hill, and Nat had joked that it was like being born again.

'Welcome to our Private Members' Club,' laughs Nat's faraway voice. 'Founding membership: two. Now expanded to three.'

Caitlin steps out onto the pebbled shore where the river bends, and skims a stone, as they had done. She can remember Nat smiling at James, in between the joshing and the competition, and how happy she had been to see their friendship. She can almost hear their laughter as she stands here again, but nothing breaks the mirror of the water now. She would give anything, she thinks, to see Nat and James sharing smiles once more.

She walks on, following the riverbank, and then suddenly he's there, by the gate ahead. It stops her feet and takes all the breath out of her chest, because it *is* him. Nat is sitting on the five-bar gate, swinging his legs, smiling and raising his hand to her. She's running then, screaming his name, needing to get to him and know that he's real, but now he's turning. She feels dizzy as she reaches the gate. She leans on it, watching Nathaniel's ghost walk across the lower field, back into the shadow of the trees, never looking back, letting her go, and then he's gone.

Caitlin sits on the grass and cries, as bitterly as she has ever cried, but there's a stillness there afterwards, and she knows with complete certainty that this was goodbye and Nat was ready to go. Birdsong fills the silence. She has no doubt (not a shred) that she has just seen her brother, and yet how could she tell that to anyone? But then she thinks of all the people who queued outside Fellside House once, long ago, and she knows that James would listen to her and not dismiss her certainty. The wings of the last butterflies flicker amongst the grass and wood pigeons call as they gather, readying to go too.

Caitlin touches the letter in her pocket. She had been about to seal the envelope as she left the house, but then had hesitated. She needed to have this space, this day, to be sure that she was doing the right thing, that her words wouldn't be too much, that it was what James wanted too. She adds one last paragraph as she sits by the bridge, and closes the envelope before she completes the circuit back up into town.

As she turns into the square, she catches her reflection in a shop window and has to stop and look again, because she sees only herself, and there is no Nat there at her shoulder; the constant echo that has been there overlaying her own reflection for the past nine years has suddenly gone. Caitlin has to blink, and check it again, but it's true – today he has left her. For a moment she wants to crouch down, and hug her arms around her knees, struck with overwhelming loneliness, but then as her breath stills, and the shadows shift, she also feels a new lightness, as if all the threads of complication are suddenly unravelling, and she knows the path ahead.

She puts the letter in the post box.

Chapter Sixty-Eight

James, Fellside House, October 1925

The last wasps make intoxicated circles around the wrinkling skins of the windfalls. The scent of the fallen apples is the condensed perfume of a whole summer of sunshine. Did Adam stand underneath these trees in the spring of this year, James wonders, and watch the air brightening with blossom? Did Eleanor stand here with him? James hopes that, at the end, Adam remembered her.

'Will you start it?'

'Yes.'

The pickaxe hits the ground and James feels the reverberation of it all through his body. He heaves it up again, up above his shoulders, and swings. After the dry summer, the ground is hard at first, but as he digs deeper it begins to yield and he finds a rhythm. Eleanor is pruning the damsons while he's making the hole for the tree, and there is a comfortable companionship in this work. He goes at the ground enthusiastically at first, he finds himself wanting to make a show of strength and energy for her, but soon he has to pause and the palms of his hands smart. He sees the tremble in his own fingers as he lights a cigarette. It is both the effort of exertion, he knows, and the words in the letter in his pocket. Eleanor leans against a tree trunk, pausing in her work too, and asks him to light one for her.

'Don't you object that he's under another man's gravestone?' James blows smoke at a blue sky streaked with high cloud. 'I hope you don't mind my asking that, only I keep asking myself the same question.'

'Mind?' She flexes the secateurs in her hands as she considers. 'In the end, there are things that matter more than words on gravestones, aren't there? I know where he is, who and what he is, and he's not answered to his own name for such a long time, has he? I think he might actually, ultimately, be amused by it. Don't you? After all, he grew to like Mrs Dakers. They had a friendship of sorts, and an understanding. He knew she only meant him well and that she missed her son terribly.'

'There really is only you and me who know where he is.'

'But does it matter? Does anyone else need to know? I think he would care far more that his garden was tended and to know that his friend James has started smiling again.'

She shrugs and smiles at him too as she turns away. He watches her working with the secateurs and thinks that she probably is right. He also thinks about Nathaniel. Is he too lying somewhere under another man's name? Or is he amongst the too-numerous ranks of the unidentified, just one more *Soldier of the Great War* on his gravestone? They have been right through the wood now, taken all the bodies out, so really one or the other must be the case. Nathaniel surely must have been found, even if he hasn't been reunited with his name.

The possibility makes the nameless men matter to James; Nathaniel could have been any one of them, and he is glad to have witnessed that they've all been reinterred with equal respect. It's not perfect, but there is some comfort and finality in that. Caitlin's letter says that she has come to an understanding with Nathaniel's ghost, that something has shifted recently, and she feels Nathaniel has let her go. As James had read those words (words that she apologized for because they might not sound quite rational), he had recognized something there that he understood too. He will come back to England now, for good, but he would like to take Caitlin to France before he finishes, and show her that the anonymous men are cared for as much as those who are named, that they too have epitaphs and flowers and will be remembered.

'Did you go to the funeral?' he asks Eleanor.

'Yes, but I didn't make myself known. There were a lot of people there.' She smiles and her eyes slide to meet his. 'There were such a lot of women there! You shouldn't laugh at a funeral, should you? But it had been in the papers and so the church was packed with them. It amused me briefly, but then it struck me how terrifically sad that was. There are holes in so many people's lives, aren't there? So much yearning and wishing and missing. But I hope that Samuel's existence, and the possibilities they saw in him, brought them some comfort.'

James thinks about Anna Mason. He had been so certain at one time that she was right, that she was telling the truth, and he's still sure that Anna saw her husband when she looked at Adam. James isn't convinced that coming to Fellside will have ended her yearning and missing, but he hopes that she did derive some comfort from being able to spend time with Adam.

Eleanor Fairleigh looks up at him with her clear eyes as she wipes the earth from her hands.

'He wanted you to be happy too. He was sad when you weren't.'

'I know,' James replies.

'He told me that he wished you could learn to forget and that you could forgive yourself.'

The walls of the garden glow in the autumn sunlight. So many walls seem to have fallen down over the past few days. James had once thought about the workings of Adam's memory in terms of these walls, but he realizes now that maybe achieving peace of mind is more about choosing a focus than building barriers; it is about both holding on and letting go; acknowledging that you have a shadow, but opting to walk forward. He smiles at Eleanor. 'I'm getting there.'

They take it in turns with the spade. When James shuts his eyes, and as he listens to it rasp at the earth, it might well be Adam digging at his side. Eleanor holds the young trunk straight, while James ties in a stake to support it, and forks the earth back in around the roots. She heels the tree in, and James sees Adam making the same action, reinforcing the damsons which are now stretching to the sky.

'It was a cutting from the old tree that came down last winter,' she tells James. 'He grafted it. Samuel took it because he wanted the tree to go on, and so it will, and so he will. It's right, isn't it? We have to look forward, don't we?'

'We do.'

Eleanor wipes the earth from her hands onto her corduroy trousers and apologizes as she examines her palms. James rather likes her for the guilelessness, and the way that she wrinkles her nose at her own hands, but then blithely polishes an apple on her trouser leg and bites into it.

'You see, he hasn't gone away,' she says. 'I can see his fingerprints in the glass of the greenhouse, I've looked at them up close and I know they're his, and his hand is on and in everything in this garden. He's in you and me too, his memory, his influence, and as long as we look for that in ourselves, he won't go away.'

They sit on Adam's garden bench and Eleanor passes James her flask of tea. It is agreeable to sit here with Eleanor Fairleigh, he feels that Adam would be pleased to see them sharing a bench and a thermos of tea, but the words of the letter in James' pocket keep circling in his head and he feels a strange sense of momentum. White moths flicker in the darkening air around them, and the shadows seem to turn too fast around the sundial.

'I promised to show you the photographs, didn't I?' Eleanor says.

She smiles as she takes them from an envelope. The men frown at the camera, lined up in a row, in rolled shirtsleeves, waistcoats and ties. There are spades and rakes arranged in front of the group, crossed like something from a heraldic shield, a line of pumpkins and watering cans. Eleanor's finger doesn't need to point to Adam before James' eyes pick his features out. There is no blur, or vagueness, or maybe about it; in crisp focus Adam Galilee looks out from the photograph. How could James ever have imagined that it could be otherwise?

Suddenly all those glimpses of Adam that he might have thought he could see in other photographs seem like foolishness. He has been here all along. Biding his time. With Eleanor. Waiting. In the second photograph he is amongst a group of men standing around a table in a glasshouse. They are potting up trays of seedlings and busy in their work. Only Adam looks up at the camera and laughs. The laughter in his eyes shines right out of the photograph and it is like connecting with him all over again. James wonders where all these men are now. Did they all go to the war? Did their spades turn different soils? How many of them have found their way home again?

'Do you know what happened to any of the rest of them?'

'I don't.' She shakes her head. 'And I'm sorry about that. Samuel was in touch with several of them at the start, with Alf and Jimmy, they were pals, but they all went their separate ways.'

How many of them, like Nathaniel, have disappeared for ever or lie under nameless gravestones? How many others have returned home with memories that they can never share? How many are still waking with nightmares and trying to remember how to forget? How many haven't yet known an armistice?

'We're the lucky ones, aren't we?'

'We are, and we should grab on to that.'

James can see Adam's husbandry in the shape of the trees all around him. Eleanor says that she means not to let this go. This garden is her husband's legacy, and she will not let that become overgrown. Walking at Eleanor's side, James feels as though Adam is there with them, he is certain of it; if he could turn around fast enough, he might catch him there, standing in his shadow. James wants to stay in the garden with Adam and Eleanor, but he also needs to get in the car, to drive up to Richmond and to walk forward.

'I'll keep it as he meant it to be,' Eleanor says. 'You must come and visit me, but, right now, there's somewhere else that you ought to be.'

He looks at her. 'Why do you say that?'

Eleanor laughs. 'Because you keep looking at your watch and rattling your keys.'

'I'm sorry.'

'Don't apologize – but go! You told me that you mean

to see Caitlin this week and it's so obvious that's where you want to be. It's what he would want you to do. Go and make it right.'

James touches the letter in his pocket and it feels as if something that was broken might yet be mended, that a false connection can be fixed, that he still has the chance to change the path ahead. He sees Adam's face glimmering in a circle of mirrors, Eleanor's portrait face all around him and their fingerprints connecting on the panes of the glasshouse, either side of life and death. James steps outside the walls of the garden and smiles as he looks ahead.

Acknowledgements

I should firstly thank my marvellous agent, Teresa Chris, without whom I wouldn't have had the opportunity to write this book. Teresa, I am grateful for your guidance, support and good humour – and for the repeated reminder to 'get on with it'! You were right, as always.

Luck was on my side when I was offered the chance to write for Simon & Schuster. I feel surrounded by allies and wise counsellors, and I'm constantly wowed by the energy, creativity and kindness of this team. I owe particular thanks to my editors, Jo Dickinson and Alice Rodgers, for championing this story and investing so much care in my manuscript. It's been an absolute pleasure working with you both.

Friends have mattered this year too. (And how!) You know who you are and why it counts. Thank you.